STORIES OF CHRIST AND CHRISTMAS

Books by EDWARD WAGENKNECHT

BIOGRAPHICAL: The Man Charles Dickens (1929); Mark Twain: The Man and His Work (1935, 1961); Longfellow, A Full-Length Portrait (1955); Mrs. Longfellow: Selected Letters and Journals (1956); The Seven Worlds of Theodore Roosevelt (1958); Nathaniel Hawthorne, Man and Writer (1961); Washington Irving: Moderation Displayed (1962); Edgar Allan Poe, The Man Behind the Legend (1963)

CRITICAL: Values in Literature (1928); A Guide to Bernard Shaw (1929); Utopia Americana (1929); Cavalcade of the English Novel (1943); Cavalcade of the American Novel (1952); A Preface to Literature (1954)

THEATRICAL: Lillian Gish, An Interpretation (1927); Geraldine Farrar, An Authorized Record of Her Career (1929); Jenny Lind (1931); The Movies in the Age of Innocence (1962)

ANTHOLOGICAL: The College Survey of English Literature, with others (1942); Six Novels of the Supernatural (1944); The Fireside Book of Christmas Stories (1945); The Story of Jesus in the World's Literature (1946); When I Was a Child (1946); The Fireside Book of Ghost Stories (1947); Abraham Lincoln: His Life, Work, and Character (1947); The Fireside Book of Romance (1948); Joan of Arc, An Anthology of History and Literature (1948); A Fireside Book of Yuletide Tales (1948); Murder by Gaslight (1949); The Collected Tales of Walter de la Mare (1950); An Introduction to Dickens (1952); Chaucer: Modern Essays in Criticism (1959); Stories of Christ and Christmas (1963)

INTRODUCTORY: The Chimes, by Charles Dickens (Limited Editions Club, 1931); Life on the Mississippi, by Mark Twain (Limited Editions Club, 1944); A Tale of Two Cities, by Charles Dickens (Modern Library, 1950); Great Expectations, by Charles Dickens (Pocket Books, 1956); The Wizard of Oz, by L. Frank Baum (Reilly & Lee edition, 1956); The Art, Humor, and Humanity of Mark Twain, edited by Minnie M. Brashear and Robert M. Rodney (1959); The Innocents Abroad, by Mark Twain (Limited Editions Club, 1962); Great Expectations, by Charles Dickens (Harcourt, 1963)

STORIES
AND

DECORATED BY
PETER BURCHARD

DAVID McKAY COMPANY, INC.

OF CHRIST
CHRISTMAS

EDITED BY
EDWARD WAGENKNECHT

NEW YORK, N.Y.

STORIES OF CHRIST AND CHRISTMAS

Acknowledgment of the right to reprint the works listed hereinafter, in the order
of their appearance in the book, is gratefully made to the following publishers and
copyright owners:

"The Man Who Gave Us Christmas" by Winifred Kirkland; copyright 1939, by
the Atlantic Monthly Company; reprinted by permission of the publisher.

"The Child" by Stanley Waterloo; from *The Wolf's Long Howl* published by
Herbert S. Stone and Co., Chicago, New York, 1899.

"Christ Legends" by Selma Lagerlöf, from *Christ Legends* by Selma Lagerlöf;
translated from the Swedish by Velma Swanston Howard; copyright 1908 by Holt,
Rinehart and Winston, Inc.; copyright renewed 1936 by Velma Swanston Howard;
reprinted by permission of Holt, Rinehart and Winston, Inc.

"Bethlehem Episodes" by Heywood Broun; from *The Collected Edition of Heywood Broun* published by Harcourt, Brace and Co.: "Frankincense and Myrhh"
copyright 1922, 1941; "Inasmuch" copyright 1921, 1941; "We, Too, Are Bidden" copyright 1938, 1941; reprinted by permission of Heywood Hale Broun and
Constance Broun. The title "Bethlehem Episodes" has been supplied by the editor.

"Christmas Fancies" by Jules Lemaître, translated by Clarence Stratton. Two
stories entitled "The Beasts of the Field" and "The Virgin of the Angels," both
from a collection entitled *On the Margins of Old Books*, published by Coward
McCann, Inc., 1929. The title "Christmas Fancies" has been supplied by the editor.

CONTENTS

[ix

EDITOR'S INTRODUCTION

Stories of Christ and Christmas is more specialized than either of the editor's earlier Christmas anthologies; it deals with religious material exclusively. Part I contains stories of the first Christmas, and Part II introduces modern fictional variations on the basic theme. Winifred Kirkland's essay on Saint Luke, who contributed more to Christmas than any other Biblical writer, seemed to me a good Prologue, and I invited Harry Emerson Fosdick to repeat one of his fine sermons in Riverside Church, New York, by way of Epilogue. Further, I sought to link Parts I and II by printing as an Interlude between them Mary Ellen Chase's first story, "His Birthday," in which we see the child Jesus looking back upon his nativity to apprehend its meaning.

The stories themselves do not seem to me to require much in the way of interpretation. I have allowed Stanley Waterloo to begin Section I because "The Child," which long anticipated more recent interesting attempts to "report" the Nativity, gives us a general, overall view, written without tendency, and therefore not stressing any one element at the expense of the others. In the succeeding tales, the shepherds, the Wise Men, and many others occupy in turn the center of the stage. There are Biblical and non-Biblical characters, and the Biblical characters appear in both Biblical and non-Biblical aspects. Some of the authors try for a realistic approach; others give the freest rein to fancy. Some stories are by distinguished writers; some by writers once known to fame but whose fame has faded; some by more or less "popular" writers, and some by writers whose names will be unfamiliar to most readers and who fall into none of these classifications. And this, I think, is

[xi

as it should be in a Christmas book, for at Christmastime none who comes in a spirit of worship should be excluded.

If the Wise Men threaten to dominate, this is not because I planned it so; availability of material was the determining factor. It may be that Henry van Dyke's "The Story of the Other Wise Man," which has become the type-tale for fictional variations on the subject of the first Christmas, exercised an influence here; in any case, it would have been absurd to omit this story from this kind of book, even though I had used it before. The Wise Men were not purer of heart than the shepherds, but since they were more complicated and sophisticated, and had the glamor of distant places about them, they lent themselves better to the stuff of fiction. But I have not tried to exclude anybody; the Innkeeper has his moment, and, in the stories by B. Z. Stambaugh and Julian Forrest, we meet characters hitherto quite unknown. Even the animals, beloved of Thomas Hardy and others, are here, and in such a tale as "The Well of the Star" by Elizabeth Goudge, both Wise Men and shepherds are so important that it would be hard to say which predominates.

Some of the generalizations I have made apply to Part II as well as Part I. In Part II, some of the stories deal with the historic past and some with our own time, for the very point to be made here is that Bethlehem is timeless, and that Christ is born again under a wide variety of circumstances. Some of these tales have a very exotic setting, while others will seem only too familiar. Some are sentimental; others have an astringency not commonly associated with Christmas. But all reassert the endless, undying possibility of theophany and recall a sentence that I read many years ago in the Christmas issue of a popular magazine and have never forgotten:

"But He is still a Child this Christmas, and in that fact lies the hope of the world."

PROLOGUE

THE MAN WHO GAVE US CHRISTMAS

BY WINIFRED KIRKLAND

I

How MANY of us in the hurry and hubbub of the holiday season steal a few silent moments to consider where our Christmas comes from? Stories as beautiful as that of Christmas do not just happen; they have a source, they come from somewhere, they come from someone. When we stop to think and search for a sure but distant origin we shall find, contrary to the evidence of this mass-made decade, that over and over again some far-off individual, man or woman, is responsible for giving the whole world some undying dream, a dream that can always be seen to have been long and courageously preserved within the dreamer's own undaunted soul. Yet this far-off bravery too often fails to stir us, because we seldom pause to look back, and remember.

From year to year we join in the singing of the old familiar carols, forgetting who recorded the very first Christmas hymns that have set the fashion for all that have followed. From year to year we listen while some voice reads, "My soul doth magnify the Lord," without remembering how high and holy and humble some far-off man must have kept his spirit before he could have perceived the ineffable loveliness of the Annunciation and shared a young mother's glory in a child-to-be. Every year we gather together, young and old, to construct the Christmas crèche. We arrange the sheep, we place the kneeling shepherds, we crown with a halo the baby's head lying on the straw, but we forget the man who so revered the sacredness of commonplace things that he dared to describe a God laid in a cattle trough for a cradle. We forget the man who gave us Christmas.

We do not know Luke well enough to say "thank you" to him across the centuries. But we might know him better, and Christmas might mean more to us, if we tried to discover what it must first have meant to the man who gave it to us, gave it in all its perennial freshness and beauty to a world racked with war in his day and still racked with war in our day, in spite of the soaring, singing message of the two thousand Christmases that have come between. While in no sense did Luke invent the Christmas narrative, one can with truth say that it was he who gave us Christmas, for it was Luke, and Luke only, who searched out and found and preserved a birth story too humble for prouder historians to touch. It is said of Jesus, the wayside preacher, that the common people heard him gladly. It may be said of Luke, the wayside doctor, that he heard the common people gladly. Was it these same common people who brought to Luke's knowledge the story of the first Christmas, revealing to him perhaps the existence of some close-kept Aramaic document, or simply transmitting to him by word of mouth sacred and secret memories? The narrative of Jesus' birth seems to have been unknown to the earliest Christian Church, concentrated as that church was on its Founder's death and Resurrection. Who else but humble people, still open to wonder and awe, could have told those old tales of miracles and angel voices? Who else but Luke would have listened? Who else in that day and hour reverenced humanity enough to accept the story of a God born in a stable and to give that story to the world?

Let us read once again the first two chapters of Luke's Gospel. Then let us pause to consider where our Christmas comes from, picture by picture, chant by chant. The most beautiful book in the world, so Renan has described the Gospel of Luke. And in that book, for sheer unearthly loveliness, the opening chapters are the most beautiful of all. Only a painter could have conceived the strange stark beauty of the scene in which the tall angel delivers his message to a wondering awestruck girl. In fact, some early statues of Luke represent him as an actual artist, carrying palette and brushes. Only a dramatist could have seen and made us see that doorway meeting of two rapt women, one young, one old, each bearing beneath her heart a little child. Only a man attuned to music like a harp could have given us those immortal chants uttered by Zacharias and Mary and Simeon. The first thing, then, that we know about Luke is that he was a genius. The second thing we know is that, from the first written word of his Gospel to the last, Luke must have dedicated all his endowment to the delineation of an invisible Master, always, from Bethlehem's manger to the supper table of Emmaus, alive and shining before his eyes.

II

We possess little enough information about Luke, but it seems to be generally accepted that he was a young doctor of Antioch, and a member of the Christian community there before he met Paul and joined that intrepid leader on his second missionary journey as his personal physician. Except for those intervals when his superior trusted him to carry out certain missionary undertakings by himself, Luke seems to have remained at Paul's side, at hand during Paul's two years' imprisonment in colonial Cæsarea, and always within call during the longer incarceration in imperial Rome. There in Rome the two must have said a last farewell before Paul's martyrdom. Paul's description of his friend has become part of the world's vocabulary: "Luke, the beloved physician."

But this compressed account of a great Christian doctor who was to become a still greater Christian historian needs to be set against the more expanded background of Luke's place and time if we are to have even the scantiest knowledge of the man who gave us Christmas. There is no period so obscure, so difficult to penetrate with accuracy, as the first century of modern times, now labeled A.D. But today these hidden decades are being penetrated with more and more patient research. Present-day scholars are suggesting fresh hypotheses about circumstances and people too long represented as already conclusively examined. Even Jesus himself comes alive with new challenge when the English scholar of today, Professor Thomas Walter Manson of Manchester, lecturing at Yale . . . presents a carefully documented and most stimulating new conception. As for Luke of Antioch, there is a vast fresh area of deeply human conjecture opened by another scholar whose monumental study of the earliest foundations of our faith, *The Four Gospels,* stands on the shelves of every religious library. Canon Streeter, whose tragic airship death will be instantly recalled by many, holds that the historian Luke must have gone up and down the Palestinian countryside garnering from the humble people of field and village priceless jewels of teaching, parable, incident, preaching, that the Great Teacher scattered prodigally to the wind as he passed by. Barely twenty years later Luke followed after him. Streeter maintains that only by such sure and reverent tracing of Jesus' footsteps could Luke have come by the wealth of biographical material that he alone of the four Evangelists has been able to retrieve from oblivion and preserve for our knowledge.

Streeter's argument flashes a great searchlight of illumination upon Luke's own soul. There must have been some strange and beautiful magnetism about the man Luke, or the lowly people of the harsh upland pastures of Judea and the sun-swept vineyards about Galilee would not have opened to him their most sacred memories of the eternal Wayfarer. If it be only guesswork to suggest that Luke actually went about gathering much material for his book from humble people who recalled Jesus, still it is guesswork based on the evidence of the type of material he gathered and the type of man he seems to have been. Certain great parables and great incidents which had deathless effect on all Christian idealism are found in Luke alone. What toilworn peasant on some solitary hillside poured into Luke's eager ears the story of the Prodigal Son? What stooping trudger-by on some burning highroad straightened before Luke's earnest inquiries and imparted to him the recollection of that thrilled long-ago moment when as a youth he had heard Jesus, steadfast on his last black journey, utter that scathing parable of rebuke to the taunting questioner who had asked, "And

6]

who is my neighbor?" It must have been in some such way that Luke came by his immortal story of the Good Samaritan. What obscure witness of a horror twenty years past recalled and described to Luke the last friend and the humblest that Jesus made on earth, one forever remembered by every one of us, but recorded by Luke alone, the Penitent Thief? And where and how and when did Luke learn of a baby God cradled in a manger?

But one cannot press on into Luke's mind and heart without first sketching what must have gone to the making of that mind and heart years before Luke had so much as heard of the hero of his great biography. Now just how did the wide-flung, powerful, but curiously disillusioned pagan Empire of Rome first come to hear about the mysterious occurrences in one of its remotest provinces? The first news the pagan world received about the Man who was destined to change the very name of history from his day to ours was sudden and sharp and unbelievable. From a mysteriously radiant and intrepid little band of Hebrew fishermen, people began to hear about a dead Leader who had utterly transformed their lives by the new laws he had laid down for all living. This Leader had died a most shameful death as a crucified criminal. But no, he had not really died at all! In spite of careful burial and a tomb sealed with the official Roman insignia, he had come back! His humble friends had seen him! They asserted that he was with them at this very moment, alive!—as he could be with anyone, so they asserted, who desired him enough to obey his laws for living, a method and practice so fresh and surprising that throughout the Empire the new sect, everywhere spreading and finally upclimbing from the humble to the high, was coming to be called simply The Way.

Nobody at first took the trouble to write the story of Jesus of Nazareth, for the simple reason that he himself had said that he would come back. His first followers took that promise of his literally. Only slowly, as the years went by, did they realize that Jesus was speaking, not of his physical return, but of his abiding spiritual presence in his world. Then the Good News of Jesus the Christ, which had first been told by flaming preaching, began to be written down here and there, wherever the message had come to be known, in scattered fugitive documents, which slowly coalesced into four books finally accepted as authoritative by the small new congregations, often secret, now swiftly forming the habit of assemblage in the name of The Way. Thus humbly the Christian Church began, steadily shaping its liturgy, its chants, its prayers.

But the Christian Church was in existence before its Gospels, as we possess them today. Our Gospels are the account of those aspects of Christ's life, and those words of his message, which had previously been tried and tested and proved to be vital by the usage of myriad little churches springing up all over the Empire, at first hidden away, for the most part, from the proud intellectual ruling classes. These classes at first regarded askance a new religious leader who had been legally executed on a charge of sedition against the brief but secure and comfortable international orderliness of that period.

But the first century was not yet half gone before the new faith was attracting the attention of some among the educated and the high-born. Of these, young Doctor Luke of Antioch was one. Another was His Excellency Theophilus of Rome. To this Theophilus Luke dedicated his twin books, his Gospel and the Acts of the Apostles. Luke addresses a preface to Theophilus indicating the nature of his researches and the purpose of his book: "Because many historians have undertaken a narrative of the mysterious events that form the basis of our faith, as these events have been transmitted to us by those who were actually present at them, I myself have now resolved to set down a record of the Christian message authenticated by all the investigation possible to me, in order that you and others like you may have a true and detailed presentation of matters you have hitherto ascertained by word of mouth."

Thus there came into existence a book which to this day presents the supreme appeal of Christianity to all paganism past or present. The universality of the Christian faith is revealed by the fact that Luke's book was written by a Greek to a Roman about a Jew.

8]

III

But what had gone into the making of Luke the man before he could become equipped to make his book? Luke had first been child and lad and man in Antioch before he had so much as heard of Jesus of Nazareth. Luke was perhaps a boy in his middle teens when in famous Jerusalem, two hundred miles distant, a certain mysterious malefactor was put to death. One cannot ascertain just how soon afterwards the news of this cruel death and the triumphant Resurrection from a felon's grave reached the receptive ears of the young Luke, but by the year 50 Luke seems to have become a well-known member of the Antioch group of Jesus' followers.

The Antioch of Luke's day was a large and prosperous city, an important transportation center for the long caravan routes, as well as the repository of a Greek culture established by Alexander the Great two centuries before. Antioch was a seaport; the boy Luke would have been familiar with ships and sailors. Many foreigners walked the streets of this flourishing metropolis; the boy Luke might have picked up the native speech of the villagers as they pressed into town, some of them speaking Aramaic, the language of Palestine, the language of Jesus. Luke, well-to-do and educated with all the liberality of Greek custom, probably had firsthand knowledge of the Old Testament, long before translated into Greek and widely circulated among Greek-speaking Jews, of whom there were very many scattered throughout the first-century Roman Empire. The large Jewish colony in Antioch was broad-minded in its outlook, and a young Greek also broad-minded in outlook would have had happy friendships that perhaps supplied Luke with his intimate understanding of Hebrew ways and customs. Luke's writing shows him to have had an eager and adventurous delight in travel. We can imagine him when a boy as taking tramps of investigation in the environs of Antioch. But both within and without the city he would have observed want and suffering to which he would never have been indifferent. Gifted, educated, well-born, and well-to-do, Luke was free to choose his own career. He looked at suffering, and he chose to be a doctor.

In Luke's after years he must often have recalled the peace and joyousness, the freedom and sanity, of his Antioch background, much as many of us today look back wistfully and gratefully to the world we knew before 1914. In Antioch, Luke in childhood and early maturity was privileged to form foundations of normal thinking and normal living. The Christian group to which he came to belong was dominated by the wise and kindly Barnabas, one of the first to trust and befriend Paul after Paul's strange sudden conversion from persecutor to missionary. Barnabas had even brought Paul to Antioch. Barnabas's warm welcome to all young Greeks was well known. In Antioch, Luke could also have known Silas and Mark. Early in his career as a Christian doctor he appears to have joined a relief expedition from the Antioch church to Jerusalem, carrying a cargo of wheat to that city stricken with famine. It may have been on this visit that Luke met people prominent among those earliest Jerusalem Christians—Peter, James, John; Mary, the mother of Mark, in whose upper room the Last Supper was celebrated; and probably that greater Mary, the mother of Jesus. Some dozen years later Luke again accompanied Paul to Jerusalem on a mission of kindliness, taking a gift of money to the Temple treasury. On one of Luke's visits to Jerusalem, many people think he must have known Mary, the mother of Jesus, and from her received directly some of the most intimate details of his story of Christmas.

The second visit to the sacred city was from the first ill omened. Paul had become most unpopular with the Jerusalem Christians because of his friendliness with the Gentiles. James, the brother of Jesus, who was at this time Bishop of Jerusalem, advised Paul to go slowly, to give proof of his fidelity, to placate his enemies. However, almost at once the dreaded circumstance occurred, and Paul was mobbed within the Temple precincts, to be rescued by the Roman guard and sent for safety, with an accompanying battalion of soldiers, to the colonial governor's seat at Cæsarea and the fortress prison there. Paul was to remain in Cæsarea for two long years, from 56 to 58. During all this time Luke was not only in constant attendance upon the prisoner, but ceaselessly working for his release. Vainly. At the end of two years Paul made his famous direct appeal to the Emperor, and was sent to Rome, never to be freed except by death.

For Luke and for us the two years at Cæsarea were to have priceless significance, for it is most probable that it was during this sojourn there, when Luke could move about freely even though in constant attendance upon a famous prisoner, that the third Evangelist gained his full knowledge of the birth story of Jesus.

If we let conjecture play a searchlight back on the middle years of the first century we may perhaps presume humbly to guess where and how and from whom Luke came to his knowledge of the first Christmas. As one of the earliest of the great research scholars of history, Luke would have followed a procedure then rare, but now long taken for granted. Luke we know made certain visits to Jerusalem, and he may well have made more such visits than we know. It seems most probable that in Jerusalem he would have sought out Mary, the mother of Jesus. Luke's own book of Acts explicitly states that Mary was one of the early church community in the holy city. If we try, we can surmise Mary's own accents as an undertone to Luke's Christmas chronicle.

At Jerusalem, Luke was within easy distance of the village of Bethlehem. From much internal evidence we know that he respected humble people, and listened to their reminiscences. It is not too far-fetched, then, to fancy his listening to some aging shepherd who recalled the angel hymn of his boyhood. In some such manner of direct firsthand research Luke may have supplemented an early Aramaic document describing the miracle of Jesus' coming into the world. All scholars seem to agree that Luke actually had in his hand some such ancient scroll, the existence of which they maintain is supported by the arresting difference between the nativity stories and the rest of Luke's Gospel. Chapter III opens to a fresh beginning; there is an abrupt break in continuity. There are also notable differences in style. There is a studied effort to use simple archaic Greek, as if the translator, who was also profoundly an artist in words, were trying to put himself and his reader back into the simple terms and manner of thought of a previous generation, hidden away in the hill country of Judea.

In Cæsarea, Luke would have had priceless leisure both to collect his material and to make some preliminary arrangement of it. In Cæsarea, too, he would have had invaluable association with Philip, and with Philip's four gifted daughters, "prophetesses"—that is to say, accepted teachers and interpreters of the new faith. Undoubtedly Philip's daughters would have known Mary in Jerusalem before they had come to settle in Cæsarea. One cannot calculate what wealth of memories they might there have transmitted to Luke.

IV

But the man Luke, the man who gave us Christmas, what deeper guesses dare we make about him, about his own soul and about his patient perfection of that soul until he was equipped to become the perpetual proclaimer of glad tidings to men? Scholarship and Biblical research afford us only a rough scaffold on which to build our conjecture, a scaffold in itself frankly conjectural. In addition to the scant life history here given, it is supposed that after Paul's death, which may have occurred in 64 as an earliest date, in 68 as a latest one, Luke eventually returned to Palestine, presumably to revise and complete his projected manuscript. At this time the long-smouldering Jewish revolt against Rome flamed to madness, and was tragically punished. The age-old citadel of the Hebrew religion was razed; of the Temple not one stone remained upon another. Luke's Gospel is now dated about 80 A.D. Luke is supposed to have died in the province of Bithynia in the first nineties.

Indeed, all this is a fragmentary basis of fact on which to build supposition that dares to penetrate the personality of the man who gave us Christmas! But he has left the world a book which reveals himself as well as his Master. Research supplies us with certain probable facts, and we may employ human insight and sympathy in interpreting them. The bare facts of Luke's life point to certain conclusions about his character. Even the most cursory examination

12]

of Luke's Gospel and the most superficial study of his life suggest at once his singular fitness for giving the world its Christmas. It was the "beloved physician" who could describe motherhood in all the holiness of our Christmas narratives. It was one who had given all his being to the service of others, and who was never to hold a child of his own in his arms, who could set down the raptured words, "My soul doth magnify the Lord." It was one whose life was consecrated to the relief of suffering who could describe with such exaltation Jesus' miracles of healing. Long before he had ever heard of the mysterious man executed in a distant city, Luke, a joyous-hearted young Greek, must have chosen a career of kindliness. He had himself gone about doing good before he was equipped to write of all the wealth of kindly deeds and sympathetic words that he records in his life of Jesus. Of all four Evangelists, it is Luke who best reveals Jesus the man, friend always of the poor and the downtrodden, comforting even the despairing thief crucified beside him, as Luke alone tells us. It is a joyous human Jesus that Luke presents, probably because he himself had learned high joy in his close contact with an unseen Master. In spite of all its tragedy, Luke's Gospel gives the reader a sense of unconquerable gladness, gladness like that of the two disciples on the walk to Emmaus when their Master returned to share a meal with them, an incident that Luke alone has saved from oblivion. Truly Luke was mysteriously fitted to transmit to us forever the joyousness of Christmas.

But it could never have been a carefree Luke who wrote down those strange sweet Christmas stories. It must have been a Luke who had drunk to the dregs the cup of despair, who had beheld evil triumph in holy places, and who had seen the dream Jesus died for apparently blotted out in blood. It was after Paul's martyrdom— after, and not before—that Luke's Gospel was finished and given to the world. It was after, not before, the destruction of Jerusalem in 70 A.D. that Luke, the doctor-scholar, ended his consecrated research into the life of his Hero, and made it public. With all the world Luke had witnessed the downfall of the old stronghold of Judaism, and the hounding of Jerusalem rebels from one precarious hiding to another. He never completed the Acts of the Apostles to include Paul's martyrdom. Was it that the "beloved physician" was too heartbroken to add the final death-dealing chapters about his dearest friend? If Luke was perhaps thirty-five, already proved a successful doctor and a trusted teacher of the new faith when he joined Paul about 50 A.D., then, when he was reverently bringing his book to a close in the seventies of the first century, he must have been aging toward his own seventies. In spirit he may have shared Simeon's delight in the vision of the newborn babe of hope. We know that the infancy narratives do not seem to have been generally known to the early church. It is Luke the doctor-evangelist who has made them a part of our Christian faith.

But what had these sacred stories of a holy little child meant to Luke himself in his darkening old age, in his darkening world? Persecution was rife. For all we know, Luke may have written in the very shadow of his own martyrdom; some ancient authorities say that he was martyred. From end to end of Palestine the armies of Rome had gone raging and avenging. No one could count the fallen dead that Luke's pen might have recorded but did not. Instead, Luke, an old unbroken man, sent forth from the stricken world of his day to our stricken world of today the deathless hope of an angel hymn, and the deathless promise of a newborn child.

PART I

BETHLEHEM WAS IN JUDAH

THE CHILD

STANLEY WATERLOO

THERE WAS a man who was called upon to write a Christmas article for a great newspaper. He had been a newspaper man himself at one time and it occurred to him, in all reverence, that if some modern daily publication could, nearly 1,900 years ago, have reported faithfully all it could learn regarding the Birth in Bethlehem, there might now be fewer doubters in the world. He imagined what a conscientious representative of the *Daily Augustinian*, had such a newspaper existed in Jerusalem, might have written concerning the greatest happening in the story of all mankind since the days of Moses and the Shepherd Kings.

Rarely has man worked harder than did this person, who, for a month or so—he had studied it all years before—sought the certain details of the historical story of the Christ. He re-read his Josephus; he sought new sources of information, and called to his aid men who knew most along the lines of the outstanding spokes of the main question. Then he lost himself as a reporter of the *Daily Augustinian*, and this, headlines and all, is what he wrote:

THE BIRTH OF THE CHILD

IS THEIR MESSIAH COME?

OLD JEWISH PROPHECY DECLARED FULFILLED IN THE BIRTH OF A GREAT PRINCE.

THE STRANGENESS OF THE STORY.

A Child Born in a Stable in Bethlehem
Asserted to be the Christ.

The Account

A strange story comes to the *Daily Augustinian* from the suburb of Bethlehem, the result of which has been to create deep feeling among the Jewish residents. It is asserted that the Messiah prophesied in their books of worship has come, and that there will be a revolution in the religious world. This belief seems to be spreading among the poor, but is not concurred in by the more wealthy nor by the rabbis who officiate in the temple, though one of them, named Zacharias, is a believer. Upon the first knowledge gained of this reported marvel every effort was made by the *Augustinian* to learn all possible concerning it. The account was that the Messiah had come in the form of a babe, born in the stable of an inn at Bethlehem, and a trustworthy member of the *Augustinian's* staff was sent to the place at once. Here is his account:

It was learned before Bethlehem was reached by the reporter that the story of the Child had first been circulated by those in charge of the flocks kept for sacrifice in the Jewish temple. These are shepherds of an intelligent class who associate with the priests, and whose pastures are very near the city on the Bethlehem road. It was thought best to interview these men before seeking the Child. They were found without difficulty, and told their story simply, a story so remarkable that it is impossible to determine what comment should be made upon it.

The head shepherd, an intelligent and evidently thoroughly honest man of about forty years of age, spoke for all present. "We were watching our flocks as usual on the night concerning the occurrences of which you ask," he said, "when all at once the sky became full of a great light. It was wonderful. We looked up, and there in the midst of the light appeared a form which I cannot describe, it was so bright and dazzling. It spoke to us; spoke in a voice like nothing that can be conceived of for its sweetness, saying that the Savior we have so long awaited had been born to us, and that we might know Him because we should find Him in Bethlehem wrapped in His swaddling clothes and lying in a manger. The wonderful figure had ceased speaking when the whole world above seemed filled with similar forms, and there came from the heavens such music, such sounds of praising as I cannot convey an idea of to you more than I can of the figure. We were awe-stricken at first, and then with one accord we started for Bethlehem. Then another strange thing happened. A great light seemed to float above and ahead of us until we reached Bethlehem, when it hung suspended over the inn. And there we found the Child."

"Is the Child the Messiah of your race? Do you believe it?"

"I *know!*" was the answer. "It is the Messiah!" And that all the shepherds believe was apparent. They appear intelligent and honest and straightforward of speech. It is incomprehensible. The next step was to visit Bethlehem.

There is but one inn in Bethlehem; there was but one place in which to seek the Child. Thither went the seeker after facts. The inn is a plain structure of the usual stonework of the hillside towns, and the stable, extending backward from the house proper, is largely an excavation in the rock. There is a narrow entrance at the side as well as one through the house. About the gates of the inn stood a number of people, the look upon their faces indicating that they were aware of the great news to their race, but all silent in their joy or disbelief or whatever sentiment affected them. The visitor was shown through the inn into the stable. There were the man, the woman, and the Child. They chanced to be alone at the time.

Of the Child it may be said that it is a beautiful male infant, nothing more, to the ordinary eye, and conducting itself not differently from any babe of its age. It clings to its mother's bosom, knowing nothing of the world, and as yet, caring nothing. The man is a sober-faced Jew, apparently about thirty years of age. The woman would attract attention anywhere, for she is one of the fair women of Nazareth, and even among those so noted for their beauty she must have ranked foremost, so sweet of face is she. She is seemingly not yet twenty years of age, with the dark hair, oriental features, and wonderful eyes of the women of her class and town, but with an added expression which makes one think of the angels of which the Jewish writers tell. That she herself believes she is the mother of the Messiah, that the Child she has borne is the Christ, does not admit of doubt. Even as she clasped Him to her breast there was awe mingled with the affection in her look, a devotion beyond even that of motherhood. The man, it was apparent, shared with her in the faith. He was asked to tell the story of the miraculous birth, and stepping aside a little from the woman and the Child, he talked gravely and earnestly, answering all questions, since, as he said, it was his duty to tell the great thing to all the world, to Jew and pagan alike.

He was betrothed to the young woman Mary, he said, months ago, in the town of Nazareth in Galilee, where he is a carpenter. They were to have been wedded, but during the interval between the betrothal and the marriage there came to her a figure, which was that of an angel of the Lord, saying to her that a son would be born to her the paternity of which would be supernatural, and that this son would be the Messiah told of in Jewish prophecy. She informed her betrothed of this, and that she had evidence that what had been told her would occur. At first Joseph was greatly troubled and resolved that the marriage should not take place lest a great disgrace should come upon him. He loved the young woman, and did not want to harm her in the eyes of the world, yet there seemed no alternative but to refuse a consummation of the betrothal. It was at this time that there came to him, as there had come to her, an angelic visitation, in which was confirmed what she had told him, and in which he was commanded to marry her. He was told this in a dream, and believed, and did as he was commanded, though as yet he has been the husband of Mary but in name.

After their marriage came the recent order from Rome for the census of all the Jews, and as it was accompanied by the direction that all should be enumerated, not where they might be living, but where they were registered at birth, Joseph, who was originally from Bethlehem, was compelled to make the journey. He was

20]

accompanied by his young wife, who rode upon a donkey, her husband walking all the way from Nazareth beside her. Upon their arrival in Bethlehem they found the place so full of those called in by the census that there was no place for them to lodge. The owner of the inn, though, who knew of Joseph's family, did all he could to relieve them, and they were given lodging in the stable. There to the patient Mary came a woman's great trial, and the Child was born. Then came the shepherds with their wonderful tale of what they had seen, followed, as related, by their adoration.

It was learned by inquiry in Bethlehem that Joseph, the carpenter, though a poor man, is a direct descendant of David, the famous Jewish king, and, strangely enough, too, that the beautiful Mary belongs to the same princely family. The Hebrew records of this great race are most complete, and there is no doubt as to the blood of the man and woman. Mary, so it is said, is the daughter of a gentlewoman named Anna and of a Hebrew who was held in great respect. There is another most singular fact to be related in this connection. It will be remembered that some months ago, when it came the turn of the venerable prophet Zacharias to offer the sacrifice in the Jewish temple—a privilege which comes to a priest but once in his lifetime—he returned before the people from the inner sanctuary stricken dumb, and manifesting by signs that he had seen a vision, the event creating great excitement among the members of his faith. Later he made it known that in the sanctuary he had a vision of an angel who declared to him that his wife, who was childless, should have a son in her old age who should be a great prophet and preacher, proclaiming the Messiah. Since that time, the aged couple, who live south of Jerusalem, have indeed been blessed with a child, the father's dumbness disappearing with its birth and the priest again praising the Lord of his people. To this child has been given the name of John.

What is most remarkable and unexplainable of all is something confirmed by Joseph and Mary, as well as by Zacharias and his wife. The wife of Zacharias, who is named Elizabeth, is a cousin of Mary, and some impulse moved the latter, after she had explained her condition to Joseph, to visit her aged kinswoman. She did so, and no sooner had she reached the home of Zacharias and entered the door than Elizabeth, who had not known of her coming, broke forth into praise of Mary as to be the mother of her Lord. The unborn babe, it is declared, recognized the presence of the Messiah, and so Elizabeth was led to adore and prophesy.

Many Nazarenes who are now in Jerusalem were seen, and all confirmed the story so far as they could know of the relations of Joseph and Mary, while many people of the hill town where Zacharias and Elizabeth live confirm all that is related of the extraordinary occurrence in their household, of the husband's recovery from dumbness when his child was born, and of his apparent inspiration at the time. There is a strong feeling among the Jews, and the belief in the real appearance of the Messiah is spreading, though, as intimated, the priests of the temple, with the exception already alluded to, seem disposed to discredit the revelation. They declare that the Messiah would scarcely come in such humble way; that the Prince of the House of David who shall renew the glory of their race will come in great magnificence and that all will recognize Him at once.

What has been related is what was learned some days ago from the interviews given and from inquiries in all quarters where it seemed likely that they would throw any light on what has really occurred. Since then something as inexplicable has happened as anything heretofore reported, something from many points of view more startling and unexplainable. There came into Jerusalem recently three Persians of the sort called Magi, or wise men, the students of the great race who have been to an extent friendly with the Jews since the time when Babylon was at its greatest. These three men, who had made a journey which must have occupied them nearly two years, seemed hurriedly intent on some great mission, and presented themselves at once before the Tetrarch, Herod, asking for information. They wanted to know where the Child was to be found who was born King of the Jews, seeming to think that the Tetrarch must know and would direct them willingly. They said they had seen the Child's star in the far east and had come to do Him homage. This was astonishing information to the Tetrarch. As is well known, there are many political intrigues in progress now, and Herod has adopted a severe policy. As between the Romans and the Jews he has been considerate in the endeavor to preserve pleasant relations with both parties, but he is most alert. His reply to the Magi was that he did not know where the Child was, but he hoped they would succeed in their mission. He required, furthermore, that when they had found the King they should inform him, that he might also visit Him. The Magi departed, and shrewd officers were at once sent to follow them, but with slight success. The Magi eluded the officers and found the Child. Joseph and Mary had moved from the stable into a house in Bethlehem, and there the three Persians bowed down before the Babe and, after the style of adoration in their country, presented gifts—gold, frankincense, and myrrh.

These last related facts were learned, as were those first given, in Bethlehem. The next step in the inquiry was naturally to seek an interview with the Magi, the three travelers from Persia who so oddly showed their belief in the supernatural nature of what had occurred, but they were found with difficulty. After visiting the Infant they had returned at once to town, and it proved a hard task to discover their whereabouts. It was ascertained, after much inquiry, that three Persians of the better class had been stopping at a small hotel near the southern gate, and a visit to the place revealed the fact that they were still there, though about to leave. They had, after their visit to Bethlehem, remained close indoors, and, the keeper of the hotel said, seemed apprehensive of a visit from the authorities. The reporter was presented to three fine-looking Chaldeans, evidently men of some importance at home, who received him with reserve, but who, after learning his occupation and object, became a little more communicative. The eldest of the three, a man past middle age, with full beard and remarkably keen eyes, acted as spokesman for all. He was asked what he thought of the Child at Bethlehem.

"It is the Messiah of the Jews," was his prompt reply.

"How do you know that?"

"We know it by His star—the star that was prophesied as heralding His coming. That the Jewish Messiah was to come was foretold by their own prophets and by our own Zoroaster. We are astronomers, and know the mystery of the heavens and the nativities. In what is called Mount Victory in our country is a cave, from the mouth of which the heavens are studied by wise men. About two years ago appeared the star of the Messiah. Then we began our journey to the city of the Jews to pay homage to the Great Ruler born."

"But why do you, who are not Jews, come on such an expedition?"

"Our belief is broad. We care very little for any old teachings which are not verified by celestial phenomena. We saw the prophecy fulfilled. That was enough."

"What about the star? Is it something which will not last?"

"No. It is a star which will last as long as any, but one which is visible on earth only at intervals of long ages. Then it foretells a great event. It appeared last just before the birth of Moses."

"What is it like?"

"It is a bright, almost red, star, visible in the sign Pisces of the zodiac only when Jupiter and Saturn are in conjunction. It is the star of the Messiah."

His companions assented to all the elder man said, but he declined to talk further on the subject. The name of the speaker was given as Melchior; the names of his two friends were Caspar and Balthasar. The first was the one who made a gift of gold to the child, while the second contributed frankincense, and the third myrrh. The reporter returned to the hotel later in the day to ask certain additional questions, but the visitors had left hurriedly. The landlord said they had gone none too soon, as agents of the authorities visited the place soon after their disappearance. It is said that they were warned in a dream that they must escape. They were all three well mounted, and are now, no doubt, some distance from Jerusalem.

Such are the facts. Such is the story as learned of the Messiah of the Jews. Were their prophets right? Has the great Prince come? Is the glory of Rome to pass away before the glory of the Hebrew Christ?

Will the Tetrarch remain undisturbed?

CHRIST LEGENDS

SELMA LAGERLÖF

*Translated from the Swedish
by Velma Swanston Howard*

1. *The Holy Night*

WHEN I was five years old I had such a great sorrow! I hardly know if I have had a greater since then.

It was then that my grandmother died. Up to that time, she used to sit every day on the corner sofa in her room, and tell stories.

I remember grandmother told story after story from morning till night, and we children sat beside her, quite still, and listened. It was a glorious life! No other children had such happy times as we did.

It isn't much that I recollect about my grandmother. I remember that she had very beautiful snow-white hair, and stooped when she walked, and that she always sat and knitted a stocking.

And I even remember that when she had finished a story, she used to lay her hand on my head and say: "All this is as true, as true as that I see you and you see me."

I also remember that she could sing songs, but this she did not do every day. One of the songs was about a knight and a sea-troll, and had this refrain: "It blows cold, cold weather at sea."

Then I remember a little prayer she taught me, and a verse of a hymn.

Of all the stories she told me I have but a dim and imperfect recollection. Only one of them do I remember so well that I should be able to repeat it. It is a little story about Jesus' birth.

Well, this is nearly all that I can recall about my grandmother, except the thing which I remember best; and that is, the great loneliness when she was gone.

I remember the morning when the corner sofa stood empty and when it was impossible to understand how the days would ever come to an end. That I remember. That I shall never forget!

And I recollect that we children were brought forward to kiss the hand of the dead and that we were afraid to do it. But then some one said to us that it would be the last time we could thank grandmother for all the pleasure she had given us.

And I remember how the stories and songs were driven from the homestead, shut up in a long black casket, and how they never came back again.

I remember that something was gone from our lives. It seemed as if the door to a whole beautiful, enchanted world—where before we had been free to go in and out—had been closed. And now there was no one who knew how to open that door.

And I remember that, little by little, we children learned to play with dolls and toys, and to live like other children. And then it seemed as though we no longer missed our grandmother, or remembered her.

But even today—after forty years—as I sit here and gather together the legends about Christ which I heard out there in the Orient, there awakes within me the little legend of Jesus' birth that my grandmother used to tell....

It was a Christmas Day and all the folks had driven to church except grandmother and I. I believe we were all alone in the house. We had not been permitted to go along, because one of us was too old and the other was too young. And we were sad, both of us, because we had not been taken to early mass to hear the singing and to see the Christmas candles.

But as we sat there in our loneliness, grandmother began to tell a story.

"There was a man," said she, "who was out in the dark night

[27

to borrow live coals to kindle a fire. He went from hut to hut and knocked. 'Dear friends, help me!' said he. 'My wife has just given birth to a child, and I must make a fire to warm her and the little one.'

"But it was way in the night, and all the people were asleep. No one replied.

"The man walked and walked. At last he saw the gleam of a fire a long way off. Then he went in that direction, and saw that the fire was burning in the open. A lot of sheep were sleeping around the fire, and an old shepherd sat and watched over the flock.

"When the man who wanted to borrow fire came up to the sheep, he saw that three big dogs lay asleep at the shepherd's feet. All three awoke when the man approached and opened their great jaws, as though they wanted to bark; but not a sound was heard. The man noticed that the hair on their backs stood up and that their sharp, white teeth glistened in the firelight. They dashed toward him. He felt that one of them bit at his leg and one at his hand and that one clung to his throat. But their jaws and teeth wouldn't obey them, and the man didn't suffer the least harm.

"Now the man wished to go farther to get what he needed. But the sheep lay back to back and so close to one another that he couldn't pass them. Then the man stepped upon their backs and walked over them and up to the fire. And not one of the animals awoke or moved."

Thus far, grandmother had been allowed to narrate without interruption. But at this point I couldn't help breaking in. "Why didn't they do it, grandma?" I asked.

"That you shall hear in a moment," said grandmother, and went on with her story.

"When the man had almost reached the fire, the shepherd looked up. He was a surly old man who was unfriendly and harsh toward human beings. And when he saw the strange man coming, he seized the long, spiked staff, which he always held in his hand when he tended his flock, and threw it at him. The staff came right toward the man, but, before it reached him, it turned off to one side and whizzed past him, far out in the meadow."

When grandmother had got this far, I interrupted her again. "Grandma, why wouldn't the stick hurt the man?" Grandmother did not bother about answering me, but continued her story.

"Now the man came up to the shepherd and said to him: 'Good man, help me, and lend me a little fire! My wife has just given birth to a child, and I must make a fire to warm her and the little one.'

"The shepherd would rather have said no, but when he pondered that the dogs couldn't hurt the man, and the sheep had not run from him, and that the staff had not wished to strike him, he was a little afraid, and dared not deny the man that which he asked.

" 'Take as much as you need!' he said to the man.

"But then the fire was nearly burnt out. There were no logs or branches left, only a big heap of live coals; and the stranger had neither spade nor shovel, wherein he could carry the red-hot coals.

"When the shepherd saw this, he said again, 'Take as much as you need!' And he was glad that the man wouldn't be able to take away any coals.

"But the man stooped and picked coals from the ashes with his bare hands, and laid them in his mantle. And he didn't burn his hands when he touched them, nor did the coals scorch his mantle; but he carried them away as if they had been nuts or apples."

But here the story-teller was interrupted for the third time. "Grandma, why wouldn't the coals burn the man?"

"That you shall hear," said grandmother, and went on:

"And when the shepherd, who was such a cruel and hard-hearted man, saw all this, he began to wonder to himself: 'What kind of a night is this, when the dogs do not bite, the sheep are not scared, the staff does not kill, or the fire scorch?' He called the stranger back, and said to him: "What kind of a night is this? And how does it happen that all things show you compassion?'

"Then said the man: 'I cannot tell you if you yourself do not see it.' And he wished to go his way, that he might soon make a fire and warm his wife and child.

"But the shepherd did not wish to lose sight of the man before he had found out what all this might portend. He got up and followed the man till they came to the place where he lived.

"Then the shepherd saw that the man didn't have so much as a hut to dwell in, but that his wife and babe were lying in a mountain grotto, where there was nothing except the cold and naked stone walls.

"But the shepherd thought that perhaps the poor innocent child might freeze to death there in the grotto; and, although he was a hard man, he was touched, and thought he would like to help it. And he loosened his knapsack from his shoulder, took from it a soft white sheepskin, gave it to the strange man, and said that he should let the child sleep on it.

"But just as soon as he showed that he, too, could be merciful, his eyes were opened, and he saw what he had not been able to see before and heard what he could not have heard before.

"He saw that all around him stood a ring of little silver-winged angels, and each held a stringed instrument, and all sang in loud tones that tonight the Saviour was born who should redeem the world from its sins.

"Then he understood how all things were so happy this night that they didn't want to do anything wrong.

"And it was not only around the shepherd that there were angels, but he saw them everywhere. They sat inside the grotto, they sat outside on the mountain, and they flew under the heavens. They came marching in great companies, and, as they passed, they paused and cast a glance at the child.

"There were such jubilation and such gladness and songs and play! And all this he saw in the dark night, whereas before he could not have made out anything. He was so happy because his eyes had been opened that he fell upon his knees and thanked God."

Here grandmother sighed and said: "What that shepherd saw we might also see, for the angels fly down from heaven every Christmas Eve, if we could only see them."

Then grandmother laid her hand on my head, and said: "You must remember this, for it is as true, as true as that I see you

30]

and you see me. It is not revealed by the light of lamps or candles, and it does not depend upon sun and moon; but that which is needful is that we have such eyes as can see God's glory."

2. The Emperor's Vision

It happened at the time when Augustus was Emperor in Rome and Herod was King in Jerusalem.

It was then that a very great and holy night sank down over the earth. It was the darkest night that any one had ever seen. One could have believed that the whole earth had fallen into a cellar vault. It was impossible to distinguish water from land, and one could not find one's way on the most familiar road. And it couldn't be otherwise, for not a ray of light came from heaven. All the stars stayed at home in their own houses, and the fair moon held her face averted.

The silence and the stillness were as profound as the darkness. The rivers stood still in their courses, the wind did not stir, and even the aspen leaves had ceased to quiver. Had anyone walked along the seashore, he would have found that the waves no longer dashed upon the sands; and had one wandered in the desert, the sand would not have crunched under one's feet. Everything was as motionless as if turned to stone, so as not to disturb the holy night. The grass was afraid to grow, the dew could not fall, and the flowers dared not exhale their perfume.

On this night the wild beasts did not seek their prey, the serpents did not sting, and the dogs did not bark. And what was even more glorious, inanimate things would have been unwilling to disturb the night's sanctity, by lending themselves to an evil deed. No false key could have picked a lock, and no knife could possibly have drawn a drop of blood.

In Rome, during this very night, a small company of people came from the Emperor's palace at the Palatine and took the path across the Forum which led to the Capitol. During the day just ended the Senators had asked the Emperor if he had any objections to their erecting a temple to him on Rome's sacred hill. But Augustus had not immediately given his consent. He did not know if it would be agreeable to the gods that he should own a temple next to theirs, and he had replied that first he wished to ascertain their will in the matter by offering a nocturnal sacrifice to his genius. It was he who, accompanied by a few trusted friends, was on his way to perform this sacrifice.

Augustus let them carry him in his litter, for he was old, and it was an effort for him to climb the long stairs leading to the Capitol. He himself held the cage with the doves for the sacrifice. No priests or soldiers or senators accompanied him, only his nearest friends. Torch-bearers walked in front of him in order to light the way in the night darkness and behind him followed the slaves, who carried the tripod, the knives, the charcoal, the sacred fire, and all the other things needed for the sacrifice.

On the way the Emperor chatted gaily with his faithful followers, and therefore none of them noticed the infinite silence and stillness of the night. Only when they had reached the highest point of the Capitol Hill and the vacant spot upon which they contemplated erecting the temple, did it dawn upon them that something unusual was taking place.

It could not be a night like all others, for up on the very edge of the cliff they saw the most remarkable being! At first they thought it was an old, distorted olive-trunk; later they imagined that an ancient stone figure from the temple of Jupiter had wandered out on the cliff. Finally it was apparent to them that it could be only the old sibyl.

Anything so aged, so weather-beaten, and so giant-like in stature they had never seen. This old woman was awe-inspiring! If the Emperor had not been present, they would all have fled to their homes.

"It is she," they whispered to each other, "who has lived as many years as there are sand-grains on her native shores. Why has she come out from her cave just tonight? What does she foretell for the Emperor and the Empire—she, who writes her prophecies on the leaves of the trees and knows that the wind will carry the words of the oracle to the person for whom they are intended?"

They were so terrified that they would have dropped on their knees with their foreheads pressed against the earth, had the sibyl stirred. But she sat as still as though she were lifeless. Crouching upon the outermost edge of the cliff, and shading her eyes with her hand, she peered out into the night. She sat there as if she had gone upon the hill that she might see more clearly something that was happening far away. *She* could see things on a night like this!

At that moment the Emperor and all his retinue marked how profound the darkness was. None of them could see a hand's breadth in front of him. And what stillness! What silence! Not even the Tiber's hollow murmur could they hear. The air seemed to suffocate them, cold sweat broke out on their foreheads, and their hands were numb and powerless. They feared that some dreadful disaster was impending.

But no one cared to show that he was afraid, and everyone told the Emperor that this was a good omen. All Nature held its breath to greet a new god.

They counseled Augustus to hurry with the sacrifice, and said that the old sibyl had evidently come out of her cave to greet his genius.

But the truth was that the old sybil was so absorbed in a vision that she did not even know that Augustus had come up to the Capitol. She was transported in spirit to a far-distant land, where she imagined that she was wandering over a great plain. In the darkness she stubbed her foot continually against something which she believed to be grass tufts. She stooped down and felt with her hand. No, it was not grass, but sheep. She was walking between great sleeping flocks of sheep.

Then she noticed the shepherds' fire. It burned in the middle of the field, and she groped her way to it. The shepherds lay asleep by the fire, and beside them were the long, spiked staves with which they defended their flocks from wild beasts. But the little animals with the glittering eyes and the bushy tails that stole up to the fire, were they not jackals? And yet the shepherds did not fling their staves at them, the dogs continued to sleep, the

[33

sheep did not flee, and the wild animals lay down to rest beside the human beings.

This the sibyl saw, but she knew nothing of what was being enacted on the hill back of her. She did not know that there they were raising an altar, lighting charcoal and strewing incense, and that the Emperor took one of the doves from the cage to sacrifice it. But his hands were so benumbed that he could not hold the bird. With one stroke of the wing, it freed itself and disappeared in the night darkness.

When this happened, the courtiers glanced suspiciously at the old sibyl. They believed that it was she who caused the misfortune.

Could they know that all the while the sibyl thought herself standing beside the shepherds' fire, and that she listened to a faint sound which came trembling through the dead-still night? She heard it long before she marked that it did not come from the earth, but from the sky. At last she raised her head; then she saw light, shimmering forms glide forward in the darkness. They were little flocks of angels, who, singing joyously, and apparently searching, flew back and forth above the wide plain.

While the sibyl was listening to the angel song, the Emperor was making preparations for a new sacrifice. He washed his hands, cleansed the altar, and took up the other dove. And although he exerted his full strength to hold it fast, the dove's slippery body slid from his hand, and the bird swung itself up into the impenetrable night.

The Emperor was appalled! He fell upon his knees and prayed to his genius. He implored him for strength to avert the disasters which this night seemed to foreshadow.

Nor did the sibyl hear any of this either. She was listening with her whole soul to the angel-song, which grew louder and louder. At last it became so powerful that it wakened the shepherds. They raised themselves on their elbows and saw shining hosts of silver-white angels move in the darkness in long, swaying lines, like migratory birds. Some held lutes and cymbals in their hands; others held zithers and harps, and their song rang out as merry as child laughter, and as carefree as the lark's trill. When the shepherds

34]

heard this, they rose up to go to the mountain city, where they lived, to tell of the miracle.

They groped their way forward on a narrow, winding path, and the sibyl followed them. Suddenly it grew light up there on the mountain: a big, clear star kindled right over it, and the city on the mountain summit glittered like silver in the starlight. All the fluttering angel throngs hastened thither, shouting for joy, and the shepherds hurried so that they almost ran. When they reached the city, they found that the angels had assembled over a low stable near the city gate. It was a wretched structure, with a roof of straw and the naked cliff for a back wall. Over it hung the Star, and hither flocked more and more angels. Some seated themselves on the straw roof or alighted upon the steep mountain wall back of the house; others, again, held themselves in the air on outspread wings, and hovered over it. High, high up, the air was illuminated by the shining wings.

The instant the Star kindled over the mountain city, all Nature awoke, and the men who stood upon Capitol Hill could not help seeing it. They felt fresh, but caressing winds which traveled through space; delicious perfumes streamed up about them; trees swayed; the Tiber began to murmur; the stars twinkled, and suddenly the moon stood out in the sky and lit up the world. And out of the clouds the two doves came circling down and lighted upon the Emperor's shoulders.

When this miracle happened, Augustus rose proud and happy, but his friends and his slaves fell on their knees.

"Hail, Caesar!" they cried. "Thy genius hath answered thee. Thou art the god who shall be worshipped on Capitol Hill!"

And this cry of homage, which the men in their transport gave as a tribute to the Emperor, was so loud that the old sibyl heard it. It waked her from her visions. She rose from her place on the edge of the cliff, and came down among the people. It was as if a dark cloud had arisen from the abyss and rushed down the mountain height. She was terrifying in her extreme age! Coarse hair hung in matted tangles around her head, her joints were enlarged, and the dark skin, hard as the bark of a tree, covered her body with furrow upon furrow.

Potent and awe-inspiring, she advanced toward the Emperor. With one hand she clutched his wrist, with the other she pointed toward the distant East.

"Look!" she commanded, and the Emperor raised his eyes and saw. The vaulted heavens opened before his eyes, and his glance traveled to the distant Orient. He saw a lowly stable behind a steep rock wall, and in the open doorway a few shepherds kneeling. Within the stable he saw a young mother on her knees before a little child, who lay upon a bundle of straw on the floor.

And the sibyl's big, knotty fingers pointed toward the poor babe. "Hail, Caesar!" cried the sibyl, in a burst of scornful laughter. "There is the god who shall be worshiped on Capitol Hill!"

Then Augustus shrank back from her, as from a maniac. But upon the sybil fell a mighty spirit of prophecy. Her dim eyes began to burn, her hands were stretched toward heaven, her voice was so changed that it seemed not to be her own, but rang out with such resonance and power that it could have been heard over the whole world. And she uttered words which she appeared to be reading among the stars.

"Upon Capitol Hill shall the Redeemer of the world be worshiped,—*Christ*—but not frail mortals."

When she had said this, she strode past the terror-stricken men, walked slowly down the mountain, and disappeared.

But on the following day, Augustus strictly forbade the people to raise any temple to him on Capitol Hill. In place of it he built a sanctuary to the new-born God-Child, and called it HEAVEN'S ALTAR—*Ara Coeli.*

3. The Wise Men's Well

In old Judea the Drought crept, gaunt and hollow-eyed, between shrunken thistles and yellowed grass.

It was summertime. The sun beat down upon the backs of un-shaded hills, and the slightest breath of wind tore up thick clouds of lime dust from the grayish-white ground. The herds stood huddled together in the valleys, by the dried-up streams.

The Drought walked about and viewed the water supplies. He wandered over to Solomon's Pools, and sighed as he saw that they still held a small quantity of water from their mountain sources. Then he journeyed down to the famous David's Well, near Bethlehem, and found water even there. Finally, he tramped with shuffling gait toward the great highway which leads from Bethlehem to Jerusalem.

When he had arrived about halfway, he saw the Wise Men's Well, where it stands close by the roadside. He saw at a glance that it was almost dry. He seated himself on the curb, which consisted of a single stone hollowed out, and looked into the well. The shining water-mirror, which usually was seen very near the opening, had sunk deep down, and the dirt and slime at the bottom of the well made it muddy and impure.

When the Well beheld the Drought's bronze visage reflected in her clouded mirror, she shook with anguish.

"I wonder when you will be exhausted," said the Drought. "Surely, you do not expect to find any fresh water source, down there in the deep, to come and give you new life; and as for rain— God be praised! there can be no question of that for the next two or three months."

"You may rest content," sighed the Well, "for nothing can help me now. It would take no less than a wellspring from Paradise to save me!"

"Then I will not forsake you until every drop has been drained!" said the Drought. He saw that the old Well was nearing its end, and now he wanted to have the pleasure of seeing it die out drop by drop.

He seated himself comfortably on the edge of the curb, and rejoiced as he heard how the Well sighed down there in the deep. He always took a keen delight in watching the thirsty wayfarers come up to the well-curb, let down the bucket, and draw it up again, with only a few drops of muddy water.

Thus the whole day passed; and when darkness descended, the

37

Drought looked again into the Well. A little water still shimmered down there. "I'll stay here all night," cried he, "so do not hurry yourself! When it grows so light that I can look into you once more, I am certain that all will be over with you."

The Drought curled himself up on the edge of the well-curb, while the hot night, which was even more cruel, and more full of torment than the day had been, descended over Judea. Dogs and jackals howled incessantly, and thirsty cows and asses answered them from their stuffy stalls.

When the breeze stirred a little now and then, it brought with it no relief, but was as hot and suffocating as a great sleeping monster's panting breath. The stars shone with the most resplendent brilliancy, and a little silvery new moon cast a pretty blue-green light over the gray hills. And in this light the Drought saw a great caravan come marching toward the hill where the Wise Men's Well was situated.

The Drought sat and gazed at the long procession, and rejoiced again at the thought of all the thirst which was coming to the well, and would not find one drop of water with which to slake itself. There were so many animals and drivers they could easily have emptied the Well, even if it had been quite full. Suddenly he began to think there was something unusual, something ghostlike, about this caravan which came marching forward in the night. First, all the camels came within sight on a hill, which loomed up, high and distinct against the horizon; it was as though they had stepped straight down from heaven. They also appeared to be larger than ordinary camels, and bore—all too lightly—the enormous burdens which weighted them.

Still he could not understand anything but that they were absolutely real, for to him they were just as plain as plain could be. He could even see that the three foremost animals were dromedaries, with gray, shiny skins; and that they were richly bridled and saddled, with fringed coverings, and were ridden by handsome, noble-looking knights.

The whole procession stopped at the well. With three sharp jerks, the dromedaries lay down on the ground, and their riders dismounted. The pack-camels remained standing, and as they assembled they seemed to form a long line of necks and humps and peculiarly piled-up packs.

Immediately, the riders came up to the Drought and greeted him by laying their hands upon their foreheads and breasts. He saw that they wore dazzling white robes and huge turbans, on the front of each of which there was a clear, glittering star, which shone as if it had been taken direct from the skies.

"We come from a far-off land," said one of the strangers, "and we bid thee tell us if this is in truth the Wise Men's Well?"

"It is called so today," said the Drought, "but by tomorrow there will be no well here. It shall die tonight."

"I can understand this, as I see thee here," said the man. "But is not this one of the sacred wells which never run dry? or whence hath it derived its name?"

"I know it is sacred," said the Drought, "but what good will that do? The three wise men are in Paradise."

The three travelers exchanged glances. "Dost thou really know the history of this ancient well?" asked they.

"I know the history of all wells and fountains and brooks and rivers," said the Drought, with pride.

"Then grant us a pleasure, and tell us the story!" begged the strangers; and they seated themselves around the old enemy to everything growing, and listened.

The Drought shook himself and crawled up on the well-curb, like a storyteller upon his improvised throne, and began his tale.

"In Gebas, in Media, a city which lies near the border of the desert—and, therefore, it has often been a free and well-beloved city to me—there lived, many, many years ago, three men who were famed for their wisdom.

"They were also very poor, which was a most uncommon state of affairs; for, in Gebas, knowledge was held in high esteem, and was well recompensed. With these men, however, it could hardly have been otherwise, for one of them was very old, one was afflicted with leprosy, and the third was a black, thick-lipped negro. People regarded the first as much too old to teach them anything; the second they avoided for fear of contagion; and the third they would not listen to, because they thought they knew that no wisdom had ever come from Ethiopia.

"Meanwhile, the three wise ones became united through their common misery. They begged during the day at the same temple gate, and at night they slept on the same roof. In this way they at least had an opportunity to while away the hours, by meditating upon the wonderful things which they observed in Nature and in the human race.

"One night, as they slept side by side on a roof, which was overgrown with stupefying red poppies, the eldest among them awoke, and hardly had he cast a glance around him, before he wakened the other two.

" 'Praised be our poverty which compels us to sleep in the open!' he said to them. 'Awake! and raise your eyes to heaven!'

"Well," said the Drought, in a somewhat milder tone, "this was a night which no one who witnessed can ever forget! The skies were so bright that the heavens, which usually resemble an arched vault, looked deep and transparent and full of waves, like a sea. The light surged backwards and forwards and the stars swam in their varying depths; some in among the light-waves; others upon the surface.

"But farthest away and highest up, the three men saw a faint shadow appear. This shadow traveled through space like a ball, and came nearer and nearer, and, as the ball approached, it began to brighten. But it brightened as roses do—may God let them all wither!—when they burst from their buds. It grew bigger and bigger, the dark cover about it turned back by degrees, and light broke forth on its sides into four distinct leaves. Finally, when it had descended to the nearest of the stars, it came to a standstill. Then the dark lobes curled themselves back and unfolded leaf upon leaf of beautiful, shimmering, rose-colored light, until it was perfect, and shone like a star among stars.

"When the poor men beheld this, their wisdom told them that at this moment a mighty king was born on earth; one, whose majesty and power should rise higher than that of Cyrus or of

Alexander; and they said to one another: 'Let us go to the father and mother of the newborn babe and tell them what we have seen! Mayhap they will reward us with a purse of coin or a bracelet of gold.'

"They grasped their long traveling staves and went forth. They wandered through the city and out from the city gate; but there they felt doubtful for a moment as they saw before them the great stretch of dry, smooth desert, which human beings dread. Then they saw the new star cast a narrow stream of light across the desert sand, and they wandered confidently forward with the star as their guide.

"All night long they tramped over the wide sand-plain, and throughout the entire journey they talked about the young, newborn king, whom they should find reposing in a cradle of gold, playing with precious stones. They whiled away the hours by talking over how they should approach his father, the king, and his mother, the queen, and tell them that the heavens augured for their son power and beauty and joy, greater than Solomon's. They prided themselves upon the fact that God had called *them* to see the Star. They said to themselves that the parents of the new-born babe would not reward them with less than twenty purses of gold; perhaps they would give them so much gold that they no longer need suffer the pangs of poverty.

"I lay in wait on the desert like a lion," said the Drought, "and intended to throw myself upon these wanderers with all the agonies of thirst, but they eluded me. All night the Star had led them, and on the morrow, when the heavens brightened and all the other stars grew pale, it remained steady and illumined the desert, and then guided them to an oasis where they found a spring and a ripe, fruit-bearing tree. There they rested all that day. And toward night, as they saw the star's rays border the sands, they went on.

"From the human way of looking at things," continued the Drought, "it was a delightful journey. The Star led them in such a way that they did not have to suffer either hunger or thirst. It led them past the sharp thistles, it avoided the thick, loose, flying sand; they escaped the burning sunshine and the hot desert storms. The three wise men said repeatedly to one another: 'God is protecting us and blessing our journey. We are His messengers.'

"Then, by degrees, they fell into my power," said the Drought. "These star-wanderers' hearts became transformed into as dry a desert as the one which they traveled through. They were filled with impotent pride and destructive greed.

" 'We are God's messengers!' repeated the three wise ones. 'The father of the newborn King will not reward us too well, even if he gives us a caravan laden with gold.'

"By and by, the Star led them over the far-famed River Jordan, and up among the hills of Judea. One night it stood still over the little city of Bethlehem, which lay upon a hilltop, and shone among the olive trees.

"But the three wise ones looked around for castles and fortified towers and walls, and all the other things that belong to a royal city; but of such they saw nothing. And what was still worse, the Star's light did not even lead them into the city, but remained over a grotto near the wayside. There, the soft light stole in through the opening and revealed to the three wanderers a little Child, who was being lulled to sleep in its mother's arms.

"Although the three men saw how the Star's light encircled the Child's head, like a crown, they remained standing outside the grotto. They did not enter to prophesy honors and kingdoms for this little One. They turned away without betraying their presence. They fled from the Child, and wandered down the hill again.

" 'Have we come in search of beggars as poor as ourselves?' said they. 'Has God brought us hither than we might mock Him, and predict honors for a shepherd's son? This Child will never attain any higher distinction than to tend sheep here in the valleys."

The Drought chuckled to himself and nodded to his hearers, as much as to say: "Am I not right? There are things which are drier than the desert sands, but there is nothing more barren than the human heart.

"The three wise ones had not wandered very far before they thought they had gone astray and had not followed the Star rightly," continued the Drought. "They turned their gaze upward to find again the Star, and the right road; but then the Star which they had followed all the way from the Orient had vanished from the heavens."

The three strangers made a quick movement, and their faces expressed deep suffering.

"That which now happened," continued the Drought, "is in accord with the usual manner of mankind in judging of what is, perhaps, a blessing.

"To be sure, when the three wise men no longer saw the Star, they understood at once that they had sinned against God.

"And it happened with them," continued the Drought furiously, "just as it happens with the ground in the autumn, when the heavy rains begin to fall. They shook with terror, as one shakes when it thunders and lightens; their whole being softened, and humility, like green grass, sprang up in their souls.

"For three nights and days they wandered about the country, in quest of the Child whom they would worship; but the Star did not appear to them. They grew more and more bewildered, and suffered the most overwhelming anguish and despair. On the third day they came to this well to drink. Then God had pardoned their sin. And, as they bent over the water, they saw in its depths the reflection of the Star which had brought them from the Orient. Instantly they saw it also in the heavens and it led them again to the grotto in Bethlehem, where they fell upon their knees before the Child and said: 'We bring thee golden vessels filled with incense and costly spices. Thou shalt be the greatest king that ever lived upon earth, from its creation even unto its destruction.'

"Then the Child laid his hand upon their lowered heads, and when they rose, lo! the Child had given them gifts greater than a king could have granted; for the old beggar had grown young, the leper was made whole, and the negro was transformed into a beautiful white man. And it is said of them that they were glorious! and that they departed and became kings—each in his own kingdom."

The Drought paused in his story, and the three strangers praised it. "Thou hast spoken well," said they. "But it surprises me," said one of them, "that the three wise men do nothing for the well which showed them the Star. Shall they entirely forget such a great blessing?"

"Should not this well remain perpetually," said the second stranger, "to remind mankind that happiness, which is lost on the heights of pride and vainglory, will let itself be found again in the depths of humility?"

"Are the departed worse than the living?" asked the third. "Does gratitude die with those who live in Paradise?"

But as he heard this, the Drought sprang up with a wild cry. He had recognized the strangers! He understood who the strangers were, and fled from them like a madman, that he might not witness how the Three Wise Men called their servants and led their camels, laden with water sacks, to the Well, and filled the poor dying Well with water, which they had brought with them from Paradise.

4. The Flight into Egypt

Far away in one of the Eastern deserts many, many years ago grew a palm tree, which was both exceedingly old and exceedingly tall.

All who passed through the desert had to stop and gaze at it, for it was much larger than the other palms; and they used to say of it, that some day it would certainly be taller than the obelisks and pyramids.

Where the huge palm tree stood in its solitude and looked out over the desert, it saw something one day which made its mighty leaf-crown sway back and forth on its slender trunk with astonishment. Over by the desert borders walked two human beings. They were still at the distance at which camels appear to be as tiny as moths, but they were certainly two human beings—two who were strangers in the desert, for the palm knew the desert folk. They were a man and a woman who had neither guide nor pack-camels; neither tent nor water sack.

"Verily," said the palm to itself, "these two have come hither only to meet certain death."

The palm cast a quick, apprehensive glance around.

"It surprises me," it said, "that the lions are not already out to hunt this prey, but I do not see a single one astir; nor do I see any of the desert robbers, but they'll probably soon come."

"A seven-fold death awaits these travelers," thought the palm. "The lions will devour them, thirst will parch them, the sandstorm will bury them, robbers will trap them, sunstroke will blight them, and fear will destroy them."

And the palm tried to think of something else. The fate of these people made it sad at heart.

But on the whole desert plain, which lay spread out beneath the palm, there was nothing which it had not known and looked upon these thousand years. Nothing in particular could arrest its attention. Again it had to think of the two wanderers.

"By the drought and the storm!" said the palm, calling upon Life's most dangerous enemies. "What is that that the woman carries on her arm? I believe these fools also bring a little child with them!"

The palm, who was far-sighted—as the old usually are—actually saw aright. The woman bore on her arm a child that leaned against her shoulder and slept.

"The child hasn't even sufficient clothing on," said the palm. "I see that the mother has tucked up her skirt and thrown it over the child. She must have snatched him from his bed in great haste and rushed off with him. I understand now: these people are runaways.

"But they are fools, nevertheless," continued the palm. "Unless an angel protects them, they would have done better to have let their enemies do their worst, than to venture into this wilderness.

"I can imagine how the whole thing came about. The man stood at his work; the child slept in his crib; the woman had gone out to fetch water. When she was a few steps from the door, she saw enemies coming. She rushed back to the house, snatched up her child, and fled.

"Since then, they have been fleeing for several days. It is very certain that they have not rested a moment. Yes, everything has happened in this way, but still I say that unless an angel protects them—

[45

"They are so frightened that, as yet, they feel neither fatigue nor suffering. But I see their thirst by the strange gleam in their eyes. Surely I ought to know a thirsty person's face!"

And when the palm began to think of thirst, a shudder passed through its tall trunk, and the long leaves' numberless lobes rolled up, as though they had been held over a fire.

"Were I a human being," it said, "I should never venture into the desert. He is pretty brave who dares come here without having roots that reach down to the never-dying water veins. Here it can be dangerous even for palms; yea, even for a palm such as I.

"If I could counsel them, I should beg them to turn back. Their enemies could never be as cruel toward them as the desert. Perhaps they think it is easy to live in the desert! But I know that, now and then, even I have found it hard to keep alive. I recollect one time in my youth when a hurricane threw a whole mountain of sand over me. I came near choking. If I could have died that would have been my last moment."

The palm continued to think aloud, as the aged and solitary habitually do.

"I hear a wondrous beautiful melody rush through my leaves," it said. "All the lobes on my leaves are quivering. I know not what it is that takes possession of me at the sight of these poor strangers. But this unfortunate woman is so beautiful! She carries me back, in memory, to the most wonderful thing that I ever experienced."

And while the leaves continued to move in a soft melody, the palm was reminded how once, very long ago, two illustrious personages had visited the oasis. They were the Queen of Sheba and Solomon the Wise. The beautiful Queen was to return to her own country; the King had accompanied her on the journey, and now they were going to part. "In remembrance of this hour," said the Queen then, "I now plant a date seed in the earth, and I wish that from it shall spring a palm which shall grow and live until a King shall arise in Judea, greater than Solomon." And when she had said this, she planted the seed in the earth and watered it with her tears.

46]

"How does it happen that I am thinking of this just today?" said the palm. "Can this woman be so beautiful that she reminds me of the most glorious of queens, of her by whose word I have lived and flourished until this day?

"I hear my leaves rustle louder and louder," said the palm, "and it sounds as melancholy as a dirge. It is as though they prophesied that someone would soon leave this life. It is well to know that it does not apply to me, since I cannot die."

The palm assumed that the death rustle in its leaves must apply to the two lone wanderers. It is certain that they too believed that their last hour was nearing. One saw it from their expression as they walked past the skeleton of a camel which lay in their path. One saw it from the glances they cast back at a pair of passing vultures. It couldn't be otherwise; they must perish!

They had caught sight of the palm and oasis and hastened thither to find water. But when they arrived at last, they collapsed from despair, for the well was dry. The woman, worn out, laid the child down and seated herself beside the well-curb, and wept. The man flung himself down beside her and beat upon the hard dry earth with his fists. The palm heard how they talked with each other about their inevitable death. It also gleaned from their conversation that King Herod had ordered the slaughter of all male children from two to three years old, because he feared that the long-looked-for King of the Jews had been born.

"It rustles louder and louder in my leaves," said the palm. "These poor fugitives will soon see their last moment."

It perceived also that they dreaded the desert. The man said it would have been better if they had stayed at home and fought with the soldiers, than to fly hither. He said that they would have met an easier death.

"God will help us," said the woman.

"We are alone among beasts of prey and serpents," said the man. "We have no food and no water. How should God be able to help us?" In despair he rent his garments and pressed his face against the dry earth. He was hopeless—like a man with a death-wound in his heart.

The woman sat erect, with her hands clasped over her knees. But the looks she cast towards the desert spoke of a hopelessness beyond bounds.

The palm heard the melancholy rustle in its leaves growing louder and louder. The woman must have heard it also, for she turned her gaze upward toward the palm-crown. And instantly she involuntarily raised her arms.

"Oh, dates, dates!" she cried. There was such intense agony in her voice that the old palm wished itself no taller than a broom and that the dates were as easy to reach as the buds on a brier bush. It probably knew that its crown was full of date clusters, but how should a human being reach such a height?

The man had already seen how beyond all reach the date clusters hung. He did not even raise his head. He begged his wife not to long for the impossible.

But the child, who had toddled about by himself and played with sticks and straws, had heard the mother's agony.

Of course the little one could not imagine that his mother should not get everything she wished for. The instant she said dates, he began to stare at the tree. He pondered and pondered how he should bring down the dates. His forehead was almost drawn into wrinkles under his golden curls. At last a smile stole over his face. He had found the way. He went up to the palm and stroked it with his little hand, and said, in a sweet, childish voice:

"Palm, bend thee! Palm, bend thee!"

But what was that, what was that? The palm leaves rustled as if a hurricane had passed through them, and up and down the long trunk traveled shudder upon shudder. And the tree felt that the little one was its superior. It could not resist him.

And it bowed its long trunk before the child, as people bow before princes. In a great bow it bent itself towards the ground, and finally it came down so far that the big crown with the trembling leaves swept the desert sand.

The child appeared to be neither frightened nor surprised; with a joyous cry he loosened cluster after cluster from the old palm's crown. When he had plucked enough dates, and the tree lay on

48]

the ground, the child came back again and caressed it and said, in the gentlest voice:

"Palm, raise thee! Palm, raise thee!"

Slowly and reverently the big tree raised itself on its slender trunk, while the leaves played like harps.

"Now I know for whom they are playing the death melody," said the palm to itself when it stood erect once more. "It is not for any of these people."

The man and the woman sank upon their knees and thanked God.

"Thou hast seen our agony and removed it. Thou art the Powerful One who bendest the palm-trunk like a reed. What enemy should we fear when Thy strength protects us?"

The next time a caravan passed through the desert, the travelers saw that the great palm's leaf-crown had withered.

"How can this be?" said a traveler. "This palm was not to die before it had seen a King greater than Solomon."

"Mayhap it hath seen him," answered another of the desert travelers.

BETHLEHEM EPISODES

HEYWOOD BROUN

Frankincense and Myrrh

ONCE THERE were three kings in the East and they were wise men. They read the heavens and they saw a certain strange star by which they knew that in a distant land the King of the World was to be born. The star beckoned to them and they made preparations for a long journey.

From their palaces they gathered rich gifts, gold and frankincense and myrrh. Great sacks of precious stuffs were loaded upon the backs of the camels which were to bear them on their journey. Everything was in readiness, but one of the wise men seemed perplexed and would not come at once to join his two companions, who were eager and impatient to be on their way in the direction indicated by the star.

They were old, these two kings, and the other wise man was young. When they asked him he could not tell why he waited. He knew that his treasures had been ransacked for rich gifts for the King of Kings. It seemed that there was nothing more which he could give, and yet he was not content.

He made no answer to the old men who shouted to him that the time had come. The camels were impatient and swayed and snarled. The shadows across the desert grew longer. And still the young king sat and thought deeply.

At length he smiled, and he ordered his servants to open the great treasure sack upon the back of the first of his camels. Then he went into a high chamber to which he had not been since he was a child. He rummaged about and presently came out and approached the caravan. In his hand he carried something which glinted in the sun.

The kings thought that he bore some new gift more rare and precious than any which they had been able to find in all their treasure rooms. They bent down to see, and even the camel drivers peered from the backs of the great beasts to find out what it was which gleamed in the sun. They were curious about this last gift for which all the caravan had waited.

And the young king took a toy from his hand and placed it upon the sand. It was a dog of tin, painted white and speckled with black spots. Great patches of paint had worn away and left the metal clear, and that was why the toy shone in the sun as if it had been silver.

The youngest of the wise men turned a key in the side of the little black and white dog and then he stepped aside so that the kings and the camel drivers could see. The dog leaped high in the air and turned a somersault. He turned another and another and then fell over upon his side and lay there with a set and painted grin upon his face.

A child, the son of a camel driver, laughed and clapped his hands, but the kings were stern. They rebuked the youngest of the wise men and he paid no attention but called to his chief servant to make the first of all the camels kneel. Then he picked up the toy of tin and, opening the treasure sack, placed his last gift with his own hands in the mouth of the sack so that it rested safely upon the soft bags of incense.

"What folly has seized you?" cried the eldest of the wise men. "Is this a gift to bear to the King of Kings in the far country?"

And the young man answered and said: "For the King of Kings there are gifts of great richness, gold and frankincense and myrrh.

"But this," he said, "is for the child in Bethlehem!"

Once there lived near Bethlehem a man named Simon and his wife Deborah. And Deborah dreamed a curious dream, a dream so vivid that it might better be called a vision. It was not yet daybreak, but she roused her husband and told him that an angel had come to her in the vision and had said, as she remembered it, "Tomorrow night in Bethlehem the King of the World will be born." The rest was not so vivid in Deborah's mind, but she told Simon that wise men and kings were already on their way to Bethlehem, bringing gifts for the wonder child.

"When he is born," she said, "the wise men and the kings who bring these gifts will see the stars dance in the heavens and hear the voices of angels. You and I must send presents, too, for this child will be the greatest man in all the world."

Simon objected that there was nothing of enough value in the house to take to such a child, but Deborah replied, "The King of the World will understand." Then, although it was not yet light, she got up and began to bake a cake, and Simon went beyond the town to the hills to get holly and made a wreath. Later in the day husband and wife looked over all their belongings, but the only suitable gift they could find was an old toy, a somewhat battered wooden duck that had belonged to their eldest son, who had grown up and married and gone away to live in Galilee. Simon painted the toy duck as well as he could, and Deborah told him to take it and the cake and the wreath of holly and go to Bethlehem. "It's not much," she said, "but the King will understand."

It was almost sunset when Simon started down the winding road that led to Bethlehem. Deborah watched him round the first turn and would have watched longer except that he was walking straight toward the sun and the light hurt her eyes. She went back into the house and an hour had hardly passed when she heard Simon whistling in the garden. He was walking very slowly. At the door he hesitated for almost a minute. She looked up when he came in. He was empty handed.

"You haven't been to Bethlehem," said Deborah.

"No," said Simon.

"Then, where is the cake, and the holly wreath, and the toy duck?"

"I'm sorry," said Simon, "I couldn't help it somehow. It just happened."

"What happened?" asked Deborah sharply.

"Well," said Simon, "just after I went around the first turn in the road I found a child sitting on that big white rock, crying. He was about two or three years old, and I stopped and asked him why he was crying. He didn't answer. Then I told him not to cry like that, and I patted his head, but that didn't do any good. I hung around, trying to think up something, and I decided to put the cake down and take him up in my arms for a minute. But the cake slipped out of my hands and hit the rock, and a piece of the icing chipped off. Well, I thought, that baby in Bethlehem won't miss a little piece of icing, and I gave it to the child and he stopped crying. But when he finished he began to cry again. I just sort of squeezed another little piece of icing off, and that was all right, for a little while; but then I had to give him another piece, and things went on that way, and all of a sudden I found that there wasn't any cake left. After that he looked as if he might cry again, and I didn't have any more cake and so I showed him the duck and he said 'Ta-ta.' I just meant to lend him the duck for a minute, but he wouldn't give it up. I coaxed him a good while, but he wouldn't let go. And then a woman came out of that little house and she began to scold him for staying out so late, and I told her it was my fault and I gave her the holly wreath just so she wouldn't be mad at the child. And after that, you see, I didn't have anything to take to Bethlehem, and so I came back here."

Deborah had begun to cry before Simon finished his story, but when he had done she lifted up her head and said, "How could you do it, Simon? Those presents were meant for the King of the World, and you gave them to the first crying child you met on the road."

Then she began to cry again, and Simon didn't know what to say or do, and it grew darker in the room and the fire on the hearth faded to a few embers. And that little red glow was all there was in the room. Now, Simon could not even see Deborah across the room, but he could still hear her sobbing. But suddenly the room was flooded with light and Deborah's sobbing broke into a great gulp and she rushed to the window and looked out. The stars danced in the sky and from high above the house came the voice of angels saying, "Glory to God in the highest, and on earth peace, good will toward men."

Deborah dropped to her knees in a panic of joy and fear. Simon knelt beside her, but first he said, "I thought maybe that the baby in Bethlehem wouldn't mind so very much."

We, Too, Are Bidden

The angel of the Lord said to the shepherds, "And this shall be a sign unto you: Ye shall find the babe wrapped in swaddling clothes, lying in a manger."

They made haste to go to Bethlehem to see the thing which had come to pass. "For unto you," the angel said, "is born this day in the city of David a Saviour, which is Christ the Lord."

But as they journeyed to Bethlehem they fell into a discussion as to just how they should find the place where the infant lay. The shepherds were not folk familiar with the town, even though it lay a short journey from the fields in which they tended their flocks. Besides, they knew that many from the country roundabout had gone to Bethlehem in compliance with the decree of Caesar Augustus that all the world should be taxed. Indeed, one of the group grumbled, "In Bethlehem there be many mangers, and how are we to find the one?"

And the youngest shepherd said, "It will be made known to us."

The night was bright wtih stars and the way more easy than they had expected. In spite of the late hour many walked in the narrow streets of Bethlehem, and from all the houses there came a clatter. The shepherds stood for a moment in some perplexity as to the appointed place. The noises of the town were confusing to men who had been standing silent under starlight.

And suddenly the volume of voices increased, and down the

street there came a caravan of camels. Upon the backs of the beasts sat great bearded men, and with them they brought sacks of precious stuffs and huge treasure chests from distant kingdoms. The air was filled with the pungent tang of spice and perfume.

The startled shepherds stood against the wall to let the cavalcade of the mighty pass by. And these wise men and kings seemed to have no doubt as to their destination. They swept past the inn and dismounted at the door of a stable. Servants took the burdens from the backs of the camels, and the kings and the wise men stooped and went in through the low door of the stable.

"It is there the child lies in the manger," said one of the shepherds and made as if to follow, but his fellows were abashed and said among themselves, "It is not meet that we should crowd in upon the heels of the mighty."

"We, too, are bidden," insisted the youngest shepherd. "For us, as well, there was the voice of the angel of the Lord."

And timidly the men from the fields followed after and found places near the door. They watched as the men from distant countries came and silently placed their gifts at the foot of the manger where the child lay sleeping. And the shepherds stood aside and let the great of the earth go out into the night to take up again their long journey.

Presently they were alone, but as they had no gifts to lay beside the gold and frankincense they turned to go back to their flocks. But Mary, the mother, made a sign to the youngest shepherd to come closer. And he said, "We are shepherds, and we have come suddenly from the fields whence an angel summoned us. There is naught which we could add to the gifts of wise men and of kings."

Mary replied, "Before the throne of God, who is a king and who is a wise man, you have brought with you a gift more precious than all the others. It lies within your heart."

And suddenly it was made known to the shepherd the meaning of the words of Mary. He knelt at the foot of the manger and gave to the child his prayer of joy and of devotion.

CHRISTMAS FANCIES

JULES LEMAÎTRE

Translated from the French by Clarence Stratton

1. The Beasts of the Fields

OLD SEPHORA lived in the village of Bethlehem.

She made her living from a herd of goats and a little orchard planted with fig trees.

As a young girl she had been servant for a priest so that she was more knowing in matters of religion than persons of her station usually are.

Returned to the village, married, several times a mother, she had lost her husband and her children. And then, though helping men according to her means, the greatest part of her sympathy she poured out on animals. She protected birds and mice; she gathered in abandoned dogs and distressed cats; and her little house was crowded with all these humble guests.

She loved animals, not only because they are innocent, because they give their hearts to those who love them, and because their trust is overwhelming, but because she was swayed by a sense of justice.

She did not understand why those who could not be wicked should suffer, nor how they could violate a rule of which they knew nothing.

She could explain better or worse the suffering of mankind. Taught by the priest, she did not believe that everything ended in the sleepy peace of *scheol*, nor that the Messiah when he should appear was merely to establish the earthly kingdom of Israel. The "Kingdom of God" would be the reign of justice beyond the tomb. It was perfectly clear that in the unknown world all suffering would deserve expiation. Unmerited and purposeless suffering (like that of little children or certain unfortunates who had sinned only a little) would seem no more than a bad dream and would be rewarded by a happiness at least to an equal degree.

But what of the beasts that suffer? Those who slowly die of cruel diseases—as men do—and raise their pleading eyes to you? Dogs to whom affection is never shown, or those who love their masters and waste away from loneliness? Horses, whose long days are nothing but heaving efforts, and weariness of bleeding under blows, whose rest, even in the darkness of narrow stalls, is so mournful? Captive beasts devoured by homesickness behind the bars of cages? All those poor beasts whose life is a hopeless agony, deprived even of a voice to utter what they endure, a voice with which to curse? What end does their suffering serve? What reward can they expect?

Sephora was a very simple old woman; but because she was sincerely hungry for justice, she often turned over these questions in her mind; and the thought of unexplained grief obscured for her the beauty of the day and the exquisite colors of the hills of Judea.

When her neighbors came to tell her, "The Messiah is born; an angel proclaimed Him to us last night; He is in a stable with His mother only a quarter of a league from here; and we have worshipped Him," old Sephora replied:

"We shall see."

For she had an idea.

That evening, after having cared for her goats, fed her other beasts, and patted all of them, she made her way toward the miraculous stable.

In the enchantment of the blue night, the plain, the rocks, the trees, and even the blades of grass seemed motionless with joy. One would have said that the whole earth slept deliciously. But old Sephora did not forget that even at the moment unjust nature was doing wrongs that no future could right; she could not put away from her thoughts the fact that at the very moment, throughout the vast world, sick persons who were not wicked were sweating with anguish in their burning beds; travelers were being killed along the roads; men were being tortured by other men; mothers were weeping over their little dead babies; and animals were suffering terribly without knowing why.

Before her she saw a light, gentle but yet so alive that it paled the light of the moon. This glow spread from the stable huddled in a fissure of the rocks and supported by pillars of stone.

Near the entrance some camels slept on their bent knees in the midst of a pile of chased and colored vases, baskets of fruit, thick carpets unrolled, and open caskets in which jewels sparkled dazzlingly.

"Now, what's all this?" asked the old woman.

"The Kings are here," a man replied.

"Kings?" said Sephora, frowning.

She went into the stable, saw the infant Jesus in the manger between Mary and Joseph, the three Magi, shepherds, and laborers with their wives, their sons, and their daughters, and in a corner an ass and an ox.

"Let us see," she said.

The three Kings advanced to the Child, and the shepherds politely stepped back before them. But the Child made a sign to the shepherds to draw near.

Old Sephora did not stir.

The Child placed his little hand first upon the heads of the wives and the daughters because they are better and suffer the more, then upon the heads of the men and the boys.

And Mary spoke to them.

"Be patient; He loves you and has come to suffer with you."

Then the white King believed his turn had come. But the Child with a gentle gesture called the black King, then the yellow King.

The black King, with hair curled close and shining with oil, and smiling with all his teeth, offered to the Newborn necklaces of bones of fish, varicolored pebbles, dates, and coconuts.

Mary spoke to him.

"You are not bad, but you do not know. Try to picture what you would be if you were not King in your country. Eat no more men, and beat no more of your subjects."

The yellow King, with slanting eyes, offered pieces of gilt embroidered with dragons, Chinese vases on which rays of the moon seemed marked in the enamel, a sphere of ivory curiously marked to represent the heavens with the planets and all the animals of creation, and sacks of tea gathered from selected bushes in the best season.

And Mary spoke to him.

"No longer hide yourself from your people. Believe no longer that all wisdom belongs to you and your race. And take care of those who have only mouldy rice to eat."

The white King in military uniform offered the Child delicate silver-ware, chiselled and inlaid weapons, statuettes carved in the form of beautiful women, and purple cases containing the writings of a sage named Plato.

And Mary spoke to him.

"Make no more unjust wars. Beware of pleasures that harden the heart. Proclaim equitable laws, and know that it is the concern of you and of all others that no one in your kingdom shall be badly treated."

And after the shepherds and the laborers, the Child blessed the Kings, in the order in which He had summoned them.

Old Sephora was thinking.

"This order is sensible. The Child began with those who need His coming most. He makes it plain that He is careful to deal with justice, that He will reestablish its reign in both this world and the other. His mother, also, talked well. Nevertheless, He doesn't think of everything. What will He do for the animals?"

But Mary understood her thoughts. She turned to her Son and the Child turned toward the ass and the ox.

The donkey, skinny and mangy, the ox, fat enough but sad, drew near to the manger and sniffed at Jesus.

The Child placed one hand on the nose of the ox while with His other hand He gently pressed one of the ears of the ass.

And the ox seemed to smile; and from the eyes of the ass dropped two tears to lose themselves in his thick hair.

At the same time one of the camels outside quietly entered the stable and stretched his trusting head toward the Child.

Old Sephora understood what all this meant:—there is also a paradise for suffering animals.

And then in her turn she stepped toward the Child.

2. *The Virgin of the Angels*

DURING THE eight days that she passed in the stable at Bethlehem Mary did not suffer very much. Shepherds brought cheeses, fruits, bread, and firewood. Their wives and daughters cared for the Child and gave to Mary the attentions needed by a new mother. Then the Magi left behind their gifts of carpets, precious stuffs, jewels, and vases of gold.

At the end of the week when she was able to walk Mary wanted to return to her home in Nazareth. Some shepherds volunteered to escort her, but she said to them:

"I don't want you to leave your flocks and fields for us. My Son will direct us."

"But," said Joseph, "shall we leave behind the gifts of the Magi?"

"Yes," said Mary, "since we can't carry them away with us."

"But they're worth a great deal of silver," said Joseph.

"So much the better," said Mary.

And she distributed the gifts of the Magi among the shepherds.

"But," persisted Joseph, "can't we keep just a few for ourselves?"

"What should we do with them?" replied Mary. "We have a greater treasure."

It was hot on the journey. Mary carried the Child in her arms; Joseph carried a basket filled with a little linen and scanty provisions. Toward noon they halted, fatigued, at the margin of a wood.

Immediately from behind the trees appeared a band of tiny angels. They were chubby youngsters, pink and round faced. On their backs were little wings which helped them to fly when they wished and which at other times made their movements easy and light. They were skillful and vigorous beyond anything their tender age and delicate figures would lead one to believe.

They offered to the travelers a jar of fresh water and fruit which they had gathered no one knew where.

When the holy family resumed their journey the angels followed. They relieved Joseph of his basket, and Joseph allowed them to carry it. But Mary would not let them have the Child.

When night fell the angels arranged beds of moss beneath a wide sycamore and all through the night they watched over the slumber of Jesus.

So Mary returned to her home in Nazareth. It was a white house with a flat roof in a populous narrow way. There was a little covered terrace where Joseph had his workshop.

The angels did not leave them but continued to make themselves useful in a thousand ways. When the Child cried, one of them gently rocked him; others made music upon tiny harps for him; or when it was necessary changed his wrappings with the wave of a hand. When Mary awoke in the mornings she found her chamber swept. After every meal they speedily carried out the dishes and bowls, ran to wash them at the nearby fountain, and ranged them in the cupboard. When the Virgin went to the washhouse they carried the package of linen, divided it among them, joyously pounded the wet garments, dried them on the stones, and carried the bundle home. And if Mary in spinning her distaff grew drowsy from the great heat, they finished her task without waking her.

They displayed no less care of Joseph. They handed him his

tools, arranged them after the work was finished, carried away the chips and shavings, and kept the shop in irreproachable order.

But, too well served by the angels and having almost nothing to do, Mary became bored.

Because she felt bored, she prayed at first; but while she prayed, she reflected.

One morning as she was getting up she saw the angels sweeping her chamber. She snatched the broom and threatened to chase them out. They scattered. But after dinner at noon, as they started to clear the table she gave one a smart rap on his fingers and this put all of them to flight. They returned shortly. When she began to spin an angel tried to take her spindle. She brandished it like a weapon and chased the intruder to the door of Joseph's shop. An hour later as she was seated beside the Child sewing she spied two angels who had slipped under the cradle and were slyly rocking it. She rose, turned them out of the room and slammed the door so violently that one of the angels was caught by the tip of a wing. He uttered a little cry. Mary released him, but she said:

"So much the worse for you. That will teach you to meddle in what doesn't concern you. Tell your companions and don't let me see any of you again!"

"But," said Joseph, "why do you drive these little creatures away? They help us a great deal."

"That's just the reason," Mary replied.

"I don't understand," Joseph continued. "Since your Son is the Messiah, it's perfectly natural that he should be served by angels, and that his mother should profit by it."

"Oh!" said Mary, "here are words with no meaning. Don't you know that the Messiah has come into the world to suffer with men and first of all to endure all the ills natural to babies? And all these sufferings, I should be able to relieve as much as is in me, since I'm his mother. But I don't want anybody else to take care of these matters. Don't other mothers care for their own children? What a coward I should be if I avoided my share of a mother's trials. Besides, I'm sure my Baby would rather be tended by me than by those winged brats. And I know that I shall be more closely associated with his redeeming spirit if as other women I suffer from accepting completely his human condition. Yes, I wish to be the only one to dress my Son, the only one to rock him to sleep, the only one to keep my house, the only one to use my distaff, the only one to go to the washhouse. And as these humble tasks are almost a joy, they will bring no great merit to me, I'm sure; but I should be blamed if I let angels do them for me. Do you understand?"

"I think I do, my dear girl.... But must I also give up the little services the angels perform for me?"

"Evidently, my friend."

"Well, I thought that being the husband of the mother of the Messiah would give me the right to some slight advantages. But you must be right: for you are more intelligent and wiser than I am, although you're only fifteen years old and I'm past sixty."

Now, the next night, as the infant Jesus cried and refused to go to sleep, suddenly there was heard in the street a delicately soothing melody.

Mary opened the casement and saw by the light of the moon, standing against the wall of the house, all the angels playing on their tiny harps.

"You again?" she called to them. "Suppose my Baby doesn't want to go to sleep? Suppose it pleases him to cry and suffer with his teeth? Isn't his mother with him, eh? Clear out, now, or I'll get angry!"

On the morrow they did not reappear during the entire day. But the day after Mary saw them in the courtyard huddled together under the fig tree, timid, shame-faced, and weeping silently.

"My little angels," she said to them, "I may seem severe to you because you are too young to understand. But listen now! Old Sephora who lives across the way is paralyzed. A little further along is good Rachel with twelve children—and a hard time in rearing them. And you will find in Nazareth enough other unfortunate women. Well, then, you should help them to keep house, to wash clothes, to tend their babies. Since you desire to please my Son, that's the best way to succeed."

And noticing their little noses wrinkled with chagrin, she added:

[63

"And when he is bigger, perhaps I'll let you play with him. But first, do what I've just told you."

And that year all the poor women and the sick of Nazareth were aided and all the little babies rocked by these invisible servants (for only Mary and Joseph could see the angels); and none of the sucking infants cried at all, except the baby Jesus who wished to suffer for them.

THE THREE KINGS

ÉMILE GEBHART

Translated from the French by James Westfall Thompson

It was in the last year of the reign of Herod the Great, Prince of Jerusalem, who governed the Jews in the name of Caesar Augustus, Emperor of the Romans. On a winter evening, two strange caravans, by the light of a multitude of torches, were slowly approaching each other along the western shore of the Dead Sea. At the head of that which came from the north barbaric music sounded —strident fifes and copper tamborines. Surrounded by warriors with flat and ferocious faces, with yellow skins and beards black as jet, their hair twisted into long braids, rode a gigantic figure, yellower of skin and haughtier of mien than any of his host, mounted upon a mail-clad horse. His beady black eyes expressed the arrogance of rule. The points of an enormous black moustache fell to his breast. In his head-dress of steel and suit of mail he loomed sinisterly like a destroyer-god above the forest of pikes, battle-axes, clubs and huge carved scimitars which flashed in the red flames of the torches as if dripping with bloody dew.

Far off at the rear guard, a string of mules laden with tents and carpets toiled heavily along the road, goaded on by the hoarse cries of half-nude slaves. By the light of the torches the royal cortège plodded across the sands and through the dark waters of the lake, an accursed expanse of monstrous shadows. But the terrible king saw neither the guards around him who watched over his mysterious pilgrimage, nor the bitter waters, smooth as the marble of a tomb, nor the violent earth from which livid vapours crept, nor the sullen mountains set in the depths of the desert. His head turned toward the right, feverish with religious frenzy, with fixed gaze he watched a great golden Star hanging above the setting sun and shining solitary in the field of the sky.

The other caravan, which was following the southern shore and came from the terrible plateaus of Arabia, was even more astonishing. The wavering lights of torches borne by bronze-skinned slaves, their heads wrapped in white veils, revealed a procession of black elephants, draped in purple, on the backs of which sat a group of pale-faced, soft-eyed men, whose crimson silken garments sparkled with gems. Old men, their brows bound with fillets of white wool, whose long beards fell to their girdles, bore ermine robes glistening with diamonds; charming pages, carrying light guitars with golden cords, were playing slow, sad melodies of yearning sweetness; anchorites with emaciated bodies, dry visages and dead eyes, in hollow tones ceaselessly chanted their somber litanies.

In the middle of the caravan, where the music yearned in saddest chords, where prayer was sombrest, stalked a colossal elephant— white at that—surmounted by an ivory tower in which lay half reclining and nearly smothered in the snow of precious furs, a young man of striking beauty, clad in ermine and crowned with rubies, who seemed languishing in mortal lassitude.

And they all marched onward, cradled in sacred chants, with priestly pose and sacerdotal mien, looking like idols lost in the weird shade of some temple. Intent upon the dreams in their brains they saw neither the mountains nor the sea, nor the desolate land nor the shining night. Alone of all, the young king followed with a gaze of infinite tenderness the course of the Golden Star, the solitary Star which gleamed in the depths of the sky.

The two fantastic caravans were but a few paces apart when of a sudden the massive foreheads of the elephants wrinkled with fury; they beat their trunks and bellowed fearfully; the fifes and tamborines clamored angrily in their ears; the yellow faces and the steel-vestured forms in the red smoke frightened them. The young

66]

king high upon his throne, cried "Halt!"; the warrior-king, amid an awful din of tom-toms, stopped his host. Each side from a distance surveyed the other in a silence filled with menaces.

The two kings exchanged ambassadors. Each of them seemed much astonished by the account which his legate brought him. An hour later, in the shelter of a purple pavilion, propped on cushions, near a brazier in which slaves were burning the most exquisite perfumes of Asia, the two travelers fell to telling how they came to be that night upon the mournful borders of the Dead Sea.

"I am the most unhappy of princes," said the King of the North. "My empire is so vast that I know not its limits toward the setting sun. Everywhere else my power ceases only at the sea, or at mountains so high that the foot of man cannot cross them. All the yellow peoples tremble under my hand. I possess provinces where the flowers are ever blooming, the fruits ever ripening, and deserts whereof the memory alone makes one shudder; the ice never melts there; the storm never ceases, and no living thing can be found there. In the heart of my realm stretches a vast magic country over which hangs an eternal fog wherein are phantoms and demons, whose voices, sweeter to hear than the singing of young girls, lure men to its abysmal depths. And yet all these misfortunes which make my subjects suffer do not in truth prevent them from living in great happiness. I am called the Son of Heaven; my ancestors were all Sons of Heaven; but unto my twelve hundred wives and my children, my name is Gaspard. Alas! the Son of Heaven knows not his Celestial Father. I am the sole priest of an Unknown God, born of the brain of a great philosopher who died hundreds of years ago. My temples, void of priests and worshippers, are ever empty. My people are sottishly content with hideous and ridiculous divinities in the presence of which, for reasons of state, I am compelled to do reverence.

"Picture to yourself, my august brother, scorpions as huge as oxen, horses with serpents' heads, dragons bristling with quills, toads whose maws might swallow the largest of your elephants. But a great god who is a figment of the imagination, and a swarm of monsters done in plaster and painted cloth, are not a serious

[67

means of public restraint. I rigorously maintain the peace of my land with my army, my spies, and my headsmen. If a province revolts or refuses tribute I let loose upon it a hundred thousand soldiers hungry for plunder. I have the most refined and curiously terrible forms of punishment. Yonder great fellow whom I stationed a short time since at the door of our tent is my minister of justice; with a blow of the sword he can make the head of a man walking fly twenty paces.

"But evil fortune sometimes causes me cruel distress. From time to time armies of savages come from I know not where—perhaps fallen from the moon—hurl themselves upon my rich dominions and pillage and massacre every one. When my generals appear they find no one, or if they find the enemy they are regularly and shamelessly beaten. Then my people whose minds are naturally superstitious, cry to my god and blame him for all their suffering; and as this god pertains to me alone, 'tis from me alone that they demand account for the blood that has been spilled, the villages and harvests burned, the children outraged. Every night the nightmare of a revolution haunts my couch. I dream that my sacred head and my inviolable arms and limbs are being paraded in fragments throughout the most remote cities of my empire. A simple laborer with his wooden plow, a humble sailor in his old craft, are more fortunate. I have consulted my astrologers and my magicians. For long their response displeased me and many of them therefore were strangled. At last one of them, a soothsayer, blind and a hundred years old, said to me:

" 'King Gaspard, Emperor of the World, mount thy warhorse and go towards the South and the setting sun. A Star yet unknown will appear unto thee. Be guided by this Star; be never discouraged; some night it will hang fixed, and in triple rays will shine upon the cradle of a god. If this god accepts thy worship thou wilt be saved and very happy.'

"I have crossed Asia, my eye fixed every night upon the Star. It has guided me through the mists and the snowstorms. For nigh unto two years I have ridden to this same music; I am wearied out. Would that tomorrow I might find this god!"

In his turn the young King of the White Race, painfully raising himself upon the gold-flowered cushions, said:

"My brother, I have yet more to weep over than thou. I am Melchior, Emperor of India, master of a realm where glow all the splendours of the earth; where precious stones glimmer in the soil like prairie flowers. But I myself and the kings my vassals, and the unheard of multitudes of my peoples are the victims of ten thousand gods, everywhere present, which never sleep, which never smile. Priests without number, of pride implacable, the wisest, the richest of my empire, priests without pity, who never soothed a human sorrow, hating my warriors and despising the poor, perform the frightful rites of these gods. There is not a valley, not a forest, not a mountain where does not rise a dazzling temple, whose domes and towers seem to defy the sky. There day and night the priests pray for them alone. Around the ferocious idols enormous reptiles curl themselves and guard treasures whereof never a piece of gold has fallen into the hand of an orphan child. Sometimes upon a scaffold as high as the temple, in order to honor the Idol of the Hundred Devouring Mouths, they burn young girls more beautiful than the dawn. My gods love only death; they give nothing but death. Every spring rivers of water sacred to them evoke the plague and throw half of my empire into waste, and then in the magnificent cities the living have no longer courage to inter the dead.

"A prophet, a saint, a long time ago sought to wrest men's souls away from these terrible gods. But he could find no other salvation save in the renunciation of life, save the deep sleep of the soul, a sleep without dreams, without love, and without hope, and the retreat of the body motionless and rigid, unto the summit of a column or in the caverns of the rock. Would that I might escape from these two lethal faiths! One evening a sage come from far, from countries of the west, said unto me:

" 'A god of good will soon be born on the far edge of Asia. Betake thyself by the road along the Persian Sea. A Star unknown to thy priests will go before thee. Its golden beams will fall upon

[69

the temple of this god and if he blesses thee, thy people will be comforted.' "

Melchior and Gaspard slept like brothers side by side near the brazier which smoked with incense. The two hosts lit their fires along the shore of the funereal lake. With the approach of day the miraculous Star paled, and vanished at the rising of the sun. Each day the two kings resumed their journey at even. Each evening, seated at the threshold of the tent, in silence they looked from the tawny mountains to the gray sea, over which the wind passed without a ripple. Melchoir listened to the plaintive music of the harp; Gaspard chanted the sombre chronicles of his grandfather, the Glorious Son of Heaven, whose eyes and tongue the sacrilegious Tartars had plucked out.

Then the tents were folded and the two commingled caravans streamed around the two kings. The Star glowed in the jeweled azure of the western skies. Of a sudden, from his high tower, the White King descried afar a newcomer, who traveled alone from the south, and signaled to the Yellow King. It was a Negro mounted upon a camel, his legs bare, his body thinly covered with tattered furs, a mean drab turban set awry upon his head, in his hand a reed. The camel, miserably worn, spent with fatigue and hunger, with bleeding knees, staggered on its long hairy legs among the rocks and briers of the path.

"Some fugitive slave," quoted Gaspard, "but his animal will not bear him farther. Will it please you, my brother, to prove in him the lightness of my headsman's axe?"

Melchior regarded the Son of Heaven with disdainful gaze.

"No," said he. "I shall take this innocent man under my protection. If he be from this country he may guide us across the ravines and marshes."

The Negro raised a shrill cry, a cry of joy. With one hand pressed over his heart and raising his turban with the other he saluted the brilliant Star. Then manifesting signs of childish pleasure he stared at the masters of Asia as they passed by. Melchior encouraged him to draw near and the tired camel bore his rider proudly between the imperial elephant and the caparisoned war-house.

"Who art thou? Whence comest thou? Whither goest thou?" cried the White King to the frightened figure.

"I am Balthazar, Emperor of the Black Men, Prince of Africa. I come from a world of desolation. I go whither the Star calls me. I bring the Divine Infant who sleeps in the light of the Star the sigh of grief of the black race."

"We will all three go together, my brother," cried Melchior, "and this will be veritably the pilgrimage of the human race."

The torches were fired and through the bitter solitudes and the mountain paths the caravans resumed their march toward Jerusalem. Until daybreak, to the sound of fife and tabors, Balthazar told of the misfortunes of his people, of endless sterile deserts where no water was; where storms scorched; where the traveler was choked in columns of burning sand; of marshes along whose edge death rose like an exhalation; of forests of gigantic trees and eternal night, whence no man could find his way; of nests of serpents, whose gaze alone gave death; of lions, hyenas, panthers; sharks in the sea, and crocodiles in the rivers and lakes; there were famines often; people of ferocious customs who devoured man. Destruction reigned everywhere; whole villages were destroyed by fire and sword and there were pirates, slave chasers, along all the coasts, who caught boys and young girls in their toils.

"And the end is not yet," cried the poor King Balthazar. "We be used to hunger and thirst, to fierce beasts and to massacres. Would that we could learn something from all these sufferings! But we cannot. Down there in the black world the old man knows no more than the child. Our whole life is passed at the bottom of a dark pit. Our gods give us no light. They are little gods and feeble, who are afraid and hide themselves under the rocks like lizards or crickets or adders. We are too ignorant to find better ones. I have summoned the ablest sorcerers. They charm the serpents, but they do not soothe the wretched hearts which are sighing for hope. But one of them said to me:

" 'King of Africa, march towards Asia. When thou reachest the

[71

borders of a sea blue like the sky, a Star will appear in the north. Shape thy course ever towards it. Some night it will stop above the roof of a new born God. Do thou adore that Babe and the evils of thy race will be cured.' "

Melchior, Gaspard, and Balthazar rested all day upon the soil of Palestine. In the evening the star glowed with a light so beautiful that they felt themselves drawing near to the goal of their travels. They climbed some arid hills. At their feet lay a valley; fires were blazing everywhere in the light of which could be seen flocks of sheep and shepherds with their dogs. In the middle of the valley near a hamlet, a rude hovel propped against a cave in the rocks shone luminous in the three golden rays which fell from the mysterious Star.

Gaspard ceased his barbaric music. Melchior commanded silence among the praying anchorites. Nothing was heard save the mournful melody of the harps, mingled with sighs and sobs. Fearlessly the flocks of sheep watched the passing of the elephants. The dogs fawned upon the slaves and men-at-arms. Some shepherds were singing in a voice so sweet that Balthazar wept and smiled together.

At midnight the Three Kings descended. Followed by slaves bearing precious gifts, they knocked at the door. Melchior carried a gold censer wherein incense smoked; Gaspard a casket of gold smelling of myrrh; Balthazar had nothing save a reed in his hand.

The door opened. It was a stable, bare and cold, into which the winter wind beat. A babe lay sleeping on straw for a cradle. An ox stood on the right, an ass upon the left, and their breath warmed the child. A young woman clad in white was sitting at the head of the humble cradle. The three Magi had found God and the three races of men prostrated themselves with foreheads on the ground before Jesus.

The blue vapors of incense and myrrh curled toward the roof. Between the rudely jointed rafters the sky could be seen and the Star and celestial palaces with great white arcades, and the whispering of angels fell upon their ears.

Gaspard first offered his presents—a heap of arms all encrusted with diamonds.

"Lord," he said, "behold me kneel before thy weakness, I, who am at the summit of human power. I have sought thee in order to obtain thy alliance in war and after war. Grant that these arms may be turned against whomsoever shall raise himself to abase my power."

But the Child slept and in the heavens celestial voices responded:

"I am the God of peace and I would have no other arms save mercy and charity. These of thine are good only for kings, who in centuries to come will slay my people like sheep without a shepherd."

Melchior folded his hands while his slaves unrolled before the cradle cloths of gold and silk, and cast upon the straw of the stable, handfuls of precious stones.

"Lord, for long I have listened unto the words of the wise men and their wisdom has seemed unto me nothing but vanity. I have venerated the saints and their sanctity is a lie. I have sought a god of life, groping in the night, and I have found nothing save grief and death. Take, Lord, all my riches, all my treasures, and make gladness to flourish among the dead ruins of my empire."

But still the Child slept. And the angels replied:

"I am the God of the poor. I would have no other treasure than purity of heart. Leave here thy presents. They shall be for my pontiffs and my priests, who, forgetful of my destitution, will robe themselves in silk and walk all radiant in emeralds and diamonds."

Balthazar knelt in turn. Between his hands he took the feet of the Child and kissed them tearfully.

"Little God, whiter and softer than the light, I have nothing to offer unto thee,—nothing save my heart and my tears. Have pity on me, Lord, have pity on my brothers, and for our great sorrow, give us thy love."

Then the little Jesus wakened and smiled. He opened his tiny arms and let fall a child's benediction upon the misery of mankind. And above the stable roof in the radiance of the Star, white-winged angels sang:

"Glory to God in the highest and on earth peace, good will to men."

VALE QUI LEGIS

BETHLEHEM, A.D. 1

JOHN OXENHAM

I

OF ALL MY journeyings—and they have been many—none stands out more clearly in my memory than the one I took, in the company of Melchior of Damascus, and Balthasar of Babylon, into the land of the Jews, over forty years ago.

And with good reason. For, though we knew it not at the time, we were brought thereby to the very beginning of a wonder, the end of which is not yet. And I alone of the three have lived long enough to see, and to understand somewhat, though perhaps not much, of the meaning and magnitude of that small and strange beginning.

Unusual happenings in the history of mankind have frequently —perhaps always, if our knowledge were complete—been heralded by equally unusual happenings in the natural world, and especially among the stars.

When therefore I, Caspar, son of Cimon, the Wise Man of Shushan in Persia, was held, night after night, in breathless amazement by the sight of that great star in the watery trigon, and actually in the constellation of the Fishes, I knew that somewhere in the world some event of unparalleled magnitude was impending.

Now that constellation of the Fishes had always in our lore been connected with those unfortunate people, the Jews. And for hundreds of years the Jews had lived in the constant expectation of the coming of One who would deliver them out of their troubles, would give them once again a place among the nations, and become rulers of the world.

Night after night I pondered these things, while the great planets Jupiter and Saturn drew closer and closer together. Then suddenly there appeared along with them that new star, larger and brighter than either and quite unknown to me, though I had studied the stars for thirty years and thought I knew them.

My father had studied them all his life. He was over ninety when he died, and he had passed on to me all that he knew; and never had such a wonder as this appeared in the heavens before.

Without a doubt it portended something stupendous, and there grew within me a great desire, which speedily strenghened into a firm determination, to find out the meaning of it.

It might betoken the end of the world, and truly the world was wicked enough and weary enough to deserve its end. It might be the coming of the One foretold by the Jewish prophets.

There was no one in Shushan, nor indeed in all Persia now, with whom I could discuss the matter. If only my father had been alive. ... Well, he would have been thinking as I was thinking, and he would have wanted to find out even as I did. For my mother had a strain of Jewish blood in her, and that, no doubt, was why I had always been so interested in that clever but unfortunate people.

There had been many Wise Men in Persia, but they had all died, and of their successors none had had a father like mine.

But counsel with someone I must take, or consume myself with my own craving. Wait quietly there, doing nothing but watching, watching, watching, and wondering ever more vehemently, I could not.

There was only one man I could think of whose opinion I would value—Balthasar, the Mage of Babylon. And he was close to three hundred miles away, beyond the great rivers, and he might well be dead, though his fame still lived.

I determined to seek Balthasar.

My dispositions were soon made, for we Magi ever cared more for the possession of knowledge and wisdom than of things. Wealth could have been ours if we had desired it, but we did not.

Fifteen arduous days brought me to what had once been Babylon —and to Balthasar.

It was a great joy to me to find him still living. The vast desolation of the once mighty city was entirely suitable for the home of one whose life was given to high thought and the study of the stars.

When I found his little house—built of the bricks made by Nebuchadnezzar, the Builder-King, whose stamp they bore—he came to the door, eyed me searchingly for a space, and said, "You must surely be a son of Cimon of Shushan. How fares it with him?"

"He died a year ago. I am Caspar, his only son."

"I see him in you . . . You have come about The Star!"

"Yes."

"I too am troubled about it. The like of it has never been seen. Come in and tell me how far you have got."

"It means something dire and dreadful, or something new and wonderful," I said eagerly, as he sank down again into the corner of his divan and I at his side.

"Yes," nodding slowly the great head which held such vast wisdom and knowledge.

I saw that he wanted to sound my depths before he gave from his own. So I continued, "It is in the sign of the Fishes, therefore it has to do with the Jews. And, according to the sayings of their wise men of old, their Deliverer and their deliverance are due. Can it be that?"

"You have thought wisely, my son," he said weightily. "It is, I am convinced, The Star of the Deliverer. . . . And now?"

He was a man of seventy or over, but tall and straight and strong, and showed no sign of age. His eyes, dark and shining, and set rather deep in his head, were the most compelling I had ever seen. There was in them some strange mysterious power. I felt that if he bade me do a thing, I must do it; if he forebade me, I must withhold.

At his quiet, earnest "And now?" I answered, "Some very great thing is coming to the world. I feel it. I know it. I would go to see for myself what it is."

"I am with you. Whatever it is, the world has never seen the like of it. We will go together. It will be a great journey, but two together will shorten it."

It was indeed a great journey. We started at daybreak, carrying each his staff and little besides, for a Mage is welcomed and honoured wherever he goes.

For fifteen days we journeyed by the caravan road up the great River Euphrates. Then for fifteen more with another caravan across the desert to Damascus, stopping one whole day amid the welcome palms of Tadmor for the relief of our desert-weary eyes and bodies. We could have traveled more quickly alone, but not with safety.

And as we walked we talked deeply of the things which meant most to us, and I learned much from Balthasar and gave him in return from the stores of my father's wisdom. And ever of a night, in the deep-blue dome over us, shone that great triple light for our guidance and encouragement, and it seemed to grow brighter and brighter with every night that passed.

III

We stopped two days at Damascus waiting for a caravan going south, and it was while we were journeying past the great Mount Hermon, and rejoicing in the wonder and majesty of his crown of snow, that we became aware of the obviously keen interest we seemed to excite in one of our fellow travelers.

He was a very old man, with snowy hair and long white beard. He wore the white pointed cap and robe and tunic peculiar to the Magi. He was mounted on a very beautiful white ass, and his still keen dark eyes were fixed so steadily upon us that our eyes kept unconsciously wandering from Hermon back to him.

"Who can he be?" said Balthasar musingly, as his mind went

groping back down the years. "Long ago I heard of a wise man who lived beyond the Great Desert, but he must surely be dead by now ... His name ... His name ... was ... yes ... Melchior ... that was it—Melchior of Damascus."

And a plodder alongside us turned, as one glad to pass on his knowledge, and said, with a jerk of the head toward the one on the white ass, "That is Melchior, the Mage of Damascus. There is nothing he does not know,"—and we made our way at once toward him.

It was a very fine old face that welcomed us, full of great joy and contentment, and his eyes were as deep and dark and compelling as Balthasar's and radiant with that which was in him.

"You are Melchior of Damascus," said Balthasar, as he walked alongside with his hand on the ass's neck, and I walked on the other side. "The fame of your wisdom has compassed the deserts. But I did not know you were still with us."

"By God's mercy I have lived to see this day. And you?"

"I am Balthasar of Babylon, and this is Caspar of Shushan, the son of Cimon the Sage."

"And, like me, it is The Star that has brought you," he said eagerly.

"Yes, it is The Star. What does it portend?"

"The coming of the Promised One, The Deliverer, without a doubt. He has been long waited for, and now, of a surety, he is at hand. It is the Bright Morning Star of the New Day."

"We were assured in our own minds that it meant something great, and we could not rest till we knew," I said.

"How great no man knows," said the old man softly.

Thenceforward we three journeyed in close company, sharing all our deepest thoughts and highest hopes, and sitting often over the fire of a night, with the wonder of The Star, blazing brightly above us till it was lost in the splendour of the dawn.

And many were our surmises as to whom The Deliverer might be, and how, and in what guise, we should find him.

As to that, even Melchior could tell us nothing. He was simply assured in his own mind and heart of the tremendous fact that he was close at hand.

IV

One night, as we sat talking over the dying fire, Melchior drew from his robe something which shone richly in the flickering light. His thin white fingers held it preciously, and gazing at it he said, "This is my offering to him we seek. It was given to me by my father, who had it from his father, and he from his. And always father has said to son, 'Keep it till you find one to whom you feel you must give it!'"

Balthasar reached out his hand for it, and I bent over with him to see.

It was a small golden cup, exquisitely shaped, with narrow, fluted stem and broad base, and chased all over with the intricate tracery of a delicately wrought design.

Balthasar pushed the embers together and examined it keenly in the spurt of light, turning it round and round, and apparently finding and following some meaning in the strange flowing lines.

"Know you what it is?" he asked at last.

"Only what I have told you. I have always supposed there might be some meaning in those curious lines, but it was beyond me."

"It is one of the cups of pure gold made for Ahasuerus the King, by one Arbanes, at the time of the King's marriage with Esther, the Jewess. It is a worthy gift indeed."

"If he whom we seek is such as we hope to find, no earthly gift is worthy of him," said the old man reverently.

"A gift indeed!" said Balthasar, "and one that makes my own seem small and inadequate," and he drew from his robe a little oblong casket of silver inlaid with gold. And, opening it, there came out a rich, sweet perfume.

"Frankincense," said Melchior, sniffing it appreciatively. "It is fitting. In this Deliverer we worship God."

"And mine is still less," I said. "But it is all I had, for we have never cared for any possession beyond knowledge and wisdom. It was given to me not long since by a Prince from Arabia, to whom I had been of service."

It also was a box, but shaped like a ball, very skilfully carved with strange devices, and made of ivory.

And from it also, when I unscrewed its two parts, there came a pungent, aromatic odour.

"Myrrh," said Melchior. "And that, too, is meet. For no man who shall lead the nations but will have his times of stress, and perhaps of bitterness. And," he said with his beneficent smile, as he stowed away the cup inside his robe, "each of us offers his best, and no man can do more."

For six days we journeyed southwards—past the great marshes, past the upper lake, and along the bank of the river Jordan, till by the fords we came to the fair, rich town of Jericho. Thence the caravan was going to Joppa, on the Western Sea, and we three went on alone up the steep, rough road to Jerusalem.

We had talked much as we walked, as to where to make for. For The Star in the heavens, though it kept alive our hopes by the brightness of its shining, could not in the nature of things indicate the place where those hopes might attain their fulfillment.

By its position in the constellation of the Fishes it pointed to the Jews and their little country, but to no particular spot in that country. From its position in the heavens it blazed and shone on every part of it alike. And so, as Jerusalem was the chief place, and an event of such magnitude would be sure to be known there first, to Jerusalem we had decided to go.

V

And it was on that last bad bit of road, when we had traversed in safety all those leagues of desert and were almost within sight of our destination, that we fell into trouble, and out of it.

For, as Old Melchior's gentle white ass picked her way cautiously up the rocky defile, with Balthasar and myself on either side of her, we were suddenly surrounded by a mob of burly ruffians armed with sticks and swords, who had stolen like shadows from their hiding places among the rocks.

"What would you?" asked Melchior quietly of their leader, who had grasped the ass by the bridle, a big, truculent fellow who looked capable of every violence.

"Whatever you have," said he, "and be quick about it!"

Melchior's deep, dark eyes gazed steadily at him with a strange unwavering intensity.

"Can you not see we are Magi?" said the old man sternly. "The Magi possess nothing—and everything. What we have is beyond your taking."

"We will see," and the burly one, advancing on him, thrust his rough hands among his robes and wrenched at his girdle, and came upon the cup.

"Oh, ho! The Magi possess nothing—"

"And everything," said Melchior. "That cup belongs to the Deliverer who is coming."

He spoke quietly. His gaze shifted from the man's face to the hand which held the cup exultantly.

And suddenly the jeering face changed, became charged with impotent fury and fear, lips twisting, eyes blinking.

"Old devil!" he foamed. "What have you done to my hand— my arm—my . . ." and he fell silent and stood stiff and motionless, unable to move, the hand and arm that held the cup outstretched as though turned to stone.

"It is dangerous to steal from a Mage," said Melchior quietly. "For though he has nothing yet he has everything. . . . Have you learned?"

The rest of the band had been surging about us, growling and muttering. Once they made as though to fall upon us. But Melchior's lightning glance swept round them and they fell back.

"Put back the cup whence you took it!" said Melchior to the rigid one. And he, with a stiff, ungainly movement, thrust it back into the old man's robe.

"And now, remember!" said Melchior, and jogged the white ass gently with his heels, and we passed on, leaving them agape and staring.

"How came you by that power, father?" I asked, as we went. "It is a useful thing to have."

[81

"It is not given to every man, but I have had it most of my life. Nor will it act on every man. But most men I can compel to my will."

"I have it also," said Balthasar.

"I must learn it of you," I said, and in time I did.

VI

When we climbed out of the rocky gorge, away in the distance we saw the golden dome of the Temple gleaming in the sun, and the great city brooding below it. But we had all of us seen too many great cities, and the ruins of still greater, to be unduly impressed by it. And, for myself, material grandeur always had in it the elements of decay, and as I looked upon such I always found myself thinking,—with a feeling of sadness not perhaps quite consistent with a philosophic mind which accounted worldly possession of small account,—"Like everything else, this too will pass."

As we jogged slowly towards the city, Melchior's mind was bent on what might await us there.

"We must go warily," he said. "For if King Herod hears of our quest it may go hardly with us. . . . And we can scarce hope to escape him, for his spies are everywhere. You see, he is an outsider and is only where he is by the grace of Rome. His life is, and always has been, one long fear of being supplanted. And to keep his throne he has lost his soul. . . ."

"What a man to be King—" I began.

"A man! He is not a man. He is a devil in the likeness of a man. And he has no more conscience than a . . . than a pig. It was Augustus himself who summed him up in one grim saying: 'Herod's pig,' he said, 'is safer than his son!'—and he was right. Three of his sons he murdered, and his wife, and her father and mother, and multitudes of others lest they should become a danger to his shaky throne. You see, I hear all these things from the travelers who come to see me in Damascus. They are always full of them. . . ."

"But what a man to be a king!" I said again.

"Kings are all the same," said Balthasar.

"It's amazing that the peoples suffer them. Why don't they rise and rend them? After all they are many, and these Kings are only men like ourselves—"

"Not like ourselves, thank the Invisible One!" said Melchior fervently.

"Well—only men anyway."

"And not much of men, at that!" said Balthasar. "But as to Herod, it was Rome put him where he is, and it is Rome that keeps him there, and Rome is strong."

"But," I argued, "Rome only means the Emperor, and I suppose he's no better."

"He is not a Herod," said Melchior. "He is more fit to rule. He has done great things . . . and had many sorrows. The worst thing he ever did was to make Herod King of the Jews. And as it is Herod we have to deal with we must go warily."

VII

And so, in the city, we cautiously questioned such as seemed of sedate and devout aspect, as to the coming of One who was to be King of the Jews and the promised Deliverer. But we met with no success.

The Deliverer had been so long promised, and had never come, that they had almost lost hope of him. Some of them had noticed the great Star, but it had meant nothing to them.

When we asked if any son had been born to Herod lately, such of the ruder sort as heard it, after a wary glance round, would say, "A *Son?* to *Herod?*" and a jeer so foul that we stopped asking that.

But most simply said, "There is no King here but Herod," and some, by their looks, added, "And may the curse of Jah rest upon his soul!"

But our quest was cut short by an officer, a Parthian by the look of him, with an armed guard, who pounced upon us and carried us off, saying briefly that the King desired to speak with us.

We were taken to the palace, up on the mount near the Temple, and led at once into the presence of King Herod.

After what Melchior had told us, we were prepared for something ill-favored and forbidding. But the man himself shocked even our minds, inured as they were to the sins and follies of mankind.

He was a dark-skinned, evil-looking old man, with lowering face and gloomy bloodshot eyes, and he sat crouching forward on his seat, as though he feared some treachery from behind or sought it in front.

By his side on the floor of the raised dais, lay a huge, ill-smelling beast, tawny yellow with black stripes—sent to him no doubt when a cub by some Eastern prince who sought his favour, for the two blood-thirsty ones seemed on good terms with one another—like to like.

The King's dangling hand played with the sleepy beast's pointed ears, and every now and again it gave a mighty yawn, half opening its eyes and displaying a great hungry cavern of red throat and hideous yellow fangs which made my flesh creep.

Any slave or official who had to go anywhere near it went very delicately and with no assurance, and made himself very small and silent till he was well out of its reach.

The King's audience chamber was large and lofty, but so dimly lighted that it took some time for our eyes to grow accustomed to it.

It was probably sumptuously decorated like all the rest of the palace,—it was he who built the Temple in six-and-forty prodigal years. But no wealth of adornment, or the smell of all the perfumes and incense burning about the room, could dispel the gloomy atmosphere of sin and death and corruption which pervaded it. About the King himself, and about every person in attendance on him, there hung a look and a feeling of fear, and mistrust, and close-impending doom. On us also; for face to face with Herod, a man's life was as a speck of dust on a windy day.

His heavy eyes burned on us grimly for a space, as though he would tear from us our inmost thoughts. His voice, when at last he spoke, was harsh and husky, but he seemed to be trying to hide his forbiddingness under a cloak of not unfriendly interest in us and our quest.

"Whence come you? And why are you come asking about a King of the Jews?" he demanded. "There is no King here but Herod."

Melchior set his strange compelling eyes on him, as probably no other man's eyes ever had been,—in a bold, unwavering gaze which even the King could not out-stare.

"We come from the East, O king,—many days' journey. A Star arose in the House of the Fishes and we had to come."

"Why?"

"In our lore of the stars, the House of the Fishes means Jewry. A Star of that magnitude portends some mighty happening in Jewry. We have come to find out."

"But why do you seek a King?"

"For hundreds of years the promised Deliverer of the Jews has been expected. We believed that this might be his Star. No greater happening could come to Jewry."

Herod brooded heavily over all this. Knowing what we did of him and his fears for his shaky throne, and the means by which he had kept it so long, it would have been quite in keeping with him if he had swept us and our Star and our coming Deliverer out of existence with a wave of the hand.

But we knew also that he was ridden by superstitious fears, and Magi of the East are dangerous folk to meddle with.

He harshly bade an attendant summon the priests and scribes from the adjoining Temple. And while we waited, a strange thing happened.

He was, as one could well suppose, not a little disquieted over this matter. The dangling hand which played with the ear of the great beast alongside him probably gave it an unconscious twitch. For the monster gave a sleepy snarl and snap, then lurched up on to its feet, stretched itself backwards and forwards till it seemed twice as big as before, and its terrible curving claws worked in and out of their sheaths and scraped and rattled on the marble floor.

Then, after another terrifying yawn, its cold inhuman eyes settled on us and it stared intently, as though contemplating a meal off us.

And then, noiseless as death, it came padding down the steps of

[85

the dais straight toward us. And my heart was in my mouth, and the skin of my back was prickly cold, for I felt sure our end had come, and a grislier end than ever I had dreamed of.

But the moment the beast sat up and looked at us, Melchior's eyes, which had never left the King's face, shifted to this new menace and held it as it had held the other.

And to the amazement of everyone there—and not least of Balthasar and myself—the monster walked softly up to Melchior and rubbed its great head confidingly against him, and prowled round and round him, pushing in between him and Balthasar and myself as though we were posts, and rumbling pleasurably in its horrible throat with sounds like distant thunder.

Round and round and in and out between us it went sinuously, insinuatingly, as though seeking his good will or expressing its own.

And, Mage though I was, as the bristling head and swinging tail brushed against me, and the fetid smell of the beast came up to me in spite of all the burning incenses and spices, I could scarce restrain myself from yelling aloud with affright. My soul was sick with fear. I felt death very near, for any moment he might rear himself up in wild, brute fury and end us all with three strokes of his mighty paws.

Herod sat gloomily watching. Perhaps he hoped the monster would make an end of us and the whole troublesome matter. On the other hand, his superstitious fears concerning this apparent threat to his shaky throne were on the boil, and he was anxious to learn if there was anything in it.

The priests came in, bowing low to the King, and stopped, amazed and staring, at sight of us and our terrifying attendant.

Herod curtly demanded of them what their tradition said of a coming deliverer. When and whence was he to come?

And they told him, from their scrolls, that such as one had been long foretold—that Bethlehem of Judea was the place named—

"Bethlehem!" said Herod scornfully.

... But as to when, they could say nothing. For hundreds of years he had been expected, and many false messiahs had appeared and disappeared. But as to the actual time of the coming of the true Messiah their records gave no indication.

Their faces showed their fears as they gave the King this unhelpful information. He was quite capable of ordering them all off to instant death, as they very well knew. But their fears for themselves still left room in them for amazement at the sight of us with that foul beast prowling in and out between us and rubbing himself against Melchior with every sign of friendliness. Whenever they dared to withdraw their eyes from the lowering face of the King, they shot furtive glances at us and at the outwardly, unruffled calm with which we bore the double ordeal of the blood-thirsty King and his blood-thirsty beast.

All this I saw out of the corners of my eyes, for I never allowed them to waver for one instant from the King's face, and in those tense moments it so wrought its evil self into my memory that I see it still, though all this happened more than forty years ago.

Balthasar told me afterwards that it was the same with him. But he also had that strange power which Melchior possessed, and he was using every bit of it that was in him to counteract the evil that was in Herod—that, indeed, was Herod. Later on that great gift came to me also and many times served me well.

And for Melchior, his strange gaze followed the prowling beast whenever it was not behind him, and at times it would look up at him and rumble in its throat as though speaking to him.

The King dismissed the priests with a wave of the hand, and with a last glance at us they scuffled away.

And after a space of gloomy pondering he glared at us and said, "Hearken, you! You will stop here this night. And tomorrow you will go to Bethlehem, and if you find your King you will return here and tell me . . . so that I too may do him homage," he added grimly.

"Satanas . . . here," he called harshly to his well-named fondling. And the beast went reluctantly, stopping to look back at us and swinging his long tail as though doubtful if he would not yet make a meal off us. But another peremptory call from the only voice he had ever obeyed, and he went, and flopped down sulkily by the King's side.

Only then did Melchior's eyes shift again from the beast to the man.

With a curt jerk of the head Herod dismissed us in charge of the officer who had brought us in, and we followed him down long, gloomy passages to a distant room; and only when we were safely in it, and he had seen to it that we were alone, did he speak.

"You are in luck to be still alive," he said. "You must have some magic power over him and that foul beast of his. For it thinks no more of leaping on a man and killing him there before him than he does of killing any who thwart him."

"By your speech you come from somewhere near my own country," I said in my own tongue. And his face lightened up at sound of it.

"I am from Parthia, on the border. And you?"

"From Shushan."

"I have been to Shushan too," he said, in an eager whisper which seemed suited to the brooding silence of the place. "I knew you were not of this country, nor like other men, or by this time you would be dead men. . . . To tell him to his face that you sought a King who was not Herod! Why, that is the one fear that rides him like a devil, that someone will supplant him. It is this that has steeped him in blood up to his lips—his own kin and every other that stood in his way."

"The King we seek will not be like Herod," said Melchior weightily. "He will be a Deliverer of his people, not a scourge."

"Then, by all your gods, find him quickly and let me know," he said eagerly. "I would serve him faithfully. I serve Herod for his pay, which is good. But I'd liefer serve a better man for less. Good pay is no good if a word can end it and you. . . . And that devil-beast! . . . No man's life is safe from it. Of a night it prowls about his chamber, and none goes near. Some night it will forget he's master, and will turn on him and rend him, and he will lie there and rot, or it will devour him. And the sooner the better if your King is ready, for the whole land quakes under this one."

"We have to find him first," said Melchior.

"And you will let me know.... And when you go tomorrow in search of him, go warily. You will be followed. Herod trusts no man."

Melchior nodded.

"Now I will send you food, and mats to lie on, and very early in the morning I will see you on your way."

VIII

"Remember!" whispered the Parthian, in my ear, and in my own tongue, as we set off at sunrise next morning. "Be wary! You will be followed."

When we were clear of the city old Melchior breathed out a great breath of relief and disgust. "I smell that foul beast and his master yet, in spite of his perfumes and incenses. He is surely the most miserable of men. His soul is steeped in blood. His body is rotten with corruption. His life is one long fear. Of a surety time is ripe for a better King."

We were so early on the road that we had it almost to ourselves. We passed a beggarman shivering in his rags by the wayside, and Melchior gave him a word of cheer and a coin which he took eagerly.

Here and there on the sides of the hills were little white villages and we wondered which was the one we sought.

As we plodded along, we came upon a shepherd with a boy and a dog, and a long stream of sheep behind them, whose path would presently cross ours. The man walked with a strong free stride and was swinging his staff in the air and singing to himself as he went. And as I thought of the horrible old man in his gloomy magnificence in Jerusalem, I said to myself, "I would sooner be this shepherd than King Herod. He is alive, and Herod would be better dead."

"You seem a happy man," said Melchior, as the joyous shepherd drew near.

"And why not? God is good, and there is still grass to be found

[89

if you know where to look for it. Whence come you?" he asked, eyeing our strange garments.

"We have come from afar in search of One who is to become the Deliverer of his people. Know you aught of him?"

His face lighted up with a great gladness.

"Your star stands high ..."

"Our star?" we cried together.

"It is a saying we have when a man is in luck. I can take you to the one you seek and none can tell you more about him than I."

He turned to the boy with the dog, and said, "Dysmas, lead them to the farther slope of the hill we had yesterday."

And when the flock had trooped slowly past, he said to us, "Now, sirs, come!"

And as we went he told us a story which filled us with wonder.

"It is many nights ago ... it is ... yes, it is exactly two-and-forty days ago, for only yesterday his little mother went up to the Temple for her purification. She is surely the most beautiful little mother the world has ever seen.

"Well, we were on the hills over there, watching our flocks that night, when we heard a sound like singing in the sky, and a great light blazed upon us and frightened us so that we fell flat on the ground. But there was one with us, Old Jeconiah, a very aged man, who all his life had been foretelling the coming of the promised One. So often had he told us of it, and it never came to pass, that we had ceased to believe in him. And as we lay there shivering with fear, we heard voices, and when they had ceased Jeconiah bade us go with him to the village, where he said the angels had told him we would find the Deliverer as a baby lying in a manger—"

"A baby ... in a manger!" said Melchior, and we shared his surprise.

"We went along and found him with his father and mother in the cave of the cattle, alongside the khan. You see, the khan itself was overfull because of the enrollment. And he was lying in the feeding-trough just as the angels had told Jeconiah.

"He is a wonderful little lad, and his mother ... well, I have a wife of my own and a boy, but I have never seen anyone like this boy and his mother. You will see for yourselves."

"And the old man—Jeconiah?" asked Melchior eagerly. "I would fain speak with him also."

"Ah ... Jeconiah! You see, he had been waiting all his life for that, and when it came his soul was satisfied, and he died as we went home. He was a very old man."

He led us straight up the terraced hillside to the khan at the top.

"That is where he was born," he said, pointing to a wide open cave. "But now they are in the house, since there is more room."

He led us to one of the arched recesses, and there, sitting on the raised floor on some straw, was a woman, very young, and beautiful beyond my power of telling, by reason of something in her and about her, a sweet and lofty innocence and graciousness which enveloped her like a garment of light and shone radiantly in her eyes and face.

And on her knee, all naked from his bathing, lay kicking a fine sturdy boy, just forty-two days old.

"You have come to see my little king again!" she cried joyously, to our shepherd friend.

"Ay! for it does me good just to look at him. And these strangers have come from afar in search of him."

The mother eyed us questioningly, but with a joyous face, as one who owns a treasure and delights to show it to others.

Our feelings were all in a turmoil of wonderment and reverence. Not for a moment did we doubt the story of Mattah, the shepherd. And the mother and the boy impressed us profoundly. That they were, in some indescribable way, far removed from the ordinary, and most loftily above, we all felt, and felt most deeply.

But ... The Promised One, the Deliverer, the One who should rule the whole people! ... how should he come in such lowly guise? It was all very amazing.

That, I know, is how we felt, for we spoke much of it afterwards. But Melchior, more far-seeing through his age and experience, permitted us no doubts in the matter. He fell on his knees, and tendered his homage to the mother and child, which he would not have done to a thousand King Herods.

And we did the same as we offered our gifts, with which the little mother was greatly delighted.

"See!" she cried to a grave-faced man, much older than herself, who had just come silently in. "See what these good men have brought for our little son! They have come from afar just to see him and to bring him these. That beautiful cup is of gold—"

"It was made for the marriage of Esther, the Queen," said Melchior. "It was made for a Queen. I bring it to a King." And she smiled her thanks to him again.

"And in that beautiful box is frankincense. Smell how sweet it is! And this lovely carved ball—it has a sweet smell also."

"It came from the south country—from Arabia," I said, as I opened it, "and this inside it is myrrh."

"Gold, frankincense, and myrrh," she said joyously. "Oh, but we are rich," and she laid the ivory ball in the hands of the boy in her lap, and he tried to grasp it and hug it to him, but it was too large for him.

I had never before seen hands so small and delicate and yet so full of life, the wonderful little fingers with their dainty, pink nails, I could not take my eyes off them.

"What is his name?" asked Melchior softly.

"His name is Jesus. It was told to me before he was born."

" 'Salvation'—it is a good name, for he is the fulfillment of the Promise," said Melchior, as he knelt closer and gazed lovingly upon the boy. "A wonder unto many, the Leader and Deliverer of his people!"

"He is my own precious little king," said the radiant mother, clasping the boy to her in her rapture. But she looked past him at the old man kneeling there with his heart in his eyes, and there was a great wonder in her face.

When Melchior rose from his knees he looked with some curiosity at the elderly man who had come in while we were offering our gifts. He seemed to be wondering how so fair a bud could have come from so austere a stem, for the man was past middle age and seemed somehow of a different texture from the fair young mother and the child.

"You are not of this country," said Melchior.

"No," said the father quietly. "We are from the north country, from Nazareth in Galilee. But being of the stock of David we had to come here for the enrollment."

"My mother's people came of the tribe of Asher," I said, knowing that that country was somewhere in the north also, and feeling glad to be able to claim even such remote race-kinship with that wonderful little mother and her child.

"Then we are almost neighbors," she laughed joyously. "Asher was on the Great Sea, and Galilee reaches to it also." And I felt a new bond of friendliness between us.

IX

While we were thus still rejoicing in the boy and his mother, Balthasar suddenly gave a warning "Tsst!"—and there came into the khan one dressed like a merchant. He gave one quick glance at us all as he passed and wandered on as though in search of the master of the khan. But the master was away on some of his daily business.

A meaning look and a quick, whispered word or two passed between Balthasar and old Melchior and then Melchior went after the stranger.

"You seek a lodging, sir?" asked the old man courteously.

"Yes, I seek a lodging for the night."

He was a well-fed, full-faced man, and looked as if he might have prospered at the expense of his fellows. His quick, dark eyes roved over Melchior and all round the place and missed nothing, I am sure.

"It is early in the day to seek a lodging for the night," said Melchior, fixing on him that same compelling gaze which had overcome the robber on the Jericho road.

"Nevertheless—" began the other, and then faltered, with a bewildered look on his face, and fell silent.

"You will go with my friend and he will find you a lodging,"

[93

said Melchior, and when Balthasar jerked his head peremptorily, the stranger followed him like one dazed. And I marveled greatly and promised myself again to acquire that strange power before I parted from Melchior and Balthasar.

Balthasar led the man outside the khan to that same stable-cave which the shepherd had pointed out as the place where the child had been born, and they disappeared inside.

Old Melchior stood watching till they were out of sight. Then he came slowly back to us, and laying his hand on the shoulder of the father of the child, said weightily:

"Listen! You are, I can see, a wise and prudent man. Take the advice of one who has seen more than most and has learned to read men's hearts and thoughts. The boy's life is in peril, and you have no time to lose. If you would save him you will leave here at once. You will take this white ass of mine and get you all into Egypt. Three days will take you to the border and there you will be safe."

"But why?" asked the man quietly, and not so surprised and startled as one might have expected.

"In Jerusalem, Herod the King heard of the quest for One who was to become King of the Jews, and sent for us to learn what we were after. He bade us return if we found him, so that he might come and pay him homage also. You know Herod?"

"All the world knows Herod," said the child's father.

"He is evil all through," continued Melchior. "We shall return by another road, but if Herod finds your boy he will of a surety kill him, as he has killed so many others who stood in his way. That man who came is without doubt one of his spies. We were warned that we would be followed."

The man nodded gravely. "You make clear to me what has been troubling me," he said. "Sometime in the night it seemed to me that one stood over me with a sword and bade me begone. And I knew not what it meant. Now I know. It was the voice of God and now He speaks through you. We will go at once. And you, good Master, will remember always that you saved three lives this day."

94]

The terrified mother was hastily gathering their belongings when still another visitor came peering cautiously round the entrance of the khan. And this was the beggar whom we had passed on the road.

"Here is another of them," said Melchior. "Herod mistrusts even his own spies."

He went to the gateway and stood in front of the beggar, and asked sharply, "What seek you, my friend?"

"An alms," whined the beggar.

"I have given you an alms already. Now you shall have a lodging to rest your weary body."

The man looked sulkily at him but quailed before the unswerving gaze. And when Melchior called to me, and bade me find a safe place for him, he followed me as one under a spell and I led him to another cave.

Within the hour they were gone, the boy clasped tightly to his mother's breast to shield him from the menace of the evil King.

Melchior patted his white ass under the neck for the last time. He had had her many years and she was dear to him. He stood watching them till they were lost in the folds of the hills, and when he spoke of her afterwards, he said, "She bears a better load now, and I would give my life for that little mother and her babe."

X

Old Melchior was feeling now the effect of all this drain upon his strength, and Balthasar and I, who had trodden the deserts for five-and-thirty days on end, felt the need of rest also.

Moreover we all desired a time for quiet thought and consideration of this whole matter.

"We will stop here for a spell," said Melchior. "But not in Bethlehem." For when we do not return Herod's spies will carry him the word and he will seek us, and if he finds us here and the child gone, we are dead men."

So toward sunset we went farther on along the hills and found another little village, and there we stayed three days, but did not find the rest we had hoped for.

Our hearts and minds were full of this strange ending to our quest. We had sought some great matter foretold by the stars. We had found a babe in the arms of a radiant laughing girl. It was not easy to reconcile the portents of the heavens with so apparently small a result.

"But," said Melchior weightily, "all things have a beginning— except the High and Invisible One, who was before all things and will be when all things are gone. There is that within me which tells me that we have been permitted to see the beginning of a matter whose end is beyond us. We will be grateful for that much."

It was on the second night that we were wakened by a babel of voices outside, and now and again sharp cries of fear and wonder. And going out into the nipping air, we found all the villagers clustered on the slope, and gazing with affright towards Bethlehem.

It was a clear, cold night, and the air was very still. A few stars snapped and sparkled as with anger or affright in the thin darkness of the sky, and a pale sickle of a moon was sinking to the horizon as though to hide itself from what it saw below.

From distant Bethlehem there rose a hideous tumult of screaming and shouting and yelling, women in desperate fear, men in furious anger. And the villagers around us buzzed with wonder and alarm.

What could it be? What was happening over there? It was not fire, for there was not a sign of glow, either above or below.

Robbers? . . . Raiders? . . . Nothing of the kind had been known these many years.

Melchior, gazing keenly, listening intently, said gravely, "It is Herod, seeking the child."

It was horrible to stand there helpless, shuddering as we listened, but unable to render any aid because of the distance and our certainty of what it meant, while the wailings and shriekings came stabbing through the still night air. The women amongst us sobbed and moaned. The men growled and cursed with the fury of their impotence.

Then the turmoil ceased, and the night became an aching mystery. Whatever the horror over yonder it was ended. The silence and darkness of death settled down on Bethlehem.

But about us the villagers still babbled their fears and their wonder.

"What was it, Wise Men?" they clamored at us.

"It was Herod the King patching his rotten throne with still more blood," said Melchior gravely.

"But why?—and what had Bethlehem done?"

"In Bethlehem was one born to be King of the Jews."

And Herod has killed him?" jerked one. "May the vengeance of the Lord smite him! Why is such a devil let live?"

"His time is running out. He will die as he has lived, a horror to himself and all the world. But, thanks be to your God, the Child is safe! ... And he will live to reign."

Before it was day one of the villagers, who had crept away to find out what had happened, came in with terrible news that confirmed Melchior's prescience. Herod, to make sure that no child lately born in Bethlehem should ever reign over the Jews, had slain that night every male child under the age of two. Bethlehem was a village of mourning and despair, with twenty slaughtered babies and many wounded men and broken-hearted women.

"Is there nothing we can do?" asked Balthasar pitifully.

"We can do nothing, save bind the wounds of those who are left. Time alone can heal the rest."

So we went along to give what help we could. But when the men of Bethlehem saw us coming they drove us off with stones and curses, shouting that it was we who had brought that trouble upon them, and we barely escaped with our lives.

"Well, God be thanked, the Child is safe!" panted Melchior, when we had got beyond their reach and he could breathe again. "Now for our own safety. We will make our way through the hills to the Salt Sea, and along its shore to Jordan, and across Jordan to the desert. There we shall be safe."

And the next day, among the hills we found some peasants who were willing to exchange some of their old rags for our good clothes. For three ragged wayfarers might pass in safety where three Wise Men from the East might have attracted undue attention.

Just thirty days after we had started from Damascus we arrived back there, in safety, but very weary, especially Old Melchior, for whom the journey on foot had been long and arduous.

But our hearts were glad, for we had learned much and had been used for the service of One whom we believed destined for great things. How great not one of us then knew, and only one of us came to know, and that not until very many years afterwards.

EPIPHANY

RICHARD SULLIVAN

THE STAR burned red and white in the early evening sky. Its shaft
of light swung very slowly, like a pendulum coming to rest, over
the hill. The frozen grass glittered in the late twilight as if salted
white.

The doorway in the side of the hill was roughly cut and braced
by beams. From top to bottom of its frame hung a rug of pale
leather, with the shape of skins seamed in ridges upon it, and one
of its bottom corners flipped back to show the dirty white curling
of sheep's wool, and to emit a spill of light from inside upon the
pebbles of the path.

Around the door, on these pebbles, and on the stiff and glittering
grass, stood a clump of people: an old man, a middle-aged man,
two little girls, a youth with raw pink pimples on his cheeks, and
a woman who bent over a shaggy black-and-white dog, scratching
its back. All these people were wrapped in heavy cloaks, and they
all—except for the two little girls, who were squatting in the path,
playing with the pebbles and giggling occasionally—stood silent
and somehow expectant, as if waiting upon an uneasy appointment.
Sometimes they shifted and sidled a step or two. The raw youth
moved over to the door and, rubbing his shoulder blades against
the rough wood of the door frame, groaned as in private excrucia-
tion. Once, when the two little girls squealed, the woman spoke
to them sharply.

From one side, moving up the hill, stepped a huge old ox with head hanging low and jaws chumping and eyes rolling up moist and bulbous under lowering brow-bones; and from the other side, from down the hill, came a swarm of sheep, rank smelling even in the cold. Behind the sheep walked daintily a small dark donkey with erect and apprehensive twitching ears. It stood quiet behind the sheep near a big rock and a spreading bush.

The dog growled. The woman murmured to it. The dog stretched and lay down on curved haunches, with straight forepaws and erect ears. The little girls were throwing pebbles at the sheep.

"Stop that!" said the old man to the children.

"You heard now!" said the woman.

One little girl went over and began to croon to the dog, petting him.

The hanging in the doorway crackled lightly as Joseph, coming from inside, swung it open with one arm. He was a stocky, sturdy man with deep-set, anxious eyes and a graying beard. Light from inside the doorway shone bright for an instant on the path as he came out. He looked up and then down the slanting path. "No sign of them yet?" said Joseph.

The old shepherd shrugged, holding his hands out with the palms up and the fingers outstretched.

"No sign," said the other man. "You're sure they're coming?"

"Are they really kings?" asked the woman. "A person hears one thing and then another. Are they really kings?"

"They're men of great wisdom from far off," said Joseph. "That's all I know. Listen!"

The youth was leaning forward, head cocked at an angle to the downhill slope of the path. "Somebody's coming!" he cried. His voice cracked pathetically over the words. He turned away in embarrassment.

"You might go down and show them the way," Joseph said to him.

Nodding, the youth ran down the path.

"From how far off do they come?" asked the old man, peering at Joseph.

"A long distance. Oh, a very long way."

"From the edge of the world?"

"A long way," said Joseph.

"But they speak our language?"

"I believe so. If these are the ones, don't worry, they know how to make themselves understood."

"I hate to hear Gentiles bungle our words," said the other man. "It does something painful to me, a thing like that. Once in Jerusalem I met a Gaul and a Celt—"

"These are your friends, these men who come?" asked the woman.

"If these are the right ones, yes," said Joseph.

"How does he know yet whether these are the right ones?" said the old man scornfully to the woman.

"He could know!" she said. "After all that's happened here, he could know, all right!"

The dog began to growl, crouching, bristling, its muzzle pointed down the path into the half-dark.

"Nah!" said the woman. "Quiet now!"

The old man tapped Joseph's arm. He tilted his head toward the down-slope of the hill. "They know?" he whispered. "These that are coming, they have heard what has happened here?"

"If these are the ones, they have heard enough to be welcome."

The dog bounded forward, barking, as Melchior and Gaspar strode up the path, the raw youth beside them.

"Down!" cried the youth, and the dog began to whine and caper, sniffing Gaspar's boots from behind, then wheeling to bark and frisk at Balthasar, who came running up behind the others.

"—certainly not going to find Him in a cave in the side of a hill!" Gaspar was saying indignantly.

"Wait and see," Balthasar told him. "You know what we decided. Ah, such a happy dog! Down now!"

"I think," said Melchior, with a somewhat taut insistence in his voice, as he glanced from the Star to Joseph, "that we've come to the right place, at last. But you'll be able to tell us."

Joseph looked at the three of them, standing side by side now in their heavy robes, each one clutching in his hands a golden box,

Melchior's with a green enameled cover, Gaspar's with a blue top, and Balthasar's with a red one.

"I think," said Joseph, "that you've come to the right place."

"The place of the King?" said Melchior.

Joseph nodded. "We've been looking for you to come."

"You *expected* us?"

"Oh, yes."

Melchior turned to his companions. Gaspar was staring, with what might have been ominous yet bland suspicion, at the two little girls, both of whom were goggling straight up at him. Balthasar had one hand stretched out toward Joseph.

"Then we can—see Him?" cried Balthasar.

"Oh, yes!"

"Now?"

The sheepskin hanging over the doorway swung open again. The light from inside came brighter now in the growing darkness. Mary, very young, slight, and quick, stepped across the sill of wood, holding the door open, the light flooding about her, so that in blue and white she was silhouetted for a moment against its brightness. She smiled at the shepherds, the woman, and the children, peered at the Magi, then looked as for confirmation to Joseph.

"They've come," said Joseph gently. He had the air of a man aware of his responsibility, even of his authority, yet momentarily puzzled. But Mary was as impulsive as he was hesitant.

"Then come *in!*" cried Mary. "Come *in!* Don't wait outside!"

She held open the hanging sheepskin until Joseph caught it, and he held it then for Melchior, Gaspar, and Balthasar, following them inside at last, and letting the covering drop over the door.

Outside, one of the little girls said: "Mama, who *are* those men?"

"They look funny!" said the other little girl.

The woman said: "Be quiet now, both of you!"

At the other side of the door, with the sheep crowding them, the old shepherd and the middle-aged one were questioning the pimpled youth.

"They were very agreeable," cried the youth. "Amiable! Eager! I found nothing suspicious at all in them."

"They do give themselves high and mighty ways, though," said the old man. "Did you notice how that little gray one sniffed when he looked at us? Anybody'd think he never got a good whiff of the stink of sheep before in his life!"

"Fancy clothes, fancy nose!" said the other shepherd, and laughed.

"They're *serious!*" said the youth. "That was what I first noticed, how *serious* they were. They couldn't quite believe that this was the right place—they were arguing among themselves."

"What did they expect, a big stone palace?"

"They've been staying with Herod, in Herod's palace."

"That old baboon! I wouldn't stay in Herod's palace if he got down on his knees and asked me!"

"Ha! I can see Herod getting down on his knees and asking you! You'd be on your knees before him, and he'd be slitting your throat, from here to here, with a wide knife—and grinning!"

"I'd kick him square in the teeth, that bloody old lizard!"

"Herod held them up," said the youth. "He delayed them. They meant to be here before."

"Something held them up," said the old man. "We know that, all right." He glanced at the crack of light coming from the hanging sheepskin over the doorway, and shook his head. "Don't ask me what they're doing in there," he said. "This all goes beyond me! Why, at first I thought—that first night, you know, with the angels—I thought it was all for *us*."

"That was very selfish of you," said the middle-aged one. "Not that I like Gentiles and foreigners crowding in this way. But to think of a thing like this as meant only for us—that is selfish."

"I have said so."

"You remember what the angels sang, in those voices?"

"I remember. Oh, I remember! All I say is I am old and slow to understand with my head. What happens here is beyond me."

"Yet you are *in* it!"

"I am in it, praise the Lord. We are all in it. Even"—he pointed with his thumb—"these new ones."

"These are good men," said the youth. "I know that much."

"They speak without fuss," said the middle-aged one. "And without pretense. Really, I am a little surprised at the way they speak. Not like foreigners at all." He thrust out his lips, looked at the doorway and nodded in commendation.

"They must be very great men in their own country," said the youth. "It must have taken a great impulse to make them come here, all that way."

"Men must be ready to give themselves, naturally."

"That's what I felt in them. A readiness to give themselves!" said the youth. "Oh, they are very good men."

"Listen!" said the old man, turning his head slowly to peer down the path.

At the same moment the dog darted forward barking.

"Somebody's coming," said the old man.

The woman, who had been talking to the two little girls, looked down the path, frowning; then she turned back to the children.

"—and so we can't always have our *own* way," she told them, quietly.

"But I want to go *in!*" cried one little girl.

"We've always gone in before!" said the other girl.

"Yes, yes, but now this is for these new ones. And we let them go in by themselves, because they—"

"What were those things they were carrying?"

"Gifts," said the woman. "Presents for Him. Little presents."

"To play with?"

"Well," said the woman, "that I don't know. The old fat one, now, with the fat little red cheeks, he's kneeling down, inside there —do you see?—and he holds out that little gold casket he was carrying, with the flashy green top on it, remember?—and he gives it to the Lord—"

"The Child?"

"The Savior. Christ. You remember what I told you about the angels that night, singing in all that brightness. Ah, the whole sky here"—she waved one hand—"was a brightness. I was afraid, just hearing about it, afterward."

"I wouldn't have been afraid," said one little girl.

"I would," said the other. "I think I would."

"You both would have been afraid, but not how you think. No, not afraid, exactly, but—full of an awe and a wonder—and a joy. Not afraid, but—touched by God. It was that way for your father" —she looked over at the middle-aged shepherd—"and for your grandfather. They were the first to see Him. And your brother there—when he saw Him, he cried."

The youth had started down the path. Near the great ox standing motionless in the grass the youth met Simon, wrapped in his black cloak. They stood whispering together. The ox moved away from them, down the hill, out of sight.

"—and now inside," whispered the woman to the girls, "the little gray one is kneeling and giving his gift—so!—and now the tall young one kneels. Imagine. Inside there now they are all kneeling, and—"

"What's *in* those boxes?"

"I've heard that what they were to bring Him was frankincense for adoration, gold for glory, and myrrh for love and for death—"

"But He isn't dead!"

"No. No. I don't understand it all, but—"

Joseph came out the doorway, flung back the sheepskin hanging. Inside, in a dazzle of brightness sat Mary with the Child in her arms; and on the straw of the floor stood the three golden boxes, their bright covers raised open and flashing; and the Magi were bending and bowing and stumbling as they backed away through the door, out onto the flashing pebbles; and the shepherds and the woman and the two little girls outside were suddenly kneeling; the youth talking to Simon at a distance bobbed about and dropped to his knees. Simon stood squinting at the light. Then Joseph dropped the sheepskin hanging; and in the dusk Joseph spoke in a low voice to the middle-aged shepherd, who nodded.

Beckoning to the woman, muttering something to the old man, the middle-aged shepherd started up the hill. The woman, the children, and the old man followed him. The dog frisked after them, then wheeled, barking sharply, and circled the sheep, snapping and growling at them. The sheep turned slowly and began to move up the hill. The youth, talking still to Simon, had turned. Simon held him by one arm. The youth broke away; he called something in an apologetic voice over his shoulder to Simon, and ran after the now hurrying sheep up the hill in the evening. He slapped the little donkey's haunch as he ran past it; the donkey reared and kicked, then ran down hill past Simon. The dog's barking sounded insistent in the distance up the hill. Simon loosened his black cloak at the throat, flung it open, and folded his arms. With the back of his hand he wiped sweat from his forehead. Then he leaned forward from the waist to squint at the three Magi, standing on the pebbles talking to Joseph outside the door.

"—but now you must go!" Joseph was telling them. "Oh, yes, yes, I know that you want to stay! But you must return to your own country. Tell them there what you have seen." He smiled; with his hands he patted the arms of Melchior and Gaspar, who stood one at each side of him; but he looked at Balthasar, across from him, straight in the eyes. "I must go now, too," he said apologetically, straight to Balthasar. "Not must but will. There are things we are all doing freely, as you three came here freely—"

"But slowly," said Balthasar. He wiped his eyes and shook his head. "So slowly!"

"But slowly," said Joseph, "yet freely, to make a design beyond us and involving us. So I will go now. You will all excuse me and understand."

And Joseph ducked back under the sheepskin hanging so quickly that there was only a whisk of light on the pebbles.

"Would God ever so lower Himself?" demanded Balthasar, not so much of the others as of the doorway swinging behind Joseph. Then he turned to Melchior. "God so degraded?" he cried. "So emptied out as to become man?" His eyes were glittering with tears; he slapped himself hard on the cheek. "Flesh? Like me?"

"You saw," said Melchior.

"But do you understand?"

"No. But I have seen!"

"You?" cried Balthasar, turning to Gaspar. "Do you understand what we—what we have been led to? God Himself among us, and we—how awful we are! How sluggish! How mean! How wavering! And yet here—here of all places!—we have come to Him!"

"A thing like this," said Gaspar, "is not meant to be understood. Naturally, I don't understand it. But I know what I've seen, and I'm not proud of what I've been." He glanced at the sky. "The Star is gone again," he said. "And how mild it's getting!" He opened his cloak at the collar.

"We're born to love!" cried Balthasar, his voice sobbing; and he laughed and hit his fist into his palm. "Men are *born to love*, do you hear me?"

"Men are born," said Melchior mildly, "to *adore*. There is no other reason for our existence. After today surely no other reason!"

Balthasar stared at him. "Yes! Of course! But that's practically what I said!"

Simon was moving slowly up the hill toward them, listening and smiling. Sweat gleamed on his face. His eyes dazzled in the dusk.

"Look," said Gaspar to his companions, "you both know me—I'm a practical man. I don't have all these rhapsodic thoughts myself, but I can see what you both have in mind, and I'd say you're *both* right, and I agree, oh, absolutely! We were born to come here, to *be* here tonight—and it was a weak enough, long enough, slow enough coming we made of it!"

"To love," said Melchior. "I agree. Yes, I agree. To *love!*"

"To adore!" cried Balthasar, fiercely. "To cry alleluia. The same thing! I agree with all my breath!"

"A most interesting thought," said Gaspar, "has just occurred to me. We are forerunners, do you realize that? Forerunners of all men to this—location." He paused and sighed. "But these are matters we must discuss alongside the night-fire on our way home. I had a warning in my sleep last night against returning to Herod—"

"That old monster! That basilisk! He worked hard on us!"

"—and you've both just heard Joseph telling us to return to our own country. A solid fellow, that Joseph. If I've learned anything in my years in business it's how to judge a man instantly. We can depend upon Joseph. If he says we're to go, we're meant to go—by our own choice, of course—and you two do what you like, but I'm going. And I say that we should *all* go, at once, now, tonight!"

Balthasar shook his head. "I'm staying," he said. "Oh, I'm going to stay!"

Melchior said: "We've been led here to the beginning. I confess I want to stay for the continuation. The Star that led us—"

"The Star is gone," said Gaspar. "I told you that before. Look. It's time for us to go. Now. Oh, I understand your feelings, both of you. We live under guidance. Free—but informed. There's a grace in things, and it's around us even if we don't feel it. That Joseph is a reliable man. And I had a dream about not going back to—"

"—to Herod!" said Simon, moving smoothly in on them. "Dear friends, how good to see you again! And how affected you've all been by this—this touching little pantomime behind the discreetly closed curtains! Really, I was affected myself, even at a distance. There was a considerable force to it. That magical little epiphany when the door was open, you know. The pretty young mother sitting there with the handsome Infant—oh, *very* moving, really! Very forceful. I wonder how they managed it. There's the making of an enduring myth here. I can see it. And I'm an expert in these things; you realize that, I'm sure."

Gaspar said to his companions: "Now do you see what I'm talking about?"

"Oh, there's not the slightest need for you to be worried about my being here!" said Simon. "I'm interested *professionally* in this kind of thing. Do you have any idea of what's behind it, really? I'd be willing to pay for information. I could feel the power. It was there, palpably, but I couldn't quite identify it. And mind you, I've had years and years of specialized experience with—"

"Go away, Simon!" said Melchior.

"Go back to Herod!" cried Balthasar.

108]

"No!" sputtered Gaspar. "He mustn't go back to—"

"Tell him what you've seen!" Balthasar said fiercely.

Simon giggled. "Tell Herod I've seen you three taken in by a sentimental charade? Oh, he'd *love* that!"

"You sniffer at camel-tracks," said Balthasar. "You skin-and-bones magician. Get away from this place!"

"What happened while you were inside? Were there some little obscure mystic rites involving the—?"

Balthasar stepped toward Simon with his hands out, his shoulders dropped.

"No!" cried Melchior. "*No!*"

"He's profaning the place!" said Balthasar, grabbing Simon. "He doesn't belong here! You vile—!"

"Stop! You may be profaning the place yourself!"

Balthasar shook Simon hard, once; then stepped away. Breathing hard, he whipped off his cloak, tossed it over one arm, and wiped sweat from his forehead.

"I tell you one thing!" screamed Simon, straightening and picking at his rumpled clothes. "You'd better treat me civilly or you'll all three be dead pigeons! *Dead* pigeons, you understand?"

"With your permission," said Balthasar to Melchior, formally, "I would feel honored to choke out this squealing voice which predicts—"

Melchior shook his head.

Down the hill, but close to the place where Simon had first appeared, there sounded a swishing of brush, dry and strident in the evening. Gaspar turned and frowned down the hill.

"If you work with me," cried Simon, "tell me what happened, I'll work with you! You have my promise! I know something went on inside there! I want to know *what!*"

"And if we don't tell you," said Melchior, sternly, "what then?"

Simon simpered. "Herod's son is already on his way back to report on your finding of your King. Naturally Herod will have the Baby killed. *And* the parents. Oh, don't take on! What would you yourselves do in Herod's case? Would you want the people all stirred up about an episode on a hillside? But of course the

[109

unfortunate thing from your point of view is that Herod surely will have you three killed, too, unless I step in and tell him that you've been—cooperative."

"Why should he have us killed?"

"Oh, use your wisdom, dear Melchior! To keep you from *talking*, of course!"

"You can't possibly stop us from leaving here right now. Or from talking hereafter!"

"I wouldn't dream of trying to stop you from going. I'm no man of action. But there are some soldiers of Herod's down below —*they* very probably would have some ideas of their own if you tried to run away!"

Down the hill again there was a rustling in the brush. Now a man walked boldly up the pebbled path, a stocky, shambling man with his arms swinging and his head lowered. They all turned to watch him. He made straight for Gaspar.

"Pomar!" said Gaspar.

"I don't mean to intrude," said Pomar, "but those soldiers of Herod's that this one has mentioned, they are—unavailable for practical purposes. We've got them tied up hand and foot and gagged to their gullets."

"That's very good of you, Pomar," said Gaspar.

"I—I heard a little of what was going on up here, and I thought I should tell you."

"Very good, Pomar. Very good. Just keep them—unavailable."

Pomar nodded, turned, and shambled back down the pebbled path, his arms swinging.

"So now," said Melchior to Gaspar, "you're sure of that dream you had?"

"Oh, yes."

"And Joseph unquestionably would direct us justly. Simon, we're going to be gone before your Herod even knows that we've been here! It seems to be intended that way!"

Balthasar ran to the closed doorway. "Joseph!" he called. "*Joseph!*"

"No point in warning *them*," said Gaspar. "They know." He

glanced at Melchior. "They must know. Oh, much more than we do. *He* knows the whole design, surely."

Simon, who had been watching them all closely, now looked at the ground. "What are you going to do with me?" he demanded, fear and importance both in his manner.

"You?" said Melchior. "Why should we do anything to you? Go back to Herod."

"He'll *kill* me!" wailed Simon.

At the doorway Balthasar was talking excitedly to Joseph.

"No.... He won't be pleased, but certainly he won't kill you."

"Yes! You don't know Herod. He'll have my liver cut out. Or he'll burn me. I know him. If you three and that Child are gone when his soldiers get here, he'll say it's my fault. I don't know why I should be expected to take part in things like this! I'm a professional, a specialist! Just because there's magic involved—"

Gaspar said: "There's no magic involved here. In my country we know what magic is. This is something quite different."

At the doorway Joseph was shaking his head and Balthasar was making wild, insistent gestures, while Joseph kept shaking his head.

"This," said Melchior to Simon, "—and perhaps now I answer a question you asked earlier—this is literally God working among men, living as man. This is no trick."

Simon smiled, gaped, and then laughed, his whole body writhing.

"Tell Herod," said Gaspar. "And don't get hysterical!"

Balthasar came stamping back at them. "All he'll say is that we are to go. He won't listen to me!"

"Look," said Melchior.

At the doorway now, holding the sheepskin half open, stood Mary. She smiled at them and nodded: it was like a very delicate and gracious and concerned thanks for their coming, and at the same time a confirmation of their going. Behind her they could all see the Child.

THE STORY OF
THE OTHER WISE MAN

HENRY VAN DYKE

YOU KNOW the story of the Three Wise Men of the East, and how they traveled from far away to offer their gifts at the manger cradle in Bethlehem. But have you ever heard the story of the Other Wise Man, who also saw the star in its rising, and set out to follow it, yet did not arrive with his brethren in the presence of the young child Jesus? Of the great desire of this fourth pilgrim, and how it was denied, yet accomplished in the denial; of his many wanderings and the probations of his soul; of the long way of his seeking and the strange way of his finding the One whom he sought —I would tell the tale as I have heard fragments of it in the Hall of Dreams, in the palace of the Heart of Man.

I

In the days when Augustus Caesar was master of many kings and Herod reigned in Jerusalem, there lived in the city of Ecbatana, among the mountains of Persia, a certain man named Artaban. His house stood close to the outermost of the walls which encircled the royal treasury. From his roof he could look over the sevenfold battlements of black and white and crimson and blue and red and silver and gold, to the hill where the summer palace of the Parthian emperors glittered like a jewel in a crown.

Around the dwelling of Artaban spread a fair garden, a tangle of flowers and fruit trees, watered by a score of streams descending from the slopes of Mount Orontes, and made musical by innumerable birds. But all color was lost in the soft and odorous darkness of the late September night, and all sounds were hushed in the deep charm of its silence, save the plashing of the water, like a voice half sobbing and half laughing under the shadows. High above the trees a dim glow of light shone through the curtained arches of the upper chamber, where the master of the house was holding council with his friends.

He stood by the doorway to greet his guests—a tall, dark man of about forty years, with brilliant eyes set near together under his broad brow, and firm lines graven around his fine, thin lips; the brow of a dreamer and the mouth of a soldier, a man of sensitive feeling but inflexible will—one of those who, in whatever age they may live, are born for inward conflict and a life of quest.

His robe was of pure white wool, thrown over a tunic of silk; and a white, pointed cap, with long lapels at the sides, rested on his flowing black hair. It was the dress of the ancient priesthood of the Magi, called the fire worshipers.

"Welcome!" he said, in his low, pleasant voice, as one after another entered the room—"welcome, Abdus; peace be with you, Rhodaspes and Tigranes, and with you, my father, Abgarus. You are all welcome. This house grows bright with the joy of your presence."

There were nine of the men, differing widely in age, but alike in the richness of their dress of many-colored silks, and in the massive golden collars around their necks, marking them as Parthian nobles, and in the winged circles of gold resting upon their breasts, the sign of the followers of Zoroaster.

They took their places around a small black altar at the end of the room, where a tiny flame was burning. Artaban, standing beside it, and waving a barsom of thin tamarisk branches above the fire, fed it with dry sticks of pine and fragrant oils. Then he began the ancient chant of the Yasna, and the voices of his companions joined in the hymn to Ahura-Mazda:

We worship the Spirit Divine,
        all wisdom and goodness possessing,
Surrounded by Holy Immortals,
        the givers of bounty and blessing;
We joy in the work of His hands,
        His truth and His power confessing.

We praise all the things that are pure,
        for these are His only Creation;
The thoughts that are true and the words
        and the deeds that have won approbation;
These are supported by Him,
        and for these we make adoration.

Hear us, O Mazda! Thou livest
        in truth and in heavenly gladness;
Cleanse us from falsehood, and keep us
        from evil and bondage to badness;
Pour out the light and the joy of Thy life
        on our darkness and sadness.

Shine on our gardens and fields,
        shine on our working and weaving;
Shine on the whole race of man,
        believing and unbelieving;
      Shine on us now through the night,
      Shine on us now in Thy might,
The flame of our holy love
        and the song of our worship receiving.

    The fire rose with the chant, throbbing as if the flame responded
to the music, until it cast a bright illumination through the whole
apartment, revealing its simplicity and splendor.
    The floor was laid with tiles of dark blue veined with white;
pilasters of twisted silver stood out against the blue walls; the clere-
story of round-arched windows above them was hung with azure

silk; the vaulted ceiling was a pavement of blue stones, like the body of heaven in its clearness, sown with silver stars. From the four corners of the roof hung four golden magic wheels, called the tongues of the gods. At the eastern end, behind the altar, there were two dark-red pillars of porphyry; above them a lintel of the same stone, on which was carved the figure of a winged archer, with his arrow set to the string and his bow drawn.

The doorway between the pillars, which opened upon the terrace of the roof, was covered with a heavy curtain of the color of a ripe pomegranate, embroidered with innumerable golden rays shooting upward from the floor. In effect the room was like a quiet, starry night, all azure and silver, flushed in the east with rosy promise of the dawn. It was, as the house of a man should be, an expression of the character and spirit of the master.

He turned to his friends when the song was ended, and invited them to be seated on the divan at the western end of the room.

"You have come tonight," said he, looking around the circle, "at my call, as the faithful scholars of Zoroaster, to renew your worship and rekindle your faith in the God of Purity, even as this fire has been rekindled on the altar. We worship not the fire, but Him of whom it is the chosen symbol, because it is the purest of all created things. It speaks to us of one who is Light and Truth. Is it not so, my father?"

"It is well said, my son," answered the venerable Abgarus. "The enlightened are never idolaters. They lift the veil of form and go in to the shrine of reality, and new light and truth are coming to them continually through the old symbols."

"Hear me, then, my father and my friends," said Artaban, "while I tell you of the new light and truth that have come to me through the most ancient of all signs. We have searched the secrets of Nature together, and studied the healing virtues of water and fire and the plants. We have read also the books of prophecy in which the future is dimly foretold in words that are hard to understand. But the highest of all learning is the knowledge of the stars. To trace their course is to untangle the threads of the mystery of life from the beginning to the end. If we could follow them perfectly, nothing would be hidden from us. But is not our knowledge of them still incomplete? Are there not many stars still beyond our horizon—lights that are known only to the dwellers in the far southland, among the spice trees of Punt and the gold mines of Ophir?"

There was a murmur of assent among the listeners.

"The stars," said Tigranes, "are the thoughts of the Eternal. They are numberless. But the thoughts of man can be counted, like the years of his life. The wisdom of the Magi is the greatest of all wisdoms on earth, because it knows its own ignorance. And that is the secret of power. We keep men always looking and waiting for a new sunrise. But we ourselves understand that the darkness is equal to the light, and that the conflict between them will never be ended."

"That does not satisfy me," answered Artaban, "for, if the waiting must be endless, if there could be no fulfillment of it, then it would not be wisdom to look and wait. We should become like those new teachers of the Greeks, who say that there is no truth, and that the only wise men are those who spend their lives in discovering and exposing the lies that have been believed in the world. But the new sunrise will certainly appear in the appointed time. Do not our own books tell us that this will come to pass, and that men will see the brightness of a great light?"

"That is true," said the voice of Abgarus; "every faithful disciple of Zoroaster knows the prophecy of the Avesta, and carries the word in his heart. 'In that day Sosiosh the Victorious shall arise out of the number of the prophets in the east country. Around him shall shine a mighty brightness, and he shall make life everlasting, incorruptible, and immortal, and the dead shall rise again.'"

"This is a dark saying," said Tigranes, "and it may be that we shall never understand it. It is better to consider the things that are near at hand, and to increase the influence of the Magi in their own country, rather than to look for one who may be a stranger, and to whom we must resign our power."

The others seemed to approve these words. There was a silent feeling of agreement manifest among them; their looks responded

116]

with that indefinable expression which always follows when a speaker has uttered the thought that has been slumbering in the hearts of his listeners. But Artaban turned to Abgarus with a glow on his face, and said:

"My father, I have kept this prophecy in the secret place of my soul. Religion without a great hope would be like an altar without a living fire. And now the flame has burned more brightly, and by the light of it I have read other words which also have come from the fountain of Truth, and speak yet more clearly of the rising of the Victorious One in his brightness."

He drew from the breast of his tunic two small rolls of fine parchment, with writing upon them, and unfolded them carefully upon his knee.

"In the years that are lost in the past, long before our fathers came into the land of Babylon, there were wise men in Chaldea, from whom the first of the Magi learned the secret of the heavens. And of these Balaam the son of Beor was one of the mightiest. Hear the words of his prophecy: 'There shall come a star out of Jacob, and a scepter shall arise out of Israel.' "

The lips of Tigranes drew downward with contempt, as he said:

"Judah was a captive by the waters of Babylon, and the sons of Jacob were in bondage to our kings. The tribes of Israel are scattered through the mountains like lost sheep, and from the remnant that dwells in Judea under the yoke of Rome neither star nor scepter shall arise."

"And yet," answered Artaban, "it was the Hebrew Daniel, the mighty searcher of dreams, the counselor of kings, the wise Belteshazzar, who was most honored and beloved of our great King Cyrus. A prophet of sure things and a reader of the thoughts of the Eternal, Daniel proved himself to our people. And these are the words that he wrote." (Artaban read from the second roll:) " 'Know, therefore, and understand that from the going forth of the commandment to restore Jerusalem, unto the Anointed One, the Prince, the time shall be seven and threescore and two weeks.' "

"But, my son," said Abgarus, doubtfully, "these are mystical numbers. Who can interpret them, or who can find the key that shall unlock their meaning?"

Artaban answered: "It has been shown to me and to my three companions among the Magi—Caspar, Melchior and Balthasar. We have searched the ancient tablets of Chaldea and computed the time. It falls in this year. We have studied the sky, and in the spring of the year we saw two of the greatest planets draw near together in the sign of the Fish, which is the house of the Hebrews. We also saw a new star there, which shone for one night and then vanished. Now again the two great planets are meeting. This night is their conjunction. My three brothers are watching by the ancient Temple of the Seven Spheres, at Borsippa, in Babylonia, and I am watching here. If the star shines again, they will wait ten days for me at the temple, and then we will set out together for Jerusalem, to see and worship the promised one who shall be born King of Israel. I believe the sign will come. I have made ready for the journey. I have sold my possessions, and bought these three jewels—a sapphire, a ruby and a pearl—to carry them as tribute to the King. And I ask you to go with me on the pilgrimage, that we may have joy together in finding the Prince who is worthy to be served."

While he was speaking he thrust his hand into the inmost fold of his girdle and drew out three great gems—one blue as a fragment of the night sky, one redder than a ray of sunrise, and one as pure as the peak of a snow mountain at twilight—and laid them on the outspread scrolls before him.

But his friends looked on with strange and alien eyes. A veil of doubt and mistrust came over their faces, like a fog creeping up from the marshes to hide the hills. They glanced at each other with looks of wonder and pity, as those who have listened to incredible sayings, the story of a wild vision, or the proposal of an impossible enterprise.

At last Tigranes said: "Artaban, this is a vain dream. It comes from too much looking upon the stars and the cherishing of lofty thoughts. It would be wiser to spend the time in gathering money for the new fire temple at Chala. No king will ever rise from the broken race of Israel, and no end will ever come to the eternal strife of light and darkness. He who looks for it is a chaser of shadows. Farewell."

And another said: "Artaban, I have no knowledge of these things, and my office as guardian of the royal treasure binds me here. The quest is not for me. But if thou must follow it, fare thee well."

And another said: "In my house there sleeps a new bride, and I cannot leave her nor take her with me on this strange journey. This quest is not for me. But may thy steps be prospered wherever thou goest. So, farewell."

And another said: "I am ill and unfit for hardship, but there is a man among my servants whom I will send with thee when thou goest, to bring me word how thou farest."

So, one by one, they left the house of Artaban. But Abgarus, the oldest and the one who loved him the best, lingered after the others had gone, and said, gravely: "My son, it may be that the light of truth is in this sign that has appeared in the skies, and then it will surely lead to the Prince and the mighty brightness. Or it may be that it is only a shadow of the light, as Tigranes has said, and then he who follows it will have a long pilgrimage and a fruitless search. But it is better to follow even the shadow of the best than to remain content with the worst. And those who would see wonderful things must often be ready to travel alone. I am too old for this journey, but my heart shall be a companion of thy pilgrimage day and night, and I shall know the end of thy quest. Go in peace."

Then Abgarus went out of the azure chamber with its silver stars, and Artaban was left in solitude.

He gathered up the jewels and replaced them in his girdle. For a long time he stood and watched the flame that flickered and sank upon the altar. Then he crossed the hall, lifted the heavy curtain, and passed out between the pillars of porphyry to the terrace on the roof.

The shiver that runs through the earth ere she rouses from her night sleep had already begun, and the cool wind that heralds the daybreak was drawing downward from the lofty, snow-traced ravines of Mount Orontes. Birds, half-awakened, crept and chirped among the rustling leaves, and the smell of ripened grapes came in brief wafts from the arbors.

Far over the eastern plain a white mist stretched like a lake. But where the distant peaks of Zagros serrated the western horizon the sky was clear. Jupiter and Saturn rolled together like drops of lambent flame about to blend in one.

As Artaban watched them, a steel-blue spark was born out of the darkness beneath, rounding itself with purple splendors to a crimson sphere, and spiring upward through rays of saffron and orange into a point of white radiance. Tiny and infinitely remote, yet perfect in every part, it pulsated in the enormous vault as if the three jewels in the Magian's girdle had mingled and been transformed into a living heart of light.

He bowed his head. He covered his brow with his hands.

"It is the sign," he said. "The King is coming, and I will go to meet him."

II

All night long, Vasda, the swiftest of Artaban's horses, had been waiting, saddled and bridled, in her stall, pawing the ground impatiently and shaking her bit as if she shared the eagerness of her master's purpose, though she knew not its meaning.

Before the birds had fully roused to their strong, high, joyful chant of morning song, before the white mist had begun to lift lazily from the plain, the Other Wise Man was in the saddle, riding swiftly along the highroad, which skirted the base of Mount Orontes, westward.

How close, how intimate is the comradeship between a man and his favorite horse on a long journey. It is a silent, comprehensive friendship, an intercourse beyond the need of words.

They drink at the same wayside springs, and sleep under the same guardian stars. They are conscious together of the subduing spell of nightfall and the quickening joy of daybreak. The master shares his evening meal with his hungry companion, and feels the soft, moist lips caressing the palm of his hand as they close over the morsel of bread. In the gray dawn he is roused from his bivouac by the gentle stir of a warm, sweet breath over his sleeping face, and looks up into the eyes of his faithful fellow traveler, ready and waiting for the toil of the day. Surely, unless he is a pagan and an unbeliever, by whatever name he calls upon his God, he will thank Him for this voiceless sympathy, this dumb affection, and his morning prayer will embrace a double blessing—God bless us both, the horse and the rider, and keep our feet from falling and our souls from death!

Then, through the keen morning air, the swift hoofs beat their tattoo along the road, keeping time to the pulsing of two hearts that are moved with the same eager desire—to conquer space, to devour the distance, to attain the goal of the journey.

Artaban must indeed ride wisely and well if he would keep the appointed hour with the other Magi; for the route was a hundred and fifty parasangs, and fifteen was the utmost that he could travel in a day. But he knew Vasda's strength, and pushed forward without anxiety, making the fixed distance every day, though he must travel late into the night, and in the morning long before sunrise.

He passed along the brown slopes of Mount Orontes, furrowed by the rocky courses of a hundred torrents.

He crossed the level plains of the Nicaeans, where the famous herds of horses, feeding in the wide pastures, tossed their heads at Vasda's approach, and galloped away with a thunder of many hoofs, and flocks of wild birds rose suddenly from the swampy meadows, wheeling in great circles with a shining flutter of innumerable wings and shrill cries of surprise.

He traversed the fertile fields of Concabar, where the dust from the threshing floors filled the air with a golden mist, half hiding the huge temple of Astarte with its four hundred pillars.

At Baghistan, among the rich gardens watered by fountains from the rock, he looked up at the mountain thrusting its immense rugged brow out over the road, and saw the figure of King Darius trampling upon his fallen foes, and the proud list of his wars and conquests graven high upon the face of the eternal cliff.

Over many a cold and desolate pass, crawling painfully across the wind-swept shoulders of the hills; down many a black mountain gorge, where the river roared and raced before him like a savage guide; across many a smiling vale, with terraces of yellow limestone full of vines and fruit trees; through the oak groves of Carine and the dark Gates of Zagros, walled in by precipices; into the ancient city of Chala, where the people of Samaria had been kept in captivity long ago; and out again by the mighty portal, riven through the encircling hills, where he saw the image of the High Priest of the Magi sculptured on the wall of rock, with hand uplifted as if to bless the centuries of pilgrims; past the entrance of the narrow defile, filled from end to end with orchards of peaches and figs, through which the river Gyndes foamed down to meet him; over the broad rice fields, where the autumnal vapors spread their deathly mists; following along the course of the river, under tremulous shadows of poplar and tamarind, among the lowed hills; and out upon the flat plain, where the road ran straight as an arrow through the stubble fields and parched meadows; past the city of Ctesiphon, where the Parthian emperors reigned, and the vast metropolis of Seleucia which Alexander built; across the swirling floods of Tigris and the many channels of Euphrates, flowing yellow through the cornlands—Artaban pressed onward until he arrived, at nightfull on the tenth day, beneath the shattered walls of populous Babylon.

Vasda was almost spent, and Artaban would gladly have turned into the city to find rest and refreshment for himself and for her. But he knew that it was three hours' journey yet to the Temple of the Seven Spheres, and he must reach the place by midnight if he would find his comrades waiting. So he did not halt, but rode steadily across the stubble fields.

A grove of date palms made an island of gloom in the pale yellow sea. As she passed into the shadow Vasda slackened her pace, and began to pick her way more carefully.

Near the farther end of the darkness an access of caution seemed to fall upon her. She scented some danger or difficulty; it was not in her heart to fly from it—only to be prepared for it, and to meet it wisely, as a good horse should do. The grove was close and silent as the tomb; not a leaf rustled, not a bird sang.

She felt her steps before her delicately, carrying her head low, and sighing now and then with apprehension. At last she gave a quick breath of anxiety and dismay, and stood stock-still, quivering in every muscle, before a dark object in the shadow of the last palm tree.

Artaban dismounted. The dim starlight revealed the form of a man lying across the road. His humble dress and the outline of his haggard face showed that he was probably one of the Hebrews who still dwelt in great numbers around the city. His pallid skin, dry and yellow as parchment, bore the mark of the deadly fever which ravaged the marshlands in autumn. The chill of death was in his lean hand, and, as Artaban released it, the arm fell back inertly upon the motionless breast.

He turned away with a thought of pity, leaving the body to that strange burial which the Magians deemed most fitting—the funeral of the desert, from which the kites and vultures rise on dark wings, and the beasts of prey slink furtively away. When they are gone there is only a heap of white bones on the sand.

But, as he turned, a long, faint, ghostly sigh came from the man's lips. The bony fingers gripped the hem of the Magian's robe and held him fast.

Artaban's heart leaped to his throat, not with fear, but with a dumb resentment at the importunity of this blind delay.

How could he stay here in the darkness to minister to a dying stranger? What claim had this unknown fragment of human life upon his compassion or his service? If he lingered but for an hour he could hardly reach Borsippa at the appointed time. His companions would think he had given up the journey. They would go without him. He would lose his quest.

But if he went on now, the man would surely die. If Artaban stayed, life might be restored. His spirit throbbed and fluttered with the urgency of the crisis. Should he risk the great reward of his faith for the sake of a single deed of charity? Should he turn aside, if only for a moment, from the following of the star, to give a cup of cold water to a poor, perishing Hebrew?

"God of truth and purity," he prayed, "direct me in the holy path, the way of wisdom which Thou only knowest."

Then he turned back to the sick man. Loosening the grasp of his hand, he carried him to a little mound at the foot of the palm tree.

He unbound the thick folds of the turban and opened the garment above the sunken breast. He brought water from one of the small canals near by, and moistened the sufferer's brow and mouth. He mingled a draught of one of those simple but potent remedies which he carried always in his girdle—for the Magians were physicians as well as astrologers—and poured it slowly between the colorless lips. Hour after hour he labored as only a skillful healer of disease can do. At last the man's strength returned; he sat up and looked about him.

"Who art thou?" he said, in the rude dialect of the country, "and why hast thou sought me here to bring back my life?"

"I am Artaban the Magian, of the city of Ecbatana, and I am going to Jerusalem in search of one who is to be born King of the Jews, a great Prince and Deliverer of all men. I dare not delay any longer upon my journey, for the caravan that has waited for me may depart without me. But see, here is all that I have left of bread and wine, and here is a potion of healing herbs. When thy strength is restored thou canst find the dwellings of the Hebrews among the houses of Babylon."

The Jew raised his trembling hand solemnly to heaven.

"Now may the God of Abraham and Isaac and Jacob bless and prosper the journey of the merciful, and bring him in peace to his desired haven. Stay! I have nothing to give thee in return—only this: that I can tell thee where the Messiah must be sought. For our prophets have said that he should be born not in Jerusalem, but in Bethlehem of Judah. May the Lord bring thee in safety to that place, because thou hast had pity upon the sick."

It was already long past midnight. Artaban rode in haste, and Vasda, restored by the brief rest, ran eagerly through the silent plain and swam the channels of the river. She put forth the remnant of her strength and fled over the ground like a gazelle.

But the first beam of the rising sun sent a long shadow before her as she entered upon the final stadium of the journey, and the eyes of Artaban, anxiously scanning the great mound of Nimrod and the Temple of the Seven Spheres, could discern no trace of his friends.

The many-colored terraces of black and orange and red and yellow and green and blue and white, shattered by the convulsions of nature, and crumbling under the repeated blows of human violence, still glittered like a ruined rainbow in the morning light.

Artaban rode swiftly around the hill. He dismounted and climbed to the highest terrace, looking out toward the west.

The huge desolation of the marshes stretched away to the horizon and the border of the desert. Bitterns stood by the stagnant pools and jackals skulked through the low bushes; but there was no sign of the caravan of the Wise Men, far or near.

At the edge of the terrace he saw a little cairn of broken bricks, and under them a piece of papyrus. He caught it up and read: "We have waited past the midnight, and can delay no longer. We go to find the King. Follow us across the desert."

Artaban sat down upon the ground and covered his head in despair.

"How can I cross the desert," said he, "with no food and with a spent horse? I must return to Babylon, sell my sapphire, and buy a train of camels, and provision for the journey. I may never overtake my friends. Only God the merciful knows whether I shall not lose the sight of the King because I tarried to show mercy."

III

There was a silence in the Hall of Dreams, where I was listening to the story of the Other Wise Man. Through this silence I saw, but very dimly, his figure passing over the dreary undulations of the desert, high upon the back of his camel, rocking steadily onward like a ship over the waves.

The land of death spread its cruel net around him. The stony waste bore no fruit but briers and thorns. The dark ledges of rock thrust themselves above the surface here and there, like the bones of perished monsters. Arid and inhospitable mountain ranges rose before him, furrowed with dry channels of ancient torrents, white and ghastly as scars on the face of nature. Shifting hills of treacherous sand were heaped like tombs along the horizon. By day the fierce heat pressed its intolerable burden on the quivering air. No living creature moved on the dumb, swooning earth, but tiny jerboas scuttling through the parched bushes, or lizards vanishing in the clefts of the rock. By night the jackals prowled and barked in the distance, and the lion made the black ravines echo with his hollow roaring, while a bitter, blighting chill followed the fever of the day. Through heat and cold, the Magian moved steadily onward.

Then I saw the gardens and orchards of Damascus, watered by the streams of Abana and Pharpar, with their sloping swards inlaid with bloom, and their thickets of myrrh and roses. I saw the long, snowy ridge of Hermon, and the dark groves of cedars, and the valley of the Jordan, and the blue waters of the Lake of Galilee, and the fertile plain of Esdraelon, and the hills of Ephraim, and the highlands of Judah. Through all these I followed the figure of Artaban moving steadily onward, until he arrived at Bethlehem. And it was the third day after the Three Wise Men had come to that place and had found Mary and Joseph, with the young child, Jesus, and had laid their gifts of gold and frankincense and myrrh at his feet.

Then the Other Wise Man drew near, weary, but full of hope, bearing his ruby and his pearl to offer to the King. "For now at last," he said, "I shall surely find him, though I be alone, and later than my brethren. This is the place of which the Hebrew exile told me that the prophets had spoken, and here I shall behold the rising of the great light. But I must inquire about the visit of my brethren, and to what house the star directed them, and to whom they presented their tribute."

The streets of the village seemed to be deserted, and Artaban wondered whether the men had all gone up to the hill pastures to bring down their sheep. From the open door of a cottage he heard the sound of a woman's voice singing softly. He entered and found a young mother hushing her baby to rest. She told him of the strangers from the far East who had appeared in the village three days ago, and how they said that a star had guided them to the place where Joseph of Nazareth was lodging with his wife and given him many rich gifts.

"But the travelers disappeared again," she continued, "as suddenly as they had come. We were afraid at the strangeness of their visit. We could not understand it. The man of Nazareth took the child and his mother, and fled away that same night secretly, and it was whispered that they were going to Egypt. Ever since, there has been a spell upon the village; something evil hangs over it. They say that the Roman soldiers are coming from Jerusalem to force a new tax from us, and the men have driven the flocks and herds far back among the hills, and hidden themselves to escape it."

Artaban listened to her gentle, timid speech, and the child in her arms looked up in his face and smiled, stretching out its rosy hands to grasp at the winged circle of gold on his breast. His heart warmed to the touch. It seemed like a greeting of love and trust to one who had journeyed long in loneliness and perplexity, fighting with his own doubts and fears, and following a light that was veiled in clouds.

"Why might not this child have been the promised Prince?" he asked within himself, as he touched its soft cheek. "Kings have been born ere now in lowlier houses than this, and the favorite of the stars may rise even from a cottage. But it has not seemed good to the God of wisdom to reward my search so soon and so easily. The one whom I seek has gone before me; and now I must follow the King to Egypt."

The young mother laid the baby in its cradle, and rose to minister to the wants of the strange guest that fate had brought into her house. She set food before him, the plain fare of peasants, but willingly offered, and therefore full of refreshment for the soul as well as for the body. Artaban accepted it gratefully; and, as he ate, the child fell into a happy slumber, and murmured sweetly in its dreams, and a great peace filled the room.

But suddenly there came the noise of a wild confusion in the streets of the village, a shrieking and wailing of women's voices, a clangor of brazen trumpets and a clashing of swords, and a desperate cry: "The soldiers! The soldiers of Herod! They are killing our children."

The young mother's face grew white with terror. She clasped her child to her bosom, and crouched motionless in the darkest corner of the room, covering him with the folds of her robe, lest he should wake and cry.

But Artaban went quickly and stood in the doorway of the house. His broad shoulders filled the portal from side to side, and the peak of his white cap all but touched the lintel.

The soldiers came hurrying down the street with bloody hands and dripping swords. At the sight of the stranger in his imposing dress they hesitated with surprise. The captain of the band approached the threshold to thrust him aside. But Artaban did not stir. His face was as calm as though he were watching the stars, and in his eyes there burned that steady radiance before which even the half-tamed hunting leopard shrinks, and the bloodhound pauses in his leap. He held the soldier silently for an instant, and then said in a low voice:

"I am all alone in this place, and I am waiting to give this jewel to the prudent captain who will leave me in peace."

He showed the ruby, glistening in the hollow of his hand like a great drop of blood.

The captain was amazed at the splendor of the gem. The pupils of his eyes expanded with desire, and the hard lines of greed wrinkled around his lips. He stretched out his hand and took the ruby.

"March on!" he cried to his men; "there is no child here. The house is empty."

The clamor and the clang of arms passed down the street as the headlong fury of the chase sweeps by the secret covert where the trembling deer is hidden. Artaban reentered the cottage. He turned his face to the east and prayed:

"God of truth, forgive my sin! I have said the thing that is not, to save the life of a child. And two of my gifts are gone. I have spent for man that which was meant for God. Shall I ever be worthy to see the face of the King?"

128]

But the voice of the woman, weeping for joy in the shadow behind him, said very gently:

"Because thou hast saved the life of my little one, may the Lord
bless thee and keep thee; the Lord make His face to shine upon
thee and be gracious unto thee; the Lord lift up His countenance
upon thee and give thee peace."

IV

Again there was a silence in the Hall of Dreams, deeper and
more mysterious than the first interval, and I understood that the
years of Artaban were flowing very swiftly under the stillness, and
I caught only a glimpse, here and there, of the river of his life
shining through the mist that concealed its course.

I saw him moving among the throngs of men in populous Egypt,
seeking everywhere for traces of the household that had come
down from Bethlehem, and finding them under the spreading sycamore trees of Heliopolis, and beneath the walls of the Roman
fortress of New Babylon beside the Nile—traces so faint and dim
that they vanished before him continually, as footprints on the wet
river sand glisten for a moment with moisture and then disappear.

I saw him again at the foot of the pyramids, which lifted their
sharp points into the intense saffron glow of the sunset sky, change-
less monuments of the perishable glory and the imperishable hope
of man. He looked up into the face of the crouching Sphinx and
vainly tried to read the meaning of the calm eyes and smiling
mouth. Was it, indeed, the mockery of all effort and all aspiration,
as Tigranes had said—the cruel jest of a riddle that has no answer,
a search that never can succeed? Or was there a touch of pity and
encouragement in that inscrutable smile—a promise that even the
defeated should attain a victory, and the disappointed should discover a prize, and the ignorant should be made wise, and the blind
should see, and the wandering should come into the haven at last?

I saw him again in an obscure house of Alexandria, taking counsel
with a Hebrew rabbi. The venerable man, bending over the rolls
of parchment on which the prophecies of Israel were written, read
aloud the pathetic words which foretold the sufferings of the prom-

ised Messiah—the despised and rejected of men, the man of sorrows and acquainted with grief.

"And remember, my son," said he, fixing his eyes upon the face of Artaban, "the King whom thou seekest is not to be found in a palace, nor among the rich and powerful. If the light of the world and the glory of Israel had been appointed to come with the greatness of earthly splendor, it must have appeared long ago. For no son of Abraham will ever again rival the power which Joseph had in the palaces of Egypt, or the magnificence of Solomon throned between the lions in Jerusalem. But the light for which the world is waiting is a new light, the glory that shall rise out of patient and triumphant suffering. And the kingdom which is to be established forever is a new kingdom, the royalty of unconquerable love.

"I do not know how this shall come to pass, nor how the turbulent kings and peoples of earth shall be brought to acknowledge the Messiah and pay homage to him. But this I know. Those who seek him will do well to look among the poor and the lowly, the sorrowful and the oppressed."

So I saw the Other Wise Man again and again, traveling from place to place, and searching among the people of the Dispersion, with whom the little family from Bethlehem might, perhaps, have found a refuge. He passed through countries where famine lay heavy upon the land, and the poor were crying for bread. He made his dwelling in plague-stricken cities where the sick were languishing in the bitter companionship of helpless misery. He visited the oppressed and the afflicted in the gloom of subterranean prisons, and the crowded wretchedness of slave markets, and the weary toil of galley ships. In all this populous and intricate world of anguish, though he found none to worship, he found many to help. He fed the hungry, and clothed the naked, and healed the sick, and comforted the captive; and his years passed more swiftly than the weaver's shuttle that flashes back and forth through the loom while the web grows and the pattern is completed.

It seemed almost as if he had forgotten his quest. But once I saw him for a moment as he stood alone at sunrise, waiting at the gate of a Roman prison. He had taken from a secret resting place in his bosom the pearl, the last of his jewels. As he looked at it, a mellower luster, a soft and iridescent light, full of shifting gleams of azure and rose, trembled upon its surface. It seemed to have absorbed some reflection of the lost sapphire and ruby. So the secret purpose of a noble life draws into itself the memories of past joy and past sorrow. All that has helped it, all that has hindered it, is transfused by a subtle magic into its very essence. It becomes more luminous and precious the longer it is carried close to the warmth of the beating heart.

Then, at last, while I was thinking of this pearl, and of its meaning, I heard the end of the story of the Other Wise Man.

V

Three-and-thirty years of the life of Artaban had passed away, and he was still a pilgrim and a seeker after light. His hair, once darker than the cliffs of Zagros, was now white as the wintry snow that covered them. His eyes, that once flashed like flames of fire, were dull as embers smoldering among the ashes.

Worn and weary and ready to die, but still looking for the King, he had come for the last time to Jerusalem. He had often visited the Holy City before, and had searched all its lanes and crowded hovels and black prisons without finding any trace of the family of Nazarenes who had fled from Bethlehem long ago. But now it seemed as if he must make one more effort, and something whispered in his heart that, at last, he might succeed.

It was the season of the Passover. The city was thronged with strangers. The children of Israel, scattered in far lands, had returned to the Temple for the great feast, and there had been a confusion of tongues in the narrow streets for many days.

But on this day a singular agitation was visible in the multitude. The sky was veiled with a portentous gloom. Currents of excitement seemed to flash through the crowd. A secret tide was sweeping them all one way. The clatter of sandals and the soft, thick sound of thousands of bare feet shuffling over the stones, flowed unceasingly along the street that leads to the Damascus gate.

Artaban joined a group of people from his own country, Parthian Jews who had come up to keep the Passover, and inquired of them the cause of the tumult, and where they were going.

"We are going," they answered, "to the place called Golgotha, outside the city walls, where there is to be an execution. Have you not heard what has happened? Two famous robbers are to be crucified, and with them another, called Jesus of Nazareth, a man who has done many wonderful works among the people, so that they love him greatly. But the priests and elders have said that he must die, because he gave himself out to be the Son of God. And Pilate has sent him to the cross because he said that he was the 'King of the Jews.'"

How strangely these familiar words fell upon the tired heart of Artaban! They had led him for a lifetime over land and sea. And now they came to him mysteriously, like a message of despair. The King had arisen, but he had been denied and cast out. He was about to perish. Perhaps he was already dying. Could it be the same who had been born in Bethlehem thirty-three years ago, at whose birth the star had appeared in heaven, and of whose coming the prophets had spoken?

Artaban's heart beat unsteadily with that troubled, doubtful apprehension which is the excitement of old age. But he said within himself: "The ways of God are stranger than the thoughts of men, and it may be that I shall find the King, at last, in the hands of his enemies, and shall come in time to offer my pearl for his ransom before he dies."

So the old man followed the multitude with slow and painful steps toward the Damascus gate of the city. Just beyond the entrance of the guardhouse a troop of Macedonian soldiers came down the street, dragging a young girl with torn dress and disheveled hair. As the Magian paused to look at her with compassion, she broke suddenly from the hands of her tormentors, and threw herself at his feet, clasping him around the knees. She had seen his white cap and the winged circle on his breast.

"Have pity on me," she cried, "and save me, for the sake of the God of Purity! I also am a daughter of the true religion which is

132]

taught by the Magi. My father was a merchant of Parthia, but he is dead, and I am seized for his debts to be sold as a slave. Save me from worse than death!"

Artaban trembled.

It was the old conflict in his soul, which had come to him in the palm grove of Babylon and in the cottage at Bethlehem—the conflict between the expectation of faith and the impulse of love. Twice the gift which he had consecrated to the worship of religion had been drawn to the service of humanity. This was the third trial, the ultimate probation, the final and irrevocable choice.

Was it his great opportunity, or his last temptation? He could not tell. One thing only was clear in the darkness of his mind— it was inevitable. And does not the inevitable come from God?

One thing only was sure to his divided heart—to rescue this helpless girl would be a true deed of love. And is not love the light of the soul?

He took the pearl from his bosom. Never had it seemed so luminous, so radiant, so full of tender, living luster. He laid it in the hand of the slave.

"This is thy ransom, daughter! It is the last of my treasures which I kept for the King."

While he spoke, the darkness of the sky deepened, and shuddering tremors ran through the earth heaving convulsively like the breast of one who struggles with mighty grief.

The walls of the houses rocked to and fro. Stones were loosened and crashed into the street. Dust clouds filled the air. The soldiers fled in terror, reeling like drunken men. But Artaban and the girl whom he had ransomed crouched helpless beneath the wall of the Praetorium.

What had he to fear? What had he to hope? He had given away the last remnant of his tribute for the King. He had parted with the last hope of finding him. The quest was over, and it had failed. But even in that thought, accepted and embraced, there was peace. It was not resignation. It was not submission. It was something more profound and searching. He knew that all was well, because he had done the best that he could from day to day. He had been true to the light that had been given to him. He had looked for more. And if he had not found it, if a failure was all that came out of his life, doubtless that was the best that was possible. He had not seen the revelation of "life everlasting, incorruptible and immortal." But he knew that even if he could live his earthly life over again, it could not be otherwise than it had been.

One more lingering pulsation of the earthquake quivered through the ground. A heavy tile, shaken from the roof, fell and struck the old man on the temple. He lay breathless and pale, with his gray head resting on the young girl's shoulder, and the blood trickling from the wound. As she bent over him, fearing that he was dead, there came a voice through the twilight, very small and still, like music sounding from a distance, in which the notes are clear but the words are lost. The girl turned to see if someone had spoken from the window above them, but she saw no one.

The old man's lips began to move, as if in answer, and she heard him say in the Parthian tongue:

"Not so, my Lord! For when saw I thee an hungered and fed thee? Or thirsty, and gave thee drink? When saw I thee a stranger, and took thee in? Or naked, and clothed thee? When saw I thee sick or in prison, and came unto thee? Three-and-thirty years have I looked for thee; but I have never seen thy face, nor ministered to thee, my King."

He ceased, and the sweet voice came again. And again the maid heard it, very faint and far away. But now it seemed as though she understood the words:

"Verily I say unto thee, Inasmuch as thou hast done it unto one of the least of these my brethren, thou hast done it unto me."

A calm radiance of wonder and joy lighted the pale face of Artaban like the first ray of dawn on a snowy mountain peak. A long breath of relief exhaled gently from his lips.

His journey was ended. His treasures were accepted. The Other Wise Man had found the King.

ALL THROUGH THE NIGHT

RACHEL FIELD

O, what mean these voices singing
  All through the night?
O, what mean these bells a-ringing
  All through the night?
                    Old Carol

ALL THAT day the Inn-Yard had been thronged with people coming
to pay their taxes in the town of Bethlehem. The small, sturdy
watchdog who slept in the stable and picked up what food he could
find had never before seen such a crowd of travelers.

When night fell he was tired from barking at so many strangers
and their beasts, and with scurrying out of the way of feet and
hoofs. But for all the barking and running about it had been a
good day. The Inn had overflowed into the yard. There had been
a fire there with meat roasting over it and pots that sent out clouds
of savory steam. Many a rich morsel had fallen his way, so he felt
well content as he crept into his corner of the stable near the oxen's
stall.

He and they greeted each other and exchanged news of the day.

"Yes, we, too, have been busy," the oxen told him. "Heavy loads
for us since daybreak and the roads round Bethlehem so choked

with carts and caravans and herds and flocks we could hardly move sometimes."

"And rude, stupid creatures they were to meet!" the ass put in from her corner. "With no manners at all or sense enough to follow their own noses. Some even dared to dispute the right of way with me, but I held my ground."

"I have no doubt you did," said the dog, for he knew the ass was not one to be persuaded against her will. He turned himself round and round in a pile of straw to make himself comfortable and fell to licking a bruised spot on his leg.

"There must have been many sheep," the old ewe joined in from her pen. "I could not see them because I was shut in here with my two lambs, but I could tell by their voices that some came from places farther away than Judea. I should have liked to see them."

"Well," the dog told her, "I found them a dusty, frightened lot. I was thankful not to have their herding in my charge. And the goats were no better," he added, that the bearded gray goat might be sure to hear. He and the goat were not upon friendly terms and took pleasure in tormenting each other.

"Peace and quiet. Peace and quiet at last," the doves cooed from the rafters. "Peace and quiet till morning, that is all we ask."

The hens made soft, clucking sounds to show that they were in complete agreement.

But the cock with his scarlet comb and burnished tail feathers, stepping about in search of stray kernels, was of a different mind. "I like noise and bustle myself." He voiced his opinion loudly. "Peace is all very well for those who haven't the spirit for something better. Now *I* can hardly wait for morning."

"Everyone to his own taste," the mild-eyed cow put in her word, shifting her cud deftly and flicking her tail as she did so. "If it were always day or always night we should not all be satisfied."

"Well said. Well said," the doves agreed in drowsy unison from the dimness of the eaves.

Darkness gathered there first. The swallows were already seeking their nests, while the bats were beginning to stretch and unfold their lean, black wings.

136]

Night was coming fast and all the birds and beasts and insects of the stable knew that it belonged to them. The world was theirs as the world of day could never be. When the sun rose man would be their master again. They would carry his burdens or feed or serve him according to their different gifts. But night was their own, when they might move or fight or take counsel together without man's interference. It was good that this should be so, the little dog thought, as he burrowed deeper into the straw.

His sworn enemy the cat slid by. She moved like a shadow with fiery-green eyes ready to pounce upon the mice who were already squeaking and scampering at their play. But the dog was too tired and comfortable to give chase, so for once he let her pass unmolested. All about him crickets chirped in rusty chorus and sometimes a bat swooped so low he could feel the stir of its wings. The darkness was warm and alive with the familiar scents of fur and feathers and grain and straw.

"Rest well. Rest well. Rest well." The doves cooed sleepily, making a soft sound in their throats that was like the bubbling of a well-filled pot over a fire.

Night had come to Bethlehem. The Inn had been full hours ago. The dog could hear late travelers being turned away. The stable door was securely bolted against intruders and the wind was rising, frosty and keen. Through an opening in the roof a star shone bright as purest silver.

"I never saw a star look so large or so near," the cock observed as he moved about with his spurred, high-stepping walk. "Somehow it makes me very restless, and there is something strange in the air. Perhaps you have felt it too?"

But the dog made no answer. He yawned and laid his pointed muzzle on his paws and prepared himself for sleep.

He woke at the sound of voices outside and roused himself to bark. But though the hair rose along his back, no sound came rumbling from his throat. The bolt was drawn and the stable door opened to lantern light and the dim shapes of two men and a donkey on whose back a woman sat, wrapped in a heavy cloak.

"Well"—the voice of the Inn-Keeper sounded sharp and impatient—"if you cannot go on, there is only the stable to offer. Coming as you have at such an hour, you are fortunate to have this shelter till morning."

"The roads were crowded," the Man answered him, "and our pace was slow because of my wife. You can see that she is nearly spent."

"Yes, yes." The Inn-Keeper was already shutting the door. "I am sorry for your plight, but I tell you there is no room left."

The dog was on his feet. He could hear the other animals rising about him, yet not one of them uttered a sound. Their throats were as silent as his own.

In the flickering lantern light he watched the Man lift the Woman from the donkey's back and set her upon her feet. She was so weary she would have fallen but for the Man's arms.

"Joseph," she said, "you must not be troubled for me, even if it should be that the time has come." She rested her head on the Man's shoulders and sighed so softly it might have been one of the doves in the rafters drawing closer to her mate.

"But, Mary," the Man went on, "it is not right and fitting that it should be here—not in a stable among the beasts."

"Who knows," she comforted him, "what is to be? These beasts are more kind than men who kill and hurt one another. I am glad to be here. Their warm breath comforts me. Their straw is clean and soft to rest upon."

Everywhere beyond the ring of light that the lantern made, bright eyes were upon the strangers. Furry ears and quivering noses pointed, alert and watchful.

The strange donkey, freed of his load, found a place beside the ass. He sank down, too tired to drink water from the trough or reach for a mouthful of hay.

A hush was on the stable. Not only were all throats silent, but no wings stirred; no claws scratched and not a hoof pounded. And in that hour nothing died. The young swallows and mice were safe from their enemies, for a mystery greater than death held them all in its power.

The lantern flickered and went out.

138]

"Our oil is gone!" the Man cried out in distress.

"There will be light enough." The Woman spoke in a faint voice, and as if in answer the star in the roof gap shone brighter than before.

How long it was after that the little dog could not tell. Morning was still far off, yet the cock suddenly lifted up his voice, so shrill and clear it seemed he would split himself in two. It was not like any other cockcrow since the world began and it rose higher than the rafters and mounted to heaven itself. At the same instant each creature found voice and joined with him. Every living thing in the stable had a part in that swelling chorus of praise. Even the bees hummed till their hive throbbed with music, sweeter than all its store of honey.

"What manner of place is this?" the Man cried out. "What beasts are these who have the tongues of angels?"

But the Woman answered him softly out of the shadows. "It was they who gave us shelter this night. Let them draw near and be the first to worship."

She drew aside the folds of her cloak and light filled the stable even to the farthest corners. The dog cowered before such strange brightness. When he dared to look more closely he saw that it encircled the head of an infant, new born.

"There is no bed for him to lie upon," the Man sighed. "Only this"—and he pointed to the manger.

"Bring it here," the Mother said. "My heart tells me there will be nights when he will have no place at all to rest his head."

So the Child lay quiet in the straw-filled wooden manger and all the animals came to view him there—the oxen, the cow, the ass, and the donkey, the ewe and her lambs, the gray goat, the dog, the hens and the proud cock ruffling his feathers. The cat left off her prowling to join them and the mice ran beside her without fear. The crickets came, too, drawn from the comfort of their warm straw; the bees, from their snug hive. The tireless ants and spiders left their toil to draw near. The swallows in the eaves flew down; the bats bent low on their dark wings, and the doves came closest of all with their soft murmurs above the manger. When they had

[139

all seen the Wonder they returned to their places and were quiet again.

All but the dog. He could not rest as he had before. He stretched himself beside the manger and lay with his head on his folded paws, his eyes wide and watchful as the hours passed.

Long before sunrise the door opened without sound of bolt being drawn and a band of shepherds came in. They bore a strange tale on their lips and they also worshipped on bended knees. One carried a lamb in his arms and the Child answered its bleating with a smile.

"Behold the Lamb of God," they said one to another as they turned to go back to their flocks on the hills.

The star grew pale and through the gap in the stable roof morning showed rosy in the east. Even before the cock hailed it, the dog knew that the sun was up. But he did not move lest he rouse the three in his care. It was then that he saw a strange thing.

The rafters high above cast their shadows as the rising sun struck through. Two of the beams crossed in sharp black bars that fell directly across the sleeping Child. The little dog could not tell why the sight should make him cower in sudden fear.

Then the cock crowed three times and the first sounds of people stirring in the Inn and yard began.

He watched the Man and the Woman preparing to go. He saw the donkey being watered and fed and the blanket fitted in place. He saw the Mother wrap her Son warmly against the cold before the Man set them upon the donkey's back and lifted a heavy bundle on his own.

"Come," he said, and opened the stable door. "We must make haste."

Stiff from his long vigil, the dog rose and followed them to the door. He watched them cross the innyard in the early light and join the other travelers who were already thronging the roads leading to and from Bethlehem. Soon they would be lost to his sight, those Three whom he had guarded through the hours of darkness.

"Ah," cried the cock, preening his burnished feathers, "what

140]

a morning!" He strutted over to where bits of food and grain lay scattered and began to forage for stray morsels.

The dog lifted his head and sniffed hungrily. He could tell that pots were already on the fires. The sharp morning air brought the savory news to him and he knew that by keeping close to the kitchen he would soon be well filled. He remembered a bone he had buried yesterday in a secluded spot. Yet he did not seek it. He trotted past the kitchen doors, and though his nose twitched at the smells that he was leaving he kept it pointed straight ahead.

"Wait. Wait." His bark rang out sharp and determined and his paws clicked over the stones as he ran.

He did not pause till he had caught up with the Man who led the plodding donkey and his burden along the dusty road.

"Here I am!" He barked again as he fell into step beside them. "Let me come with you."

AN INNKEEPER'S TALE

PETER HOWARD

My wife says I made a mistake over the whole business. I do not see it quite that way. Looking back on it all, I think I did the right thing.

But there you are. Village people will gossip, and there's no denying that the doings of that night have harmed my good name in those parts. Perhaps you would like to hear just what happened and tell me what you think.

Our house is well known around here—comfortable rooms, good cooking, and some of the best drink you can buy in the whole country. That is why we are always busy and why I've managed to lay aside a big nest-egg in the bank. I've worked hard for it, mind you. But it's a comfort to me to think of it as I grow past middle age.

Well, we were hard at it that night, drinks going all round the bar and in the public room, luggage being lugged into the bedrooms by the man, and my wife with her apron on and the sweat glistening like stars in a red sky on her face as it always does when she has finished cooking a big dinner.

Later on, things quietened down, and when most of the guests had turned in and I was thinking of bed myself, suddenly the dog began to growl and bark. He's a surly beast, but a watchdog. We reckon he hears or sniffs folk when they are halfway down the road. I listened. Presently there came a knock on the door. So I silenced the dog, took the chain off the door and peered out in the moonlight. An oldish fellow stood there with his arm around a woman—she was little more than a girl, I guess—and asked if they could have a bed for the night.

Now in my trade you get the habit of summing up folk pretty quickly. I noticed they had no luggage with them. They were covered with dust from the road and looked as if they had been traveling all day, and on foot, too. They were modestly dressed, of humble background, good people, no doubt, but not what I call good cash customers.

In any case, my wife had had a hard day, and I've been stung before by travelers who get in late at night and leave quietly in the dawning without paying their bills.

So I just told them that I was sorry we had no room for them. The best room, Number Five, at the back of the house, happened to be free. But a room of that kind would have been quite out of place for people like them. They certainly could never have afforded it even if it had been convenient at that time of night, which it wasn't.

The old fellow looked at the girl, who was wrapped around with some sort of long over-cloak and could not be seen very clearly as her back was towards the moon. Then he muttered something to me about "... come a long way ... my wife needs rest ... please." But I just said once more that I was sorry, and shut the door quietly. My wife says I slammed it, but you know what women are. They always exaggerate when things upset them. And my wife has never stopped nagging me about how I should have done things differently.

Anyway, I went to bed. My wife snored away as usual. But somehow I could not get to sleep very soon. And when I did drop off, I was full of dreams. I dreamed that I was running away from something terrible, without knowing just what I was running from. I was afraid. Then a lot of people were chasing me too, and some of them were singing the songs the rough fellows sing around the bar fire on a Saturday winter night when the drink has overflowed a little.

I woke with a jump, and through the window, clear as a mountain stream, came the sound of singing. Only it was not the rough men's voices I am used to, and it was a song I have never heard before. I pulled on my trousers and boots, and crept out to the hall. There, believe it, or not, his ears pucked, his tail wagging, and one eye cocked on me, sat the dog.

Not a growl or a bark came out of him, though the singing was clearer and even I, with my man's slow ears, could hear the rustle and murmur of people moving in the street. I looked out of the window.

It was two o'clock in the morning, and the moon was on the wane. But one great star still shone up above the horizon and in its light I saw scores of people moving along the road. They all seemed to be moving towards an old shed just beyond the annex to our inn, where the horses used to live in the coaching days, which has been cluttered up for years with odds and ends, and where the few cows that we keep for our milk and butter supply at the inn are still housed. As I watched, I saw the light of a lantern flicker across the doorway of the shed, I heard the low of one of the cows, and a figure that reminded me in some ways of the old fellow who had asked for a bed seemed to move across the doorway of the shed.

By this time I was fully awake and really angry. I put on my coat and reached for my stick. "Kicking up a row at this time of the night," I muttered to myself. "It's disgraceful. It will spoil the good name of the place and waken the neighborhood. They've had a drop too much, I suppose."

That, or the possibility that there had been some kind of accident, crossed my mind and I opened the door and shouldered my way toward the shed.

Some of the people greeted me as I passed them. I recognized one or two of the farmhands and the drovers who live up in the hill country. But, though I know most of the people for miles around this area, there were many, many faces in the street that I did not recognize. I pushed my way towards the shed door, meaning to clear out whoever was making the disturbance, and to shut the place up for the night. In the light of the lanterns that people were carrying I saw through the half-open door the shape of one of the cows, a great heap of straw which somebody had thrown down beside the manger, and there was the old fellow who had tried to get a bed in my inn, bending over the girl who had been with him. She was lying on the straw, and in her arms was a newborn baby. "So this was it," I thought, "they just made free of my shed and she's had a baby and they've upset half the neighborhood"; and I was going to force my way in and tell them to be off, when something happened which made me change my mind.

The singing which I had heard in my bedroom grew louder, though I still could not make out whence it came from, and inside the shed I saw a very distinguished-looking gentleman—we get to recognize the real gentry in our trade, you know—and he bent forward and gave some parcel to the old fellow. I caught the glow of gold in the lantern light as he did so. The gentleman said something I did not catch. The old fellow who had asked for a bed in the inn put the parcel down where I saw a great heap of other packages in the background. He said something to the gentleman, and I caught the words: "Your Highness." Then, believe it or not, the gentleman knelt down in the dirt and the straw of the shed, and for about a minute did nothing that I could see except look at the girl and the baby lying there.

Well, I did not know whether I was awake or dreaming. But, whichever it was, I reckoned it would do no good to kick up a fuss. "Your Highness" means only one thing any time of night or day, and it was clear to me that royalty had come to see whatever it was that was going on in my shed in the middle of the night.

Royalty do the oddest things, you know. They don't behave like ordinary people. Why, when I was a lad, we had a prince of the land, the heir-apparent, stop at our place for supper once, after a day's hunting—and what did he do when he'd finished his meal but come into the kitchen and talk in quite a familiar way with the staff, as he thanked them. Very bad it was for the staff too, I remember, and my father had to sack one of the kitchenmaids for impertinence the next week.

Anyway, I went back through the crowd without saying a word, and the dog walking at my heels all the way wagging his tail, and with not a growl out of him in the middle of all the strangers. Which more and more convinced me that the whole thing must be some sort of a dream or nightmare.

My wife was there still snoring away, and I lay down beside her.

But, you know, it was all true. First thing I heard next morning was a knocking at the door. When I opened it, the same old fellow was there as had come the night before. Behind him, sitting on a horse that somebody must have given or left them, was the young girl looking so tired but so happy, and in her arms a baby. It is a funny thing to say, but peace seemed to flow out of them.

Standing beside them were quite a crowd of people, including the gentleman whom I had heard the old fellow call "Your Highness" in the middle of the night.

Before I could decide whether it was better policy to tell them off for making free of my shed and kicking up such a row in the night, or to pretend I hadn't noticed at all and to ask them in, the old fellow took off his hat and apologized very humbly for using the shed. "You see," he said, "when we could not get a bed in your inn, it was so late and we were too tired to go any further. And you see how it was with my wife?" and he pointed to the girl sitting there smiling at me with the baby in her arms. You'll think it wrong of me, but we hotelkeepers do get cynical, you know. And it was only the fact that he talked about the girl as his wife in front of royalty that made me really believe they were married to each other.

I scarcely knew what to say when the gentleman who had been kneeling in the straw the night before stepped forward and pulled out one of those old-fashioned leather purses. "I would like to pay for the use of the shed," he said, and he slipped into my hand nearly three times as much as the best room, Number Five, would have cost them.

Well, my wife says I should not have taken the money, but what I say is that trade is trade, and as they say in these parts, a soft heart means a soft head. After all, they had used my shed and upset the cattle as well as leaving straw all over the place.

So I pocketed the money, and then the old boy took the horse by the bridle and began to walk off down the road away from the city, with half the village following him.

Things don't seem the same around here since all this happened. As I say, my wife is forever scolding me. But if women had their way, a business like ours would soon beggar us. In any case, it's all a long time ago now, and the old inn still keeps going. I'm not so young as I was, but I'm sure of one thing:

People will still be talking and drinking and eating around my place long after the old fellow and his family are forgotten.

THE STABLEBOY AT THE INN

B. Z. STAMBAUGH

STEPHEN the stableboy, was often lonely, but seldom unhappy. The reason for this was not usually apparent to those who knew him, for he had not been favored by fortune. The venerable rabbi was often amazed at the gaiety of the ragged urchin who came so regularly for instruction at the little synagogue of Bethlehem. He remembered how the child's mother had sent for him, as she lay dying in the poorest quarter of the town, and had committed the sleeping baby to his care. Sometimes he regretted the haste with which he had, in turn, given the child to Simeon, the innkeeper's stable servant. For Simeon was scarcely able to feed and clothe his own children, and his wife was a woman of violent temper and shrewish tongue. He thought sometimes that the boy's sunny disposition must be an inheritance from his father, a vagabond Greek, who had deserted his wife and child in their time of need, leaving nothing for his son but his name—Stephen—which is Greek for "the crown," or "the crowned one." The name had stuck. It had appealed to a twisted sense of humor in the community, and the pauper child continued to be called "Stephen."

But Stephen's Greek paternity could not entirely account for his contentedness. The determining factor was his general good-will toward everybody and his particular sympathy for those who seemed more unfortunate than himself. And as there were not many humans who could lay claim to such sympathy, this quality manifested itself chiefly toward the animals—the cattle and asses at the cave-stables of the inn; the great hulking camels, whose Arab drivers beat them so unmercifully at times, when the long caravans passed through the village toward the desert far southward; and especially the sheep and lambs that abounded on the plain of Bethlehem and in the hill country near, whose shepherds drove them in flocks through the village on their way to the market at Jerusalem. Stephen loved animals, and as often as he could escape the watchful eye and sharp tongue of his foster-mother, he followed Simeon about his duties. There were the cows and the she-asses and the goats to be milked every morning and evening. There were the stately oxen who came in from the fields at night, very tired and very hungry, and very grateful for their care. And there were the flock of sheep that belonged to the innkeeper, whose shepherd brought them in from the pasture at nightfall, instead of keeping them in the sheepfold on the hill. As the boy grew older, Simeon found him more and more useful. One day the innkeeper himself watched, as he cleaned out the stall for the oxen, carefully spread the clean straw, and filled the manger—and after that Stephen was numbered among the servants, and Simeon received an extra shekel each month for the lad's work.

On the last day before the Great Taxation, Stephen had been very busy. Bethlehem for several days had been filling with visitors —people who were conforming to the emperor's edict by returning to their birthplace for the enrollment; and while many had come on foot, the majority had brought with them beasts of burden. A great caravan had come from Egypt, with asses and camels, footsore from the long desert journey. Some of the younger Jews, who had come from Caesarea, had made the journey Roman fashion, in chariots, with beautiful Arabian horses harnessed to the pole. Stephen had never seen many horses, and was nearly overawed by their regal appearance. The whole village was buzzing with excitement. There had never been so much buying and selling since any-

[149

body could remember. There were errands for all the boys in the place, and many of the visitors were able and willing to pay handsomely for service. Simeon had been short-handed all day, because so many of the stable servants had yielded to the lure of easier and quicker money.

Stephen had been tempted in the earlier part of the day, as he saw other boys no older than himself with their fists already full of coppers. But he could not forget the weariness of the poor beasts, footsore and lame, that were bringing the people into the town. So he worked the harder to keep the inn stables clean and sweet, for the comfort of the animals. "The people," he said, "can always manage for themselves. But the poor beasts have no comforts except what we give them." So he whistled, after the immemorial manner of boys, as he gathered up armfuls of the fresh, dusty straw to carry into the farther corners of the great caves, the parts long disused. And then he stopped whistling, and choked and sneezed as the dust filled his eyes and nose.

He heard the innkeeper and other men talking. There was an air of expectancy upon them. "I have heard a soothsayer," said one, "who declareth that tonight the Messiah will appear in Bethlehem, to set Israel free and drive away the Roman eagles that hover over Judah." Another volunteered the information: "There is a grizzled Chaldean astrologer who came in the caravan today who saith that a star hath risen in great splendor to declare the coming of a King in Judah." And the innkeeper, a devout Pharisee, said, "I know nothing of your Chaldeans nor your soothsayers, but I know the prophets, and clearly they foretell the coming of the Messiah. They tell of Bethlehem, saying, 'And thou, Bethlehem, art not the least among the princes of Judah, for out of thee shall come a governor that shall rule my people Israel.' And surely the time is ripe. The cup of Roman iniquity is full. Jehovah cannot longer turn away His face from His people." Stephen heard others talking about the same thing throughout the day. Bethlehem was all agog. The resentment of the people against the Roman tax had become intense. The garrison had trouble to keep order. The tax-gatherers were threatened with violence, and did not dare to stir without armed guards.

Stephen learned that the innkeeper had begun to charge an excessive rate for lodging, and that every nook and cranny of the town was being filled with latecomers. Toward evening the roads were crowded with people, hurrying into Bethlehem before the closing of the town gate. Then the shepherd came in with his flock, and Stephen had no time for other things, while he attended to the brier scratches and bruises that the sheep always brought back from pasture.

A group of boys scuffled noisily past the entrance of the cave. One of them chanced to spy Stephen as he finished scattering clean straw on the floor of the stall for the oxen and was starting after fresh hay from the manger. "Ah, there, 'Crowned One'!" he shouted, and the others took up the cry, "The Messiah! The Messiah!" they screamed. "Here is the King! Here is the Anointed of Israel! The manger is his throne! The pitchfork is his scepter!" Amid the bedlam they told him of the growing excitement. Apparently there was nothing being done in the town except the plotting and scheming for the advent of the King. Some were saying that it would be Abiud, son of Jotham of Caesarea, who would set up the standard of revolt in Bethlehem that night, would lead forth the men of Israel to battle, and would drive the Roman jackals from the land of their fathers. Some said, however, that Abiud's descent from King David had been questioned—that Mattathias, of the house of Maccabees, still lived and would certainly appear in Bethlehem that night. For on his mother's side he was a prince of the House of David.

"I shall be at hand!" exclaimed one of the boys, "I shall carry a bow and arrows and a sword." And the others all shouted at the tops of their voices trying to be heard above one another, telling what they would do to help the King. Then they hurried out, so as to be in the midst of things when the King should declare himself.

Indeed, it seemed as if everyone had been of the same mind. The stalls had been neglected. The stable was in a disgraceful condition. Stephen was tired. He stood in the failing light with arms akimbo, half-minded to slip away himself and join in the excitement. Then he remembered the oxen who would be weary from their journey to Jerusalem, carrying the heavy, wooden cart that had been sent in loaded with cheese and butter and eggs. And he remembered the cows who were already due for milking, and must have good, warm beds, clean and dry. So he set about it to do what the others had been neglecting. "After all," he said to himself, "if the King is really a wise King, he would rather find me at work, taking care of the beasts who are a part of his realm, than out yonder before the inn, throwing up my hat and shouting for him. And who knows? Maybe the King will have horses and asses and camels with him, and they must have room, and a good bed, and something to eat."

So he redoubled his efforts. The stalls were all cleaned carefully. The mangers were filled. A heavy blanket was hung over the doorway to keep out the cold night air.

Then he heard voices coming along the path which led down from the courtyard of the inn overhead. He recognized the voice of Simeon—usually it was a jovial, good-natured voice, but now it had taken a more serious tone. Stephen thought he must be bringing in an injured lamb, although he had counted them all carefully, and was certain that none was missing. Then there was another voice, a deep, rather pleasant voice, with the highland burr in it that he had so often noticed in the voices of Galileans. And then he heard a woman's voice, the clearest, sweetest voice that had ever come to his ears. It was like what he had often tried to imagine as his mother's voice—the voice that had named him Stephen, the "Crowned One," when he was eight days old.

The blanket over the door was drawn back, and by the dim light of his lantern Stephen could see Simeon, leading an ass, on which was seated a woman; while behind them loomed the full figure of a Galilean peasant. "There was no room for them in the inn," said Simeon. "We must make a place for them here." The woman drew the mantle from her face a bit, so that the lad could see her dark eyes, the broad white brow, and the soft curve of her cheek. She seemed wan and tired, he thought. She smiled at Stephen, and then the big Galilean lifted her from the back of the beast and carried her in his arms as he strode after the boy, who was already leading the way to the stall which he had prepared so carefully for the oxen. It was all so clean and smelled so fragrantly of the fresh hay, that the girl (for she was scarcely more than that) gave a cry of pleasure; and the Galilean turned to Simeon, saying, "You are very kind to us, and we are grateful. I am Joseph, the carpenter, of Nazareth in Galilee, and this is Mary, my wife. We were born in Bethlehem, and we are of the house and lineage of David. But without your hospitality Mary would have perished this night." Stephen hastened to spread a blanket in the straw for Mary, and brought a small bale of cotton that had come in the caravan from Egypt and put it under her head. She smiled her gratitude, and Stephen hastened away to look after their beast, which still stood patiently near the door.

The lad was busy till very late. The cows had been brought up, and the goats for milking. The four horses of Prince Abiud, whose chariot had rumbled up just in time for him to take the last room at the inn, under the very nose of Joseph, had to be provided with stalls and food. The grooms tried to drive Mary and Joseph from their place, but Stephen had threatened them in a shrill voice of rage that brought Simeon running, and they had been satisfied with other stalls. And finally the oxen themselves had come in from their long journey, and it had taken a great deal of soothing and petting to make them content with a strange corner of the great cave, where there was no manger, and where no oxen had ever been stalled before. But at last everything seemed to be done. Simeon said it was best—with so many strangers about, and maybe thieves—to sleep at the stable. Stephen tiptoed back to the secluded stall where he had left Joseph and Mary. Mary was asleep, but Joseph was alert. He seemed to be expecting something. He smiled gravely at Stephen, and whispered good night, with his finger on his lips, to indicate that his wife must not be disturbed. The flickering lantern still hung on the post above his head, and the lad thought it ought to be extinguished for fear of fire and to save

[153

the expense. But he did not dare to say anything. He dragged his weary feet across the stone floor of the cave to the dark corner where the oxen were now placidly chewing their cuds, lay down in the hay, and was instantly asleep.

Stephen could not tell what it was. But he felt that something wonderful was happening. He was certain it was something concerning the King, the Messiah. Yes, that was it. The King had come. There He was—on a great white throne with a glory of light about His head—with an unearthly splendor radiating from Him. Bright figures stood about, angels and archangels and all the company of heaven. And yet, in the most glorious of them all, there was something vaguely familiar. Why, of course! It was Mary, full of grace, blessed above women! And the other was Joseph, regal and majestic. And there was a marvelous melody rising from the angelic host. It seemed to fill all the spaces of the unseen universe. Higher and higher rose the sound till the words of the song filled his soul: "Glory be to God on high, and on earth, peace, good will to men!"

Stephen sat up and blinked, and rubbed his eyes. Then he began to stretch, just as any sleepy boy who had been awakened in the middle of the night. Then he stopped and listened again. Surely, he *was* hearing that song. There was a murmur of voices at the door of the stable—perhaps this was what he had heard—but that melody was still very real. He could even remember the words. He hastened out to see what had happened. Simeon was leading a group of shepherds, who brought with them the chill of the Judean hills under the frosty stars. And they were going straight toward the stall where Joseph and Mary were. Stephen came up just in time to see the shepherds fall on their knees before the manger. And in the manger he saw, by the lantern's glow, the face of a Baby. As he looked again at Mary he saw her as he had seen her in his dream, full of grace, transfigured, and wonderful. And Joseph was a person of dignity and grandeur. Then he looked again at the sleeping Babe, and behold, it was the face of the King. He knelt there in the straw, and all the people knelt, while the shepherds repeated the song of the angels: "Glory be to God on high, and on earth peace, good will toward men." Then Stephen realized that, as he had prepared comfort and happiness for the humble beasts of the field, he had been readying the manger-throne for the King of Kings.

Outside the walls of Jerusalem, near the gate that was ever after to be called "St. Stephen's Gate," a man was being stoned to death. But the pain of the pelting stones was gone now. He could not feel them any more, as he knelt there in the sand. He was living only in memory. He remembered the day when he had seen the King a Babe in a manger. He remembered the after years, when the King had come out of Galilee to establish His kingdom. He remembered the wonder of those years of the ministry, as he had humbly tried to bring in the sick and the suffering to the healing touch of the Master. He remembered the horror of the crucifixion, the glory of the resurrection, and the splendor of Pentecost. He remembered the day when the new Church had seen how the Apostles and elders themselves could not administer the charities if they were to care well for the souls of those entrusted to them. And he remembered his joy when he, Stephen, had been chosen a deacon— one whose duty it was to look after the needy, to tend the sick, to distribute the alms, and to prepare the holy table for the Breaking of the Bread. And now the enemies of the King had taken him, as they had taken his Master. And he, looking steadfastly up into heaven, saw the glory of God, and Jesus standing on the right hand of God. And he cried, "Lord Jesus, receive my spirit." Then he remembered again those who were taking his life, and prayed, "Lord, lay not this sin to their charge." And when he had said this, he fell asleep. He first, of all the followers of the Christ-Child, had won the crown of martyrdom. Stephen had fulfilled his name. So I think maybe that is one reason why we keep the Feast of Stephen on the day nearest after the Feast of the Nativity of our Lord.

THE SOLDIER WHO
SAVED THE CHILD

JULIAN FORREST

THIS IS a very specialized kind of story. I heard it many years ago from the only really gifted oral storyteller I have ever known. It was in Hollywood of all places, where he had some kind of connection with the research department of a motion-picture studio. I don't really know much about this man; I was never even quite sure just what he did. He never talked about himself, and kind as he was, there was something about him which rather discouraged your asking him personal questions, especially when you were so much younger than he was, as for some reason most of his friends seemed to be. In the little group that listened to him the night I am now trying to recall were a well-known script writer, a lovely girl destined to a sensational career as a star, and three or four more.

The Tale Teller was obviously of European origin, Eastern European, I should think, but though many of his tales involved religious themes, I was never sure what his particular religion might be. He never claimed originality for the stories he told; instead he had a way of attributing them to very recondite sources. But these were always very vaguely indicated, and I always suspected that he made them up himself.

From the specimen I am about to give the reader will have no difficulty in seeing that even when he used very familiar material, he knew how to give it a very special twist. This is not a comfortable

156]

tale—few of his stories were that—and not everybody will like it, but I do, perhaps because it shows that from the very beginning those who wished to serve the Child had to pay a price for it, sometimes even a price whose necessity they must have quite failed to understand.

This is the story the Tale Teller told us more than a dozen years ago.

"When the Three Wise Men failed to return to Herod and report the whereabouts of the Child, that monster moved in his own fashion to secure himself against the menace he sensed to his position and his power. When you have a mind like Herod's it always seems that when in doubt the safest thing is to kill somebody; so it is not really surprising that he acted as he did on this occasion. Some monarchs would have been balked by the fact that they did not know whom to kill, but this did not trouble Herod, who simply decided that if he killed everybody he would be sure to get the Somebody he wanted to kill. So he sent his soldiers to Bethlehem and ordered them to kill all the male children two years old and under. A really humane monster would have set the limit lower, for the Child whom Herod feared was only a few days old, but Herod was one of those who, as the saying goes, would rather be safe than sorry, and he did not mind making other people sorry. In fact, he rather enjoyed it.

"Yet Herod was not completely ruthless; he saved the girls. You or I might have thought that if we could not give a soldier credit for enough intelligence to distinguish between a new baby and a two-year-old, then he might also conceivably be confused about the sex of the child. And if only one escaped, it might very well be the One whom Herod regarded as a danger. So Herod really ran a great chance when he spared the girls. And, as you will see when I tell my story, if he hadn't issued the order in that way, the Child could not have been saved at all. Of course Herod didn't know that—nor plan it either. Still, we ought always to give the devil his due, and we ought to give Herod credit too for his gallantry and chivalry in sparing the girls. It's more than modern

[157

soldiers do. Herod will need all the credit he can get. And he is
not going to be the only one either.

"Now Saint Matthew says that the Child Jesus was saved because
an angel appeared to his father Joseph in a dream, and Joseph took
the Child and Mary his mother and fled to Egypt, and there they
stayed until after Herod was dead. So it may have been; I have
no desire to contradict Saint Matthew. But there is another version
of the story which has been preserved among the Copts, and which
is so ancient that nobody knows where it began or upon what authority it may rest. According to this story, God, having permitted
His Son to become flesh, used a purely human agency to preserve
him, about the unlikeliest human agency He could have found.
Communication was made not through a Shining Being from the
skies but in the infinitely devious, indefinable way in which God
moves into the heart of a man.

"The name of the soldier who saved the child was Celsus, and he
was the captain of Herod's guard. Celsus was a Roman who had
been assigned to service in Palestine in connection with some up-
rising or other there, and there he had stayed. He didn't like Palestine, and he didn't like the Jews, but he didn't like Rome as it was
then constituted either. It was the ideals of the old Rome, the pre-
imperial Rome, that were cherished in the family of Celsus; they
were backward people, and, as you know, backward people are of no
use in this world. The thing to do is to keep moving; it doesn't
really make much difference which way you move, for of course all
change is progress.

"Celsus and his family accepted the Empire, at home and abroad,
because that was the only thing they could do, but they did not
love it, and they had no influence in it. Otherwise they might have
been able to bring Celsus home from Palestine and get him assigned to a more important post. The tradition of serving the state
was strong in this family, and it would hardly have occurred to
Celsus that there was anything else he could do. So Celsus served,
faithfully, but increasingly, as time went on, with many questions

158]

in his heart. I think you can understand that a man who was beginning to have doubts about the Empire would not be helped to resolve them by having the Empire represented for him by somebody like Herod.

"It was pure chance—or was it?—that Celsus and his friend Gaius (the only other member of the guard with whom he had anything in common) happened to be in Bethlehem on an errand the day the Holy Family rode into town. They came at dusk, and the two Romans were just in the act of refreshing themselves at the town well in the marketplace when Mary and Joseph rode up. Or rather Mary rode up, and Joseph walked. Celsus was just about to raise the dipper to his lips when he looked up and saw her.

"I don't know what it was that happened, but I do know that Celsus was never the same man again. You know Mary was very beautiful. She was the most beautiful person that ever lived in this world—except her Son—and at this time she was only a girl. Celsus didn't know that she was a pregnant girl; the way she sat on the donkey he couldn't see that; so there was no appeal to him from her Divine Motherhood; he didn't even see how tired she was. Maybe it was her lovely hair, which had all the gold of the sun in it, or her deep blue eyes with their silent pledge of truth and utter devotion, or her smooth skin, which was white as only perfectly pure things can be. Ah, but who can tell what a man sees in any woman, even in a purely human way, and who can control it?

"Celsus never drank from the uplifted dipper. His eyes steadily fixed upon her face, he handed it to her silently. Silently she received it, and put it to her lips and drank, and handed it back to him. He emptied the surplus water left in it upon the ground, reached again into the bucket, filled the dipper again and handed it to Joseph, who, in his turn, drank and returned it to him. Celsus never took his gaze from Mary until she rode away. Though no word had passed between them, they both understood that he had offered her his whole heart.

"He did not see her again until—well, until the day Herod made

[159

up his mind that the Wise Men were not coming back, but I am sure he never ceased to cherish her in his heart. And, of course, by now you have guessed. It was Celsus who commanded the company that was sent into Bethlehem.

"He could have avoided going. He could have sent the soldiers out under Gaius, who was his second-in-command. But for some reason which he did not understand he had to go. He did not have his own hand in at the butchery, but he went and saw it through.

"Nothing happened until they came to the inn. Oh, that's all wrong! Everything happened. Tragedy and slaughter and agony happened. The destruction of life and hope happened. But that is not what our story is about.

"The company rode up to the inn and summoned the innkeeper. Basil was a sullen man, but by this time he too had felt Mary's spell. He began to feel it that first night or he would never have allowed them the use of the stable, with the inn being full and all.

"Celsus asked, 'Are there any male children in this inn under two years of age?'

"And Basil answered, 'No.'

"That might have been the end of it if the inn had not been so small or the stable so near. But just as the soldiers turned, the Baby cried.

"Celsus look sternly upon Basil.

" 'Is there a child in the stable?'

" 'There may be,' said Basil.

" 'Why didn't you tell me?'

"Basil looked him straight in the eye. 'You didn't ask me,' he replied. Then, after a pause barely long enough to be discernible he added, 'Besides the baby in the stable is a girl.'

"Once again that might have been the end of it, but there was one brutal soldier who was not yet sated with killing. He hurried to the stable, Celsus hot on his heels, pulled the Baby out of his cradle in the manger by his feet, and with one sweep of his left hand tore his clothes off to reveal his sex. It all happened in an instant, but in that instant Joseph hurried forward as if he wished to throw himself upon the soldier's sword, and if the Child had been killed, I think an invisible sword would have reached Mary's heart before the sword of steel reached the heart of the Child. Celsus did not need more than an instant to recognize the face he had carried in his heart these two weeks or more. He needed hardly more than that to take in the fact of the Child, *her* Child. The bloodthirsty soldier had not yet quite drawn his sword when he stepped forward, took the Child with a swift, sure, gentle movement, and held him with his face close to himself.

" 'Fool! he cried. 'Dolt! Have you no eyes in your head? This Child is a girl!'

" 'Girl?!' The soldier was justifiably stupefied. The Baby's little genitals had been dangling before his face not a moment before. But Celsus had not learned the habit of command for nothing. Perhaps he had learned it, he and his whole family before him, for this moment alone.

" 'Yes, girl! Don't you know the difference between a boy and a girl? Didn't the innkeeper tell you? On your way!'

"Celsus turned to Mary and gave her the Child. Their eyes spoke together again, now with tenfold more eloquence than in the marketplace.

" 'You must take your little girl to Egypt,' he said quietly. 'Herod has ordered the slaughter of all the boys in Bethlehem, and it may be that there will be other soldiers who cannot tell the difference between a boy and a girl. Go to Egypt—to Alexandria— and stay there until Herod is dead.'

" 'Egypt!' cried Joseph. 'Alexandria! And what shall we do there? How can I earn a living for the Child? Must he be saved from Herod to perish of hunger?'

"Mary had said nothing. Mary *knew*.

" 'I have friends in Alexandria,' replied Celsus, drawing out a tablet. 'There are Romans there. What is more important from your point of view, there are many Jews. Take this tablet, and give it to my friend whom I have named there. He will see that you get work.'

"Back in Mary's arms, the Baby had stopped crying. With one last look at her and at the Child, Celsus was gone."

At this point the Tale Teller paused and looked searchingly at his listeners. There was a challenge in the look, and it would have been unnatural if one of us had not asked, "And is that the end of the story?"

Even then he did not reply at once. When his answer came it was spoken very slowly.

"No, not quite. At least it was not the end for Celsus."

It was clear that he was waiting, as actors say, to be "fed" his lines. So I asked, "And what did happen to Celsus?"

He had fished for this like a "ham." But not many "hams" get the response he got when he replied, "He killed himself."

"*Killed* himself!"

"What!"

"Why?"

And one of us, the girl whom the old man dearly loved and who looked so much like the way he had described Mary that he might have been suspected of borrowing her coloring for the purpose, said nothing but merely shuddered all through her body as if, as the saying is, somebody had walked across her grave.

But the Tale Teller had got just the response he wanted.

"Yes, he killed himself. Only a few weeks afterwards. He went out one day into the palace courtyard, and drew his sword out of its scabbard, and braced it against a corner of the wall, and leaned upon it. It was quite like Brutus in Shakespeare's *Julius Caesar.*"

And again came the cries of "Why?"

The Old Man continued.

"That troubles you; doesn't it? You expected me to invent a shining future for Celsus. He ought to have become a Christian, shouldn't he? And you wouldn't have minded if, at the end of his noble life, he had been martyred for the Cause. That would have been appropriate enough. It's not the blood you mind, really. But that he should confess himself baffled and defeated...."

"It doesn't seem right," said one, "that the man who saved the Child should have been lost himself."

The Tale Teller shrugged and replied rather sternly, "Oh, as to that I express no judgment. I am not one of those who seek to set bounds to the Mercy of God."

"But why should he kill himself, just after . . . ?"

"Just after having found a new and much greater meaning for his life? Well, I don't suppose he had, you know. I don't know why Celsus killed himself, but I can think of a lot of good reasons. I'm sure that what he saw in Mary's face and in the face of the Child charmed him greatly, but don't you think it must also have troubled him greatly? It passed judgment upon his whole life and upon everything to which his life had been given. It made everything he had done until now, everything he could hope to do in the future, all wrong. It left him without a pilot to show him the way. You must not forget that the Empire herself had been slipping out from under him, leaving him without the faith he had grown up on. Then, too, though he had saved the Child, there were all those other children who had been slaughtered under his command, and perhaps that troubled him. At the same time, he must have felt that when he saved the Child, he had betrayed the Empire and his faith as a soldier. Whichever way he turned he saw guilt, and nowhere could he find any possibility of freeing himself of it. To do right he had to do wrong. He was—what is it your Matthew Arnold says?—wandering between two worlds, one dead, the other powerless to be born. He may have felt, deep down in his heart, where men feel the most illogical things, he may have felt that to die was the least he could do for the Empire, and, contradictorily, for those poor slaughtered children too. Or he may, in that final moment, just have been so tired of turning the whole thing over and over in his mind that he didn't care any more.

"You see, you must not forget that the Child was still—the Child. If Celsus had encountered him after he had become the Teacher (but Celsus would have been a very old man by that time), perhaps it might have been different. Perhaps even he might have become a Christian and ended his life in what obviously all of you would have considered so much more suitable a manner. But none of these things happened. Celsus was needed at this particular moment, and this is where he was brought in. He couldn't have done what he did if he hadn't been sensitive enough and heart-hungry enough to respond to the Child and his Mother just as he did. But, for that very reason, the disturbance which that response occasioned couldn't have been resolved. The price he paid in ignorance was the price he had to pay. It was his share of the Passion. You see, my children, life is a great deal more complicated than any of the churches or philosophers or theologians have ever fully realized. It is even a great deal more complicated than the psychologists realize, though it would be too much to expect them to find that out."

"Do you think Celsus might have feared that what he had done might become known and he punished for it?"

"I don't think so. Roman soldiers were not in the habit of telling tales behind their backs on their commanding officers. Then, too, you must not forget that Basil the innkeeper had already said that the Child in the stable was a girl. No, I don't think it was that. If the simple soldier continued to puzzle the matter in his mind at all, probably he was more inclined to wonder whether he hadn't made a mistake in the first place. He was very stupid, you know. Otherwise he wouldn't have been a soldier."

"The most interesting question of all is whether Christ ever knew who had saved him and what it had cost him."

"Yes, from the human point of view at any rate. From the divine point of view, perhaps it is no question at all. You see, if He was Incarnate God, then He must have known everything."

"And Mary?"

"Was not Incarnate God, to be sure. But she was a very wise woman nevertheless. And I think we may be sure that she has long since interceded for Celsus."

THE WELL OF THE STAR

ELIZABETH GOUDGE

On the road to Bethlehem there is a well called the Well of the Star. The legend goes that the Three Wise Men, on their journey to the manger, lost sight of the star that was guiding them. Pausing to water their camels at the well they found it again reflected in the water.

DAVID sat cross-legged by himself in a corner of the room, separated from the other children, clasping his curly toes in his lean brown hands, and wished he were a rich man, grown-up and strong, with bags full of gold and thousands of camels and tens of thousands of sheep. But he was not rich, he was only a diminutive, ragged, shepherd boy who possessed nothing in the world except the shepherd's pipe slung round his neck, his little pipe upon which he played to himself or the sheep all day long and which was as dear to him as life itself.

At the moment he was very miserable. Sighing, he lifted his hands and placed them on his stomach, pushing it inward and noting the deflation with considerable concern. How soon would he be dead of hunger? How soon would they all be dead of hunger, and safely at rest in Abraham's bosom? It was a very nice place, he had no doubt, and suitable to grandparents and people of that type,

who were tired by a long life and quite ready to be gathered to their
fathers, but hardly the place for a little boy who had lived for only
a few short years in this world, who had seen only a few springs
painting the bare hills purple and scarlet with the anemone flowers,
only a few high summer suns wheeling majestically through the
burning heavens.

If only it were summer now, instead of a cold night in midwinter! If only mother would light a fire for them to warm themselves by, a bright fire that would paint the walls of the dark little
one-roomed house orange and rose color, and chase away the
frightening shadows. But there was no light in the room except
the flickering, dying flame that came from a little lamp, fast burning up the last of their oil, set on the earth floor close to his mother,
where she sat crouched beside her sick husband, swaying herself
ceaselessly from side to side, abandoned to her grief and oblivious
of the wails of four little cold and hungry children, younger than
David, who lay all together on their matting bed.

If only he were a rich man, thought David, then it would not
matter that storms had destroyed the barley, that their vines had
failed, or that their father, the carpenter of this tiny village on a
hill top, could no longer ply his trade. Nothing would matter if he
were a rich man and could buy food and wine and oil and healing
salves; they would be happy then, with food in their stomachs,
their father well, and comforting light in this horrible darkness
of midwinter.

How could he be a rich man?

Suddenly there came to David's mind the thought of the wishing
well far down below on the road to Bethlehem. It was a well of
clear sparkling water, and it was said that those who stood by it at
midnight, and prayed to the Lord God Jehovah from a pure heart,
were given their heart's desire. The difficulty, of course, was to *be*
pure in heart. They said that if you were, and your prayer had been
accepted, you saw your heart's desire mirrored in the water of the
well; the face of someone you loved, maybe, or the gold that would
save your home from ruin, or even, so it was whispered, the face
of God himself. . . . But no one of David's acquaintance had ever

seen anything, though they had visited and prayed time and again.

Nevertheless he jumped up and crept noiselessly through the shadows to the door. He had no idea whether his heart was pure or no, but he would give it the benefit of the doubt and go down to the well. He pulled open the door and slipped out into the great cold silent night.

And instantly he was terribly afraid. All around him the bare hills lay beneath the starlight in an awful, waiting, attentive loneliness, and far down below the terraces of olive trees were drowned in pitch-black shadow. But the sky was streaming with light, so jeweled with myriads of blazing stars that it seemed the weight of them would make the sky fall down and crush the waiting earth to atoms. The loneliness, the darkness, the cold and that great sky above, turned David's heart to water and made his knees shake under him. He had never been out by himself so late at night before, and he had not got the courage, hungry and cold as he was, to go down over the lonely hills and through the darkness of the olive trees to the white road below where they said that robbers lurked, wild sheep stealers and murderers who would cut your throat as soon as look at you just for the fun of it.

Then he bethought him that just over the brow of a nearby hill a flock of sheep were folded, and their shepherds with them. His own cousin Eli, who was teaching David to be a shepherd, would be with them, and Eli would surely be willing to leave the sheep to the other shepherds for a short time and go with David to the well.... At least David would ask him to.

He set off running, a little flitting shadow beneath the stars, and he ran hard because he was afraid.... For surely, he thought, there was something very strange about this night.... The earth lay so still, waiting for something, and overhead that great sky was palpitating and ablaze with triumph. Several times, as he ran, he could have sworn he heard triumphant voices crying, "Glory to God! Glory to God!" as though the hills themselves were singing, and a rushing sound as though great wings were beating over his head. Yet when he stopped to listen there was nothing, only the frail echo of a shepherd's pipe and a whisper of wind over the hills.

[167

He was glad when he saw in front of him the rocky hillock behind which the sheep were folded. "Eli!" he cried, giving a hop, skip and a jump, "Are you there? Jacob? Tobias? It's David."

But there was no answering call from the friendly shepherds, though there was a soft bleating from the sheep, only that strange stillness with its undercurrent of triumphant music that was heard and yet not heard. With a beating heart he bounded round the corner and came out in the little hollow in the hills that was the sheepfold, his eyes straining through the darkness to make out the figures of his friends.

But they were not there; no one was there except a tall, cloaked stranger who sat upon a rock among the sheep leaning on a shepherd's crook. . . . And the sheep, who knew their own shepherds and would fly in fear from a stranger whose voice they did not know, were gathered closely about him in confidence and love. . . . David halted in blank astonishment.

"Good evening to you," said the stranger pleasantly. "It's a fine night."

David advanced with caution, rubbing his nose in perplexity. Who was this stranger? The sheep seemed to know him, and he seemed to know David, yet David knew no man with so straight a back and so grand a head or such a deep, ringing, beautiful voice. This was a very great man, without doubt; a soldier, perhaps, but no shepherd.

"Good evening," said David politely, edging a little closer. " 'Tis a fine evening, but cold about the legs."

"Is it? Then come under my cloak," said the stranger, lifting it so that it suddenly seemed to spread about him like great wings, and David, all his fear suddenly evaporated, scuttled forward and found himself gathered in against the stranger's side, under the stranger's cloak, warm and protected and sublimely happy.

"But where are the others?" he asked. "Eli and Jacob and Tobias?"

"They've gone to Bethlehem," said the stranger. "They've gone to a birthday party."

"A birthday party, and didn't take me?" ejaculated David in powerful indignation. "The nasty, selfish brutes!"

"They were in rather a hurry," explained the stranger. "It was all rather unexpected."

"Then I suppose they had no presents to take?" asked David. "They'll feel awkward, turning up with no presents. . . . Serve them right for not taking me."

"They took what they could," said the stranger. "A shepherd's crook, a cloak, and a loaf of bread."

David snorted with contempt, and then snorted again in indignation. "They shouldn't have gone," he said, and indeed it was a terrible crime for shepherds to leave their sheep, with those robbers prowling about in the shadows below and only too ready to pounce upon them.

"They were quite right to go," said the stranger. "And I have taken their place."

"But you're only one man," objected David, "and it takes several to tackle robbers."

"I think I'm equal to any number of robbers," smiled the stranger. He was making a statement, not boasting, and David thrilled to the quiet confidence of his voice, and thrilled, too, to feel the strength of the arm that was round him and of the knee against which he leant.

"Have you done a lot of fighting, great lord?" he whispered in awe.

"Quite a lot," said the stranger.

"Who did you fight?" breathed David. "Barbarians?"

"The devil and his angels," said the stranger nonchalantly.

David was momentarily deprived of the power of speech, but, pressing closer, he gazed upward at the face of this man for whom neither robbers nor devils seemed to hold any terrors, and once he began to look he could not take his eyes away, for never before had he seen a face like this man's, a face at once delicate and strong, full of power yet quick with tenderness, bright as the sky in early morning yet shadowed with mystery. . . . It seemed an eternity before David could find his voice.

"Who are you, great lord?" he whispered at last. "You're no shepherd."

"I'm a soldier," said the stranger. "And my name is Michael. ...What's your name?"

"David," murmured the little boy, and suddenly he shut his eyes because he was dazzled by the face above him. . . . If this was a soldier, he was a very king among soldiers.

"Tell me where you are going, David," said the stranger.

Now that they had told each other their names David felt they were lifelong friends, and it was not hard to tell his story. He told it all: his father's illness, his mother's tears, the children's hunger and the cold home where there was no fire and the oil was nearly finished; his longing to be a rich man that he might help them all, and the wishing well that gave their hearts' desire to the pure in heart.

"But I hadn't meant to go down to the road alone, you see," he finished. "I thought Eli would have gone with me, and now Eli has gone to that birthday party."

"Then you'll have to go alone," said Michael.

"I suppose the sheep wouldn't be all right by themselves?" hinted David gently.

"They certainly would not," said Michael firmly.

"I'm not afraid, of course," boasted David and shrank a little closer against that strong knee.

"Of course not," concurred Michael heartily. "I've noticed that Davids are always plucky. Look at King David fighting the lion and the bear when he was only a shepherd boy like you."

"But the Lord God Jehovah guided and protected him," said David.

"And the Lord God will protect you," said Michael.

"I don't *feel* as though he was protecting me," objected David.

"You haven't started out yet," said Michael, and laughed. "How can he protect you when there's nothing to protect you from? Or guide you when you don't take to the road? Go on now. Hurry up." And with a gentle but inexorable movement he withdrew his knee from beneath David's clinging hands, and lifted his cloak from

David's shoulders so that it slid back with a soft rustling upward movement, as though great wings were folded against the sky.... And the winter wind blew cold and chill about the little boy who stood ragged and barefoot in the blackness of the night.

"Good-bye," said Michael's deep voice; but it seemed to be drifting away as though Michael too were withdrawing himself. "Play your pipe to yourself if you are afraid, for music is the voice of man's trust in God's protection, even as the gift of courage is God's voice answering."

David took a few steps forward, and again terror gripped him. Again he saw the bare, lonely hills, and the shadows down below where the robbers lurked. He glanced back over his shoulder, ready to bolt back to the shelter of Michael's strong arm and the warmth of his cloak.... But he could no longer see Michael very clearly, he could only see a dark shape that might have been a man but that might have been only a shadow.... But yet the moment he glanced back he knew that Michael was watching him, Michael the soldier who was afraid neither of robbers nor of the devil and his angels, and with a heart suddenly turned valiant he turned and scuttled off down the hill toward the valley.

Nevertheless he had the most uncomfortable journey. Going down the hill he cut his feet on the sharp stones, and fell down twice and barked his knees, and going through the olive grove below he saw robbers hiding behind every tree. There were times when he was so frightened that his knees doubled up beneath him and he came out in a clammy perspiration, but there were other times when he remembered Michael's advice and stopped a minute to play a few sweet notes on his precious pipe, and then he was suddenly brave again and rushed through the terrifying shadows whooping as though he were that other David going for the lion and the bear.... But all the same it was a most uncomfortable journey, and he was overwhelmingly thankful when with final jump he landed in the road and saw the water of the well gleaming only a few feet away from him.

He leaned against the stone parapet and looked at it gravely....

Water.... In this land that in the summer months was parched with drought and scorched with heat water was the most precious thing in the world, the source of all growth and all purification, the cure of sickness, the preserver of life itself. It was no wonder that men came to water to pray for their hearts' desire, to water, the comforter and lord of all life. "Comfort ye, comfort ye, my people." It seemed to him that he heard voices singing in the wind among the olive trees, as though the trees themselves were singing, voices that sang not to the ear but to the soul. "He shall feed his flock like a shepherd: he shall gather the lambs with his arm, and carry them in his bosom. Wonderful! Counselor! The mighty God! The everlasting Father! The Prince of Peace!" Surely, he thought, if the Lord God Jehovah cared so for the little lambs he would care also for David's sick father and weeping mother and the little hungry children, and covering his face with his brown fingers he prayed to the Lord God that he might have gold to buy food and wine and oil for that stricken house up above him on the hill. And so hard did he pray that he forgot everything but his own longing, forgot his fears and the cold wind that nipped him through his rags, saw nothing but the darkness of his closed eyes and heard nothing but his own desperate whispering.

Then, sighing a little like a child awaking from sleep, he opened his eyes and peeped anxiously through his fingers at the water in the well. Would he have his heart's desire? Had he prayed from a pure heart? Was that something glittering in the well? He dropped his hands from his face and leaned closer, the blood pounding so in his ears that it sounded like drums beating. Yes, it was gold! Circles of gold lying upon the surface of the water, as though the stars had dropped down from heaven. With a cry of joy he leaned nearer, his face right over the water, as though he would have touched with his lips those visionary gold pieces that promised him his heart's desire.... And then, in an instant of time, his cry of joy changed to a cry of terror, for framed in those twinkling golden points of light he saw the reflection of a man's face, a bearded swarthy face with gleaming teeth and eyes, the face of a foreigner.

So the Lord God had not protected him. So the robbers had got him. He stared at the water for a long minute, stark with terror, and then swung round with a choking cry, both his thin hands at his throat to protect it from the robber's knife.

"Do not cry out, little son. I will not hurt you." The man stretched out a hand and gave David's shoulder a reassuring little shake. "I but looked over your shoulder to see what you stared at so intently."

The voice, deep-toned, kindly, strangely attractive with its foreign inflection, chased away all David's fears. . . . This was no robber. . . . His breath came more evenly, and he wiped the sweat of his terror off his forehead with his tattered sleeve while he looked up with bulging eyes at the splendid stranger standing in front of him.

He was tall, though not so tall as that other splendid stranger keeping the sheep up on the hill, and he wore a purple robe girdled at the waist with gold and a green turban to which were stitched gold ornaments that shook and trembled round his proud, hawk-nosed face. David had one pang of agonized disappointment as he realized that it was only the reflection of these gold ornaments he had seen in the water, and not God's answer to his prayer, and then amazement swept all other thoughts from his mind.

For the star-lit road to the well that a short while ago had been empty was now full. While David prayed, his ears closed to all sounds, a glittering cavalcade had come up out of the night. There were black men carrying torches, richly caparisoned camels, and two more splendid grave-faced men even more richly dressed than his friend. The torchlight gleamed on gold and scarlet, emerald green and rich night blue, and the scent of spices came fragrant on the wind. This cavalcade might have belonged to Solomon, thought David, to Solomon in all his glory. . . . Surely these men were kings?

But the camels were thirsty, and the first king drew David gently away from the well that they might drink. Yet he kept his hand upon his shoulder and looked down upon him with kindly liking.

"And for what were you looking so intently, little son?" he asked.

[173

"For my heart's desire, great lord," whispered David, nervously pleating his ragged little tunic with fingers that still shook from the fright he had had.

"So?" asked the stranger. "Is it a wishing well?"

"They say," said David, "that if you pray to God for your heart's desire from a pure heart, and if God has granted your prayer, you will see a vision of it in the water."

"And you saw yours?"

David shook his head. "You came, great lord," he explained. "I saw you."

One of the other kings, an old white-bearded man in a sea-green robe, was listening smiling to their talk. "We three have lost a star, little son," he said to David. "Should we find it again in your well?"

David thought it must be a joke, for what could three great lords want with a star? But when he looked up into the fine old eyes gazing down into his he saw trouble and bewilderment in them.

"If your heart is pure, great lord."

A shadow passed over the old man's face and he turned back to the third king, a young man with a boy's smooth skin and eyes that were bright and gay.

"Gaspar," he said. "You are young and pure of heart, you look."

Gaspar laughed, his white teeth flashing in his brown face. "Only an old wives' tale," he mocked. "We've lost the star twenty times in the blaze of the night sky and twenty times we have found it again. Why should we look for it now in a well?"

"Yet pray," said the old man sternly. "Pray and look."

Obediently Gaspar stepped up to the well, his scarlet robe swirling about him and the curved sword that he wore slapping against his side, bowed his head in prayer, then bent over the well.

"I can see only a part of the sky," he murmured, "and each star is like another in glory—no—yes." He paused and suddenly gave a shout of triumph. "I have found it, Melchior! It shines in the center of the well, like the hub of a wheel or the boss of a shield."

He straightened himself and flung back his head, his arms stretched up toward the sky. "There! There!" he cried, and David and the elder kings, gazing, saw a great star blazing over their heads, a star that was mightier and more glorious than the sister stars that shone around it like cavaliers round the throne.... And as they gazed it suddenly moved, streaking through the sky like a comet.

"Look! Look!" cried David. "A shooting star!" And he danced out into the middle of the road to follow its flight. "Look! It is shining over Bethlehem!"

The three kings stood behind him, gazing where he pointed, and saw at the end of the road, faintly visible in the starlight, slender cypress trees rising above the huddled roofs of a little white town upon a hill, and above them the blazing star.

Gaspar, young and excited, suddenly swung round and began shouting to the servants to bring up the camels, but the two older kings still stood gazing.

"Praise be to the Lord God," said the old king tremulously, and he bowed his head and crossed his hands upon his breast.

"Bethlehem," said the king who was David's friend. "The end of our journey."

His voice was infinitely weary, and for the first time it occurred to David that these great lords had come from a long way off. Their beautiful clothes were travel-stained and their faces drawn with fatigue. They must, he decided suddenly, be lunatics; no sane men, he thought, would come from so far away to visit an unimportant little place like Bethlehem; nor be in such a taking because they had lost sight of a star. Nevertheless he liked them and had no wish to lose their company.

"*I'll* take you to Bethlehem," he announced, and flung back his head and straddled his legs as though it would be a matter of great difficulty and danger to guide them the short way along the straight road to a town that was visible to the naked eye.

"And so you shall," laughed his friend. "And you shall ride my camel in front of me and be the leader of the caravan."

David jigged excitedly from one foot to the other. He had never ridden a camel, for only well-to-do men had camels. He could not contain himself and let out a shrill squeak of joy as a

[175

richly caparisoned beast was led up and made to kneel before them; a squeak that ended rather abruptly when the camel turned its head and gave him a slow disdainful look, lifting its upper lip and showing its teeth in a contempt so profound that David blushed hotly to the roots of his hair, and did not recover himself until he was seated on the golden saddle cloth before his friend, safe in the grip of his arm, rocking up toward the stars as the camel got upon its feet.

It was one of the most wonderful moments of that wonderful night when David found himself swaying along toward the cypresses of Bethlehem, the leader of a caravan. Because he was so happy he put his pipe to his lips and began to play the gay little tune that shepherds have played among the hills since the dawn of the world, and so infectious was it that the men coming behind began to hum it as they swung along under the stars.

"It is right to sing upon a journey, great lord," said David, when a pause fell, "for music is the voice of man's trust in God's protection, even as the gift of courage is God's voice answering."

"That is a wise child you have got there, Balthasar," said old Melchior, who was riding just behind them.

"I didn't make that up for myself," David answered truthfully. "A man up in the hills told it to me. A man who came to mind the sheep so that Eli and the other shepherds could go with their presents to a birthday party in Bethlehem."

"Does all the world carry gifts to Bethlehem tonight?" questioned Balthasar softly. "Wise men from the desert with their mysteries, shepherds from the hills with their simplicities, and a little boy with the gift of music."

"Do you mean that we are all going to the same place?" asked David eagerly. "Are *you* going to the birthday party too? And am I going with you? Me too?"

"A king has been born," said Balthasar. "We go to worship him."

A king? The world seemed full of kings tonight, and kings doing the most unsuitable things, too, keeping sheep on the hills

176]

and journeying along the highway travel-stained and weary. On this wonderful topsy-turvy night nothing surprised him, not even the news that the birthday party was a king's; but desolation seized him as he realized that he wouldn't be able to go to it himself. . . . For how could he go inside a grand palace when his clothes were torn and his feet were bare and dirty? They wouldn't let him in. They'd set the dogs on him. . . . Disappointment surged over him in sickening waves. He gritted his teeth to keep himself from crying, but even with all his effort two fat tears escaped and plowed two clean but scalding furrows through the grime on his face.

They were at Bethlehem before he realized it, for he had been keeping his head bent for fear Balthasar should see his two tears. Looking up suddenly he saw the white walls of the little town close in front of him, the cypress trees like swords against the sky and that star shining just ahead of them, so bright that it seemed like a great lamp let down out of heaven by a string. The gate of the town was standing wide open and they clattered through it without hindrance, which surprised David until he remembered that just at this time Bethlehem would be full of people who had come in from the country to be taxed. They would not be afraid of robbers tonight, when the walls held so many good strong countrymen with knives in their girdles and a quick way with their fists. The visitors were still up and about, too, for as they climbed the main street of the little hill town David could see lines of light shining under doors and hear laughter and voices behind them. . . . And a good thing too, he thought, for at any other time the arrival of this strange cavalcade in the dead of night might have caused a disturbance. . . . The Lord God, he thought, had arranged things very conveniently for them.

"Which way are we going?" he whispered excitedly to his king.

"We follow the star," said Balthasar.

David looked up and saw that the star must have been up to its shooting tricks again, for it had now moved over to their right, and obediently they too swerved to their right and made their way up a narrow lane where houses had been built over caves in the limestone rock. Each house was the home of poor people, who kept their animals in the cave below and lived themselves in the one room above reached by its flight of stone steps.

"The king can't be *here!*" said David disgustedly, as the cavalcade, moving now in single file, picked its way over the heaps of refuse in the lane. "Only poor people live *here.*"

"Look!" said Balthasar, and, looking, David saw that the star was hanging so low over a little house at the end of the lane that a bright beam of light caressed its roof.

"The star is making a mistake," said David firmly, "if it thinks a king could be born in a place like that."

But no one was taking any notice of him. A great awe seemed to have descended upon the three kings, and a thankfulness too deep for speech. In silence the cavalcade halted outside the house at the end of the lane, and in silence the servants gathered round to bring the camels to their knees and help their masters to the ground. David, picked up and set upon his feet by a sturdy Nubian whose black face gleamed in the torchlight like ebony, stood aside and watched, something of the awe that gripped the others communicating itself to him, so that the scene he saw stamped itself upon his memory forever. . . . The torchlight and starlight lighting up the rich colors of the kings' garments and illumining their dark, intent faces, as though they were lit by an inner light; the stir among the servants as three of them came forward carrying three golden caskets, fragrant with spices and so richly jeweled that the light seemed to fall upon them in points of fire, and gave them reverently into their masters' hands. . . . The birthday presents, thought David, the riches that Balthasar had spoken of, and he looked hastily up at the poor little house built above the stable, incredulous that such wealth could enter a door so humble.

But the door at the top of the stone steps was shut fast and no line of light showed beneath it, or shone out in welcome from the window. The only light there was showed through the ill-fitting door that closed in the opening to the cave below, and it was toward this that Melchoir turned, knocking softly on the rotten wood and standing with bent head to listen for the answer.

178]

"But that's the *stable!*" whispered David. "He couldn't be there!"

But no one answered him, for the door opened and the three kings, their heads lowered and their long dark fingers curved about their gifts, passed into the light beyond, the door closing softly behind them, shutting David outside in the night with the strange black servants and the supercilious camels.

But his curiosity was too strong for him to feel afraid. There was a hole quite low in the door and kneeling down he pressed his dirty little face against the wood and squinted eagerly through it.

Of course there was no king there; he had said there wouldn't be and there wasn't; looking beyond the kings he saw there was nothing there but the stable and the animals and a few people, poor people like himself. The animals, a little donkey with his ribs sticking through his skin and an old ox whose shoulders bore the marks of the yoke they had carried through many hard years, were fastened to iron rings in the wall of the cave, but both of them had turned their sleepy heads toward the rough stone manger filled with hay, and toward a gray-bearded man who held a lighted lantern over the manger and a woman with a tired white face, muffled in a blue cloak, who lay on the floor leaning back against the wall.... But though she was so tired she was smiling at the men who were kneeling together on the hard floor, and she had the liveliest and most welcoming smile that David had ever seen.

And then he saw that the men she was smiling at were Eli, Jacob, and Tobias, kneeling with heads bent and hands clasped in the attitude of worship. And before them on the hard floor, just in front of the manger, they had laid their gifts: Eli's shepherd's crook that had been his father's, Jacob's cloak lined with the lamb's wool that he set such store by, and Tobias's little loaf of bread that he always ate all by himself in the middle of the night when he was guarding sheep, never giving a crumb to anyone else no matter how hard they begged. And beside these humble men knelt the ings in their glory, and beside the simple gifts were the three h, fragrant caskets, just as though there were no barrier between

[179

rich people and poor people, and no difference in value between wood and bread and gold and jewels.

But what could be in that manger that they were all so intent upon it? David had another peep through his hole and saw to his astonishment that there was a baby in it, a tiny newborn baby wrapped in swaddling clothes. Normally David took no interest at all in babies, but at the sight of this one he was smitten with such awe that he shut his eyes and ducked his head, just as though he had been blinded by the sight of a king with eyes like flame sitting upon a rainbow-encircled throne.

So this was the king, this tiny baby lying in a rough stone manger in a stable. . . . It struck David that of all the extraordinary places where he had encountered kings this night this was the most extraordinary of all. . . . And then he gave a joyous exclamation. On the journey here he had cried because he had thought a barefoot dirty little boy would not be able to go to a king's birthday party, but surely even he could go to a birthday party in a stable. He leaped to his feet, dusted his knees, pulled down his rags, laid his hands on the latch of the door, and crept noiselessly in.

And then, standing by himself in the shadows by the door, he bethought him that he had no present to give. He had no possessions in the world at all, except his beloved shepherd's pipe, and it was out of the question that he should give that for he loved it as his own life. Noiseless as a mouse he turned to go out again, but suddenly the mother in the blue cloak, who must have known all the time that he was there, raised her face and smiled at him, a radiant smile full of promise, and at the same time the man with the gray beard lowered the lantern a little so that it seemed as though the whole manger were enveloped with light, with that baby at the heart of the light like the sun itself.

And suddenly David could not stay by himself in the shadows, any more than he could stay in a dark stuffy house when the sun was shining. No sacrifice was too great, not even the sacrifice of the little shepherd's pipe that was dear as life itself, if he could be in that light. He ran forward, pushing rudely between Balthasar and Tobias, and laid his shepherd's pipe joyously down before the

180]

manger, between Balthasar's jeweled casket and Tobias's humble loaf of bread. . . . He was too little to realize, as he knelt down and covered his face with his hands, that the birthday gifts lying there in a row were symbolic of all that a man could need for his life on earth: a cloak for shelter, a loaf of bread for food, a shepherd's crook for work, and a musical instrument to bring courage in the doing of it; and those other gifts of gold and jewels and spices that symbolized rich qualities of kingliness and priestliness and wisdom that were beyond human understanding. "Wise men from the desert with their mysteries," Balthasar had said, "shepherds from the hills with their simplicities, and a little boy with the gift of music." But David, peeping through his fingers at the baby in the manger, did not think at all, he only felt, and what his spirit experienced was exactly what his body felt when he danced about on the hills in the first hot sunshine of the year; warmth was poured into him, health and strength and life itself. He took his hands away from his face and gazed and gazed at that baby, his whole being poured out in adoration.

And then it was all over and he found himself outside Bethlehem, trailing along in the dust behind Eli, Jacob, and Tobias, footsore and weary and as cross as two sticks.

"Where's my camel?" he asked petulantly. "When I went to Bethlehem I was the leader of a caravan, and I had three great lords with me, and servants and torches."

"Well, you haven't got them now," said Eli. "The great lords are still at Bethlehem. . . . When Jacob and Tobias and I saw you there in the stable we made haste to take you home to your mother, young truant that you are."

"I don't want mother," grumbled David. "I want my camel."

Eli glanced back over his shoulder at the disagreeable little urchin dawdling at his heels. Was this the same child who had knelt in the stable wrapped in adoration? How quick can be the fall from ecstasy! "You keep your mouth shut, little son," he adjured him, "and quicken your heels; for I must get back to those sheep."

"Baa!" said David nastily, and purposely lagged behind.

So determinedly did he lag that by the time he had reached the well he found himself alone again. The well! The sight of it brought home to him his desperate plight. From his night's adventure he had gained nothing. Up there on the hill was the little house that held his sick father, his weeping mother, and his hungry little brothers and sisters, and he must go home to them no richer than he went.... Poorer, in fact, for now he had lost his shepherd's pipe, thrown away his greatest treasure in what seemed to him now a moment of madness.... Now he had nothing, nothing in all the world.

He flung himself down in the grass beside the well, and he cried as though his heart were breaking. The utter deadness of the hour before dawn weighed on him like a pall, and the cold of it numbed him from head to foot. He felt himself sinking lower and lower, dropping down to the bottom of some black sea of misery, and it was not until he reached the bottom that comfort came to him.

His sobs ceased, and he was conscious again of the feel of the earth beneath the grass where he lay, hard and cold yet bearing him up with a strength that was reassuring. He thought of the terraces of olive trees above him and of the great bare hills beyond, and then he thought of the voices he had heard singing in the wind up in the hills, and singing down below among the trees, and then suddenly he thought he heard voices in the grass, tiny voices that were like the voices of all growing things, corn and flowers and grasses. "They that sow in tears, shall reap in joy," they whispered. "He that goeth forth and weepeth, bearing precious seed, shall doubtless come again rejoicing, bringing his sheaves with him."

He got up, his courage restored, and stumbled over to the well, faintly silvered now with the first hint of dawn. He did not pray to be a rich man, he did not look in it for his heart's desire, he simply went to it to wash himself, for he did not intend to appear before his mother with dirty tear stains all over his face.... If he could not arrive back home with bags full of gold and thousands of camels and tens of thousands of sheep he would at least arrive with a clean and cheerful face to comfort them.

182]

Like all small boys David was a noisy washer, and it must have been the sound of his splashings that prevented him from hearing the feet of a trotting camel upon the road; nor could the surface of the well, much agitated by his ablutions, show him at first the reflection of the man standing behind him; it had to smooth itself out before he could see the swarthy face framed in the twinkling golden ornaments. When he did see it he blinked incredulously for a moment and then swung round with a cry of joy.

"So you thought I had forgotten you, did you, little son?" smiled Balthasar. "I would not forget so excellent a leader of a caravan. When you left the stable I followed after you as quickly as I could. See what I have for you."

He gave a bag to David, and the little boy, opening it, saw by the first light of the dawn the shine of golden pieces.... Lots of golden pieces, enough to buy medicines and healing salves for his father and food and warmth for all of them for a long time to come.... He had no words to tell of his gratitude, but the face that he tilted up to Balthasar, with eyes and mouth as round in wonder as coins themselves, was in itself a paean of praise.

Balthasar laughed and patted his shoulder. "When I saw you give your shepherd's pipe to the little King," he said, "I vowed that you should not go home empty-handed.... I think it was the little King himself who put the thought into my head.... Now I must go back to my country, and you to your home, but we will not forget each other. Fare you well, little son."

As he went up through the shadows of the olive trees David was no longer frightened of robbers, for he was far too happy. The trees were singing again, he thought, as the dawn wind rustled them. "Comfort ye, comfort ye, my people," they sang. And when he got out beyond the trees, and saw the great bare stretches of the hills flushed rose and lilac in the dawn, it seemed as though the hills themselves were shouting, "Glory to God!"

INTERLUDE

HIS BIRTHDAY*

MARY ELLEN CHASE

Could every time-worn heart but see Thee once again,
A happy, human child among the homes of men,
The age of doubt would cease, the vision of Thy face
Would silently restore the childhood of the race.

Henry van Dyke

I

The Boy Jesus in Nazareth

It was late afternoon in Nazareth of Galilee. Through the narrow streets the laborers from the fields without the village hurried homeward. Workmen, their heavy tools resting on their roughly clad shoulders, passed weary footed over the rude stones paving the road. Here and there a bronzed and bearded shepherd, crook in hand, led his flock to safer shelter, for the nights were chill even in the lower hillfolds. Small groups of the soldiers of Augustus, scornful of these silent Hebrews and disgruntled over their own station in this impoverished and remote province of the Empire, sauntered idly along the streets, or gave rude proofs of their authority to the quiet Nazarenes, to whom the grandeur of Rome meant little save much discomfort and too heavy taxation.

---

* *His Birthday* was published as a small book by the Pilgrim Press in 1915. In granting permission to have it reprinted here, the author has stipulated that the editor of this volume make it clear to his readers that it was her very first story.

Eastward from the village led a footpath, worn by the feet of many generations; and along this path through the awakening fields the girls and women of Nazareth went in companies of twos and threes to fill their jars and pitchers of clay and goatskin at the fountain, whose clear water had for centuries given refreshment, not only to the Nazareth folk, but also to the traveler and wayfarer on the dusty, stone-strewn roads of Palestine. It was a joyful little procession at this evening hour, for the heavy rains of early winter had granted one day's respite, and the sun was sinking into the western Mediterranean in a sky as clear and blue as the sea itself. Gladly the women in their bright-colored garments trooped along, some driving small flocks of herds, others holding their pitchers lightly upon their shoulders, or balancing them easily upon their dark, shapely heads; gaily they exchanged greetings or shared some village incident, while the children darted from the path to snatch eagerly after field flowers, whose petals the day's long sunshine had opened in the new grass.

At the fountain other and strange faces greeted their own; other and strange words returned their evening welcome; for this fountain without Nazareth was the daily resting-place of many a caravan from Egypt and the farther Eastern deserts, bound for Ephesus or other rich cities of Asia Minor, of companies of white-robed Arabs, bent on ever inscrutable errands, of dark-skinned Numidians, henchmen of Rome, of footsore, many-tongued pilgrims from the lands far beyond Jordan. But simple gratitude for the water which gushed into the stone-built well and trough, a common joy in the sunlit hills, and that strange reverence which all men feel in the mysterious hush of twilight, shattered the barriers of race and speech, and made of the Nazarenes and the travelers comrades in a common fellowship. And as Rebekah gave the servant of Abraham to drink, so the maidens of Nazareth gave drink from their pitchers to the weary and wayworn who had no jars of their own; and so, also, did many a Jacob from Egypt or Rome or beyond the Jordan help to water the sheep and fill the jars of the Rachels of Nazareth.

Then as the blue melted into the gold of the later sunset time, and as the Galilean hills deepened and darkened in the glow, those clustered about the fountain went again upon their ways, the travelers to continue their journeyings until time to camp for the night, the dwellers in Nazareth to go again to their homes. Yet the evening was so rare for the wintry season and the twilight so beautiful, that several, perhaps unhampered by urgent duties at home and loath to lose the sun sooner than necessary, chose to climb the hill back of the village and view the Galilean country at this loveliest time of the day.

Two had preceded them in thought and action—a woman and her child. Already they were halfway up the hill, the woman's white-gowned figure moving lightly, unhaltingly; the child clinging to a fold of her robe, and trying to equal her long, easy steps with his own small feet. On one shoulder she carried a brown water jar, which she steadied with a firm hand, and which seemed no impediment to her ascent, for she soon and easily gained the summit and turned her face southward, the child's eyes following her own.

She was a type rare in Galilee—a woman well-knit, of large frame, though lithe and graceful of movement. Her skin was fine of texture, clear, and olive in color, save for a healthy glow in her cheeks; her nose and chin, cleanly cut and strong with an emotional kind of strength; her mouth, sweet, appealing, almost sad; her forehead, full and somewhat high, though its height was softened by brown hair parted upon it; her eyes, blue-gray and far apart, were wistful with undiscernible longing, joyous with motherhood, strange with a vision of the Unseen. It was as if they had looked upon the intangible, which is at the heart of things, and had understood—for a moment.

She stood upon the summit of the hill—her hand, long, slender, and finely-cut, beyond the imagination or the skill of any worshipping artist, resting upon the shoulder of her son. He was very like her—this little boy of hers. He stood leaning against her, one brown hand clutching the fold of her garment, the other playing with her long fingers on his shoulder. His tunic of white wool reached only to his knees, which were sturdy, brown, and bare, as were his legs and loosely-sandaled feet. His throat was slender, and the lines of his nose and chin were, even at six years, very like his mother's in strength and sweetness. His hair, heavier and darker than her own, though still brown like the brown of a ripe filbert nut, grew back from his forehead and fell in curls about his neck. His skin was of the same fine texture as that of his mother, but somewhat lighter in color, and his cheeks were tinged with the clear pink of flax blossoms in the fields around Nazareth. Behind the child's joyousness in his deep-blue eyes lay the same mystery that haunted her own; the same wistful longing; the same mystic vision. Was that which lay in his a bequest from her, or had he brought both from whence he came?

So they stood together and watched the sunset glow touch the blue line of the hills of Moab on the southeast, gild the summit of Tabor, and suffuse with purple light the far distances of the Jordan Valley. Snow-clad Hermon reached to Carmel on the South, Carmel swept away to the sea on the southwest, and thus surrounded by a tumbled mass of hills stretched the great Plain of Esdraelon, on whose vast surface Gideon had put to flight the Midianites and Sisera had been conquered. Esdraelon—that great battleground of ages past and of ages yet to come, when southern hordes should attempt to exterminate by the sword a religion born in this very Nazareth!

Now in the half-light shadowy, slow-moving forms crept here and there in long lines across Esdraelon—caravans plodding northward.

"They are bearing wealth to Rome," she told him, while his eyes, big with wonder, counted the camels in the dim, uncertain light.

From the southeast, beyond the white roofs of Nain, came a gleam of light, then another and another—the sun's lingering rays flashing upon Roman spears and shields. A legion was coming up the Valley of the Jordan, journeying homeward after the Parthian conquests perhaps.

"Soldiers!" cried the child, his eyes shining. "Soldiers of Augustus! When I am grown, I, too, perhaps may bear a spear and shield. Would that please thee, mother?"

She looked at him tenderly, caressed his cheek, and drew his dark head closer.

"The Holy City of thy fathers lies southward," she said, "and Bethlehem where thou wast born; far beyond Esdraelon and the hills of Samaria and the waste places of Judah. Thou hast been in Jerusalem with thy father and me at the time of the Passover, but thou rememberest it little. When thou art older grown, thou wilt perhaps journey there again, and learn to become a priest in the great temple."

Her eyes, vague with dreams, sought the southern mountains. The child laughed thoughtfully.

"My father would wish me to be a carpenter in Nazareth," he said, "and thou a priest in the great temple, and I, a soldier of Augustus, but braver than those who dwell in our village."

Hs mother's eyes gleamed with an instant's fleeting vision; his mother's arms drew him closer.

"The dreams of a mother are strangely real," she said at last. "Some day thou shalt be at Jerusalem in the great temple. Of that I am very sure. But the darkness is hastening. We must go down to thy father who awaits us, and to the stories I promised thee. Thou hast not forgotten?"

"No," he answered eagerly, as they descended in the half-light. "All day I have been waiting, and my father's gift was all but ready for me when we went to draw the water. It must be now quite complete."

"And mine, also."

"Hast thou a gift besides, mother?" he cried joyfully, his face aglow. "Hast thou one truly besides? Shall I know tonight? I need not wait till morning! Say that I need not!"

She smiled, glad in his happiness. "Thou needst not wait," she promised, his hand in hers. "Thou mayest have it tonight. Take care, dear, lest the stones pierce thy feet. Thy sandals are worn, and I would not have thee hurt."

Slowly the western glow died away. The hills, darker grown,

seemed to withdraw farther into the shadows, as though the sun had unlocked their mysteries, they all unwilling. One star gleamed over Carmel as the boy and his mother left the hill path for the narrow village street. A few minutes and the street had widened into a kind of village gathering ground and meeting place where town councils were held and where the boys of Nazareth enjoyed their sports and games. Of late years, much to the discomfort of the Nazarenes, the Roman guards had made this their rendezvous; and the lads of Nazareth, like the other lads of all countries and all times, could not refrain from gathering here to gaze with mingled hatred and admiration upon the shining helmets, the carven shields, and the mighty spears of Rome.

Tonight, as was not unusual, there was apparently trouble. A crowding together of boys and soldiers, a shout of triumph followed by indignant cries, betokened its presence as the boy and his mother approached. The child saw quickly what had happened.

"It is Joel!" he cried. "The lame son of Isaac, the sheepherder! They have broken his new ball, which but yesterday his father bought from a trader, and they play with the halves!"

He sprang from his mother's side, and ran with all his might into the shouting group of men and boys. The shouting ceased, the soldiers of Augustus fell back, the boys stood still. The child's eyes were dark with anger, his lips quivered, his hands were clenched tightly.

"What is this thou doest?" he cried, addressing the foremost soldier. "Thou hast broken Joel's ball by rough handling, and he a cripple! And thou a soldier of the great Augustus!"

The soldier stared stupidly. "Nay, it was but in sport," he mumbled, unable to fathom the strange awe with which this child inspired him. "It was but in sport."

"It is but poor sport," cried the child again, "and unworthy! Wouldst thou call it sport if thou wert Joel and he a soldier of Augustus? Give me the halves. My father will join them in his workshop if I ask him. Come thou with me, Joel!"

He passed to the center of the silent, astonished circle, and placed his arm about the shrunken shoulders of a crippled boy with sad, drawn features.

"Come thou with me, Joel," he whispered. "My father will tomorrow mend thy ball. It shall be as good as new then, I promise thee. Come!"

They moved away across the open space to the entrance of a narrow street beyond. The crowd dispersed, the soldiers half-scornful, half-subdued; the boys, perplexed, incredulous. The child's mother followed him, pride and wonder in her heart.

"Some day all will be well with thee, Joel," she heard him say. "Something tells me that some day thou shalt be a cripple no longer. Wait and see if I do not tell thee true."

Shy, half-embarrassed, very grateful, the crippled boy gazed at this child, who was younger than himself, but whom he strangely revered and loved. Then turning on his rough crutches, he started down the narrow street, looking back every now and then until the child and his mother disappeared around another and sharper curve of the crooked road.

II

The Birthday Gifts

Hurriedly now the two went homeward, she holding him closely within a fold of her garment, for the night grew cold, and soon they reached the western outskirts of Nazareth, where their home lay, together with the adjoining workshop of Joseph, the carpenter.

It was into this workshop that they entered first, the child throwing aside the restraining garment fold, and drawing his mother eagerly after him. The low room was small and confusedly littered by stray tools and loose scraps of wood and iron. In one corner several pieces of unfinished work, patiently waiting completion, were huddled together; in another, nearest the door, stood a table, on whose rough, unplaned surface was heaped a motley collection of bruised and battered toys—headless spears, dilapidated kite frames, broken chariots.

A man, bent and heavily bearded, sat on a rude bench in the center of the little shop, and by the flickering and uncertain glare of a torchlight polished and re-polished something which he held upon his knees. He raised his head as the two entered, his dark eyes, so common to his race, giving them welcome. Then without comment he would have resumed his task, had not the child laid a resisting hand upon his arm.

"See, father, here are the halves of Joel's ball." And he held in either outstretched hand the cracked and mutilated pieces of wood. "The soldiers of Augustus tore it from him, and broke it by rough play. But I said thou couldst mend it for him. And thou canst, father?"

The man looked from the child's mother to the child, and then toward the table with its load of sad, broken things.

"Place Joel's ball there with the other toys, my son," he said. "Tomorrow I will mend them all for thy friends. But today I have given up all to complete thy gift. Come nearer to the light. Art thou pleased?"

The boy stood beneath the light which glowed around his dark head and eager face. In his outstretched arms his father placed a long, narrow box, made of Lebanon cedar and sweet to the smell. It was polished well, and fastened by a shining clasp. The child's eyes shone, as he held, examined, and opened it.

"Art thou pleased?" his father asked again, almost wistfully.

"It is beautiful, father!" he cried. "Is it not, mother?" She nodded, smiling, glad in his joy. "And now my treasures need lie no longer in the great chest, but may be in my new box. May I have it? Is it quite complete?"

"It needs but one more dressing of oil, and then a little polishing to make it quite complete," the man answered. "Go with thy mother and get thy treasures ready. I will soon bring it to thee."

They passed through the workshop and a little inner court to the dimly-lighted house, low-storied and white-walled, built somewhat after the manner of the rich homes of Rome with atrium and rooms opening on either side, but small, crude in its workmanship, and primitive in its furnishings. The woman, followed by the eager child, walked hurriedly the length of the poor center room to a chest near the farther door, pulled from it a rude cover of goatskins, raised the lid, and drew forth with careful fingers a small bundle, wrapped in white wool, and tied with thongs of skin.

"Here are thy treasures, dear," she said, unknotting the tough thongs. "Here are the gold coins which the strange and wise men from the Far East brought thee, and the alabaster boxes of frankincense and sweet myrrh: and here the olive branch which the shepherds from the hills without Bethlehem gave thee, and the dried flower placed in thy hand by the sweet-voiced herdsboy on the hills north of Nazareth. And the wool in which I wrapped thee to keep thee from the cold."

She gave the loosened bundle into his hands, and watched him, as, sitting on a low stool by her side, he drew out each gift separately and gazed at it lovingly, then arranged each in order in the lap of his tunic.

"They must be tired of the great chest," he mused with quaint fancy. "Weary of lying so often unnoticed among so many other things. They will like the new box, will they not, mother?"

"Yes," she said, "I am sure they will. But I forget. There is yet something in the great chest. My own gift for thee."

He would have sprung from the stool in his eager excitement had he not remembered the treasure in his lap.

"Draw it from the chest, mother," he entreated, "but slowly, while I bind these again in the wool."

She obeyed, opening the lid slowly, and awaiting his preparation.

"Now!" he cried, laying the bundle upon the stool, and standing beside her. "Now!"

She drew a second and larger bundle from the chest, and unfolded its contents, bringing before his shining eyes a little coat of red-and-blue wool, the colors curiously intermingled. He put it on at once over his white tunic, and embraced her rapturously.

"Oh!" he cried. "A new coat! And bright like that which Joseph's father gave him in the stories thou tellest me!"

She laughed as joyously as he. "And I made if for thee as

[195

Hannah of old made that of little Samuel in the same stories of our people. Dost remember?"

He nodded. Then—

"See!" he whispered. "An old man begs entrance at our door. He is like the prophets of our race of which thou tellest me."

Quite unconscious in their joy they had not heeded the entrance of a stranger, who now rested wearily against the doorpost—a very old man with the long white beard of the patriarchs and the searching eyes of the seers. He stood staff in hand, and gazed in strange incredulity at the woman and the child, who, half in fear, half in awe, clung to his mother's garment.

"It is even so the same child and his mother," spoke the old man in deep tones, more to himself than to them, while his eyes ever scanned their faces. "Verily, the Spirit hath led me to this house, as six years since it led me to the temple where I first beheld his glory."

Still lost in wonder he stood there. So deep in meditation was he that he did not heed the woman's greeting of welcome; did not perceive that the child, his shyness conquered, had left his mother's side and with pretty courtesy had come forward to add his solicitation to her own: did not note in the shadows behind the two the dark figure of the silent Nazarene carpenter.

The woman spoke first. "My father," she said, gently and reverently, "thou art wayworn and weary. Rest with us this night, and on the morrow continue thy journey. Lay thyself upon this couch. Thou honorest our house by thy presence. My son, wilt thou bring water and oil, while I prepare food and drink?"

The child started eagerly to obey, but the old man came forward and placed his hand upon the boy's head.

"Thou dost not know me, my son."

"Nay, master," said the child. "Yet in my father's house is no man a stranger, but a friend."

"Dost thou know me, my daughter?"

"I know thee." She spoke quietly, but intensely, and as though these simple words brought memories, rushing over her, engulfing her in their sacredness. "I know thee. Thou art one Simeon—he who was in the temple when we brought the child to do sacrifice before the Lord. Thou raised him in thine arms and blessed him." She turned toward the bent figure of her husband, who had come to her side, and whose years seemed strangely multiplied in contrast with her own fresh youthfulness.

"Thou rememberest, my husband?"

"Yea, verily," said the Nazarene carpenter. And then to his guest, "Father, thou wilt abide with us in peace, tonight? My son already brings water for thy feet, and his mother will give thee food."

The old man sank gratefully upon the couch toward which they had led him.

"I will rest and partake of thy food," he said, "that a blessing may be upon this house, and a greater upon mine own head. But then must I resume my journey. I go to Cana in Galilee to assist there in the consecration of a temple. I have been wondrously led to this house. May God's blessing rest upon it!"

The carpenter bent his dark, heavy head; the child, drawing near with basin and water jar, paused a moment to bend his own. Then he came and knelt by the couch.

"I would unloose thy sandals, my father, and wash and anoint thy feet," he said.

"Thy service to the wayworn hath already begun, my son—that I perceive. And thine age? Is it in truth six years since thou wast born?"

The child, kneeling before him, raised his eager, flushed face.

"This is my birthday eve, my father. It is six years to-night since I was born in Bethlehem of Judea." He bent to his task, his curls falling around his face, in every sensitive line of which was written the pride he felt because he, a little boy, was allowed to do graciously for the stranger within his father's house.

Painstakingly he untied the dusty sandal knots, removed the sandals, and placed the tired feet in the deep, water-filled basin. Gently he kneaded the weary, aching muscles with his child's fingers, then dried the feet upon the towel with which he had girded himself, and lastly anointed them with soothing oil. Mean-

[197

while his mother brought nourishing cakes and fresh goat's milk, of which the old man gratefully partook.

The boy, his task finished, carried away his basin, jar, and oil flask, and then, returning, stole to his father, who sat silently apart.

"Was it well done, father?" he whispered. "Thou couldst have better served him, that I knew, but I tried to pattern after thee. Was it well done?"

"Yes, my son, thy father is proud of thee."

The voice of the old man rose through the quiet room.

"My son, I now resume my journey to Cana of Galilee. I would bless thee before I go. Draw near with thy father."

The boy came at once across the stone floor, his father following more slowly. Their guest had arisen and stood facing the door. The child knelt before him, his father and mother behind their son on either side. Then the old man placed his thin, trembling hands on the boy's bent head. His voice, deep with strange and strong emotion, rang through the room.

"As six years past in Jerusalem I held this child in my arms and blessed him, even so now do I bless him in his father's house.

" 'Lord, now lettest Thou Thy servant depart in peace, for mine eyes have again seen Thy salvation,

" 'Which Thou hast prepared before the face of all people.

" 'A light to lighten the Gentiles and the glory of Thy people Israel.' "

And in the stillness which followed, Joseph and the child's mother marvelled much at those things which were spoken.

Thereafter, the old man blessed them also, while the child still knelt, and said to his mother strange words—words heard six years before and, as then—poignant with suffering.

" 'Yea, my daughter, a sword shall pierce through thine own soul also.' "

Then gathering his garment in one hand and taking his staff in the other, he passed over the threshold and into the darkness without.

III

The Story of Jesus' First Birthday Retold

Silently the carpenter withdrew to the corner of the little atrium; silently the child watched his mother who stood, her hands pressed against her heart, and gazed with wide-open, frightened eyes into the darkness whence had passed their guest. She saw there neither the lights of Nazareth nor the moon that silvered the Galilean hills; but before her eyes rose the white pillars of the temple at Jerusalem, the purple altar cloth, the smoke of incense ascending; and in her ears above the voices of the chanting priests, sounded the piteous cries of doves brought for sacrifice. Her son watched her, his own face troubled.

"Mother," he said, his arms around her. "Thou lookest sad. Our guest was very strange. Didst thou understand his words?"

Her arms held him close, drew him closer.

"Didst thou?" he persisted.

"Not fully, dear," she said at last. "Yet they were all a part of his blessing, I doubt not. But come, it draws late. The moon is rising over the hills of Moab, and it is already past thy bedtime."

"But the stories! We need not give them up? Say we need not, mother!"

Her eyes, smiling at his eagerness, lost their look of fear.

"We need not," she told him, "but hasten! Thy treasures are on the stool by the great chest; and the new box I saw thy father place upon thy bed in the eastward room. Run, give him thy thanks, and bid him good-night."

He ran eagerly to where his father sat, still apart and alone, and kissed his dark, bearded face.

"I am going to put them in it now, father," he whispered. "Come and see, and hear the stories. Wilt thou?"

"Later, perhaps, my son, but I have tasks yet to do. Go to thy mother who awaits thee. I am glad the box pleases thee."

The child bounded away, hop-skipping in his eagerness across the rough floor to the room where his mother awaited him. Hastily he prepared for the night, folding with great precision his new coat and placing it at the foot of his bed, changing his woollen tunic for a lighter gown, and washing his dusty little feet in the same basin in which he had bathed the traveler's, though his own were less carefully done. Lastly, he knelt beside his mother, and, with her arm close around him, with his hands folded and his eyes closed, he said his evening prayer—a prayer which, like that of every child, ascended to Heaven an offering, not a petition. Then clambering into her lap, he placed his new box upon his knees, and from the bundle on the bed drew the first of his treasures.

"The olive branch, mother. Tell about that."

She cuddled him close in her arms. "That olive branch," she began, but he interposed hastily.

"Thou forgettest the beginning, mother. 'Long years ago, on the very day that thou wast born—' "

She laughed. Then she began again.

"Long years ago, on the very day that thou wast born—six years ago this very night, dear—thy father and I were traveling toward Jerusalem to pay our tax to the great emperor Augustus. The roads were hard for the winter rains had been heavy, and as at nightfall we reached Bethlehem, I grew tired and ill. Like many others going up to Jerusalem for the same purpose, we stopped at the inn just without the village, and asked shelter for the night, but—"

"There was no room for thee." Again the child interrupted, his eyes dark with pity. "This part always makes me sad, mother—to think there was no room for thee when thou wast ill and weary."

She kissed him. "Nay, dear, do not be sad. The innkeeper was kind, but there were others who had come before us, also weary and very likely ill. He could not ask of them to give us their beds; but he offered us the only shelter left, the stable without the inn. Thy father was loath to accept it, thinking it too poor shelter for me, but it was late and we dared look no farther.

"It was not uncomfortable, dear, nor very cold. Many of the innkeeper's sheep were still upon the hills, so that there was room for the asses and horses of the travelers, and one large, straw-filled manger in which I could rest. And the breath of the kind creatures standing about made the air warmer, so that I did not suffer from the cold."

He was smiling again and listening eagerly. "And there I was born."

"There thou wast born." She spoke softly, her face suffused with joy. "Very, very early in the morning while it was still dark without. Through an opening in the roof, I could see from where I lay the sky, filled with stars. And one star, bigger and brighter than all the rest, seemed to be looking down upon me, and thee in my arms, and thy father standing near."

The child was sitting upright in his excitement, his eyes glowing, his breath coming quickly.

"And didst thou see angels, mother? Tell me truly this time! Were there angels in the sky? Didst thou see them?"

Thoughtfully she studied his face, while he, impatient, awaited her answer.

"Dear," she said at last, "I cannot tell thee truly, for I do not know. Angels are very near to every mother when she first realizes that her baby has been born. But whether the angels were truly in the sky or just as truly in my own heart, I cannot tell. Dost thou wish greatly that there had been angels?"

"I am sure there were, mother," he answered positively. "Remember thou wast tired and ill, and thou couldst not see clearly perhaps. But my father saw them and heard them sing. He told me but today in the workshop. And the shepherds—thou rememberest them, and what they told thee about the angels?"

"Truly, I remember them. I was just about to tell you of them. As I lay looking at the star, there appeared in the open doorway of the stable a light, and the dim figures of shepherds. They seemed half-frightened and shy of approach, but as thy father went forward to greet them, they asked if a child had not been born in that very place. Then he told them of thee, and they crowded around thee and me, bent and bearded men, but kindly. One held his rude lantern above thy face so as to see thee more clearly, and the others knelt and strangely honored thee, a simple babe. And one, the eldest and most bent, placed this olive branch within thy tiny hand."

"And they said?" the child persisted.

She read his thought. "They said that as one of their number watched their flocks upon the hillside, a star, brighter than all other stars, shone in the sky, and angels sang of thy birth in a Bethlehem manger. And that the one watching aroused the others, heavy with sleep, and following the star, they found thee as the angels had sung."

"And thou believest my father and the shepherds, dost thou not, mother?"

"I have always believed thy father, dear. In his great joy over thee, I am sure he saw and heard the angels, and the shepherds of our land have often talked with angels in their lonely watches on the hills."

Thoughtfully he placed the olive branch in his new box; and then from the bundle drew the alabaster boxes of frankincense and myrrh and the little bag filled with the strange coins.

"Now about these, mother, which the strange men from the East brought me."

"That was later," she told him. "Thou wast twelve days old when they came. They were strange men from the countries far to the east of us, with the long beards of patriarchs and singular white robes and hats. Their eyes were dark and piercing and very deep, as though they were wise and learned, and they had read of thy coming in the stars, they said, for they possessed strange knowledge of the heavens—knowledge which our people do not understand."

"And had they also seen the same bright star in their far homes?" he asked.

"They told a wonderful story of how a star had guided them long days and nights across the deserts, as they journeyed on their beautiful horses, while camels bore their goods and food, and dark servants waited upon their needs. There were three of them, but so strangely alike were they in their white robes that I could ill distinguish one from the others. They came and knelt before thee, and from the deep folds of their garments drew these gifts which they had brought from afar to proffer thee. They made strange signs to one another, and spoke words which I did not understand, and their wisdom frightened me somewhat. But they loved thee— I, thy mother, could perceive that—even as the Judean shepherds loved thee."

"And were the camels even larger than those that cross Esdraelon?"

"I could hardly say truly, dear, for I saw but dimly through the stable door as they were kneeling in the courtyard. But they were great creatures, I know, and their trappings were of rich cloths, gold-trimmed and of bright colors."

He sighed—a long, deep sigh. "I wish I could remember it all," he said wistfully. "Thou hast told me so often it seems as though I do remember. I will place these treasures with the olive branch in the box, and now there is left but the flower. It has grown so withered I wonder that it does not break. It will fare better in the new box."

Gently he unwound the wrappings from the tiny, withered remnant of a seeded flower, which he held carefully in the palm of his hand.

"Every time I look at thee I fear thou wilt have crumbled away," he whispered. And then, "Tell me about it, mother."

"Thou wast little more than a year old when it was given thee," she said. "I took thee in my arms one day and went with thee upon the hills. It was a day very like this one, the rains having ceased for a little. Thou wast so joyful at the sight of the new blossoms and so happy in the sunshine that I wandered far with thee over the hills toward the north. And in a little valley there, bright with many-colored flowers, I found a shepherd boy with his flock.

"He was an earnest-faced lad of Joel's age perhaps, roughly clad, but gentle and gracious of manner, and when he saw thee laughing at the flowers, he left his crook upon the ground and came toward thee. And as he came he pulled from among the many blossoms all about, this one which was not a blossom at all, but a seed-ball covered with tiny winged seeds of thistledown. Then he knelt in the soft grass and passed the flower up to thee, and thy little hands were outstretched eagerly as though it were fresh and bright of hue. Then thou pursed thy little lips and blew against the seeds, and they sailed away over the meadow. But thy fingers clung to this, and when I saw thy love for it, I put it away for thee. He was a strange lad, I think," she finished musingly, "else he would have given thee a flower."

The child was silent for a moment. "Perhaps, an angel told him I would like the little seedball," he whispered. "Just as the angel told me that some day Joel would be a cripple no longer. Dost think an angel told him, mother?"

"It is not unlikely," she said. "Angels would tell us much if we would but listen. Dear, place the little seed-ball with the other treasures in thy box, and then I must put thee in thy bed to sleep. Thou art tired and must rest if tomorrow we are to go upon the hills."

"May I not keep my treasure-box by me while I sleep?" he pleaded. "Then I shall know that it is safe. Say that I may, mother."

"Thou mayest," she promised him. "But lay thee down, dear. One song I will sing thee before thou sleepest. Which shall it be?"

He pondered, deciding, as she smoothed the coverlet, and tucked him in securely against the cold night air. Then, as she kissed him,

"Sing the shepherd song of our fathers. That pleases me, I think, the most of all. Perhaps the shepherd boy who gave me the flower sings it when he is alone with his sheep. Dost think so, mother?"

"I am sure he does," she said.

Sitting by him, she held one hand in hers, while the other rested on his precious box, which he had encircled closely with his arm. Then his mother watching sang him to sleep:

" 'Jehovah, the Lord, is my shepherd. I shall want for nothing. In green pastures He maketh me to rest; by still waters He leadeth me. Through His mercy is my soul restored.' "

Almost at once he slept, wearied by happiness. Gently she placed the hand which she held beneath the coverlet; very gently she brushed back a lock of hair, which had fallen across his forehead. Then, bending forward, she watched her little boy asleep. Across

204]

the threshold of the doorway a shadow fell, and Joseph, the carpenter, came to sit beside her. Together they gazed upon him, his hair dark upon the pillow, a smile upon his face, in the circle of his arm his precious box. Together they loved him.

The hours of the night waned; the moon journeyed toward its resting-place in Mediterranean waters; the hills of Moab waited— patient, undistracted, faithful. It was very still. But when the stillness was at its height, when all discordant sounds had ceased, there gleamed and quivered over those hills of Moab a star!

And who shall say that angels did not sing—behind the veil which faithlessness has woven? Perhaps the child's heart, listening, heard them, for the two watching saw him smile, and hold his treasures yet more closely as he slept.

PART II

BETHLEHEM IS FOREVER

THE MYSTIC THORN

ELVA SOPHRONIA SMITH

Adapted from Traditional Sources

Three hawthornes also that groweth in Werall
Do burge and bere grene leaves at Christmas
As fresshe as other in May.

IT WAS Christmas day in the year 63. The autumn colors of red and gold had long since faded from the hills, and the trees which covered the island valley of Glastonbury, the Avalon or Apple-tree isle of the early Britons, were bare and lifeless. The spreading, glass-like waters encircling it round about gleamed faintly in the pale afternoon light of the winter's day. The light fell also on the silver stems of the willows and on the tall flags and bending reeds and osiers which bordered the marsh island. Westward the long ranges of hills running seaward were purple in the distance and their tops were partly hidden by the misty white clouds which rested lightly upon them. To the south rose sharply and abruptly a high, pointed hill, the tor of Glastonbury.

It was nearing the sunset hour when a little band of men in pilgrim garb, approaching from the west and climbing the long, hilly ridge, came within sight of this "isle of rest." Twelve pilgrims there were in all, in dress and appearance very unlike the fair-haired Britons who at that time dwelt in the land. One, he who led the way, was an old man. His hair was white and his long, white beard fell upon his breast, but he was tall and erect and bore no other signs of age. In his hand he carried a stout hawthorn staff.

The men were climbing slowly up the hill, for they were all weary with long traveling. And here at the summit of the ridge they stopped to look out over the wooded hills, the wide-spreading waters and the grassy island with its leafless thickets of oak and alder. Sitting down to rest, they spoke one to another of their long journeying from the far-distant land of Palestine and of their hope that here their pilgrimage might have end.

Those who were with him called their leader Joseph of Arimathea. He it was who had been known among the Jews many years before as a counsellor, "a good man, and a just," and who, when the Saviour was crucified on Calvary, had given his sepulchre to receive the body of the Lord.

From this tomb upon the third day came the risen Saviour but the people, thinking that Joseph had stolen away the body, seized and imprisoned him in a chamber where there was no window. They fastened the door and put a seal upon the lock and placed men before the door to guard it. Then the priests and the Levites contrived to what death they should put him; but when they sent for Joseph to be brought forth he could not be found, though the seal was still upon the lock and the guard before the door.

The disciples of Joseph as they gathered about their fire of an evening often told how, at night, as he prayed, the prison chamber had been filled with a light brighter than that of the sun, and Jesus himself had appeared to him and had led him forth unharmed to his own house in Arimathea.

And sometimes they told how, again imprisoned, he had been fed from the Holy Cup from which the Saviour had drunk at the "last sad supper with his own" and in which Joseph had caught the blood of his Master when he was on the cross, and how he had been blest with such heavenly visions that the years passed and seemed to him as naught.

Now after a certain time he had been released from prison but there were people who still doubted him and so with his friends,

Lazarus and Mary Magdalene and Philip and others, he had been driven away from Jerusalem. The small vessel, without oars, rudder or sail, in which they had been cast adrift on the Mediterranean, had come at last in safety to the coast of Gaul. And for many years since then had Joseph wandered through the land carrying ever with him two precious relics, the Holy Grail and "that same spear wherewith the Roman pierced the side of Christ." Now at last with a chosen band of disciples he had reached the little-known island of the Britons.

Landing from their little boat in the early morn on this unknown coast, they had knelt upon the shore while Joseph "gave blessing to the God of heaven in a lowly chanted prayer." Then, "over the brow of the seaward hill" they had passed, led by an invisible hand and singing as they went. All day through dark forests and over reedy swamps they had made their way and now at nightfall, tired and wayworn, they rested on the ridgy hill which has ever since been known by the name of Wearyall.

During the long day's march they had seen but few of the people of the land and these had held aloof.

Now, suddenly, the silence was broken by loud cries and shouts, and groups of the native Britons, wild and uncouth in appearance, their half-naked bodies stained blue with woad, were seen coming from different directions up the hill. They were armed with spears, hatchets of bronze, and other rude weapons of olden warfare and, as they came rapidly near, their threatening aspect and menacing cries startled the pilgrim band. Rising hastily, as though they would flee, the men looked in terror, one toward another. Joseph alone showed no trace of fear and obedient to a sign from him, they all knelt in prayer upon the hillside.

Then, thrusting his thorny staff into the ground beside him and raising both hands toward heaven, Joseph claimed possession of this new land in the name of his Master, Christ.

> "This staff hath borne me long and well,"
> Then spake that saint divine,
> "Over mountains and over plain,

On quest of the Promise-sign;
For aye let it stand in this western land,
And God do no more to me
If there ring not out from this realm about,
Tibi gloria, Domine."

His voice ceased and the men rose from their knees, looking ex-
pectantly for the heavenly sign, but ready, if need be, to meet with
courage the threatened attack.

But stillness had again settled over the hill. Only a few rods
distant the Britons had stopped and grouped closely together were
gazing in awestruck silence upon the dry and withered staff, which
had so often aided Joseph in his wanderings from the Holy Land.
Following their gaze, Joseph and his companions turned toward
it and even as they did so, behold! A miracle! The staff took root
and grew and, as they watched, they saw it put forth branches and
green leaves, fair buds and milk-white blossoms which filled the
air with their sweet odor.

For a moment, awed and amazed, all stood silent. Wondrously
had Joseph's prayer been answered! This was indeed the heavenly
token which had been foretold! Then with tears of joy all cried
out as with one voice, "Our God is with us! Jesus is with us!"

Marveling much at the strange things they had just seen and
heard, the Britons dropped their weapons and fled in haste from
the hill.

Then did Joseph and his disciples go down across the marsh
into the valley and there they rested undisturbed.

Word of the miracle which had thus been wrought on Wearyall
Hill was brought soon to Arviragus, the heathen king of the time,
and he welcomed gladly the holy men and gave them the beautiful
vale of Avalon whereon to live. There they built "a little lonely
church," with roof of rushes and walls of woven twigs and "wattles
from the marsh," the first Christian church which had ever been
built in Britain.

There they dwelt for many years, serving God, fasting and

praying, and there Joseph taught the half-barbarous Britons, who gathered to listen to him, the faith of Christ.

Time passed and the little, low, wattled church became a great and beautiful abbey. Many pilgrims there were who came to worship at the shrine of St. Joseph; to drink from the holy well which sprang from the foot of Chalice Hill where the Holy Cup lay buried; and to watch the budding of the mystic thorn, which, year after year, when the snows of Christmas covered the hills, put forth its holy blossoms, "a symbol of God's promise, care and love."

Now long, long afterward there came a time then there was war in the land and one day a rough soldier who recked not of his heavenly origin cut down the sacred tree. Only a flat stone now marks the place where it once stood and where Joseph's staff burst into bloom. But there were other trees which had been grown from slips of the miraculous thorn and these, "mindful of the Lord" still keep the sacred birthday and blossom each year on Christmas Day.

THE MAGI IN THE WEST AND
THEIR SEARCH FOR CHRIST

FREDERIC E. DEWHURST

Now IT happened a long time ago, in the year ——, but the exact
year does not matter, because you will not find this story written
in the history of any of the nations of the world. But in one of the
countries of Europe bordering on the Mediterranean Sea was a
lofty mountain, which, to the dwellers in the plains below, seemed
to reach to the very sky. At times its summit was covered with clouds,
so that it could not be seen; at other times it stood out fair and
clear, as though silently asking the people to look up and not down.
The lower slopes of the mountain were covered with olive trees,
with groves of oranges and lemons, and with vineyards, and they
were dotted here and there with the little white cottages of the
peasants who made their living from these groves and vineyards,
the fruit of which they sold in the city not far away.

Along the mountainside wound a foot trail even to the summit,
and nowhere, in all the region, was there a finer view of the Mediterranean than from the summit of this mountain. In the long summer afternoons the peasants and children would climb to the top,
and look on the lovely picture of land and sea. Then they would
eat their simple lunch of bread and dates and olives, quenching

their thirst from the spring on the mountainside, which they called "Dew-of-heaven," so clear and fresh and sparkling was it; and when the sun began to touch the western sky with his pencils of gold and carmine and purple, they hastened down, that they might reach their cottages before the night shut in.

On the day when this story begins a man was standing on the summit of the mountain looking across the sea in the direction where you will find Tyre and Joppa on the map. He was, very plainly, not one of the peasants who lived on the mountainside. He looked about sixty years of age; he was tall and erect, though he carried a staff in his hand. His hair and beard were long and flowing, and almost gray, but his eyes were clear and penetrating, and he was looking across the sea as though he expected someone to appear.

And while he stood there gazing seaward, there appeared a second man on the summit, helping himself up with his staff, and panting with the effort of the long climb. From his dress and manner it was plain that this man, too, was not one of the peasants, for, like the first comer, he seemed to belong to another age and clime. The two men glanced at each other and gave such greeting as strangers might who should meet in so solitary a spot as a mountain summit. Then both lapsed into silence and looked across the sea.

Presently the last comer seemed to wake from his reverie; he walked over to the place where the other was sitting, still gazing off toward Joppa, and touched him on the shoulder.

"A thousand pardons, my friend," he said, "but my mind is haunted with some far-off recollection, as though in some other land and some far-off time I had seen thy face. Wilt thou have the kindness to tell me thy name?"

Without lifting his eyes from the sea, and in a tone which seemed regretful and sad, the stranger replied: "My name is Gaspard."

"Gaspard! Indeed, then I have seen thee! Look at me, my friend; dost thou not remember me? My name is Melchior. Dost thou not recall that time, how long ago I know not, when thou and I and Balthazar followed a star which led us to a little Jewish hamlet, thou bearing gold and I frankincense, and Balthazar myrrh? Dost thou not remember how, on the long journey thither, we talked about the young Prince, whom we expected to find in a royal palace, and how at last when we reached the village, following the star, we were led not to a palace, but to a little inn, and not even to a room within the inn, but to the stable-yard, where we found a sweet-faced peasant woman bending over a babe cradled in a manger; and standing near, a sturdy peasant, proud and happy, whose name was Joseph? Dost thou not remember, too, that when we had recovered from our surprise, we left our gifts and greetings, and went our way as men who had been dreaming? Gaspard, dost thou not remember?"

And Gaspard, looking now intently in the other's face, replied: "Yes, Melchior, I remember thee, and I remember the journey of which thou hast spoken better than I remember aught else. Neither have I forgotten the surprise and disappointment with which we came to the place whither the star led us, nor how, after leaving our gifts, we went away as in a dream; and, Melchior, I have been dreaming ever since. Even here hast thou found me in a dream of perplexity. I am still Gaspard, the wandering magician; for how many years I know not, I have wandered up and down these lands of Europe. I have crossed the seas; in every place I have sought to find the kingdom over which we were told this young prince was one day to reign. Dost thou not remember that we were told his kingdom was to last forever, that he would reign in it himself forever and would never die? Alas! I have lost the old power of the magician's art. I can summon no star to guide me to the place where I shall find this kingdom and its king."

"Truly, Gaspard," answered Melchior, "the story of your wanderings is but the repetition of my own; and even now was I drawn to this mountain summit on the self-same errand that brought you here—to see if I could not discover in the direction of yonder land, where Bethlehem was, some star which might prove to be His star, and which might guide me in the new quest. If only our old companion, Balthazar, were with us now, he might give us the clew

216]

to our search, for not only was he more skillful in the magician's art, but he was braver and more courageous, and withal more serene in spirit."

Now, even while Melchior was speaking, a voice was heard a little way down the mountain. Gaspard and Melchior stopped to listen. The voice was singing, and the words of the song floated up to them distinctly:

If the sun has hid its light,
If the day has turned to night,
If the heavens are not benign,
If the stars refuse to shine—
   Heart of man lose not thy hope;
   Door, there's none that shall not ope;
   Path, there's none that shall not clear;
   Heart of man! why shouldst thou fear!

If for years should be thy quest,
If for years thou hast no rest,
If thou circlest earth and sea,
If thou worn and weary be—
   Heart of man, lose not thy hope;
   Door, there's none that shall not ope;
   Path, there's none that shall not clear;
   Heart of man! why shouldst thou fear!

"That," exclaimed Gaspard and Melchior together, "is the voice of Balthazar," and they hastened to meet him, for he was now almost at the summit, and the refrain of his song was still upon his lips. At that moment Balthazar sprang up from the sloping path into full view of the two men, and, giving each a hand, exclaimed: "Gaspard, Melchior, beloved companions, I have found you at last. The peasants below were not mistaken. From their description, I was certain I should find you here. And you, too, have been searching these long years for the kingdom of the Christ! And, like me,

[217

you have met with disappointment; but, comrades, be not of faint
heart:

> Door, there's none that shall not ope;
> Path, there's none that shall not clear.

Let us hasten down the mountain, for see! the sky is already growing gold and crimson beyond the pillars of Hercules. Let us seek
the wayfarers' lodging with the hospitable peasants in the valley,
and tomorrow let us begin our search for the Christ anew. We have
wandered alone; let us invoke now the stars to guide us together."

That night, therefore, the three strangers lodged with the simple
peasant people in the valley, partaking with thankfulness of the
coarse bread, the dates and the red wine—the common fare of their
daily life. Nor did they fail to notice a motto inscribed above the
fireplace in rude Greek letters:

ΤΗΣ ΦΙΛΟΞΕΝΙΑΣ ΜΗ
ΕΠΙΛΑΝΘΑΝΕΣΘΕ

On the morrow they were ready to begin their search together
for the Christ, and they hoped not to wander far before they
should find at least the outskirts of His kingdom. But whither
should they go? In what direction should they first turn their
steps?

While they were thus wondering and debating, Balthazar suddenly exclaimed: "I see the star!" And behold, a little way before
them, and at no great distance above their heads, they discerned in
the gray of the early morning a star of pale, opal light, which
seemed to move forward as the men moved toward it.

"We must follow the star!" Balthazar said, in a whisper. Silently
and breathlessly his companions followed on.

Now, so intently did the three men keep their eyes fixed upon
the star, and so eagerly did they follow in the direction where it
seemed to lead, that it was only after a considerable time they discovered that they had become separated from each other, and that
their paths were getting farther and farther apart. Yet, there before

each of them was the star, shining with its soft, opalescent light, and still ringing in their ears were the words of Balthazar, "We must follow the star."

So each followed the star, each by himself alone. Gaspard's path wound along near the shore of the gulfs and bays of the Mediterranean, until at last the star turned southward and drew him nearer and nearer to a great city, and finally stood still over the dome of a vast cathedral. "It must be," thought Gaspard, "that I have come to the end of my search. This must be the capital and palace of the eternal king."

The square in front of the cathedral was thronged with people; multitudes were pouring in through the great portals. Gaspard joined the throngs, and at last found himself under the mighty dome, which seemed to him as far away as the sky itself. Everything in this wonderful place appealed to his imagination. There were great rows of massive columns, symbol of a strength eternal, and they seemed like wide-open arms holding out a welcome to the human race. There were statues and paintings by great masters in art. The light of the sun poured in through many-colored windows, on which were blazoned the deeds of heroes and saints. Strains of music from the great organ in the distance floated out upon the air. Touched and thrilled by all he saw, Gaspard exclaimed to himself: "The place on which I stand is holy ground."

Soon, however, he perceived that the throngs of people were not lingering, like himself, in awe and wonder over the great columns and the dome, and the statues, and the paintings, and the windows. Their eyes were fixed intently upon something that was going on in the far end of the cathedral. An altar was there, and priests in white robes passing up and down before it, and tall tapers burning around it. Near the altar was the image of a man hanging from a cross; his hands and feet were pierced with nails, and a cruel wound was in his side. The people were gazing at this altar, and at the image, and at what the white-robed priests were doing. The strains of solemn music from the organ blended with the voices of priests chanting the service. Clouds of incense rose from censers, swung with solemn motion by the altar boys, and the fragrance of

[219

the incense was wafted down the long aisles. At last, the tinkling of a bell. The organ became silent for an instant, as though it felt within its heart the awful solemnity of the moment; and then it burst forth into new rapture, and the people began pouring out through the great doors.

Gaspard went forth with the throng into the cathedral square. "And this," he said, "is the end of my search. I have found the Christ. His kingdom is in the imagination of a man. How beautiful, how wonderful, how strange it was! *'Dominus vobiscum,'* did not the priests say? Here, then, at last I have found the city of the great King."

But as he lingered, behold! the star which had stood over the dome of the cathedral was now before him, as at first, and seemed to waver and tremble, as if beckoning him on. So, although his feet seemed bound to the spot, and his heart was still throbbing with the deep feelings the cathedral service had created in him, remembering the words of Balthazar, "we must follow the star," he slowly and reluctantly walked on.

In the meantime Melchior also had followed faithfully the path along which the star seemed to lead. Through forests in which he almost lost his way, across rivers difficult and dangerous to ford —still he followed on. At length Melchior's star seemed to tarry over the spire of a Gothic church, into which the people were going in throngs. Waiting a moment, to be sure that the star was actually standing still, Melchior went in with the rest. In this place was no altar, such as Gaspard saw; no image on the cross; no white-robed priests; no swinging censers. But, as Melchior entered he heard strains from the organ, and a chorus of voices was singing an anthem beginning with the words, *"Te Deum laudamus."* And when the anthem came to a close, a man clothed in a black robe, such as scholars were wont to wear, rose in his place upon a platform elevated above the people, and began to speak to them about the kingdom of the Christ. Melchior listened in eager expectancy. "The kingdom of the Christ," the preacher said, "is the kingdom of the truth, and the truth is to be continued and kept alive by the strength and constancy of man's belief. Those things which have been handed down by holy men and sacred oracles since Christ was here upon the earth, are the truths by which we live. How can Christ live, except He live in our beliefs? Why did the Father of all entrust us with our reasons, unless it were that we should make them the instruments of our faith and our salvation? Let us therefore stand in our places, while we recite together the articles of our holy faith."

These and many such words did the scholar-preacher declare. And as he sat there with the people, Melchior felt the weight of the solemn and earnest words, and he said: "So at last have I come to the end of my search. The kingdom of Christ is in the mind of man. His kingdom is the kingdom of the truth."

Then he followed the throngs as they went forth from the church; but the star which had tarried over the lofty spire was now before him, and the opal light wavered and trembled, as if beckoning him on; and the words of the preacher, "we must believe," seemed to blend with the words of Balthazar, "we must follow the star." So, reluctantly and slowly, he followed on.

But Balthazar—whither went he, following the star? Over many a rugged way, through many a tangled thicket, through valleys and over hills. His star tarried over no cathedrals; it lingered over no Gothic spires. It seemed capricious and restless and tireless. At times it seemed intent on coming to a pause over the head of some human being, but perhaps it was because these human beings themselves were so restless and so busy that the star could not accomplish its intent. For Balthazar saw these men and women hurrying hither and thither on errands of mercy, or deeds of justice; he saw them ferreting out great wrongs, laying heavy blows on the backs of men who oppressed and defrauded their fellow men.

At length Balthazar seemed to understand the movements of the star, and, drawing nearer, he would seem to hear these men repeating cheering and encouraging words to one another. "Pure religion and undefiled," he heard one exclaiming, "is to visit the fatherless and widows in their affliction, and to keep himself unspotted from the world." And another echoed: "Inasmuch as we do it to the least of these, we do it unto Christ."

"Ah!" thought Balthazar as he listened, "I see the meaning of it now; I am coming to the end of my search. The kingdom of Christ—I have found it. It is in the deeds of men; it is in the conscience and the serving will. Devotion to right, this is the law of the kingdom of Christ."

Then Balthazar turned to go in search of his comrades again; but behold! the opal star was trembling, as if beckoning him on. So, still doubting if he had reached the end of his search, he followed the star.

Thus Gaspard, Melchior and Balthazar, each following the star, at last approached each other. The star of each seemed to melt and blend into the star of the others, and the opal light stood at last in the center of the group. Gaspard exclaimed: "I have found that which we all were seeking. The kingdom of Christ is in the imagination; Christ lives in what man feels."

"Nay," said Melchior, "I have followed the star, and I have found what we sought. The kingdom of Christ is in the reason of man. Christ lives in what man believes."

"But," cried Balthazar, "my star has led me to a different end. The kingdom of Christ is in the will of man. Christ lives in what man does."

"The truth," once more exclaimed Melchior, "is the law of the kingdom."

"Not truth," declared Balthazar, "but justice, righteouness, goodness and purity—these are its laws and its marks."

"Nay, comrades beloved, hearken to me," answered Gaspard; "it is the miracle of the divine presence. It is God among men, realized in the holy mass. I beheld it all in yonder cathderal."

But lo! once more the star began to tremble and to change its place.

"Let us follow the star!" Balthazar whispered. "We will follow it," echoed the other two.

222]

Then the star led them on, and they followed together until they came at length to the doorway of a little cottage; and within the cottage they saw a woman bending over a cradle, and in the cradle a little child lay sleeping. She was a peasant woman; her clothing was not rich; the furnishing of the cottage was humble and scanty. The cradle itself was rude, as if put together by hands unskillful in tasks like that. But when the mother looked at her babe a sweet smile played about her lips, and a light was in her eyes. Then all suddenly the three men remembered another scene long before, when they were bearers of gold and frankincense and myrrh to another babe.

And while they stood and wondered by the door, there came a strong and sturdy peasant, broad-shouldered, roughly clad, his face browned in the sun, his hands hardened with toil. He came and stood beside the woman, and they bent together over the cradle of the sleeping child, and the man drew the woman tenderly toward him and kissed her brow.

And still the three men lingered; for behold! the star stood still above the child, and they dared not speak. But the heart of Gaspard was saying in silence, "There is something greater than the repeated miracle of the mass."

And Melchior was thinking, "There is something mightier even than the mind; something superior to naked truth."

And Balthazar was confessing to himself that he had found something more potent even than the righteous deed. For here they all beheld how life was made sweet and blessed and holy by the power of love; and by love for a little child, in whom was all weakness and helplessness, whose only voice was a cry, but who was all strong and mighty with the power of God, because he could transform toughness into tenderness, and selfishness into loving care, and poverty itself into gifts of gold and fragrant myrrh.

"Truly, my comrades," Balthazar said, "love is the greatest of all."

"And now I understand," said Gaspard, "how the weak things of the world can confound the mighty."

"And I," added Melchior, "see what it means for God to come to earth in the form of a little child."

And so they turned away, and the radiance of the star was round about them, and they were saying to each other: "Our search at last is ended."

THE THREE WISE MEN OF TOTENLEBEN

ALEXANDER LERNET-HOLENIA

Translated by Judith Bernays Heller

IN THE month of November of the year 1647, the commander-in-chief of the French forces during the Thirty Years War, Marshal Turenne, set out on a long journey on horseback. He wished to inspect, in person, certain advance positions of his army, at that time occupying the Palatinate. On that occasion, his horsemen picked up two young people who were traveling through the country, poorly clad and on foot. One was a young man, the other a blonde young woman; both looked miserable. The woman was pregnant, perhaps already in her seventh or eighth month. Questioned, they replied they were husband and wife, who had been forced to leave the place where they had hitherto been living with the wife's parents, where the husband had plied his trade, because everything had been put to the torch by the soldiers. They were now on their way to the husband's home—a village called Totenleben on the lower Main River, where they hoped to find living quarters and perhaps some means of livelihood as well, for they possessed nothing but the clothes on their backs, and their hopes for the child about to be born.

Marshal Turenne, whose mind had been otherwise occupied during this recital, took in only a few snatches of this cross-examination, conducted as it was in German. Nevertheless he noted the odd name of the village which was the goal of the two young people. He dismissed them, and then reached a strange decision.

One night of this same extraordinarily severe winter, he suddenly appeared, accompanied by a troop of horsemen, in the region of the lower Main.

Both he and his men were armed to the teeth and wrapped in warm coats and furs. The moon glistened on their helmets. All the land around was devastated. Preceding the troop by some hundred paces, two horsemen with rifles in their hands stopped now and again in front of a clump of snow-covered bushes or at the ruins of a burned farm and cried out: "Who goes there?" But there was no one to answer. The whole region lay still as in death, only a few savage dogs fled across the snowy fields, continuing their howling from the distance. As they passed by a place of execution, the remains of a corpse dangled from the gallows. As the cavalcade pressed steadily forward, silver hoarfrost spun its web in the icy ruts.

The riders stopped at the edge of a wood. Turenne dismounted from his steed and two henchmen apparently according to orders previously given, approached him and removed his fur coat and hat. The moonlight gleamed on his cuirass and on the gold chain he wore around his neck.

Meanwhile, several of his officers had gotten off their horses and approached him while the serving men pulled a very strange garment over his armor. It was a white robe, bespangled with golden stars. They covered his face with a black veil. The whole was the costume for the eve of Twelfth Night, such as waits or carol singers wear.

And now the servants took the pistols from his saddlebag, and placed them in his hands.

"I am going now," he said to his officers. "Do you, my lords, wait for me here. If I have not returned by three o'clock in the morning, then have the village searched for me."

"Yes, your excellency," was the officers' reply. The Marshal departed alone, trudging over the field of snow.

He had walked several hundred paces when the silhouette of a village suddenly appeared before him. At its northern boundary a light was shining. Toward this he made his way. The beam came from a peculiar lantern made out of oiled paper in the shape of a star, and attached to a pole some eight feet high.

Two men, one of whom carried the pole, stood by the light. They, too, wore the costume of waits, though the veils they wore were white.

Turenne raised his pistols and stepped up to them as he gave his own name. The two answered, giving their names: "Wrangel," and "Melander." They were, respectively, the commander-in-chief of the Swedes, newly appointed after Torstenson's retirement, and the Supreme Chief of the Imperial Armies, Count Melander of Holzapfel.

All three of them now raised their veils and looked into one another's eyes, then let the veils fall once more over their faces. Turenne hid his pistols under the silk sash that he wore under his robe, and said: "I have asked you gentlemen to come here in this disguise so that we may be able to discuss the matters that concern us, undisturbed and in secret. This is the eve of Twelfth Night and we shall be taken for waits. We would do best to proceed to the village now, to find quarters where we can begin our deliberations."

"There is no longer any village," said Melander. "It has been burned to the ground. Your own troops, Count, may have set fire to it."

"It may have been done by your troops, Count," replied Turenne.

"Be that as it may," said Wrangel, "we ought to see to it that we find some shelter somewhere. Surely we do not want to stand about here in the cold."

Accordingly they began to move on with their star. Along the village street there were only heaps of rubble where once there had been houses. But near the burned-out church they managed to find a house passably preserved, with its windows boarded up. A faint light shone from between the boards.

They went up to the door and knocked. They had to do this

repeatedly before a voice from within inquired what they wanted.

"Open the door," they called, whereupon the door, which no longer had any hinges, was pulled back a bit with a creak. A man stuck his head out.

"What's your business?" he asked.

"We are waits," said Melander. "Let us in."

"Waits?" the man asked. "So early?"

"Yes," said Melander. Let us in."

And with these words, he crossed the threshold, followed by the two others, after they had put aside the pole with the lantern.

"But look here," said the man, after closing the door behind them, "today is only Christmas Eve."

"No, indeed," said Wrangel, "it's Twelfth Night. Do you people here still go by the old calendar? We've already got a new one."

"What sort of a new one?" the man asked.

"The pope has changed the calendar," said Melander. "It was already fourteen days behind, and no longer agreed with the position of the stars. Don't you know that? Didn't your priest tell you that?"

"Our priest has been dead for a long time," said the man. "The Swedes killed him; the village is in ruins; the whole countryside is desolate. How should we know whether the pope has changed the calendar or not? We are celebrating Christmas Eve today, if you can still call it celebrating."

"Well," said Wrangel, "never mind. We would like to stay here for a while. Bring us something to eat and a couple of glasses of wine. We'll pay you in good honest coin."

"I used to be the innkeeper here," said the man, "and my business prospered. But now I have scarcely bread enough for my own family, and if we are thirsty, we have to drink melted snow, for our wells are all stopped up. Sit down, for a seat is all I have to offer. What manner of men are you to believe that you can get alms by singing as waits? Where do you come from? Here, in this village, we are the only ones left alive; and there is not a grain of wheat or a single beast left in the whole region. Everything has been destroyed by the war. They say that in the Henneberg district

228]

people have even eaten the corpses of the dead. How much longer will this war go on?"

The three commanders shrugged their shoulders and looked about them. All they saw was a hearth on which a fire cast its flickering light, and a table with a few benches around it. Smoke filled the room. The innkeeper's wife and a half-grown boy—both of them alarmingly emaciated—were watching the strangers. In addition, there were two other people in the room—a young man and his young, blonde wife. Turenne recognized them as the same two whom he had encountered on his reconnaissance trip.

"Who are they?" he asked in faulty German.

"They are poor people," said the innkeeper, "who came to this place but who could find no shelter anywhere. The man was originally from here; he moved away and got married. But he had to come back, and now I've given them a lodging in the stable. The wife is expecting a child."

"You don't say!" said Turenne. The three strangers sat down at the table.

In the meantime, the others busied themselves near the hearth setting up a Christmas crèche of moss and small wooden figures. The innkeeper still had the figures, since the marauding soldiers had not thought them worth taking. They were brightly colored and represented the Holy Family, the angels, the adoring Magi, the shepherds, the ox and the ass.

For a while the three generals looked on; then they began their talk. They spoke in French.

"The peace talks that started at Muenster last year," said Turenne, "are not being conducted in the interest of the armies. If peace were really to come, there would be no need to have armed forces. But the soldier has grown accustomed to making his living by soldiering, and we, his leaders, have the responsibility for his livelihood. And to speak frankly, war has become a trade like any other. I do not know what you gentlemen may think about this, but I, for my part, will leave nothing undone to prevent the war from ending in such a way as to cause us and our men to lose our predominant role, and run the risk of being driven away at a moment's notice. To discuss together what measures should be taken against the conclusion of an overhasty peace is the purpose of my invitation. For even though we are enemies, we are all in the same boat; however you look at it, what's good for one is good for all three of us."

When those who were setting up the crèche heard the talk in a foreign language, they looked over at the three in surprise. For a time the innkeeper listened anxiously, then he approached the table. "Who are you?" he asked. "You are no ordinary waits. You are foreigners and perhaps soldiers as well. What is your business here? Haven't you convinced yourself by this time that this country, this village, this house are in ruins and that there's nothing more for you to carry off? What do you want from us? Are you freebooters or spies? Have you been sent by those who want to take our very lives? That is the only thing you can still take from us."

"Be still," said Melander, "we are the Three Wise Men, and that's all. Don't disturb us, we have to discuss something here." And he threw him a golden coin.

The innkeeper looked at the shining gold piece, for he had not seen its like for many a long year. He took it quickly and tested it with his fingers. At the same time, his bearing changed completely. He wanted to look into the faces of the three, yet his glance could not penetrate their veils. Only now did he notice the boots and spurs visible below their robes, and the metal ends of their leather sword sheaths.

"Your pardon, My Lords!" he said, bowing obsequiously, "I would not for the world—I did not know—"

"Very well, very well," said Melander, "leave us alone."

"May we at least," said the innkeeper, "sing the Christmas song for the gentlemen? It will not disturb you?"

"Sing it, for all I care," said Melander, "but do it quietly. Don't make a hullaballoo."

Retreating backwards and continuing to bow very low, the innkeeper withdrew. He whispered to his people, showing them the gold piece. The others looked over at the three, then the innkeeper's wife advanced and kissed Melander's hand, to thank him.

"Never mind, never mind," said Melander, and took no notice whatever of her. Meanwhile the talk in French went on. After some time, those around the crèche began to sing the Christmas song. They sang it softly in moving, tender tones.

Toward the end of the song, the young wife stopped singing; she tottered, and clung to her husband. Her pains had begun.

Had it not been for the strangers, the innkeeper would have allowed her to remain in the room and have her baby there. But in the presence of the others he did not dare to do this. The woman was led into the stable where she lay on a pile of moss and dead leaves.

The generals had not noticed when the song was interrupted nor when the woman was led out the room. They were in the habit of disregarding the others as so much chaff. They went on with their talk; the French sentences were interrupted by the names *Torstenson, Jan of Werth, Max Emanuel.* For some unknown reason, suddenly the generals appeared to be at odds now, and their voices rose in excitement. It was Melander who pronounced himself most emphatically as against continuation of the war. He said that surely the country was sufficiently desolate, it was plain to see how poverty-stricken the people had become here as well as elsewhere; there was undoubtedly some truth in the innkeeper's story of cannibalism. For some time reports had been coming in that after certain battles people had appeared at night on the battlefields to dismember the dead bodies and roast and consume them.

And so the three went on quarreling until a cry and then another was heard coming from the stable. They looked up.

"What's the matter?" asked Wrangel. But now all was quiet. "Wherever are those fellows?" he asked. He rose from the table, went to the door leading to the stable, and beat on it with the butt of his pistol.

Some little time passed before the innkeeper appeared.

"Who screamed out there?" asked Wrangel. "What is going on out there?"

"Oh, Sir!" said the innkeeper. "Oh, Sir!" and a very strange expression came over his face.

[231

"What is it?" Wrangel cried. "What's the matter?"

"Just imagine, Sir," said the innkeeper, "while you were sitting there, something happened. It's been such a long time since anything like that has happened here. There were always strange soldiers who murdered, struck down and burned and then there were always fewer and fewer people here. But now another soul has been added, once more. The young wife gave birth to a child, a boy. Perhaps, after all, peace will come soon. Don't you want to come and look at the child, gentlemen?"

The three looked at one another. At first they perhaps intended asking the innkeeper if he had lost his mind—bothering them like this—and telling him to go to the devil. But then perhaps one or the other of them recalled the time when a child was born in his own family and what rejoicing there had been. Or perhaps they thought of the day when they themselves had been children. And Turenne may have been thinking for a moment of the woman's blonde hair.

For a long time they had not heard anyone speak in tones such as the innkeeper used. The child was the child of strangers, it was no concern of his, and yet he was as moved as if it had indeed been his own. For here, in this destroyed countryside, resembling an icy waste covered with the corpses of the dead, a child had begun to live—breathing a breath of spring. In the midst of the triumph of death, which was the daily business of the generals, a child had been born, and it seemed as if it had been born also unto them.

The first to step through the threshold of the stable door was Melander. He was followed by Wrangel, and then Turenne. There lay the woman on her bed of straw, her face was white as snow, in the light of the pine torch her hair shone like spun gold. The others knelt around her as they wrapped the baby in a few odds and ends of old rags and laid the child in her arms.

The generals stood there in silence and gazed upon the mother and child for a long time. Then Turenne removed the golden chain which he wore under his Twelfth Night robe, and placed it near the child. Melander pulled off his glove and took a ruby ring

232]

from his finger, and Wrangel laid a pouch full of money down on the bed of straw.

To those who received the gifts it seemed as if a miracle had happened. The young man wanted to express his faltering thanks, but was not able to utter a single word. For the generals suddenly declined such thanks almost disdainfully. Altogether they appeared to be somewhat embarrassed by what they had just done. They found an excuse for themselves in looking upon it as a mere whim, such as highborn gentlemen sometimes indulge in. They soon departed, leaving behind them their strange lantern, and ordered the innkeeper, who was chattering and laughing and who continued to wipe his eyes, to stay behind when he wanted to accompany them.

At the outskirts of the village, they saluted one another curtly, and each one went on his way, their talk unfinished.

But in their hearts was peace.

THE CARPENTER'S CHRISTMAS

PETER K. ROSEGGER

Translated by Eric Posselt

At last it was over, this vigorous sweeping and scrubbing and chasing of dirt, this week-long turmoil during which nothing, not a piece of furniture, not a single wall decoration, remained in its place, until every piece of wood had been cleaned, every stone whitewashed, every bit of metal polished. Now the house shone in purest cleanliness.

The calm after a storm has a solemn effect in any case, but particularly when the Christ child is about to arrive. Somewhere in the house stands the cradle in which the God child sleeps. Those who wear shoes take them off; and those in their stocking feet must walk on tiptoe, for—He sleeps.

The goodwife bustled around in her rooms purposefully; she had to see that everything was right without marking the floor; check all the chests and closets and windows without touching anything, so that everything would retain its pristine beauty. The wind rattled the windowpanes, blowing snow into every nook and cranny, and the darkness of the skies almost turned the room into night. In the living room, on a table covered with white linen, were a crucifix, a burning blessed candle, and a crock holding a branch cut from the cherry tree three weeks ago on St. Barbara's Day, which was to bloom that night. Its buds glistened and swelled and would burst into flower any moment.

The goodwife ran to the door, opened it softly, raised her forefinger and hissed, "Pssst!" into the kitchen, where the servant girl wasn't quiet enough with the dishes. "Pssst! The Christ child is asleep!"

The woman was in a deeply pious mood. Her graying hair was wound around her head in two braids; she had donned her red kerchief and her silk apron. With a rosary in her folded hands she sat in the armchair next to the table and could think of nothing except: Christmas Eve! The Christ child!

Suddenly there was a noise in the corner. Her husband, the carpenter, who was lying on the bench against the wall, turned around and bumped his elbow so hard against the back rest of the chair that it crashed to the floor.

"Pssst!" she hissed, getting up. "Man alive, but what a restless person you are!"

"I? Restless?" He brushed his hand over his face. "Can't a person sleep any more? Can't you leave me alone?"

"If you don't want to pray, you should at least be quiet, man. And you shouldn't sleep, either!"

"But, old lady, when a man sleeps he makes the least noise."

"So you think! That's when you make the most noise, when you sleep! If you're not upsetting a chair beating about with your arms you're poking a hole in the wall. Anyone would think there were at least two sawmills and a threshing machine in here."

"Yea, the sawmills and that threshing machine ought to be turned off on Christmas Eve," he answered calmly, sitting up.

"Oh, don't talk nonsense, please! Here, find yourself a nice Christmas prayer!" She reached for the prayer book on the shelf, wiped the old, worn binding with her apron—yes, it was already dusty again!—and laid it on the table.

"What's the matter with you?" he asked tranquilly. "When they ring the bell, I'll pray all right. Just now I want to sleep some more."

"Stop arguing!" she cried impatiently, kicking at a footstool below the table.

He looked at her and grinned. "Woman," he said. "Not even old age helps you—you simply won't change!"

"You're the one to talk!" she answered. "A man ought to remember at least on a day like this that he has holy water on him. Haven't you any piety in you at all? Don't you know that tomorrow is Christmas?"

"Am I doing anything wrong?"

"Nor are you doing anything right, either. Go on, find that Christmas prayer!"

"I've never let anyone order me to be pious. If it doesn't come by itself . . ."

"Come by itself? To you? Mary Joseph, that'd be a long wait! All week long you are so unchristian that it's a scandal. Holidays are made for piety!"

"Oh, phhht!" the carpenter replied crossly. "If a man works hard all week and does his duty in God's name and does nobody any wrong, he's supposed to be extra-pious on Sundays, eh? Why, woman, how is a man to do that?"

"Pray, I said, and keep quiet! Holy Christ will be awakened soon enough when He comes to judge the quick and the dead. . . . Jesus Mary, what's that?!"

For a moment it was quite dark in the room, as if a black cloth had been drawn across the window; then, a heavy thud, and the wild whirling of the snow outside. The carpenter went to the window and looked out. The storm had broken off a heavy limb from the old fir tree standing in front of the house.

"Oh God, oh God, what a day!" the woman whined, wringing her hands. "That's a bad sign for a year without peace!"

"If the devil doesn't fetch you, it'll be just that," the carpenter growled amiably.

"Today I refuse to argue with you!" she answered with cold superiority. "But just you wait until the day is over. Then you'll see whom the devil will fetch!"

She took the little vessel of holy water from the doorjamb and sprinkled everything in the room, especially her husband. He stared at her grumpily and refused to stir.

"He doesn't even make the sign of the cross when he is sprinkled with holy water!"

She rushed to the kitchen, returned with a basin of glowing embers, sprinkled incense over it and carried it around, according to the old Christmas custom, close to the table, to the bed and, finally, to her husband, whose nostrils the incense attacked so vehemently that he began to curse and opened a window.

He opened the window just in time. From the road, over the whistling of the wind, came excited voices. The wind had done quite a bit of damage in the village. "Ditch-Cenzi's" roof had been torn off so that you could look from above it into the crawling children's warren.

"That's because they don't pray, those people," the carpenter's wife sneered. "Mary Joseph, that's how it is in this world. The entire Christmas Eve spoiled! And instead of saying his Christmas prayers now, he runs away! Who, I ask you, is to protect us, if not our dear Lord in heaven?"

"Ditch-Cenzi" was a widow with three small children, the oldest of which was sick in bed with scarlet fever. She wasn't much liked in the village and it was said that in the fall she sometimes harvested potatoes where she hadn't planted any. Now the roof of her hut was torn down, with the shingles lying in the road. Cenzi stumbled around with her children in the darkness and succeeded, just barely succeeded, in placing them with neighbors. Nobody wanted to harbor the child sick with scarlet fever until the teacher offered to take it in; but the teacher was ruled out because he might carry the infection into the school. The childless wife of the carpenter, too, was approached, but she didn't want her Christmas Eve spoiled by a sick child. Finally, the village priest remembered that He who was expected that very night had said that whoever takes in a child, takes in Him—even though he wasn't quite certain how the quotation really ran. And so, with kindness and the help of the quotation, he arranged with his housekeeper for the sick child to stay at the vicarage until the roof of the old home could be fixed at least temporarily.

The carpenter had gone outside. His voice was louder than the wind as he called together his neighbors and his journeymen. They came with ladders, tools and boards. There was a hammering and sawing in the village that lasted all night under the light of the improvised torches—very much to the horror of Mrs. Carpenter, who esteemed the holy calm and heavenly peace of this night above all else.

"How can the cherry branch bloom in all this turmoil? And how is the Christ child to rest?"

When the bells in the church tower began to chime for Midnight Mass the men still shouted and hammered on Ditch-Cenzi's roof. And while the parish sang in the church, the pounding and the clanking of nails and tools still vied so with the noise of the storm that the women, thus cheated out of their Christmas humor, were positively horrified. At last, when all the bells tolled in unison and the organ jubilated at the high point of the Midnight Mass, the men who were helping to build the roof jumped down and strolled into the church, too; and the carpenter found himself alone with two of his journeymen on the skeleton of the roof. The storm seemed to blow harder now, to tear down again what the hands of men had just put up.

The carpenter had expected to have the roof ready before morning. When he saw that most of the others had deserted him and that even the boys who had held the torches had thrown them in the snow and run to church, he began to curse mightily.

"To —— with these —— hypocrites! I like that! Here they practically chew off the toes of our good Lord, and in the meantime these poor wretches can go and die with the cold. Who cares? They squat around the corners of the church until they rot. He up there in heaven can really be proud of this brood! Hear them sing, 'Praise God in the highest!' They kiss the waxen image of the Christ child and cuddle it like a doll—and let these poor little human creatures—croak, I almost said, God forgive me my sins!"

When Midnight Mass was over and the people came out of the

church, the carpenter was still cursing and kicking up on his roof. One man said to the other, "Poor fellow, he'll go completely mad if we don't help him; and maybe we are a little to blame for his swearing at that! Come on, let's pitch in. We can have that roof up in less than an hour."

Then another planted himself firmly in front of the speaker and said: "Do you really think, neighbor, that I would be so unchristian as to work on Holy Christmas Morn?" But his manner was so overbearing that the effect was far from what he intended.

"Did you hear that one?" someone asked. "In the face of such hypocrisy, I prefer the carpenter and all his cussing; and I for one am going to help him finish that roof!"

Others joined him. The torches were lit again and the sawing and hammering began once more with such renewed vigor that the carpenter's wife, in desperation, covered both her ears with her hands.

"You can't sleep and you can't pray with all this noise going on. And that—that heathen husband of mine prefers this beggar woman to our Jesus Child, so that he won't even let Him rest in His cradle. . . . God forgive him!"

On Christmas Day when the sun rose, the icy wind still rushed over the rooftops, and over many a gable snow clouds still danced. But the roof of the Ditch-Cenzi house was fixed and nailed down tight, a good fire crackled in her stove, and the woman with her children had returned to their home. The carpenter was lying on his bed, jacket and boots and all, snoring with a right good will. His wife stood in the doorway, staring at him in disgust.

She herself could not settle down. She was miserable. Even before the solemn High Mass she went over to the vicarage, but she could hardly say a single word between her sobs. What an unhappy woman she was, she finally managed to stammer, to have such husband! True, he was usually quiet and industrious, but he simply had no religion! Just no religion at all! And if she were to live to be a hundred, she would never forget that night!

"Not a single Our Father did he say, nor did he welcome the Christ Child with so much as a single little prayer! What an end such a man will come to! Even this morning people are going from house to house telling each other that they have never heard anyone curse as much as this husband of mine on Holy Night! You must have heard it yourself, Your Reverence, after Midnight Mass! I was actually shivering in my soul!"

The priest sat with his hands folded in his lap and smiled benevolently at the distracted woman.

"To be sure, I heard something," he said. "But I thought it was a prayer!"

"Prayer?" the woman moaned, raising her hands and folding them high above her head, then letting them fall again as if she had had a stroke.

"My dear woman," the priest replied. "Some people have queer ways of praying. The Jews, for example. They wind their prayer-belts around their heads and arms when they pray. Others just turn the leaves of their prayer books. And still others pass the beads of their rosaries through their fingers. Well, our carpenter simply hammers nails into wooden shingles during his Our Father."

The woman again clasped her hands in despair.

"Did you say 'Our Father' Your Reverence? Some Our Father that would be! How he cursed and shouted during Holy Mass! If our dear Lord weren't so kind, the earth would have opened up and swallowed him!"

"I admit," the priest replied, "that his words may have been chosen somewhat—unfortunately. But his intentions were certainly good. And that's really what counts. All the while he was cursing and shouting, I'm sure he didn't have another thought in his head other than to provide a roof for the poor widow and her children and his conviction that other men ought to be helping him. We probably all prayed devoutly last night, but I have an idea that the carpenter's prayer with his saw and hammer pleased Our Good Lord the most."

"And now," the woman cried, "when the others are on their way to High Mass, he lies sleeping like a . . . a dormouse!"

"Let him sleep, my dear woman. Just as his work was a prayer, so is his rest."

As the carpenter's wife departed she kept shaking her head. She could make neither head nor tail of all this. What was the world coming to? If cursing was praying, what then was praying?

But she didn't get quite that far in her meditations.

THE CHRISTMAS FLOWER

JOSEPH HENRY JACKSON

FATHER CLEMENTE stood in the door of his church, his worn gray robe tucked up in an extra fold under its cord so that it might not sweep the earthen floor. He lifted his round, good-humored face to the sunlight, feeling the breeze cool on his cheek and breathing the early morning freshness it brought down from the high peaks into his little valley.

From the church steps the road ran straight and dusty between small fields of winter stubble, through a narrow belt of mountain forest, oak and cedar and stunted pine all tangled in weedy undergrowth. For a brief space it became the village street, the brown, thatched adobes clustering along it on both sides, two or three of them stringing out past the village into the hills where the road shrank to dry ruts and wandered irresolutely toward Mexico City somewhere over the ridge.

Standing in the doorway, Father Clemente could see thin blue smoke beginning to leak from the roofs beyond the trees, and he smiled to himself as its pungent, resinous odor reached his nostrils.

This was the day of the year he liked best, the Christmas morning when he held early service especially for the village children.

They would come—his bright blue eyes grew softer as he remembered—bringing their small gifts as he had taught them; and they would sit, hushed and solemn, listening to the story of the Infant Jesus. Father Clemente had told it each Christmas for almost thirty years, ever since he had come to this remote valley in the high country of New Spain and shown the Indians how to build the strange, tall house in which they would find the Truth he had been sent to bring them.

Sometimes the priest thought unhappily that he had failed. The children grew up. They continued to come obediently to church; they accepted their penances, sinned and came again; they were docile and in this sense devout, no more frail perhaps than any Christians anywhere. Yet after they were grown it was not the same. Somehow, Father Clemente knew, he had lost them. The little ones watched him so seriously when he told them of the Child, one like themselves but King and Savior too. But then all at once they were men and women, and although the dark, liquid eyes were trusting still, they were without depth; a door had closed behind them.

Father Clemente understood what it was, and now he sighed as he became once more aware of the little belt of forest between the church and the houses of the village. He had learned eventually to ignore the carved stone image that stood there, back from the road under the dark trees. The evilly grinning thing, he knew, was Tlaloc, old Aztec god of the rains. The priest felt suddenly colder in the wind from the mountains as he thought of those days before the Spaniard had brought the true Faith to Mexico, and of the sacrifice that Tlaloc had required—the blood of the littlest ones, the living hearts of the children.

Remembering the ancient, dreadful story, Father Clemente drew in his breath and shivered under his robe.

All that was past and done. The Conquest was nearly a century old, the priest reminded himself; there was no longer any question of living sacrifices. Yet he knew that his people did not forget the squat, hideous stone figure in the half-darkness of the forest. Sometimes, passing the spot, he would see that the earth before the god had been swept smooth, and there would be the cold ashes of a tiny fire in the clearing and the wild, sweet perfume of *copal* in the air. And there was that other, almost daily, reminder that his Indians, even the children following their elders, remembered their god. A hundred, a thousand times Father Clemente had seen it—the slight but unmistakable crook and dip of the knee, as they passed the image, the turned head and quick nod that symbolized what long ago had undoubtedly been an abject prostration before Tlaloc the Powerful.

At first the young priest had fought this vigorously. He had exhorted his Indians, had tried to show them the wickedness of their hearts that spoke with two voices, one to the true God and one to the false and evil Tlaloc. His Indians had listened, but it had never been any use. The day before, the month before, a woman had forgotten her gesture of respect to Tlaloc; the child she carried had been stillborn. Only last year a man had returned weary from the fields and had slept, refusing to go out with the rest on the Night Of The God to sweep the earth smooth and to burn incense; the next morning he did not wake at all. These things were in the minds of his people, the priest knew, unspoken but deeply rooted. And though he spoke to them with all the eloquence he could summon, and though the impassive brown faces watched him seriously, as if it were all clearly understood, the eyes remained flat and dead. The obeisance to the stone image went on, a part of his Indians' inward life, forever shut away from their priest. Father Clemente had been able, not to accept the gesture but to put it out of his mind for most of the time. Now and then he could not avoid seeing the pause, the crook of the knee, the little tip of the head. At such times he averted his eyes, saddened momentarily by what he thought of as his own failure.

Father Clemente was never sad for very long, for he would remember the children.

If the elders clung to their old gods, there would still be a new generation without such memories. All his Indians were children in a manner of speaking, simple and childlike in their scattering of rose-petals and the token drops of strong aromatic *aguardiente* on the church floor, their acknowledgment, along with Christian observance, of the age-old ritual their priest had never known. But the little ones—Father Clemente's heart would grow lighter as he felt his faith in the children spring up once more. When he thought of them it did not matter so much that the men went secretly at night to clear the ground and burn incense before the hidden god. Always the priest held fast to the hope that one day he would reach at least a child so surely that the heathen image would be forgotten. There would be one—one was all he asked—who would keep to the Faith. One boy would grow strong in the Truth as he grew older; his open look would never change; he would sponge utterly from his heart all memory of the evil of Tlaloc. In some way, the priest had often thought, he must show, clearly and in terms that such a boy and all of the children would understand, the folly of their homage to the idol in the forest. He had never been able to find the way, but he thought of it always. Perhaps this would be a miracle. Father Clemente thought now it could be nothing less. But surely God might grant him such a sign. He had labored long and hard; had he not earned this one small miracle? Then he bent his head humbly, knowing his folly, and the words of the prophet Daniel came to him: "Those that walk in pride He is able to abase." Yet the stubborn hope remained. One child brought to God; could it be a sinful thing to wish this?

Father Clemente put the thought from him and lifted his face again to the sun, warmer now, and he thought with pleasure of how it would soon strike through the quatrefoil window high above the door.

In his boyhood there had been such a window in the church in Spain where he had first heard the story of the Christ Child, and he had taken quiet happiness in reproducing the shape here from memory when, as a strong young priest, he had worked with his hands beside his Indians in the raising of God's house. Like the window of his childhood recollection, this one opened toward the morning sun, and Father Clemente had placed it so that the long golden finger of light would fall directly upon the altar. He had always been glad that at Christmastide the illumination was strongest. He turned from the doorway, pleased to see his small altar growing brighter. Even the first shallow gleam felt warm and good on his back as he moved down the aisle.

The altar was in order as he had known it would be. Below it, a little in front of the first row of wooden benches, was the small table Father Clemente set out each year to receive the children's gifts to the Child on His day. He smiled as he remembered how the sunlight would pour down upon the little heap of gifts. These would be unimportant in themselves, a few tiny mats raggedly woven of reeds or perhaps of threads raveled from some useless scrap at home; maybe a crude, miniature bowl or two, pressed out of clay by inexpert fingers and baked in the sun. But each child would bring something; mothers would see to it that they did not forget.

The priest remembered now that the candles must be lighted, and he brought a flaming pine splinter from the small fire in his sacristy and touched the tall wax tapers into life. Then he walked, more quickly this time, to the front of the church and across to where the bell-rope hung, smiling again as he thought of how the voice of the bell, quickening the bright morning air, would bring his children trooping down the road.

As he bent to the rope, Father Clemente allowed himself once more to slip for a moment into his cherished dream.

His dream, as it always did, centered on one boy for whom he held a special hope.

There had been a long procession of them over the years, good, eager children who had grown older and slipped away from him into the part-Christian, part-Indian worship that was not enough. The disappointment pricked him in the same way each time. Yet some days there would be one who would remain steadfast. One would reject the evil image and accept the Faith entire. This time— at the thought Father Clemente leaned strongly to the rope and the bell above him pealed joyously in response—it might be the shy, sensitive Pablo, small for his nine years but so responsive, so quiet, so earnest and quick to learn.

For months now, Father Clemente had built his hopes on Pablo, instructing and guiding the boy with special love. The child was lonely; the others played their games without him, made sport of him excepting when they left him to himself. The priest knew why, though the children did not fully understand. The boy's mother, widowed young and bitter from her loss, had rejected the church. In the meanest abode of the village, where the road lost itself in the hills, she had given Pablo a succession of "uncles" about whom the other children gibed unpleasantly, repeating what they heard from their elders. Pablo accepted their harshness and his own solitary state, as he did the fact that his mother never came to services. Father Clemente had tried to reason with her but without success.

"Hah!" she had spat once. "Your strong god! Can he bring back my husband whom Tlaloc took away? You tell us of miracles! Show me, then, one small miracle! Your god can do such a thing, no?" She had laughed loudly and turned away. The priest knew he should have gone back and back again, and shame came over him when he thought of how he had not.

But there was Pablo, who came to listen and to learn what the priest could teach, who sat so attentively and answered questions so intelligently, whose wide, dark eyes were so eager and candid, who would grow up—how could it be wrong to hope for this?—firm and unwavering in the Faith. It must happen, Father Clemente told himself. This time it must.

Yet, like the others, Pablo too always made the automatic obeisance to Tlaloc as he passed through the narrow forest strip where the stone god stood. Once, when the priest had asked him why, the boy had said only, "One does this, Father, in our village!" and when it was explained that a Christian boy must put aside the savage superstitions of his parents, Pablo had murmured "Yes, Father, surely!" But he had continued to make the gesture. In some way about which he was not quite certain, Father Clemente had begun to think of Pablo as the symbol of his own stubborn hope. If, just once, the boy would pass the stone god without acknowledgment, would not this be a sign? Could it not be, in itself, the miracle for which he had hoped so long? And—the thought surged powerfully in him—might not this be the year it would happen, even the very day?

As he swayed forward with the rope and the last note of the bell sounded sonorously in the tower, Father Clemente shook himself from his dream and stood up, flexing his shoulders, the rope falling from his hands to sway and then hang still and straight. He listened to the last long humming in the tower and patiently put away the thought of miracles and symbols. The children would be coming, and because he loved to watch their straggling, innocent procession he moved quickly to the doorway once more, letting the hem of his robe fall its full length to his ankles and tightening the cord about his waist. His stocky frame in the heavy, shapeless garment, almost filled the space as he stood, his arms spread wide and his hands braced on the doorposts, his eyes warm and happy as he saw the small, distant figures come into the road beyond the trees and turn toward the church.

The early breeze had died, and little puffs of gray dust rose and hung, dispersing slowly in the clear, quiet air behind the children as they emerged into the brief, straight stretch of road that led to the church door. Through the floating haze, the priest's eyes found the figure they sought, walking a little after the rest as always. With a momentary pang, he watched Pablo give the dip and nod toward the image of Tlaloc. Then the first little group was at the steps below him, and Father Clemente turned and moved rapidly down to the altar to watch them lay their gifts on the low table and seat themselves in chirping bird-rows on the long benches.

The children were very quiet on this special morning, tiptoeing down to leave their gifts and back again to sit solemnly, their eyes on their priest. Father Clemente lifted his hands and the children bowed with him. As he began the brief prayer that he knew would draw them into the spirit of the story he was to tell, he sensed that Pablo had come softly down the aisle, hesitated for a moment at the low table, and walked back to his place on a bench all to himself. Then suddenly the cadence of the prayer which had filled the church was interrupted by a quick confusion of sound among the benches, and Father Clemente looked up, shocked to see the even, hushed rows broken into shifting leaning groups, and to hear the sound of half-suppressed, mocking laughter. The words of the prayer died on his lips and his voice rose.

"Children!" he said. "What is this? You must not! Why do you laugh?"

The whispering quieted, and a child, bolder than the others spoke shrilly. "It is the stupid Pablo, Father! See what he brings!"

As the priest looked down, following the pointing finger, the light, cruel laughter rose again among the benches, and the mocking words came, "Leaves! Foolish little weed-leaves from the forest! A gift for the Christ Child! Leaves! Only leaves!"

The single young voice shrilled again. "It was last night, Father! All of us saw! It was Pablo beneath the trees, leaving there his small straw basket. We saw, and heard him ask that it be filled in the morning with gold—gold for the Child! And this morning it was not even there anymore!" The shrill little voice paused, then finished, sharp-edged with malice. "The god remembered! It was the father of Pablo who would not burn incense last year—his father who slept instead and did not wake afterward!"

Father Clemente raised his hand and the church grew still. He saw on the small table what Pablo had brought, the drooping clusters of dull, dusty leaves, broken in haste and desperation from one of the tall, rank weeds that grew so profusely along the road where the trees gave them shade. Then he was aware of Pablo's small figure sitting apart from the rest on the last bench, not huddled and tearful, the priest noted, as in his childhood he would have been in such a case, but only very still, staring straight before him.

The priest's voice was gentle as he said, "Tell us, Pablo, why do you bring leaves?" Pablo looked up at him and Father Clemente saw that the boy's eyes were all Indian now, the eyes that said nothing, answered nothing, that had defeated him in a generation of reaching for his people. He said again, "Pablo, the leaves of the forest weed! Why do you bring them to the Child?"

The boy's words came slowly. "There was nothing...I could not...I had no other gift, Father!"

Father Clemente's face was grave and his voice rang loudly in the small room.

"Children!" he said. "Children! You have heard. Pablo has brought what he could, as all of you have done. Would one mock at you..." his finger pointed among them, "...or you...or you ...because you did not bring a fine silver candlestick but only a small bowl of clay or a mat of reeds?"

His tone softened. "Children," he said, "Pablo brings his gift as you bring yours, in love for the Child!" He lifted his hands. "Pray, then," he said, "to be forgiven, for the Christ Child receives one gift as He receives another, because it is the gift of the heart!"

He bent his head and the children, stilled by the ringing voice, followed his motion. As Father Clemente began to pray, he felt the full warmth of the sun through the window, and his serenity returned. The children were thoughtless, even cruel, though without comprehension of their cruelty. But they were his children— not Pablo only, but all of them. His spirit grew tranquil as, behind his rolling words and on another level of his mind, he remembered another Light, the Star the shepherds had seen in the dark blue evening sky in Galilee. This was the Story, and he knew he would reach the children with it as he had never done before. As he shaped in his mind the words with which he would close his prayer, he sensed that the sunlight had grown in intensity. His body and mind were bathed in the warm brilliance, and fresh strength flowed through him.

Then, all at once, there was a new sound from the benches. This time it was not laughter, but a swift whisper like a wind sweeping through the church, growing more insistent each moment. Father Clemente said "Amen!" loudly, and raised his head.

Once more the even rows of children were broken into little groups, and once more there were pointing fingers and the high susurration of small voices. But now there was no mockery, only the rising, sighing rush of excited whispering in which at last the

250]

priest could distinguish words: "The leaves! Pablo's weed-leaves! See! The leaves!"

Father Clemente looked down at the low table that held the gifts, and his heart leaped. In the full, golden flood of light that streamed from the window lay the miracle, Pablo's pitiful little handful of desperately snatched leaves, their dusty green now a deep glowing emerald, and the topmost cluster a spreading, shining scarlet star.

As Father Clemente looked up, the whispering died. The children sat motionless, upright and silent, their enormous eyes fixed on their priest as his voice sounded triumphantly in the small room, telling them of the miracle they had seen, and of that other miraculous, heavenly Star that had guided men, both simple and wise, to the birthplace of the Child that was to be their King. He knew now, too, that this was the opportunity he had sought so long, and he spoke to them of what they had seen and how it was no greater than the miracle of all God's world, of His Heaven and His earth and His law. The seed that swelled in the ground and grew into a tall green weed that had become, by God's will, a scarlet flower—this was like the seed of true belief that, once planted in the heart, would grow and flourish and blossom at last into the Flower of Faith which would fill them wholly, leaving no space for the false god, the cold stone image in the forest that old men had made long ago when they did not know the Truth. As he finished, he felt his new peace flow ever more strongly in him, and his heart was warm with gratitude and love for the Power that had shown him the way to reach his children at last.

The service was over, and Father Clemente stood again at the church door, his heart overflowing as he watched the children scatter down the road to the village.

The sun was warm now, the sky was cloudless and endlessly deep, and the priest thought again of the children's eyes, so alive and shining with wonder at the thing they had seen. He knew that they would remain so, would never grow opaque and dead again in the ancient Indian way. He thought of the miracle, and he understood, as by a revelation, what his sin of pride had been and where it had lain. It had been rooted in his wish, his obstinate and selfish hope that he might reach one child only, Pablo or another, instead of all the children, all his people who were his children too.

It had flourished, that sin, like a forest wheel in his mind when he foolishly dreamed of the private miracle he had wanted— arrogantly demanded of God, he saw now—as though he had earned a special reward for something accomplished alone. In his new, profound humility, he understood at last that he also had been granted a miracle, and that it was in his own heart, which had been cleansed of pride.

He lifted his head and his eyes followed the small, diminishing figures. Somewhere among them was Pablo, he knew, but the priest could no longer distinguish one from another as they came to the trees.

Then he saw that the band of forest was no longer dark and chill, the shadowy dwelling-place of Tlaloc Of The Rains. For beneath the oak and cedar, springing up under the pines, cutting off the evil image from sight and memory, there glowed a thousand dazzling spearpoints of flaming crimson.

As he watched, he saw the children break into a run in which there was no pause, no nod, no acknowledgment to the old god hidden somewhere behind the multitudinous scarlet glory of the Christmas Flower.

Father Clemente turned and knelt in his doorway, the light from the window above him flooding down upon the altar. Below it, on the crude wooden table, the Flower seemed to grow and spread until its burning radiance filled the little church. He bent to pray, his heart filled with peace, warm and steady in its submission to a newly encompassing love.

As he prayed, he could hear behind him from the village beyond the trees the tiny, far echo of young voices, high and soft, "The Flower!" they cried. "The miracle! The miracle!"

A CHRISTMAS MYSTERY

WILLIAM J. LOCKE

THREE MEN who had gained great fame and honor throughout the world met unexpectedly in front of the bookstall at Paddington Station. Like most of the great ones of the earth they were personally acquainted, and they exchanged surprised greetings.

Sir Angus McCurdie, the eminent physicist, scowled at the two others beneath his heavy black eyebrows.

"I'm going to a God-forsaken place in Cornwall called Trehenna," said he.

"That's odd; so am I," croaked Professor Biggleswade. He was a little, untidy man with round spectacles, a fringe of grayish beard and a weak, rasping voice, and he knew more of Assyriology than any man, living or dead. A flippant pupil once remarked that the Professor's face was furnished with a Babylonic cuneiform in lieu of features.

"People called Deverill, at Foullis Castle?" asked Sir Angus.

"Yes," replied Professor Biggleswade.

"How curious! I am going to the Deverills, too," said the third man.

This man was the Right Honourable Viscount Doyne, the renowned Empire Builder and Administrator, around whose solitary and remote life popular imagination had woven many legends. He looked at the world through tired gray eyes, and the heavy, drooping, blond moustache seemed tired, too, and had dragged down the tired face into deep furrows. He was smoking a long black cigar.

"I suppose we may as well travel down together," said Sir Angus, not very cordially.

Lord Doyne said courteously: "I have a reserved carriage. The railway company is always good enough to place one at my disposal. It would give me great pleasure if you would share it."

The invitation was accepted, and the three men crossed the busy, crowded platform to take their seats in the great express train. A porter, laden with an incredible load of paraphernalia, trying to make his way through the press, happened to jostle Sir Angus McCurdie. He rubbed his shoulder fretfully.

"Why the whole land should be turned into a bear garden on account of this exploded superstition of Christmas is one of the anomalies of modern civilization. Look at this insensate welter of fools traveling in wild herds to disgusting places merely because it's Christmas!"

"You seem to be traveling yourself, McCurdie," said Lord Doyne.

"Yes—and why the devil I'm doing it, I've not the faintest notion," replied Sir Angus.

"It's going to be a beast of a journey," he remarked some moments later, as the train carried them slowly out of the station. "The whole country is under snow—and as far as I can understand we have to change twice and wind up with a twenty-mile motor drive."

He was an iron-faced, beetle-browed, stern man, and this morning he did not seem to be in the best of tempers. Finding his companions inclined to be sympathetic, he continued his lamentation.

"And merely because it's Christmas I've had to shut up my laboratory and give my young fools a holiday—just when I was in the midst of a most important series of experiments."

Professor Biggleswade, who had heard vaguely of and rather

looked down upon such new-fangled toys as radium and thorium and helium and argon—for the latest astonishing developments in the theory of radioactivity had brought Sir Angus McCurdie his worldwide fame—said somewhat ironically:

"If the experiments were so important, why didn't you lock yourself up with your test tubes and electric batteries and finish them alone?"

"Man!" said McCurdie, bending across the carriage, and speaking with a curious intensity of voice, "d'ye know I'd give a hundred pounds to be able to answer that question?"

"What do you mean?" asked the Professor, startled.

"I should like to know why I'm sitting in this damned train and going to visit a couple of addle-headed society people whom I'm scarcely acquainted with, when I might be at home in my own good company furthering the progress of science."

"I myself," said the Professor, "am not acquainted with them at all."

It was Sir Angus McCurdie's turn to look surprised.

"Then why are you spending Christmas with them?"

"I reviewed a ridiculous blank-verse tragedy written by Deverill on the Death of Sennacherib. Historically it was puerile. I said so in no measured terms. He wrote a letter claiming to be a poet and not an archaeologist. I replied that the day had passed when poets could with impunity commit the abominable crime of distorting history. He retorted with some futile argument, and we went on exchanging letters, until his invitation and my acceptance concluded the correspondence."

McCurdie, still bending his black brows on him, asked him why he had not declined. The Professor screwed up his face till it looked more like a cuneiform than ever. He, too, found the question difficult to answer, but he showed a bold front.

"I felt it my duty," said he, "to teach that preposterous ignoramus something worth knowing about Sennacherib. Besides I am a bachelor and would sooner spend Christmas, as to whose irritating and meaningless annoyance I cordially agree with you, among

[255

strangers than among my married sisters' numerous and nerve-racking families."

Sir Angus McCurdie, the hard, metallic apostle of radioactivity, glanced for a moment out of the window at the gray, frost-bitten fields. Then he said:

"I'm a widower. My wife died many years ago and, thank God, we had no children. I generally spend Christmas alone."

He looked out of the window again. Professor Biggleswade suddenly remembered the popular story of the great scientist's antecedents, and reflected that as McCurdie had once run, a bare-foot urchin, through the Glasgow mud, he was likely to have little kith or kin. He himself envied McCurdie. He was always praying to be delivered from his sisters and nephews and nieces, whose embarrassing demands no calculated coldness could repress.

"Children are the root of all evil," said he. "Happy the man who has his quiver empty."

Sir Angus McCurdie did not reply at once; when he spoke again it was with reference to their prospective host.

"I met Deverill," said he, "at the Royal Society's Soirée this year. One of my assistants was demonstrating a peculiar property of thorium and Deverill seemed interested. I asked him to come to my laboratory the next day, and found he didn't know a damned thing about anything. That's all the acquaintance I have with him."

Lord Doyne, the great administrator, who had been wearily turning over the pages of an illustrated weekly chiefly filled with flamboyant photographs of obscure actresses, took his gold glasses from his nose and the black cigar from his lips, and addressed his companions.

"I've been considerably interested in your conversation," said he, "and as you've been frank, I'll be frank too. I knew Mrs. Deverill's mother, Lady Carstairs, very well years ago, and of course Mrs. Deverill when she was a child. Deverill I came across once in Persia—he had been sent on a diplomatic mission to Teheran. As for our being invited on such slight acquaintance, little Mrs. Deverill has the reputation of being the only really successful celebrity hunter in England. She inherited the faculty from her mother, who entertained the whole world. We're sure to find arch-bishops, and eminent actors, and illustrious divorcées asked to meet us. That's one thing. But why I, who loathe country-house parties and children and Christmas as much as Biggleswade, am going down there today, I can no more explain than you can. It's a devilish odd coincidence."

The three men looked at one another. Suddenly McCurdie shivered and drew his fur coat around him.

"I'll thank you," said he, "to shut that window."

"It is shut," said Doyne.

"It's just uncanny," said McCurdie, looking from one to the other.

"What?" asked Doyne.

"Nothing, if you didn't feel it."

"There did seem to be a sudden draught," said Professor Biggleswade. "But as both window and door are shut, it could only be imaginary."

"It wasn't imaginary," muttered McCurdie.

Then he laughed harshly. "My father and mother came from Cromarty," he said with apparent irrelevance.

"That's the Highlands," said the Professor.

"Ay," said McCurdie.

Lord Doyne said nothing, but tugged at his moustache and looked out of the window as the frozen meadows and bits of river and willows raced past. A dead silence fell on them. McCurdie broke it with another laugh and took a whisky flask from his handbag.

"Have a nip?"

"Thanks, no," said the Professor. "I have to keep to a strict dietary, and I only drink hot milk and water—and of that spar-ingly. I have some in a thermos bottle."

Lord Doyne also declining the whisky, McCurdie swallowed a dram and declared himself to be better. The Professor took from his bag a foreign review in which a German sciolist had dared to question his interpretation of a Hittite inscription. Over the man's ineptitude he fell asleep and snored loudly.

To escape from his immediate neighborhood McCurdie went to the other end of the seat and faced Lord Doyne, who had resumed his gold glasses and his listless contemplation of obscure actresses. McCurdie lit a pipe, Doyne another black cigar. The train thundered on.

Presently they all lunched together in the restaurant car. The windows steamed, but here and there through a wiped patch of pane a white world was revealed. The snow was falling. As they passed through Westbury, McCurdie looked mechanically for the famous white horse carved into the chalk of the down; but it was not visible beneath the thick covering of snow.

"It'll be just like this all the way to Gehenna—Trehenna, I mean," said McCurdie.

Doyne nodded. He had done his life's work amid all extreme fiercenesses of heat and cold, in burning droughts, in simooms and in icy wildernesses, and a ray or two more of the pale sun or a flake or two more of the gentle snow of England mattered to him but little. But Biggleswade rubbed the pane with his table napkin and gazed apprehensively at the prospect.

"If only this wretched train would stop," said he, "I would go back again."

And he thought how comfortable it would be to sneak home again to his books and thus elude not only the Deverills, but the Christmas jollities of his sisters' families, who would think him miles away. But the train was timed not to stop till Plymouth, two hundred and thirty-five miles from London, and thither was he being relentlessly carried. Then he quarreled with his food, which brought a certain consolation.

The train did stop, however, before Plymouth—indeed, before Exeter. An accident on the line had dislocated the traffic. The express was held up for an hour, and when it was permitted to proceed, instead of thundering on, it went cautiously, subject to continual stoppings. It arrived at Plymouth two hours late. The travelers learned that they had missed the connection on which they had counted and that they could not reach Trehenna till nearly ten o'clock. After weary waiting at Plymouth they took their seats in the little, cold local train that was to carry them another stage on their journey. Hot-water cans put in at Plymouth mitigated to some extent the iciness of the compartment. But that only lasted a comparatively short time, for soon they were set down at a desolate, shelterless wayside junction, dumped in the midst of a hilly snow-covered waste, where they went through another weary wait for another dismal local train that was to carry them to Trehenna. And in this train there were no hot-water cans, so that the compartment was as cold as death. McCurdie fretted and shook his fist in the direction of Trehenna.

"And when we get there we have still a twenty-miles' motor drive to Foullis Castle. It's a fool name and we're fools to be going there."

"I shall die of bronchitis," wailed Professor Biggleswade.

"A man dies when it is appointed for him to die," said Lord Doyne, in his tired way; and he went on smoking long black cigars.

"It's not the dying that worries me," said McCurdie. "That's a mere mechanical process which every organic being from a king to a cauliflower has to pass through. It's the being forced against my will and my reason to come on this accursed journey, which something tells me will become more and more accursed as we go on, that is driving me to distraction."

"What will be, will be," said Doyne.

"I can't see where the comfort of that reflction comes in," said Biggleswade.

"And yet you traveled in the East," said Doyne. "I suppose you know the Valley of the Tigris as well as any man living."

"Yes," said the Professor. "I can say I dug my way from Tekrit to Baghdad and left not a stone unexamined."

"Perhaps, after all," Doyne remarked, "that's not quite the way to know the East."

"I never wanted to know the modern East," returned the Professor. "What is there in it of interest compared with the mighty civilizations that have gone before?"

McCurdie took a pull from his flask.

"I'm glad I thought of having a refill at Plymouth," said he.

At last, after many stops at little lonely stations, they arrived at Trehenna. The guard opened the door and they stepped out on to the snow-covered platform. An oil-lamp hung from the tiny penthouse roof that, structurally, was Trehenna Station. They looked around at the silent gloom of white undulating moorland, and it seemed a place where no man lived and only ghosts could have a bleak and unsheltered being. A porter came up and helped the guard with the luggage. Then they realized that the station was built on a small embankment, for, looking over the railing, they saw below the two great lamps of a motor car. A fur-clad chauffeur met them at the bottom of the stairs. He clapped his hands together and informed them cheerily that he had been waiting for hours. It was the bitterest winter in these parts within the memory of man, said he, and he himself had not seen snow there for five years. Then he settled the three travelers in the great roomy touring-car covered with a Cape-cart hood, wrapped them up in many rugs and started.

After a few moments, the huddling together of their bodies—for, the Professor being a spare man, there was room for them all on the back seat—the pile of rugs, the serviceable and all but air-tight hood, induced a pleasant warmth and a pleasant drowsiness. Where they were being driven they knew not. The perfectly upholstered seat eased their limbs, the easy swinging motion of the car soothed their spirits. They felt that already they had reached the luxuriously appointed home which, after all, they knew awaited them. McCurdie no longer railed, Professor Biggleswade forgot the dangers of bronchitis, and Lord Doyne twisted the stump of a black cigar between his lips without any desire to relight it. A tiny electric lamp inside the hood made the darkness of the world to right and left and in front of the talc windows still darker. McCurdie and Biggleswade fell into a doze. Lord Doyne chewed the end of his cigar. The car sped on through an unseen wilderness.

Suddenly there was a horrid jolt and a lurch and a leap and a rebound, and then the car stood still, quivering like a ship that has been struck by a heavy sea. The three men were pitched and tossed and thrown sprawling over one another on to the bottom of the car. Biggleswade screamed. McCurdie cursed. Doyne scrambled from the confusion of rugs and limbs and, tearing open the side of the Cape-cart hood, jumped out. The chauffeur had also just leaped from his seat. It was pitch dark save for the great shaft of light down the snowy road cast by the headlamps. The snow had ceased falling.

"What's gone wrong?"

"It sounds like the axle," said the chauffeur ruefully.

He unshipped a lamp and examined the car, which had wedged itself against a great drift of snow on the offside. Meanwhile Mc-Curdie and Biggleswade had alighted.

"Yes, it's the axle," said the chauffeur.

"Then we're done," remarked Doyne.

"I'm afraid so, my lord."

"What's the matter? Can't we get on?" asked Biggleswade in his querulous voice.

McCurdie laughed. "How can we get on with a broken axle? The thing's as useless as a man with a broken back. Gad, I was right. I said it was going to be an infernal journey."

The little Professor wrung his hands. "But what's to be done?" he cried.

"Tramp it," said Lord Doyne, lighting a fresh cigar.

"It's ten miles," said the chauffeur.

"It would be the death of me," the Professor wailed.

"I utterly refuse to walk ten miles through a Polar waste with a gouty foot," McCurdie declared wrathfully.

The chauffeur offered a solution of the difficulty. He would set out alone for Foullis Castle—five miles farther on was an inn where he could obtain a horse and trap—would return for the three gentlemen with another car. In the meanwhile they could take shelter in a little house which they had just passed, some half-mile up the road. This was agreed to. The chauffeur went on cheerily enough with a lamp, and the three travelers with another lamp started off in the opposite direction. As far as they could see they were in a long, desolate valley, a sort of No Man's Land, deathly silent. The eastern sky had cleared somewhat, and they faced a loose rack through which one pale star was dimly visible.

"I'm a man of science," said McCurdie as they trudged through the snow, "and I dismiss the supernatural as contrary to reason; but I have Highland blood in my veins that plays me exasperating tricks. My reason tells me that this place is only a commonplace moor, yet it seems like a Valley of Bones haunted by malignant spirits who have lured us here to our destruction. There's something guiding us now. It's just uncanny."

"Why on earth did we ever come?" croaked Biggleswade.

Lord Doyne answered: "The Koran says, 'Nothing can befall us but what God hath destined for us.' So why worry?"

"Because I'm not a Mohammedan," retorted Biggleswade.

"You might be worse," said Doyne.

Presently the dim outline of the little house grew perceptible. A faint light shone from the window. It stood unfenced by any kind of hedge or railing a few feet away from the road in a little hollow beneath some rising ground. As far as they could discern in the darkness when they drew near, the house was a mean, dilapidated hovel. A guttering candle stood on the inner sill of the small window and afforded a vague view into a mean interior. Doyne held up the lamp so that its rays fell full on the door. As he did so, an exclamation broke from his lips and he hurried forward, followed by the others. A man's body lay huddled together on the snow by the threshold. He was dressed like a peasant, in old corduroy trousers and rough coat, and a handkerchief was knotted round his neck. In his hand he grasped the neck of a broken bottle. Doyne set the lamp on the ground and the three bent down together over the man. Close by the neck lay the rest of the broken bottle whose contents had evidently run out into the snow.

"Drunk?" asked Biggleswade.

Doyne felt the man and laid his hand on his heart.

"No," said he, "dead."

McCurdie leaped to his full height. "I told you the place was uncanny!" he cried. "It's fey." Then he hammered wildly at the door.

There was no response. He hammered again till it rattled. This time a faint prolonged sound like the wailing of a sea creature was heard from within the house. McCurdie turned round, his teeth chattering.

"Did ye hear that, Doyne?"

"Perhaps it's a dog," said the Professor.

Lord Doyne, the man of action, pushed them aside and tried the door-handle. It yielded, the door stood open, and the gust of cold wind entering the house extinguished the candle within. They entered and found themselves in a miserable stone-paved kitchen, furnished with poverty-stricken meagreness—a wooden chair or two, a dirty table, some broken crockery, old cooking utensils, a fly-blown missionary society almanac, and a fireless grate. Doyne set the lamp on the table.

"We must bring him in," said he.

They returned to the threshold, and as they were bending over to grip the dead man the same sound filled the air, but this time louder, more intense, a cry of great agony. The sweat dripped from McCurdie's forehead. They lifted the dead man and brought him into the room, and after laying him on a dirty strip of carpet they did their best to straighten the stiff limbs. Biggleswade put on the table a bundle which he had picked up outside. It contained some poor provisions—a loaf, a piece of fat bacon, and a paper of tea. As far as they could guess (and as they learned later they guessed rightly) the man was the master of the house, who, coming home blind drunk from some distant inn, had fallen at his own threshold and got frozen to death. As they could not unclasp his fingers from the broken bottleneck they had to let him clutch it as a dead warrior clutches the hilt of his broken sword.

Then suddenly the whole place was rent with another and yet another long, soul-piercing moan of anguish.

"There's a second room," said Doyne, pointing to a door. "The sound comes from there."

He opened the door, peeped in, and then, returning for the lamp, disappeared, leaving McCurdie and Biggleswade in the pitch darkness, with the dead man on the floor.

"For Heaven's sake give me a drop of whisky," said the Professor, "or I shall faint."

[263

Presently the door opened and Lord Doyne appeared in the shaft of light. He beckoned to his companions.

"It is a woman in childbirth," he said in his even, tired voice. "We must aid her. She appears unconscious. Does either of you know anything about such things?"

They shook their heads, and the three looked at each other in dismay. Masters of knowledge that had won them world fame and honor, they stood helpless, abashed before this, the commonest phenomenon of nature.

"My wife had no child," said McCurdie.

"I've avoided women all my life," said Biggleswade.

"And I've been too busy to think of them. God forgive me," said Doyne.

The history of the next two hours was one that none of the three men ever cared to touch upon. They did things blindly, instinctively, as men do when they come face to face with the elemental. A fire was made, they knew not how, water drawn they knew not whence, and a kettle boiled. Doyne, accustomed to command, directed. The others obeyed. At his suggestion they hastened to the wreck of the car and came staggering back beneath rugs and traveling bags which could supply clean linen and needful things, for amid the poverty of the house they could find nothing fit for human touch or use. Early they saw that the woman's strength was failing, and that she could not live. And there, in that nameless hovel, with death on the hearthstone, and death and life hovering over the pitiful bed, the three great men went through the pain and the horror and squalor of birth, and they knew that they had never yet stood before so great a mystery.

With the first wail of the newly born infant a last convulsive shudder passed through the frame of the unconscious mother. Then three or four short gasps for breath, and the spirit passed away. She was dead. Professor Biggleswade threw a corner of the sheet over her face, for he could not bear to see it.

They washed and dried the child as any crone of a midwife would have done, and dipped a small sponge which had always

264]

remained unused in a cut-glass bottle in Doyne's dressing-bag in the hot milk and water of Biggleswade's Thermos bottle and put it to his lips; and then they wrapped him up warm in some of their own woolen undergarments, and took him into the kitchen and placed him on a bed made of their fur coats in front of the fire. As the last piece of fuel was exhausted they took one of the wooden chairs and broke it up and cast it into the blaze. And then they raised the dead man from the strip of carpet and carried him into the bedroom and laid him reverently by the side of his dead wife, after which they left the dead in darkness and returned to the living. And the three grave men stood over the wisp of flesh that had been born a male into the world. Then, their task being accomplished, reaction came, and even Doyne, who had seen death in many lands, turned faint. But the others, losing control of their nerves, shook like men stricken with palsy.

Suddenly McCurdie cried in a high-pitched voice, "My God! Don't you feel it?" and clutched Doyne by the arm. An expression of terror appeared on his iron features. "There! It's here with us."

Little Professor Biggleswade sat on a corner of the table and wiped his forehead.

"I heard it. I felt it. It was like the beating of wings."

"It's the fourth time," said McCurdie. "The first time was just before I accepted the Deverills' invitation. The second in the railway carriage this afternoon. The third on the way here. This is the fourth."

Biggleswade plucked nervously at the fringe of whisker under his jaws and said faintly, "It's the fourth time up to now. I thought it was fancy."

"I have felt it too," said Doyne. "It is the Angel of Death." And he pointed to the room where the dead man and woman lay.

"For God's sake let us get away from this," cried Biggleswade.

"And leave the child to die, like the others?" said Doyne.

"We must see it through," said McCurdie.

A silence fell upon them as they sat round in the blaze with the newborn babe wrapped in its odd swaddling clothes asleep on the pile of fur coats, and it lasted until Sir Angus McCurdie looked at his watch.

"Good Lord," said he, "it's twelve o'clock."

"Christmas morning," said Biggleswade.

"A strange Christmas," mused Doyne.

McCurdie put up his hand. "There it is again! The beating of wings." And they listened like men spellbound. McCurdie kept his hand uplifted, and gazed over their heads at the wall, and his gaze was that of a man in a trance, and he spoke:

"Unto us a child is born, unto us a son is given—"

Doyne sprang from his chair, which fell behind him with a crash.

"Man—what the devil are you saying?"

Then McCurdie rose and met Biggleswade's eyes staring at him through the great round spectacles, and Biggleswade turned and met the eyes of Doyne. A pulsation like the beating of wings stirred the air.

The three wise men shivered with a queer exultation. Something strange, mystical, dynamic had happened. It was as if scales had fallen from their eyes and they saw with a new vision. They stood together humbly, divested of all their greatness, touching one another in the instinctive fashion of children, as if seeking mutual protection, and they looked, with one accord, irresistibly compelled, at the child.

At last McCurdie unbent his black brows and said hoarsely:

"It was not the Angel of Death, Doyne, but another Messenger that drew us here."

The tiredness seemed to pass away from the great administrator's face, and he nodded his head with the calm of a man who has come to the quiet heart of a perplexing mystery.

"It's true," he murmured. "Unto us a child is born, unto us a son is given. Unto the three of us."

Biggleswade took off his great round spectacles and wiped them.

"Gaspar, Melchior, Balthazar. But where are the gold, frankincense, and myrrh?"

"In our hearts, man," said McCurdie.

The babe cried and stretched its tiny limbs.

Instinctively they all knelt down together to discover, if possible, and administer ignorantly to, its wants. The scene had the appearance of an adoration.

Then these three wise, lonely, childless men who, in furtherance of their own greatness, had cut themselves adrift from the sweet and simple things of life and from the kindly ways of their brethren, and had grown old in unhappy and profitless wisdom, knew that an inscrutable Providence had led them, as it had led Three Wise Men of old, on a Christmas morning long ago, to a nativity which should give them a new wisdom, a new link with humanity, a new spiritual outlook, a new hope.

And, when their watch was ended, they wrapped up the babe with precious care, and carried him with them, an inalienable joy and possession, into the great world.

THE SHEPHERD WHO WATCHED
BY NIGHT

THOMAS NELSON PAGE

THE PLACE had nothing distinguished or even perhaps distinctive about it except its trees and the tapering spire of a church lifting above them. It was not unlike a hundred other places that one sees as one travels through the country. It called itself a town but it was hardly more than a village. One long street, now paved on both sides, climbed the hill, where the old post-road used to run in from the country on one side and out again on the other, passing a dingy, large house with whitewashed pillars, formerly known as the tavern, but now calling itself "The Inn." This, with two or three built-up cross streets and a short street or two on either side of the main street, constituted "the town." A number of good houses, and a few very good indeed, sat back in yards dignified by fine trees. Three or four churches stood on corners, as far apart apparently as possible. Several of them were much newer and fresher painted than the one with the spire and cross; but this was the only old one and was generally spoken of as "The Church," and the rector was meant when the people spoke of "The Preacher." It sat back from the street, and near it, yet more retired, was an old dwelling, also dilapidated, with a wide porch, much decayed, and an out-building or two to the side and a little behind it, one of which was also occupied as a dwelling. The former was the rectory and the smaller dwelling was where the old woman lived who took care of the rectory, cleaned up the two rooms which the rector used since his wife's death, and furnished him his meals. It had begun as a temporary arrangement, but it had seemed to work well enough and had gone on now for years and no one thought of changing it. If an idea of change ever entered the mind of any one, it was only when the old woman's grumbling floated out into the town as to the tramps who would come and whom the preacher would try to take care of. Then, indeed, discussion would take place as to the utter impracticability of the old preacher and the possibility of getting a younger and livelier man in his place. For the rest of the time the people were hopeless. The old preacher was past his prime; no one else wanted him, and the people could not turn him out. He was saddled on them for life. They ran simply by the old propulsion; but the church was going down, they said, and they were helpless. This had been the case for years. And now as the year neared its close it was the same.

Such was the talk as they finished dressing the church for Christmas and made their way homeward, the few who still took interest enough to help in this way. They felt sorry for the old man, who had been much in their way during the dressing, but sorrier for themselves. This had been a few days before Christmas and now it was Christmas eve.

The old rector sat at his table trying to write his Christmas sermon. He was hopelessly behindhand with it. The table was drawn up close to the worn stove, but the little bare room was cold, and now and then the old man blew on his fingers to warm them, and pushed his feet closer to the black hearth. Again and again he took up his pen as if to write, and as often laid it down again. The weather was bitter and the coal would not burn. There was little to burn. Before him on the table, amid a litter of other books and papers, lay a worn Bible and prayer book—open, and beside them a folded letter on which his eye often rested. Outside, the wind roared, shaking the doors, rattling the windows, and whistling at the keyholes. Now and then the sound of a passing vehicle was borne in on the wind, and at intervals came the voices of boys shouting to each other as they ran by. The old man did not hear the former, but when the boys shouted he listened till they had ceased and his thoughts turned to the past and to the two boys whom God had given him and had then taken back to Himself. His gray face wore a look of deep concern, and, indeed, of dejection, and his eye wandered once more to the folded letter on the table. It was signed "A Friend," and it was this which was responsible for the unwritten Christmas sermon. It was what the world calls an anonymous letter and, though couched in kindly terms, it had struck a dagger into the old man's heart. And yet he could not but say that in tone and manner it was a kind act. Certainly it had told the truth and, if in tearing a veil from his eyes it had stunned him, why should he not face the truth!

He took up the letter again and reread it, not that he needed to read it, for he knew it by heart.

He reread it hoping to find some answer to its plain, blunt, true statements, but he found none. It was all true, every word, from the ominous beginning which stated that the writer felt that he had "a clear duty to perform," down to the close when with a protestation of goodwill he signed himself the old man's "friend."

"You must see, unless you are blind," ran the letter, "that your church is running down, and unless you get out and let the congregation secure a new and younger man, there will soon be no congregation at all left. No men come to church any longer and many women who used to come now stay away. You are a good man, but you are a failure. Your usefulness is past."

Yes, it was true, he was a failure. His usefulness was past. This was the reason no Christmas things had come this year—they wanted to let him know. It pained him to think it, and he sighed.

"You spend your time fooling about a lot of useless things, visiting people who do not come to church, and you have turned the rectory into a harbor for tramps," continued the anonymous friend.

"You cannot preach any longer. You are hopelessly behind the times. People nowadays want no more doctrinal points discussed;

they want to hear live, up-to-date, practical discourses on the vital problems of the day—such as the Rev. Dr.——delivers. His church is full." This also was true. He was no longer able to preach. He had felt something of this himself. Now it came home to him like a blow on the head, and a deeper pain was the conviction which, long hovering about his heart, now settled and took definite shape, that he ought to get out. But where could he go? He would have gone long since if he had known where to go. He could not go out and graze like an old horse by the roadside. There was no provision made for those like him. No pensions were provided by his church for old and disabled clergymen, and the suggestion made in the letter had no foundation in his case. It ran, "You must or, at least, you should have saved something in all this time."

This sounded almost humorous, and a wintry little smile flickered for a moment about the old man's wrinkled mouth. His salary had never been a thousand dollars, and there were so many to give to. Of late, it had been less than two-thirds of this amount and not all of this had been paid. The smile died out and the old man's face grew grave again as he tried to figure out what he could do. He thought of one or two old friends to whom he could write. Possibly, they might know of some country parish that would be willing to take him, though it was a forlorn hope. If he could but hold on till they invited him, it would be easier, for he knew how difficult it was for a clergyman out of a place to get a call. People were so suspicious. Once out, he was lost.

At the thought, a picture of a little plot amid the trees in the small cemetery on the hill near the town slipped into his mind. Three little slabs stood there above three mounds, one longer than the others. They covered all that was mortal of what he had loved best on earth. The old man sighed and his face in the dim light took on an expression very far away. He drifted off into a reverie. Ah, if they had only been left to him, the two boys that God had sent him and had then taken back to Himself, and the good wife who had borne up so bravely till she had sunk by the wayside! If he were only with them! He used to be rebellious at the neglect that left the drains so deadly, but that was gone now. He leant forward on his elbows and gradually slipped slowly to his knees. He was on them a long time, and when he tried to rise he was quite stiff; but his face had grown tranquil. He had been in high converse with the blessed of God and his mind had cleared. He had placed everything in God's hands, and He had given him light. He would wait until after Christmas and then he would resign. But he would announce it next day. The flock there should have a new and younger and abler shepherd. This would be glad tidings to them.

He folded up the letter and put it away. He no longer felt wounded by it. It was of God's ordaining and was to be received as a kindness, a ray of light to show him the path of duty. He drew his paper toward him and, taking up his pen, began to write rapidly and firmly. The doubt was gone, the way was clear. His text had come to his mind.

"And there were in the same country, shepherds abiding in the field, keeping watch over their flock by night. And, lo, the angel of the Lord came upon them, and the glory of the Lord shone round about them: and they were sore afraid. And the angel said unto them, Fear not: for behold, I bring unto you good tidings of great joy, which shall be to all people. For unto you is born this day in the City of David a Saviour which is Christ the Lord. And this shall be a sign unto you; Ye shall find the Babe wrapped in swaddling clothes lying in a manger."

Unfolding the story, he told of the darkness that had settled over Israel under the Roman sway and the formalism of the Jewish hierarchy at the time of Christ's coming, drawing from it the lesson that God still had shepherds watching over His flocks in the night to whom he vouchsafed to send His heavenly messengers. On and on he wrote, picturing the divine mission of the Redeemer and His power to save souls, and dwelling on Christmas as the ever-recurrent reminder of "the tender mercy of our God whereby the Day Spring from on High hath visited us."

Suddenly he came to a pause. Something troubled him. It flashed over him that he had heard that a woman in the town was very sick and he had intended going to see her. She had had a bad reputation; but he had heard that she had reformed. At any rate she was ill. He paused and deliberated. At the moment the wind rattled the shutters. She did not belong to his flock or, so far as he knew, to any flock, and once when he had stopped her on the street and spoken to her of her evil life, she had insulted him.

He turned back to his paper, pen in hand; but it was borne in on him that he was writing of watching over the flock by night and here he was neglecting one of his Father's sheep. He laid aside his pen and, rising, took down his old overcoat and hat and stick, lit his lantern, turned down his lamp, and shuffling through the bare, narrow passage, let himself out at the door.

As he came out on to the little porch to step down to the walk, the wind struck him fiercely and he had some difficulty in fastening the door with its loose lock; but this done he pushed forward. The black trees swayed and creaked above him in the high night wind, and fine particles of snow stung his withered cheeks. He wondered if the shepherds in the fields ever had such a night as this for their watch. He remembered to have read that snow fell on the mountains of Judea.

At length he reached the little house on a back street where he had heard the sick woman lived. A light glimmered dimly in an upper window and his knocking finally brought to the door a woman who looked after her. She was not in a good humor at being disturbed at that hour, for her rest had been much broken of late; but she was civil and invited him in.

In answer to his question of how her patient was, she replied gloomily: "No better; the doctor says she can't last much longer. Do you want to see her?" she added presently.

The old rector said he did, and she waved toward the stair. "You can walk up."

As they climbed the stair she added: "She said you'd come if you knew." The words made the old man warmer. And when she opened the door of the sick room and said, "Here's the preacher, as you said," the faint voice of the invalid murmuring, "I hoped you'd come," made him feel yet warmer.

He was still of some use even in this parish.

Whatever her face had been in the past, illness and suffering had refined it. He stayed there long, for he found that she needed him. She unburdened herself to him. She was sorry she had been rude to him that time. She had been a sinful woman. She said she had tried of late to live a good life, since that day he had spoken to her, but she now found that she had not. She had wanted to be a believer and she had gone to hear him preach one day after that, but now she did not seem to believe anything. She wanted to repent, but she could not feel. She was in the dark, and she feared she was lost.

The old man had taken his seat by her side, and he now held her hand and soothed her tenderly.

"Once, perhaps," he said doubtfully, "though God only knows that, but certainly no longer. Christ died for you. You say you wanted to change, that you tried to ask God's pardon and to live a better life even before you fell ill. Do you think you could want this as much as God wanted it? He put the wish into your heart. Do you think He would now let you remain lost? Why, He sent His Son into the world to seek and to save the lost. He has sent me to you tonight to tell you that He has come to save you. It is not you that can save yourself, but He, and if you feel that it is dark about you, never mind—the path is still there. One of the old Fathers has said that God sometimes puts His children to sleep in the dark. He not only forgave the Magdalen for her love of Him, but He vouchsafed to her the first sight of his face after His resurrection."

"I see," she said simply.

A little later she dozed off, but presently roused up again. A bell was ringing somewhere in the distance. It was the ushering in of the Christmas morn.

"What is this?" she asked feebly.

He told her.

"I think if I were well, if I could ever be good enough, I should like to join the church," she said. "I remember being baptized—long ago."

"You have joined it," he replied.

Just then the nurse brought her a glass.

274]

"What is that?" she asked feebly.

"A little wine." She held up a bottle in which a small quantity remained.

It seemed to the old preacher a sort of answer to his thought. "Have you bread here?" he asked the young woman. She went out and a moment later brought him a piece of bread.

He had often administered the early communion on Christmas morning, but never remembered a celebration that had seemed to him so real and satisfying. As he thought of the saints departed this life in the faith and fear of the Lord, they appeared to throng about him as never before, and among them were the faces he had known and loved best on earth.

It was toward morning when he left. As he bade her goodbye he knew he should see her no more this side of heaven.

As he came out into the night the snow was falling softly, but the wind had died down and he no longer felt cold. The street was empty, but he no longer felt lonely. He seemed to have got nearer to God's throne.

Suddenly, as he neared his house, a sound fell on his ears. He stopped short and listened. Could he have been mistaken? Could that have been a baby's cry? There was no dwelling near but his own, and on that side only the old and unoccupied stable in the yard whence the sound had seemed to come. A glance at it showed that it was dark and he was moving on again to the house when the sound was repeated. This time there was no doubt of it. A baby's wail came clear on the silence of the night from the unused stable. A thought that it might be some poor foundling flashed into his mind. The old man turned and, stumbling across the yard, went to the door.

"Who is here?" he asked of the dark. There was no answer, but the child wailed again, and he entered the dark building, asking again, "Who is here?" as he groped his way forward. This time a voice almost inarticulate answered. Holding his dim little lantern above his head, he made his way inside, peering into the darkness, and presently, in a stall, on a lot of old litter, he descried a dark and shapeless mass from which the sound came. Moving for-

[275

ward, he bent down, with the lantern held low, and the dark mass gradually took shape as a woman's form seated on the straw. A patch of white, from which a pair of eyes gazed up at him, became a face, and below, a small bundle clasped to her breast took on the lines of a babe.

"What are you doing here?" he asked, breathless with astonishment. She shook her head wearily, and her lips moved as if to say: "I didn't mean any harm." But no sound came. She only tried to fold the babe more warmly in her shawl. He took off his overcoat and wrapped it around her. "Come," he said firmly. "You must come with me," he added kindly; then, as she did not rise, he put out his hand to lift her, but, instead, suddenly set down the lantern and took the babe gently in his arms. She let him take the child, and rose slowly, her eyes still on him. He motioned for her to take the lantern and she did so. And they came to the door. He turned up the walk, the babe in his arms, and she going before him with the lantern. The ground was softly carpeted with snow; the wind had died down, but the clouds had disappeared and the trees were all white, softly gleaming, like dream-trees in a dreamland. The old man shivered slightly, but not now with cold. He felt as if he had gone back and held once more in his arms one of those babes he had given back to God. He thought of the shepherds who watched by night on the Judean hills. "It must have been such a night as this," he thought, as his eyes caught the morning star, which appeared to rest over his home.

When they reached his door he saw that some one had been there in his absence. A large box stood on the little porch and beside it a basket filled with things. So he had not been forgotten after all. The milkman also had called, and for his customary small bottle of milk had left one of double the usual size. When he let himself in at the door, he took the milk with him. So the shepherds might have done, he thought.

It was long before he could get the fire to burn; but in time this was done; the room was warm and the milk was warmed also. The baby was quieted and was soon asleep in its mother's lap, where she sat, still hooded, before the stove. And as the firelight fell from the open stove on the child in its mother's arms, the old man thought of a little picture he had once seen in a shop window. He had wanted to buy it, but he had never felt that he could gratify such a taste. There were too many calls on him. Then, as the young woman appeared overcome with fatigue, the old man put her with the child in the only bed in the house that was ready for an occupant and, returning to the little living room, ensconced himself in his armchair by the stove. He had meant to finish his sermon, but he was conscious for the first time that he was very tired; but he was also very happy. When he awoke he found that it was quite late. He had overslept and though his breakfast had been set out for him, he had time only to make his toilet and to go to church. The mother and child were still asleep in his room, the babe folded in her arm, and he stopped only to gaze on them a moment and to set the rest of the milk and his breakfast where the young mother could find it on awakening. Then he went to church, taking his half-finished sermon in his worn case. He thought with some dismay that it was unfinished, but the memory of the poor woman and the midnight communion, and of the young mother and her babe, comforted him; so he plodded on bravely. When he reached the church it was nearly full. He had not had such a congregation in a long time. And they were all cheerful and happy. The pang he had had as he remembered that he was to announce his resignation that day was renewed, but only for a second. The thought of the babe and its mother, warmed and fed in his little home, drove it away. And soon he began the service.

He had never had such a service. It all appeared to him to have a new meaning. He felt nearer to the people in the pews than he ever remembered to have felt. They were more than ever his flock and he more than ever their shepherd. More, he felt nearer to mankind, and yet more near to those who had gone before— the innumerable company of the redeemed. They were all about him, clad all in white, glistening like the sun. The heavens seemed full of them. When he turned his eyes to the window, the whole earth seemed white with them. The singing sounded in his ears like the choiring of angels. He was now in a maze. He forgot the notice he had meant to give and went straight into his sermon, stumbling a little as he climbed the steps to the pulpit. He repeated the text and kept straight on. He told the story of the shepherds in the fields watching their flocks when the angel of the Lord came upon them and told of the Babe in the manger who was Christ the Lord. He spoke for the shepherds. He pictured the shepherds watching through the night and made a plea for their loneliness and the hardship of their lives. They were very poor and ignorant. But they had to watch the flock and God had chosen them to be His messengers. The Wise Men would come later, but now it was the shepherds who first knew of the birth of Christ the Lord. He was not reading as was his wont. It was all out of his heart and the eyes of all seemed to be on him—of all in pews and of all that innumerable white-clad host about him.

He was not altogether coherent, for he at times appeared to confuse himself with the shepherds. He spoke as if the message had come to him, and after a while he talked of some experiences he had had in finding a child in a stable. He spoke as though he had really seen it. "And now," he said, "this old shepherd must leave his flock, the message has come for him."

He paused and looked down at his sermon and turned the leaves slowly, at first carefully and then almost aimlessly. A breath of wind blew in and a few leaves slid off the desk and fluttered to the floor.

"I have been in some fear lately," he said, "but God has appeared to make the way plain. A friend has helped me, and I thank him." He looked around and lost himself. "I seem to have come to the end," he said, smiling simply with a soft, childish expression stealing over and lighting up his wan face. "I had something more I wanted to say, but I can't find it and—I can't remember it. I am a very old man and you must bear with me, please, while I try." He quietly turned and walked down the steps, holding on to the railing.

As he stooped to pick up a loose sheet from the floor, he sank to his knees, but he picked it up. "Here it is," he said with a tone of relief. "I remember now. It is that there were shepherds abiding in the fields, keeping watch over their flocks by night, and the light came upon them and the glory of the Lord shone round about them and they were sore afraid, and the angel said unto them: 'Fear not, for behold, I bring unto you good tidings of great joy which shall be unto all people; for unto you is born this day in the city of David a Saviour which is Christ the Lord.'"

They reached him as he sank down and, lifting him, placed him on a cushion taken from a pew. He was babbling softly of a babe in a stable end and of the glory of the Lord that shone round about them. "Don't you hear them singing?" he said. "You must sing too; we must all join them."

At the suggestion of some one, a woman's clear voice struck up,

"While shepherds watched their flocks by night,"

and they sang it through as well as they could for sobbing. But before the hymn was ended the old shepherd had joined the heavenly choir and had gone away up into heaven.

As they laid him in the little chamber on the hill opening to the sunrise, the look on his face showed that the name of that chamber was Peace.

They talk of him still in his old parish—of the good he did, and of his peaceful death on the day that of all the year signified Birth and Life.

Nothing was ever known of the mother and babe. Only there was a rumor that one had been seen leaving the house during the morning and passing out into the white-clad country. And at the little inn in the town there was vague wonder what had become of the woman and her baby who had applied for shelter there the night before and had been told that there was no place for her there, and that she had better go to the old preacher, as he took in all the tramps. But in heaven it is known that there was that Christmas Eve a shepherd who kept watch over his flock by night.

WHEN THEY SAW THE STAR

ANNIE B. KERR

Morris stood in the kitchen with his nose pressed against the windowpane. The window looked out upon a narrow shaft which supplied air and light to the back rooms of the tall tenement house where Morris and his mother lived.

Because their three rooms were on the top floor he could look up into the blue sky, where white clouds drifted past in the daytime and stars shone out at night. The stars gave him a feeling of their friendliness and protection when his mother was away working and he was left alone at night.

But it was not his patch of sky that had kept him standing by the window for so many hours on this particular Christmas Eve. It was the Christmas preparations of the Kalenski family, whose kitchen window was just opposite.

All day long Mrs. Kalenski had been busy cooking and making ready for the feast which was about to take place, right there before the fascinated gaze of the little Jewish boy.

She stood now, with her broad back to the window, attending to the food cooking on the stove. The window was open a few inches and Morris sniffed hungrily the fish soup, which was boiling merrily in one big kettle, the cabbage and mushrooms which filled another to the very top, and the fish with stewed prunes, which was to be the high point of the celebration.

Mrs. Kalenski lifted a corner of her apron and wiped the perspiration from her round, smiling face. Then she cleared off the big table and called Jadwiga and Helen to come and help her set it.

They spread smoothly the heavy linen cloth, having first arranged handfuls of yellow straw all around the edge of the table. Morris pushed back his mop of curly hair from his eyes and flattened his nose against the pane until it hurt, so surprised was he at the straw. The girls saw him standing there and ran to their own window and beckoned him. He shook his head mournfully.

The Kalenskis were very kind, but his mother had forbidden him ever to go inside their apartment. They were Christians. They hated the Jews. In Poland, even now, the Christians killed the Jews; he must promise never to go to their house. Morris had promised, although he was sure the Kalenskis didn't hate anybody. And so he shook his head sadly when Jadwiga held up a plate of twisted pastries with gestures indicating that he was to have some.

They were such kind people, the Kalenskis. There was Mr. Kalenski, who worked in a tailor shop in the next block, and Mrs. Kalenski always ready to help a sick neighbor or a lonely little boy, and Jadwiga (named for a queen), and Helen and Janina, and the three boys. Sometimes, when his mother was away at work and the hours from five to twelve dragged on endlessly, Morris would tap on the pane and one of them would run to the bright window opposite, and smile and wave to him. They were such comforting people, thought Morris, and it comforted mother too, to know that they were there, ready to come to their window, whenever he tapped on his.

And yet mother had said, "They are Christians. You must never go to their house."

Mother was a very wonderful person. Ever since father died she had had to work very hard. Morris would not think of disobeying her but there were many puzzling things she did not seem able to explain. For instance, Christmas.

The shop windows were filled with fascinating toys, warm sweaters, beautiful dresses, all marked "For Christmas." In the bakery windows were Christmas cakes and candies and other delicious things to eat. At school all the children sang "Silent Night, Holy Night" and "Tannenbaum, O Tannenbaum," and when they trooped out of the building for the last time till "next year," teacher had called "Merry Christmas, children."

"Why don't *we* have Christmas?" Morris had asked his mother one evening over a week ago, as they ate their early supper on the white enamel table in the kitchen.

"It is not for the Jews," Rachel said, gazing proudly into the small puzzled eyes of her small son.

"We have *Chanukah,* and we have lights and presents then. If you are a good little boy mother will bring you a red sweater to wear to school like the one we saw in the window this morning."

Morris gave a little gasp. The sweater cost three dollars! And mother did not have enough money to buy the coat she greatly needed when she went out to work on cold winter nights. Then his eyes filled with sudden tears.

"It's not the sweater I want," he sobbed.

"Why, Morris! Don't cry, dear," she pleaded. "What is it you want so badly?"

He pointed across the shaft to the Kalenskis' lighted kitchen. Mrs. Kalenski was, as usual, preparing supper for Mr. Kalenski and Jadwiga and Helen and Janina and the three boys. Her movements were somewhat hampered by the fact that Stanislas, aged two, was draped across her shoulder, fast asleep.

"I want a baby brother," said Morris.

"Darling!" cried Rachel, and ran around to his chair and gathered him up in her arms.

"Or else," pondered Morris, snuggling his dark head against his mother's neck, "or else the baby Jesus, to play with when you are away at night."

"Don't, Morris." His mother unclasped his arms from around her neck, and went back to her chair.

"But the baby Jesus was a Jew, mother."

"When you are older, Morris, you will understand about Christmas and the little Jesus. And next month, when they are not so busy, you may invite the Kalenski boys to come here and play with you. But you must never go to their house. Now remember."

"Yes, mother," promised Morris with a little sigh.

Rachel was away all day, the day before Christmas, as well as at night, because one of the stores in the neighborhood needed extra help. It was a chance to earn a few more dollars to make up for the wages she had lost those days when she was sick. She had left crackers and milk for Morris and promised to bring something more substantial home with her at eleven o'clock, and they would have a little feast together, if Morris thought he could stay awake that long.

He had forgotten to eat his early supper, and the sight and smell of the Kalenskis' feast reminded him of how hungry he was.

The Christmas Eve feast of his Polish neighbors appeared to be ready and the entire family was assembled. A small Christmas tree stood on a shelf in one corner of the room and two tall candles, in gaily decorated candlesticks, gave an additional touch of festivity to the bright, crowded kitchen.

Morris turned away from the window reluctantly. A light snow had fallen and the flakes had made beautiful shapes and patterns against the windowpane. He dragged his feet to the cupboard and took out the milk and crackers. How bare and dreary the room seemed! He would set the table for two and then wait for his mother's return. There was a lump in his throat, and in spite of himself he turned back to the window.

The Kalenskis were crowded against their own windowpane, gazing up at the small patch of sky. Jadwiga opened the window and leaned out, her blue eyes searching the heavens eagerly.

"I see it!" she cried. "The evening star! *Now* we can have our feast!"

She saw the wistful little face at the other window and called across to him, "Come and eat with us, Morris. We have much to eat tonight—see?" She pushed the children aside and pointed to the loaded table.

But he shook his head. They had invited him before and he had always refused, as gently as possible. He could never tell them the real reason. That would be impolite. Better let them think he was shy and afraid, though he smiled to himself at the idea of being afraid of the kind, friendly Kalenskis.

Jadwiga brushed the snow from her fair hair and flushed face. Then before she shut the window she called once more across the darkness that separated them:

"Then we'll save some supper for you and bring it when your mother comes home, before we go to church tonight."

Morris opened his own window and leaned out in a vain effort to see the star for whose appearance the Kalenskis had evidently been waiting. Tears of loneliness filled his eyes as he watched the happy family across the way. He put out the light and drew a chair close to the window. There they were, standing behind their chairs, Mr. Kalenski, tall and thin with gray hair and a worried look on his face. It was the same kind of look that mother had sometimes. Perhaps he was afraid there wouldn't be enough money to pay for all the food, thought Morris. And Mrs. Kalenski, who didn't look at all worried, was very beautiful indeed in a new silk dress with a lace collar which fell in ruffles down the front. And Jadwiga, her smooth yellow braids wound round her head, her two hands holding little Stanislas, who stood upright in his chair at her side. The other four—Josef and Ignace and Janina and Helen—watched their mother break a thin wafer in eight pieces and hand a piece to each member of the family. As they ate the wafer Mrs. Kalenski spoke to each one. Then they bowed their heads reverently while Mr. Kalenski said a long prayer. Morris bowed his head also.

The Kalenskis pulled back their chairs and broke into a merry chatter, while Mrs. Kalenski filled their plates from the big kettles on the stove. Then Morris saw that one chair was empty. Not Mrs. Kalenski's, which was at the end of the table nearest the stove, but the one between little Stanislas and Josef. He counted carefully. They were all there. *Who* could the chair be for? Jadwiga had explained to him that the family would be alone tonight. Tomorrow there would be many guests for the big Christmas Day feast. How strange that there should be an empty chair! Morris slid down from his own chair in order to press closer against the window.

How good the supper looked and how happy they all were! Surely his mother wouldn't mind if he accepted their invitation just this once, on Christmas Eve. He was hungry and cold and lonely, and there, just around the other side of the hall, were food and warmth and fellowship. But they were Christians and he was a Jew. What difference did that make, really? The Kalenskis had never been unkind to the Jews, either in Poland or in America, he was sure of that. They had tried very hard to be kind to Morris and his mother, ever since they came there to live, six months ago. His mother didn't understand. She wouldn't mind his being with them tonight if she knew them as he did. Yet he had promised her.

He looked at the empty chair. Surely no one could come now to be their guest. Josef came to the window and looked across to where Morris was standing; but he could not see beyond the darkness. Morris opened the window a crack. A gust of wind blew the snow inside from the sill and he closed it hastily. Then he jumped up and down in excitement. The empty chair—who could it be for but himself, Morris Lewisohn? *He* was the guest they had invited —the chair was set for him. That being so, his mother could not object to his going. It would be impolite to leave it empty. He snapped on the light, washed his thin little hands at the kitchen sink, straightened his collar, smoothed down his rumpled hair and slipped out into the dim hall. His timid knock at the Kalenskis' door was not heard because of the merriment inside. Finally Morris pushed open the door and stood blinking in the bright light of the Kalenskis' kitchen.

Then he walked quietly around the table and slipped into the empty chair.

A sudden startled silence fell upon the children. At last Ignace voiced the dismay which they were all feeling.

"He has taken the chair belonging to the Christ child!"

"Hush." Mrs. Kalenski leaned across the end of the table and gave the unexpected guest a reassuring pat.

"We are so glad to have you come, Morris. And now I give you soup and mushrooms and fish hot from the stove."

"I thank you," said Morris politely, his eyes fixed on the generous dishes which Mrs. Kalenski was placing in front of him. "I think my mother would like to have me come to your party." He spoke hesitatingly, trying to curb his eagerness. He had not understood Ignace and was quite unaware of the consternation he had caused.

The assumption of adult politeness vanished and a very hungry little boy fell upon the appetizing food with gusto.

"Let us sing," cried Mrs. Kalenski, anxious to put their guest at ease and divert attention from him. And so they sang an old Christmas carol, the last verse of which is something like this:

> We too await Thee, Lord,
> As once they did of old,
> And when Thou comest,
> On our knees we'll fall before Thee
> And in spirit we'll adore Thee.

Morris settled back in his chair with a little sigh of satisfaction, while the girls cleared away the plates and brought pastries, various kinds of fruit and a pudding of noodles, honey and poppy seed. His eyes gazed around the cheerful room, with its gay linoleum, its curtains and pictures. On the wall opposite hung a portrait of an interesting looking man in uniform.

"Our great hero—Kosciusko." Mr. Kalenski, following the little boy's gaze, spoke for the first time.

"Yes," explained Jadwiga; "he helped fight in the war, here in America, long ago. He is in my history book. Once when my teacher sassed me in school and called me *Polak* I asked her: 'What did your old Ireland ever do for this country? But Kosciusko and Pulaski fought for it and you don't dast to call me a Polak!'"

"Jadwiga very sassy to her teacher," apologized Jadwiga's mother.

"You can't understand, mama," explained Jadwiga hotly. "The

286]

teacher was sassy first. And she made me call myself Julia instead of Jadwiga 'cause she don't like Polish names!"

"I think the Polish people are the most grandest in all the world," announced Morris fervently, his mouth full of crisp Polish pastry.

"God bless him!" cried Mrs. Kalenski, filling a plate with goodies for him to carry home. "Now we pull out the straw. What for do you wish, Morris?"

Morris looked around at them with a question on his face and Jadwiga explained, "We tell our fortune by the straw. We each make a wish and if it is a very long straw, or if there is any grain on it, then the wish will come true. See?" She held up a long straw. "Now I know I'll be married soon to a rich husband."

"And I," cried Morris, excitedly waving two straws over his head—"I shall have a brother—*two* brothers, like Josef and Stanislas!"

The children looked at their mother questioningly, but she shook her head.

"I tink—not, Morris." Then seeing the tears slowly gathering in his eyes, she added hastily, "But Jadwiga not tell why we have the straw. It is because the little Jesus was born in stable, where are cattle—and straw. In church we have the stable, and the—what you call?"

"Manger," said Jadwiga.

"Oh—and do you have Santa Claus—like in Dabrowski's store?"

"No," explained Mrs. Kalenski. "In Poland we have Saint Nicholas on December sixth. And if all the children be good, he will send presents for Christmas."

"Yes," broke in Josef, "tomorrow we will have our presents— 'little stars,' because a beautiful lady, all dressed in white, brings them. She is the Good Star from Heaven like we saw in the sky tonight."

"Oh, I love the stars!" Morris' own eyes were starry as he lifted them to Mrs. Kalenski's. "And please, may I come tomorrow?"

"God bless him!" exclaimed Mrs. Kalenski again. "If your

mother say yes, we like to have you come. But now it is for church we must make ready."

"But see the tree first." Janina caught her mother by the hand and pulled her toward the corner where stood the little tree, Morris following in their wake.

"We have put on the balls and the ornaments and all the little lights, with the star on top. Oh, mother, we must turn on the lights before Morris goes home!"

Jadwiga turned off the big center light overhead and flashed on the tiny lights of the Christmas tree. Morris stood in rapt admiration. Then he turned and looked slowly around at each one.

"I thank you, one and all," he said quaintly.

But they did not answer. They only gazed at him breathlessly. His dark, childish head blotted out the little Christmas tree, but the yellow bulbs threw a light around it which glowed softly, and just above, the star shone down upon him.

A CHRISTMAS GIFT

T. F. POWYS

IT IS a harmless wish to like a little notice to be taken of one's name, and a number of people, besides Mr. Balliboy, the Dodder carrier, like attention to be paid to their names when they are written down. Children will write their names upon a fair stretch of yellow sand, young men will carve their names upon an old oak in the forest, and even the most simple peasant will like to see his name printed in a newspaper.

For most of his life Mr. Balliboy was satisfied with having his name written upon the side of his van, and he was always pleased and interested when anyone paused in the street to read his name.

But Mr. Balliboy's pride in his name made him do more than one foolish thing.

Once he cut "Mr. Balliboy, Carrier," with his market knife upon one of the doors of Mr. Told's old barn, and again upon the right-hand post of the village pound. But, on his going to see how the names looked the next Sunday—and perhaps hoping that a stranger might be found regarding them—he discovered, to his sorrow, that the rude village boys had changed the first letters of his name into an unpleasant and ill-sounding word.

Mr. Balliboy was a lonely man, and a bachelor—for no young woman would ever look at his name twice and none had ever wished to have his name written beside hers in a church register.

One Christmas Mr. Balliboy journeyed, as was his wont, to Weyminster. His van was full of countrywomen, each one of whom thought herself to be of the highest quality, for each had put on the finest airs with her market clothes and, so dressed, could talk in a superior manner.

Mr. Balliboy had certainly one reason for happiness—other than the ordinary joyfulness of the merry season—which was that his rival, John Hawkins, had passed by with his van empty of customers, yet Mr. Balliboy was sad. His sadness came, strangely enough, only because he wished, for the first time in his life, to give a Christmas present.

It might have been only to give himself pleasure that he wished to do this. For whatever the present was that he should buy, he determined that a label should be tied on it, with his name written clearly upon it—"From Mr. Balliboy."

What the present would be, and to whom it should be given, Mr. Balliboy did not know. He decided to buy something that he fancied, and then allow destiny to decide to whom the gift should go.

When Mr. Balliboy reached the town he walked about the streets in order to see what could be bought for money. Many a shop window did he look into and many a time did he stand and scratch his head, wondering what he should buy.

There was one oddity that he fancied in a toyshop—a demon holding a fork in his hand, upon which he was raising a naked young woman. Mr. Balliboy thought the demon might do, but over the young woman he shook his head.

Mr. Balliboy moved to another window. Here at once, he saw what pleased him—a little cross, made of cardboard and covered with tinsel, that shone and glistened before Mr. Balliboy's admiring eyes.

Mr. Balliboy purchased the cross for a shilling and attached a label to it, with his name written large. . . .

Sometimes a change comes over a scene, now so happy and gay but in one moment altered into a frown. As soon as Mr. Balliboy had buttoned the cross into his pocket the streets of Weyminster showed this changed look. The shoppers' merriment and joyful surprise at what they saw in the windows gave place to a sad and tired look. The great church that so many hurried by in order to reach their favorite tavern, appeared more dark and somber than a winter's day should ever have made it.

Even the warm drinks served out by black-haired Mabel at the "Rod and Lion" could not make the drinkers forget that care and trouble could cut a Christmas cake and sing a Christmas carol as well as they.

The general gloom of the town touched Mr. Balliboy, and had he not had the present hid in his coat, he might have entered an inn, in order to drown the troubled feelings that moved about him, in a deep mug.

But, having bought the Christmas present, he had now the amusement of seeking the right person to give it to. And so, instead of walking along the street with downcast eyes, he walked along smiling.

While he was yet some way off his van, he could see that a figure was standing beside it, who seemed to be reading his name. And, whoever this was, Mr. Balliboy determined as he walked, that it should be the one to receive his Christmas gift.

As he drew nearer he saw that the figure was that of a young woman—wrapped in a thin cloak—who showed by her wan look and by her shape that she expected soon to be a mother.

At a little distance from his van Mr. Balliboy waited, pretending to admire a row of bottles in a wine merchant's shopwindow, but, at the same time, keeping an eye upon the woman.

"Was she a thief—was she come there to steal?" A passing policeman, with a fine military strut, evidently thought so.

"Don't stand about here," he shouted. "Go along home with you!"

The policeman seized her roughly.

"I am doing no harm," the woman said, looking at the name again, "I am only waiting for Mr. Balliboy."

"Go along, you lying drab," grumbled the policeman.

He would have pushed her along, only Mr. Balliboy, who had heard his name mentioned, came nearer.

"Baint 'ee poor Mary," he asked, "who was to have married the carpenter at Shelton?"

The policeman winked twice at Mr. Balliboy, smiled and walked on.

"What was it," asked Mr. Balliboy, kindly, as soon as the policeman was out of hearing, "that made 'ee wish to study and remember the name of a poor carrier?"

"I wished to ask you," said the young woman, "whether you would take me as far as the 'Norbury Arms.' Here is my fare," and she handed Mr. Balliboy a shilling—the price of the cross.

Mr. Balliboy put the shilling into his pocket.

"Get up into van," he said, "and 'tis to be hoped they t'others won't mind 'ee."

That day the most respectable of the people of the village had come to town in Mr. Balliboy's van. There was even rich Mrs. Todd, clad in warm furs, whose own motor car had met with an accident the day before. There were others too, as comfortably off—Mrs. Potten and Mrs. Biggs—and none of these, or even his lesser customers, did Mr. Balliboy wish to offend. He looked anxiously up the street and then into the van.

The young woman's clothes were rags, her toes peeped from her shoes, and she sighed woefully.

Mr. Balliboy gave her a rug to cover her. "Keep tight hold of 'en," he said, "for t'other women be grabbers."

The change in the town from joy to trouble had caused the women who had journeyed with Mr. Balliboy that day to arrive at the van a little late, and in no very good tempers. And, when they did come, they were not best pleased to see a poor woman—worse clothed than a tramp—sitting in the best seat in the van, with her knees covered by Mr. Balliboy's rug.

" 'Tis only Mary," said Mr. Balliboy, hoping to put them at their ease. " 'Tis only thik poor toad."

"Mary, is it?" cried Mrs. Biggs angrily, "who did deceive Joseph with her wickedness. What lady would ride with her? Turn her out at once, Mr. Balliboy—the horrid wretch."

"Out with her!" cried Mrs. Todd. "Just look at her," and she whispered unpleasant words to Mrs. Potten.

Mr. Balliboy hesitated. He hardly knew what to do. He had more than once borrowed a little straw from Mrs. Todd's stackyard and now he did not want to offend her.

He had a mind to order Mary out, only—putting his hand under his coat to look at his watch—he felt the Christmas present that he had purchased—the cardboard cross.

"Thee needn't sit beside her," he said coaxingly to Mrs. Todd, "though she's skin be as white and clean as any lamb's."

"We won't have no lousy breeding beggar with we," shouted Mrs. Biggs, who had taken a little too much to drink at the tavern.

"Let she alone," said Mr. Balliboy, scratching his head and wondering what he had better do.

"Thrust her out," cried Mrs. Potten, and, climbing into the van, she spat at the woman.

"Out with her," screamed Mrs. Todd. "Away with her, away with her!" cried all the women.

Now, had it not been that Mr. Balliboy had taken Mary's shilling and so made her free of his van, with the right to be carried as far as the 'Norbury Arms,' he might have performed the commands of the drunken woman and thrown Mary into the street. But, as he had taken her shilling, Mr. Balliboy bethought him of what was his own.

The woman had read his name; he had taken her fare.

"Let she alone," said Mr. Balliboy gruffly to Mrs. Biggs, who had laid hands upon the woman.

"We'll go to John Hawkins; he'll take us home," said Mrs. Todd angrily.

Mr. Balliboy winced. He knew how glad his rival would be to welcome all his company.

"Why, what evil has she done?" Mr. Balliboy asked in a milder tone.

With one accord the women shouted out Mary's sorrow.

"Away with her, away with her!" they called.

Mr. Balliboy put his hand into his coat, but it was not his watch that he felt for this time—it was his Christmas gift.

"Away with your own selves," he said stoutly. "Thik maiden be going wi' I, for 'tis me own van."

Mr. Balliboy took his seat angrily and the women left him. He knew that what had happened that afternoon was likely to have a lasting effect upon his future. Everyone in the village would side with the women with whom he had quarreled, and the story of his kindness to Mary would not lose in the telling.

But, before very long, an accident happened that troubled Mr. Balliboy even more than the loss of his customers. In the middle of a long and lonely road his van broke down.

Mr. Balliboy tried to start the car, but with no success. Other carriers passed him by, among whom was John Hawkins, and many were the taunts and unseemly jests shouted at him by the Christmas revelers who sat therein. But soon all was silence, and the road utterly deserted, for the time was near midnight.

For some while Mr. Balliboy busied himself with the aid of the car lamps, trying to start the engine. But, all at once and without any warning, the lamps went out.

Mr. Balliboy shivered. The weather was changed, a sharp frost had set in and the stars shone brightly. Someone groaned. Mary's pains had come upon her.

"I be going," said Mr. Balliboy, "to get some help for 'ee."

Mr. Balliboy had noticed a little cottage across the moor, with a light in the window. He hurried there, but before he reached the cottage the light had vanished, and, knock as he would at the door, no one replied.

"What be I to do?" cried Mr. Balliboy anxiously, and looked up at the sky. A large and brightly shining star appeared exactly above his van.

Mr. Balliboy looked at his van and rubbed his eyes. The van was lighted up and beams of strange light seemed to emanate from it.

" 'Taint on fire, I do hope," said Mr. Balliboy. He began to run and came quickly to the car.

Mary was now resting comfortably, while two shining creatures with white wings leaned over her. Upon her lap was her newborn babe, smiling happily.

Mr. Balliboy fumbled in his coat for his Christmas gift. He stepped into the van and held out the cross to the babe.

Mary looked proudly at her infant, and the babe, delighted with the shining toy, took hold of the cross.

The angels wept.

HAPPY CHRISTMAS

DAPHNE DU MAURIER

THE LAWRENCE family lived in a large house just outside town.

Mr. Lawrence was a big heavy man, with a round face and a smile. He motored into town every day to his office, where he had a roll-top desk and three secretaries. During the day he used the telephone, and had a business lunch, and then used the telephone again. He made a lot of money.

Mrs. Lawrence had fair hair and china-blue eyes. Mr. Lawrence called her Kitten, but she was not helpless. She had a lovely figure and long fingernails, and she played bridge most afternoons. Bob Lawrence was ten. He was like Mr. Lawrence, only smaller. He was fond of electric trains, and his father had got some men to fix up a miniature railway in the garden. Marigold Lawrence was seven. She was like her mother, only rounder. She had fifteen dolls. She kept breaking them somehow.

If you met them anywhere you would not recognize the Lawrences as being different from any other family. Perhaps that was the trouble. They were just a bit too much like all the rest. Life was a comfortable and easy thing, which was, of course, very pleasant.

On Christmas Eve the Lawrence family did much the same as every other family. Mr. Lawrence came home early from town so that he could stand around and watch the household get ready for tomorrow. He smiled more than usual and put his hands in his pockets and shouted, "Look out, you damn fool!" when he tripped over the dog who was hiding behind some evergreen. Mrs. Lawrence had cut bridge for once and was threading lanterns across the drawing room. Actually it was the garden boy who threaded the lanterns, but Mrs. Lawrence stuck little frills of colored paper round them and handed them to him, and as she was smoking all the time the smoke got in the garden boy's eyes, but he was too polite to brush it away. Bob Lawrence and Marigold Lawrence kept running around the sofas and chairs and calling out, "What am I going to have tomorrow? Am I going to have a train? Am I going to have a doll?" until Mr. Lawrence got fed up and said, "If you don't stop that row you won't get anything," but he said it in a way that did not mean much, and the children were not deceived.

It was just before the children's bedtime that Mrs. Lawrence was called to the telephone. She said "Damn!" and some more smoke got into the garden boy's eyes. Mr. Lawrence picked up a piece of evergreen and stuck it behind a picture. He whistled cheerfully.

Mrs. Lawrence was away five minutes, and when she came back her blue eyes were full of sparks and her hair was rumpled. She looked like a kitten. The kind you pick up and say "Sweet Puss!" to and then quickly put down again.

"Oh, it's a bit thick, it really is," she said, and for a moment the children thought she was going to cry.

"What the hell's the matter?" asked Mr. Lawrence.

"It's that refugee officer for the district," said Mrs. Lawrence. "You know—I told you the place was swarming with refugees. Well, like everybody else, I had to put our names down as receivers when the thing started, never thinking seriously that anything would happen. And now it has. We've got to take in a couple, here, tonight."

Mr. Lawrence stopped smiling. "Look here," he said, "the refugee officer can't do that sort of thing to people without proper warning. Why didn't you tell him to go to blazes?"

"I did," said Mrs. Lawrence indignantly, "and all he could say was that he was very sorry, but it was the same for everybody, and people in every house were having to do it, and he said something about a 'compulsory measure,' which I did not understand, but it sounded nasty."

"They can't do it," said Mr. Lawrence, sticking out his jaw. "I'll get on the phone to someone in authority. I'll see that officer is sacked, I'll go into town myself, I'll—"

"Oh, what's the use?" said Mrs. Lawrence. "Don't let's get ourselves all heated over it. You forget it's Christmas Eve and everyone's out of town by now. Anyway, the creatures are on their way, and we can't very well lock the doors. I suppose I shall have to break it to the servants."

"What will the refugees do?" clamored the children excitedly. "Will they want to take our things? Will they want our beds?"

"Of course not," said Mrs. Lawrence sharply. "Don't be such little idiots!"

"Where are we going to put them?" asked Mr. Lawrence. "We shall have every room full as it is with the Dalys and the Collinses coming over tomorrow. You surely don't suggest we put them off now?"

"No fear," said Mrs. Lawrence, her blue eyes sparkling. "That's one comfort, we can truthfully say the house *is* full. No, the refugees can have the room over the garage. It's been very dry up to now, so the damp won't have got through. There is a bed that we turned out of the house two months ago—the springs had gone. But there's nothing wrong with it. And I think the servants have an oil stove they don't use."

Mr. Lawrence smiled. "You've got it all taped, haven't you?" he said. "No one can get the better of you, Kitten. Oh well, as long as it doesn't hurt us, I don't care." He swooped down in sudden relief and picked up Marigold. "Anyway, we won't let it spoil our Christmas, will we, honey?" he said. And he tossed Marigold in the air, and she shrieked with laughter.

"It's not fair," said Bob Lawrence, his round face flushed. "Marigold is younger than me and she wants to hang up the same size stocking. I'm eldest, I ought to have the biggest, oughtn't I?"

Mr. Lawrence rumpled his son's hair. "Be a man, Bob," he said, "and don't tease your sister. I've got something for you tomorrow better than any toy you'll find in your stocking."

Bob stopped scowling. "Is it something for my railway?" he asked eagerly.

Mr. Lawrence winked and would not answer.

Bob began to jump up and down on his bed. "My present's going to be bigger than Marigold's," he shouted in triumph, "much, much bigger."

"It's not, it's not," cried Marigold tearfully. "Mine is just as nice, isn't it, Dad?"

Mr. Lawrence called to the nurse: "Come and quieten the kids, will you? I think they're getting too excited." He laughed and went down the stairs.

Mrs. Lawrence met him halfway. "They've arrived," she said. Her voice had a warning note.

"Well?" he asked.

She shrugged her shoulders and made a little face. "Jews," she said briefly—and went into the nursery.

Mr. Lawrence said something, and then he straightened his tie and put on an expression that he considered right for refugees. It was a mixture of sternness and bravado. He went round the drive to the garage and climbed the rickety stairs.

"Ha, good evening!" he said in loud, jovial tones as he entered the room. "Are you fixed up all right?"

The room was rather dim, for the one electric-light bulb had not been dusted for many months and it hung in one corner, away from the bed and the table and the stove. The two refugees stared for a moment without speaking. The woman was sitting at the table, unpacking a basket, from which she brought a loaf of bread and two cups. The man was spreading a blanket over the bed, and when Mr. Lawrence spoke he straightened his back and turned toward him.

"We are so grateful," he said, "so very grateful."

Mr. Lawrence coughed and half laughed. "Oh, that's all right," he said. "No trouble at all."

They were Jews and no mistake. The man's nose was enormous, and his skin that typical greasy yellow. The woman had large dark eyes, with shadows beneath them. She looked unhealthy.

[299

"Er—anything else you want?" asked Mr. Lawrence.

The woman answered this time. She shook her head. "We want nothing," she said. "We are very tired."

"Everywhere was full," said the man. "No one could take us in. It is most generous of you."

"Not at all, not at all," said Mr. Lawrence, waving his hand. "Good thing we had this room empty. You must have had a stiff time where you've been."

They said nothing to this.

"Well," said Mr. Lawrence, "if there's nothing more I can do, I'll say good night. Don't forget to turn the stove down if it smokes. And—er—if you should need more food or blankets or anything, just give a knock on the back door and ask the servants. Good night."

"Good night," they echoed, and then the woman added, "A Happy Christmas to you."

Mr. Lawrence stared. "Oh yes," he said. "Yes, of course. Thanks very much."

He turned up the collar of his coat as he walked round to the front door. It was cold. There would be a sharp frost. The gong was just sounding for dinner as he went into the hall. The garden boy had finished stringing up the lanterns, and they fluttered from the ceiling with a jaunty air. Mrs. Lawrence was mixing a drink at the table by the fire.

"Hurry up," she called over her shoulder; "dinner will be spoiled, and if there's anything I loathe it's lukewarm duck."

"Kids asleep?" asked Mr. Lawrence.

"I shouldn't think so," said Mrs. Lawrence. "It's difficult to get them to settle on Christmas Eve. I gave them both some chocolate and told them to be quiet. Want a drink?"

Later, when they were undressing for the night, Mr. Lawrence poked his head round from the dressing room, a toothbrush in his hand.

"Funny thing," he said; "that woman wished me a Happy Christmas. I never knew the Jews kept Christmas before."

"I don't suppose she knows what it means," said Mrs. Lawrence, and she patted some skin food into her round smooth cheek.

One by one the lights in the house were extinguished. The Lawrence family slept. Outside the sky was bright with stars. And in the room over the garage there was one light burning.

"I say, gosh, just look at this, I've got an airplane as well as a new engine for my railway," shouted Bob. "Look, it works like a real one. Look at the propeller."

"Have I got two things from Dad as well?" asked Marigold, fumbling feverishly among the litter of paper on her bed, and she threw aside the large doll she had just unpacked. "Nurse," she shrieked, "where's my other present from Dad?" Her cheeks were hot and flushed.

"Serves you right for being so greedy," mocked Bob. "Look what I've got."

"I'll break your silly horrid plane," said Marigold, and tears began to fall down her cheeks.

"You mustn't quarrel on Christmas Day," said Nurse, and she drew a small box triumphantly from the heap of waste paper. "Look, Marigold, what's in here?"

Marigold tore aside the paper. Soon she held a glittering necklace in her hands. "I'm a princess!" she shouted. "I'm a princess!"

Bob threw her a glance of contempt. "It's not very big," he said.

Downstairs Mr. and Mrs. Lawrence were being served with their morning tea. The electric stove was lighted, the curtains drawn, and the room was flooded with sunlight. The letters and the parcels remained unopened, though, for both Mr. and Mrs. Lawrence listened aghast to the tale that Anna, the servant, had to tell.

"I can't believe it, it's preposterous," said Mr. Lawrence.

"I can. It's just typical of the sort of thing these people do," said Mrs. Lawrence.

"Won't I give that refugee officer hell!" said Mr. Lawrence.

"I don't suppose he knew," said Mrs. Lawrence. "They took jolly good care not to let on that anything might happen. Well, we can't keep them here now, that's certain. There's no one here to look after the woman."

"We must telephone for an ambulance and have them removed," said Mr. Lawrence. "I thought the woman had a bad color. She must be pretty tough to have stood it, all alone."

"Oh, those sort of people have babies very easily," said Mrs. Lawrence. "They scarcely feel it. Well, I'm very thankful they were in the garage room and not in the house. They can't have done much damage there. And, Anna," she called, as the maid was leaving the room, "be sure and tell Nurse that the children are not to go near the garage until the ambulance has been."

Then they settled down to the letters and parcels.

"We'll make everyone laugh at the story, anyway," said Mr. Lawrence. "It will go down well with the turkey and the plum pudding."

When they had breakfasted and had dressed, and the children had been in to tumble about on the beds and show their presents, Mr. and Mrs. Lawrence went round to the garage to see what could be done about the refugees. The children were sent up to the nursery to play with their new things, because, after all, what had happened was not very nice, as Nurse agreed with Mrs. Lawrence. And besides, you never knew.

When they came to the garage they found a little crowd of servants in the yard talking. There were the cook, and the parlor man, and one of the housemaids, and the chauffeur, and even the garden boy.

"What's going on?" asked Mr. Lawrence.

"They've cleared out," said the chauffeur.

"How do you mean, cleared out?"

"The fellow went off while we were having breakfast and got hold of a taxi," said the chauffeur. "He must have gone to the stand at the end of the road. Never a word to any of us."

"And we heard wheels by the back gate," chimed in the cook, "and he and the taxi driver were lifting the woman into the car."

"The fellow asked for the name of a hospital, and we told him there was a Jewish hospital just before you get into town," said the chauffeur. "He said he was very sorry to have given us all this trouble. Cool sort of customer, hadn't turned a hair."

"And the baby. We saw the baby," giggled the housemaid, and then she blushed furiously for no reason.

"Yes," said the cook, "a proper little Jew, the image of his father."

And then they all laughed and looked at one another rather foolishly.

"Well," said Mr. Lawrence, "there's nothing more any of us can do, I suppose."

The servants melted away. The excitement for the moment was over. There was the Christmas party to prepare for, and what with one thing and another they felt they had been run off their legs already, and it was only ten o'clock.

"We'd better have a look," said Mr. Lawrence, jerking his head at the garage. Mrs. Lawrence made a face and followed him.

They climbed the rickety stairs to the little dark room in the loft. There was no sign of disorder. The bed had been placed back against the wall, and the blanket was neatly folded at the foot. The chair and table were in the usual place. The window in the room had been opened to let in the fresh morning air. The stove had been turned out. Only one thing showed that the room had been used. On the floor, beside the bed, was a glass of cold water.

Mr. Lawrence did not say anything. Mrs. Lawrence did not say anything, either. They went back to the house and into the drawing room. Mr. Lawrence wandered to the window and looked out across the garden. He could see Bob's miniature railway at the far corner. Mrs. Lawrence opened a parcel she had not seen at breakfast. Overhead, shouts and yells told that the children were either enjoying themselves or not.

"What about your golf? Weren't you meeting the others at eleven?" asked Mrs. Lawrence.

Mr. Lawrence sat down on the window seat. "I don't feel very keen," he said.

Mrs. Lawrence put back the vanity case she had just drawn from sheet after sheet of tissue paper.

"Funny," she said, "I feel sort of flat too, not a bit Christmasy."

Through the open door they could see the table in the dining room being prepared for lunch. The decorations looked fine, with the little bunches of flowers amidst the silver. Round the center was a great heap of crackers.

"I really don't know what else we could have done," said Mrs. Lawrence suddenly.

Mr. Lawrence did not answer. He arose and began walking up and down the room. Mrs. Lawrence straightened the evergreen behind a picture.

"After all, they didn't ask for anything," said Mrs. Lawrence. "The man would have said," went on Mrs. Lawrence, "if the woman had been very ill, or the baby. I'm sure they were both all right. They are so tough, that race."

Mr. Lawrence took out a cigar from his waistcoat pocket and put it back again.

"They'll be much better off in the Jewish hospital than they would have been here," said Mrs. Lawrence, "—proper nursing and everything. We couldn't possibly have coped with it. Besides, going off in a hurry like that, so independent, we did not have a chance to suggest a thing."

Mr. Lawrence picked up a book and then shut it. Mrs. Lawrence kept twisting and untwisting the belt on her dress.

"Of course," she said hurriedly, "I shall go and inquire how they are, and take fruit and things, and perhaps some warm woollies, and ask if there is anything else they want. I'd go this morning, only I have to take the children to church. . . ."

And then the door opened and the children came into the room.

"I've got my new necklace on," said Marigold. "Bob hasn't anything new to wear." She pirouetted round on her toes. "Hurry up, Mummy, we shall be late, and we shall miss seeing all the people come in."

"I hope they sing 'Hark the Herald Angels,'" said Bob. "We learned the words in school and I shan't have to look at the book. Why was Jesus born in a stable, Dad?"

"There wasn't room for them at the inn," said Mr. Lawrence.

"Why, were they refugees?" said Marigold.

Nobody answered for a moment, and then Mrs. Lawrence got up and tied her hair in front of the looking glass.

"Don't ask such silly questions, darling," she said.

Mr. Lawrence threw open the window. Across the garden came the sound of the church bells. The sun shone on the clean white frost, turning it to silver. Mr. Lawrence had a funny, puzzled look on his face.

"I wish . . ." he began, "I wish . . ." But he never finished what he was going to say, because the two cars carrying the Daly family and the Collins family drove in at the gate and up the drive, and the children with shouts of delight were running out onto the steps and calling, "Happy Christmas, Happy Christmas!"

THE STORY OF THE LOST STAR

GRACE LIVINGSTON HILL

ABOUT a week before Christmas in a small city of the East there appeared in the Lost and Found column this advertisement:

Lost. Sometime between the World War and the present morning, The Star of Bethlehem. The finder will confer everlasting favor and receive a reward of ten thousand dollars if returned to the owner between the hours of sundown and midnight on Christmas Eve.

(Signed) George K. Hamilton,
Eleven, Harvard Place.

The typesetter blinked and paused in his busy work, read it again and wondered. Ten thousand dollars! Was it a joke? It must be a mistake! But no, it was paid for. It must go in. He punched away at his machine and the lines appeared in the type, but his thoughts were busy. Ten thousand dollars! With that he could, with self respect, marry Mary! He would not have been John if he had not thought of that first.

George K. Hamilton! That was the rich guy who lived in the big house, with one blind wall stuck on its side that everybody said was a picture gallery. He was rolling in wealth so it must be real. But what was this thing he had lost that was worth everlasting favor and ten thousand dollars? A jewel? A silver tablet? Something of intrinsic historic value perhaps? Something that must be well known, or the writer would not have spoken of it in that offhand indefinite way as *the* Star of Bethlehem, as if there were but one. Bethlehem—Bethlehem—that was the place where they made steel! Steel! why—steel, of course. George K. Hamilton. Hamilton the steel king! Ah! Why hadn't he thought of it at once?

And why couldn't he go to Bethlehem and find out all about it? He was the first one, excepting the editor of the Lost and Found column, to see this ad. Why wouldn't he stand first chance of the reward if he worked it right?

To be sure there was a possibility that someone, who knew just what this star was, would be able to get on its track sooner, but if he caught the first train in the morning he would have a good start before anyone read the morning papers.

He would be through with his work by three A.M. at the latest, and there was a train at five. He would have time to get back to his boarding place and clean up a bit, perhaps scribble a note to Mary telling her to be ready for the wedding.

His fingers flew over the keys of his machine as he laid his plans, and his heart throbbed with excitement over the great opportunity that had flung its open door right in his humble path. Ten thousand dollars!

Early dawn saw him dressed in his best and hurrying on his way to Bethlehem amid a trainload of laborers going out for the day's work. But he saw not pick nor shovel nor dinner pail, nor noted greasy overalls and sleepy-eyed companions. Before his shining eyes was a star, sometimes silver, sumptuously engraved, sometimes gold, and set in sparkling jewels, leading him on into the day of adventure.

He essayed to question his fellow seatmate about the star:

"You live in Bethlehem? Did you ever see the Star of Bethlehem?"

But the man stood his head dumbly:

"Me no spak L'angla!"

Arrived in the City of Steel he went straight to the news agent:

"Have you been here some time?"

"Born here."

"Then tell me, have you a Star of Bethlehem?"

The agent shook his head.

"Don't smoke that kind. Don't keep that kind. Try the little cigar store down the street." And he swung himself under the shelf and, shouldering a pile of morning papers, rushed off down the platform.

Out in the street John stopped a man whose foot was just mounting the running board of his car:

"Do you know anything about the Star of Bethlehem?"

"Never heard of it, man. A Ford's good enough for me!" and he swung into his car and shot away from the curb hurriedly.

He asked a little girl who was hurrying away from the bakery with a basket of bread.

"Why, Star-of-Bethlehem is a flower," she said, "a little green-and-white starry flower with pointed petals. It grows in the meadow over there in the summertime, but it's all gone now. You can't find Stars-of-Bethlehem this time of year!" And she stared after him for a silly fool.

He asked a passer on the street:

"Can you tell me how to find out about Star of Bethlehem?"

The man tapped him lightly on the shoulder with a wink and advised him knowingly, with a thumb pointing down a side alley:

"You better not mention that openly, brother. There's been several raids around here lately and the police are wise. It ain't safe."

And about this time the Bishop back at home was opening the morning paper at the breakfast table as he toyed with his grapefruit and coffee:

"He, ha!" he said as his eye traveled down the column idly and paused at the Lost and Found, "Listen to this, Bella. Poor old George has got 'em again. He probably thinks he is going to die this time. I'll just step in and have a little talk on theology with him this morning and set his mind at rest. No need for that ten thousand dollars to go out of the church. We might as well have it as some home for the feeble minded."

Bella left her coffee and came around to read the advertisement, her face lighting intelligently:

"Oh, Basil! Do you think you can work it?" she cried delightedly.

"Why, sure, he's just a little daffy on religion now because he's been sick. The last time I saw him he asked me how we could know any of the creeds were true when they were all so different. I'll smooth it all out for him, and make him give another ten thousand or so to the social service work of our church, and he'll come across handsomely, you'll see. I'd better go at once. It won't do to wait, there are too many kinds of crooks on the lookout for just such a soft ten thousand as this." And he took his hat and coat and hurried out.

The Professor at his meager breakfast table, worrying about his sick wife, and how he could afford to keep his eldest son in college, happened on the item.

He set down his coffee cup untasted and stepped to his book shelves taking down several wise treatises on astronomy.

A sweet-faced saint in an invalid chair read and pondered and murmured thoughtfully: "Poor soul! What's happened to the man's Bible?"

Before night the one little shop in the city that made a specialty of astronomical instruments had been drained of everything in the shape of a searcher of the heavens, and a rush order had gone to New York by telegraph for more telescopes of various sizes and prices, while a boy in the back office who was good at lettering was busy making a copy of the advertisement to fasten up in the plate-glass window, with special electric lights playing about it and a note below:

"Come in and order your telescope now before they are all gone, and get into line for the great sky prize! We have 'em! All prices!"

Far into the evening the crowd continued around that window and many who had glasses at home hurried away to search for them, and build air castles of how they would spend the ten thousand dollars when they got it.

Even before the day was half over the office of the University was besieged by eager visitors come to question wise ones, a folded newspaper furtively held under each applicant's arm.

As evening drew on shadowy figures stole forth to high places and might have been seen scanning the heavens, and now and then consulting a book by means of a pocket flashlight. More than one young student worked into the small hours of the night with reference books scattered about him, writing a many-paged treatise on the Star of Stars, some to prove that the star was a myth, and others that it was still in existence and would one day appear again as bright as of old. Even the police, coming suddenly upon the lurking stargazers far toward morning, began to question what had taken hold of the town.

Coming home on the late train from a fruitless search for an unknown quantity which was not there, John Powers sat wearily back in the fusty seat of the common car and took out the worn advertisement from his pocket to read it once more.

The lost Star of Bethlehem! What could it be? He had searched the steel city from end to end without finding so much as a trace of tradition or story about a star in connection with that town. He had met with more rebuffs and strange suggestions than ever before in his life together, and he was dog-weary and utterly discouraged. If only he had not written that hopeful letter to Mary in the morning!

Now perhaps she would already be planning to have the wedding soon, and where was the money coming from to provide the little home?

Of course it just might happen that after all the star had been lost up in the city, else why should the advertisement have been put in the city paper and not in the Bethlehem local? But even so he had hoped great things from this trip to Bethlehem and now he had only wasted a day and the carfare, and had gotten nowhere at all.

At a local station a loud-mouthed traveler got off, leaving his recent seatmate without anyone to talk to, and presently he joined John Powers and entered into conversation, being one of those men who is never happy unless his tongue is wagging. In the course of their talk, John found himself asking the old question again:

"You say you are from Bethlehem? Did you ever hear of a star in connection with that town? Was there any memorial tablet or monument or emblem or anything in the shape of a star, that has been stolen away? Star of Bethlehem it was called, do you know anything about it?"

The stranger stared blankly and shook his head.

"Sounds to me as if it might be a song, or a book mebbe. If you knowed who wrote it you might find out at one o' the schools. My Johnny says you can find out almost anything if you know who wrote it. Ever been a Mason? Might be some kind of a Masonic badge, mightn't it?"

The man got out at the next station and Powers leaned back wearily and thought how he had failed. His mind seemed too tired to think any longer on the subject.

An old lady with a queer bonnet with many bundles at her feet and a basket beside her out of which stuck a pair of turkey's feet, leaned over suddenly and touched him on the shoulder.

"Laddie, hae ye tried the auld Buik?" she asked timidly, "I'm thinkin' ye'll find it all there."

"I beg your pardon!" said Powers lifting his hat courteously and thinking how the blue of her eyes had a light like that in Mary's eyes.

He arose from his seat and went back to sit beside her. Then somehow the blue of her eyes made him unafraid, and he told her all about the ten thousand dollars and his fruitless trip to Bethlehem.

"Oh, but laddie, ye're on the wrong track entirely," said the old lady. "The Star of Bethlehem's in the auld Buik. I ken it's no the fashion to read it these days, but the worruld lost sight of a lot besides the things it wanted to forget when it set out to put its Bibles awa! Hunt up yer mither's Bible, lad, and study it out. The star arose in the East ye ken, and the folks who saw it first was those that was lookin' fer its arisin'. The star's *na* lost. It led to the little King ye ken, an' it'll always lead to the King if a body seeks with all the heirt, fer that is the promise: 'An' ye shall find Me, when ye shall seek fer Me with all yer heirts.' Many like the puir buddy who wrote the bit lines in the paper was longin' fer the King hisself an' wanted the star to guide him, but ye ken ye can't purchase the gifts of God wi' silver ner gold. The mon may lay his ten thousand baubles at the fut of the throne, but he'll find he must go his own self across the desert, and wait mayhap, before he'll ever see the shinin' of the Star. But you'll not turn back yerself now you've started, laddie! Go find the King fer yerself. Look in the Gospels an' read the story. It's passin' wonderful an' lovely. This is my station now, and I'll be leavin' ye, but it'll be a glad Christmas time fer you ef you find the little King, an' *ye'll find Him sure*, if ye seek with all yer heirt."

The doorway to the fine old Hamilton mansion on Harvard Place was besieged by applicants from morning to night all that week, wishing to speak with the Master, but to all the grave and dignified servitor who answered the door replied:

"My master is away. He cannot speak with you until the time appointed. If any then have found the lost treasure they may come and claim the reward. But they must come bringing it with them. None others need present themselves."

Even the Bishop had not been able to gain admittance. He was much annoyed about it. He was afraid others would get ahead of him. He had written a letter, but he knew it had not yet been opened for the last time he called he had seen it lying on the console in the hall with a lot of other unopened letters. The Bishop was very certain that if he could have audience *first* all would be well. He was sure he could explain the philosophy of life and the mystery of the star quite satisfactorily and soothingly.

Before John Powers had gone back to work that night on his return from Bethlehem, he had gone to the bottom of an old chest and hunted out his mother's Bible. It was worn and dropping apart in places, but he put it tenderly on his bed, and following an impulse, dropped to his knees beside it, laying his lips against its dusty covers. Somehow the very look of the old worn covers brought back his childhood days, and a sense of sin in that he had wandered so far from the path in which his mother had set his young feet.

All that week he gave all the extra time he had to studying about the star. He did not even go to see Mary. He lost sight of the ten thousand dollars in his interest in the star itself. He was now seeking to find that star for himself, not for the reward that had been offered. He wanted to find the King who was also a Saviour.

The last night before it came time for him to go to his work, he dropped upon his knees once more beside the little tattered book, and prayed:

"Oh Jesus Christ, Saviour of the world, I thank Thee that Thou has sent Thy star to guide me to Thee. I worship Thee, and I give myself to Thee forever."

On Christmas Eve when the door of the mansion was thrown open a large throng of people entered, and were speedily admitted, one by one, to audience with the master of the house, until in an incredibly short space of time, the waiting room was emptied of philosophers and dreamers and ambitious ones. Even the Bishop had been courteously sent his way. Only three were left. Three wise ones, and two of them were women!

One was an old woman with a burr upon her tongue and a Bible in her hand; one was a young girl with blue, starry eyes and a bit of a Testament in the folds of her gown where she kept her fingers between the leaves to a place. The third was John Powers, standing within the shadow of a heavy curtain beside a deepset window looking out at the great shining of a bright star, with peace upon his face. He turned about as the door closed after the Bishop and glanced at the two women. The girl looked up and their eyes met.

"Mary!"

"John!"

There was scarcely time to recognize the old woman before the door opened and George K. Hamilton, keen of eye, sharp of feature, eager of expression, walked in and looked from one to the other searching each face questioningly.

[31]

The young man stepped forward to meet him and Mary saw for the first time that a worn little Bible was in his hand.

But John was speaking in such a ringing voice of certainty:

"Sir, I want to tell you first that I have not come for your money. When I began this search it was in hope of the reward, but I've found the Star itself, and it led me to the King, and now I've brought it to you because I want you to have it too. You'll find it in this Book. It has to be searched for, but it's there. And when you have found it I've been thinking you'll maybe want to sell all that you have and give to the poor and go and follow *Him*. But *I* am not one of those poor any longer, for I *have found the King!* Come, Mary, shall we go?"

Then up rose the old Scotch woman from her place near the door:

"I've just one more word to say, an' ye'll find it in yon Buik: 'Arise, shine; for thy light is come, and the Glory of the Lord is risen upon thee.' That star isn't lost, sir, an' never was! Never will be! It's up in the heavens waiting till the King has need of it again, and someday it will burst upon the world again and they will all know that it has been there all the time!"

The Master was left alone in his mansion with the book in his hand and a strange awed feeling of the Presence of God in his room.

He looked wonderingly, doubtfully, down at the book, and then wistfully out through his richly draped window to where a single star shone softly through the Christmas night.

THE HOUR OF STARS

HERMANN HAGEDORN

One moment they were outside the high wire fence, the next they were within, three bearded old men in fur caps and overcoats, steaming like engines in a switching yard as their breath froze in the bitter December cold. They ploughed over the broken snow inside the enclosure. Low, black barracks lay across their path. One moment they were outside them, the next they were within, huddling over an iron stove whose sides glowed red.

"You are strangers," said one of the men, "and yet I think I have known you before."

"Yes," murmured another dreamily, "I think we were once companions on a journey. It was a long time ago."

"Yes," mused the third, "and very far away."

"That, too, was a winter night," said the first, a big man with a big head, "but not like this."

"Not like this," said the second, who was round and small and full of dreams.

"No," said the first, "that night was clear."

"There were stars, if I remember correctly," said the other man, who was lean and precise.

"Many stars," the little man agreed.

"I remember only one," the big man declared flatly.

"There were many stars, I tell you!" the lean old man insisted.

"Many stars," echoed the little man, "but—"

"I remember only one."

"One!" In the little man's mind amorphous shapes were beginning to take outline and color.

"Yes, I remember now," the lean man grudgingly assented, "one was brighter than all the others."

"One was brighter than all the others put together."

"It was strange, that star."

"It seemed alive."

"It was alive. It moved across the sky like a man's hand, pointing..."

"A man's hand..."

"God's hand..."

"God's hand pointing."

"What was it pointing at? Do you remember?"

"It was a long time ago." The little fellow's mind had gone vague again.

"I remember," cried the bean pole, "it was pointing at a stable."

"A stable!"

"That was an odd thing for the finger of God to be pointing at!"

"Not so odd. It was not really pointing at the stable. Don't you remember? It was pointing at something inside the stable."

The fat man nodded vacantly. "That was far away and very long ago."

The big man was staring past the stove into the darkness of the long room. "My memory seems to hold nothing except a sense of light."

"That was all there was," cried the lean fellow. "Light!"

"No, there was more," cried the other, struggling to recall. "The light was alive."

"Of course, foolish old man. Light is always alive."

"You don't understand. This light had hands and feet."

"I begin to remember," said the fat little man, coming to life. "It had eyes."

"Why do I want to kneel when I think of those eyes?"

"Why do I want to die when I think of that heart?"

The lean man looked frightened. "To die?"

"I too want to die."

316]

"Yes, yes, to die that we may live."

"I see it all now!" exclaimed the big man. "A dark room, dark as this."

"An ox, an ass...."

"A manger. There was a manger. I am sure there was a manger."

"There was a Child in the manger, a Child, lying on straw."

"There was the Light."

"Of course!" The fat man's little eyes were alive and alert. "The Child was the Light."

"A woman was near, and a man. How it all comes back!"

"You brought gifts, Melchior."

"You, too, Balthasar."

"And you, Ka-Spar."

"Gold and rubies."

"Frankincense and myrrh."

"Silks from India and Cathay."

"Pearls from the sea, pearls from the depths of the sea."

"I thought my gifts worthy of a king," murmured the big man, "and was proud of them on the long journey, but they seemed trash when I laid them at the Child's feet."

"He wanted something else," cried the little man.

"Something to Him more precious."

"Me?"

"Yes. And *me*."

"And *me*."

"I did not know it was me He wanted, not then," said the big man who had been called Melchior, "and I have been wandering since, through all space and all time, trying to find Him again and offer what I then held back."

"What *I* held back."

"What *I* held back."

"Do you remember ... ?" cried the little man, whose eyes were beginning to dance.

"What?"

"Was there not singing?"

"Why, yes, now you speak of it. I do remember singing."

[317

"It sounded like the singing of children."

"Not children. Angels."

"Angels . . ." the little man was back in dreams.

"Do you remember what they sang?"

"I have forgotten. It was very long ago."

"I remember . . ." whispered lean Balthazar.

"What was it?"

"Glory to God in the highest . . ."

"Now I remember. On earth, peace, to men of good will."

"Peace. What is peace?" asked the little man. "I have forgotten."

"I never knew until that night," answered big Melchior, "but kneeling beside the manger, I knew."

"I, too, kneeling beside the manger."

"Yes, kneeling beside the manger."

"I have wandered far since that night, and studied deeply and gained much knowledge, but I have not known peace again."

"I have ruled a kingdom, but I never knew peace again."

The eyes of Ka-Spar, the little man, were sad as falling leaves. "I have gathered great riches, but I have never again known peace."

The long dark room was suddenly filled with a thousand men, crowding around the three. "Santa Claus! Santa Claus in person!"

"No. It is three Santa Clauses! St. Nicholas in triplicate, whiskers and all!"

"You must be Russian swine! Nobody hides his dirty face in the bushes like that except in Russia."

"Who are you, strange young men?"

"We five are Nazi Storm Troopers. These cattle are Russians. They are prisoners. We are guarding them."

"What is that in your hand?"

"Why, that's a gun, of course, you old fool. What else would it be?"

"What is a gun?"

Derisive laughter clattered against the low roof.

"What is a gun? That's a question! A gun is power. A gun is a king."

"A king?" said lean old Balthasar. "I was a king once."

"You were a king, you were! Tell that to the rats!"

"I'll tell you what a gun is," cried another of the guards. "A gun is God."

The old men shook their heads. "A gun is not God," said old Melchior, with quiet grandeur. "God alone is God."

Once more, the derisive laughter beat like bats against the low rafters.

"There is just one thing in this place we all agree on, we Nazis who are to rule the world, and these swine who are to be our slaves. God is a myth, an impertinence, a bad joke, a fifth wheel, a fifth column invented by the Devil to undermine national morale."

Huge old Melchior lifted his face suddenly, and the derision died. "I saw God once," he said.

Whistles and catcalls answered him. The guards snorted and one of them made a lunge for the old man and swept a cat-o'-nine-tails sharply across his face.

"Nevertheless," said Melchior with composure, "I did see Him."

The room was suddenly still, as still as the northern plains when the green fires danced on the horizon. "It was a winter night like this," great Melchior went on. "I had been told in a dream to follow a star. I followed it for days and nights and weeks and weary moons. It shone at last on a stable. And in the stable I found a Child in a manger, with his mother beside Him. And the Child was all Light, and I bowed down and worshipped Him."

"You're a fake!" growled one of the prisoners. "A rotten fake! I know that story. My mother used to tell it to me."

"Yes," whispered a guard to his neighbor, "my mother told me that story too. At the foot of the Christmas tree."

"Nothing ever was like Christmas at home," the other guard whispered, "the tree with the white candles flickering, the smell of the pine needles, the presents, the *Honigkuchen,* the songs, the beautiful songs, *Stille Nacht . . . O Tannenbaum . . .* The transparency of the Christ child, the tender thoughts for one another, the loving and the giving. Will there ever be a Christmas again?"

"My mother told me all about the Christ-child!" said one of the prisoners.

"I saw the Christ-child," said big Melchior.

"And I," said Ka-Spar.

"And I," murmured Balthasar.

"Jewish propaganda!" shouted the guard with the whip. "Filthy, Jewish mythology! Beat them and throw them out!"

"There were angels singing," went on the old man, as though the guards were on another planet, "singing Glory to God in the Highest, peace on earth, to men of good will."

"Did the angels say peace?" asked one of the prisoners.

"You'll get all the peace you want," the guard retorted, reaching again for his whip. "Peace is for swine like you, and you shall rot in it! Peace is for those who can't take it. Strong men want no peace."

"I am strong," cried the guard whose mother had told him the story of the Magi. "I can take it, and I want peace. I want it as I never wanted anything in my life, not food, or drink, or fire, or money. I want it above me and below me, around me, and inside of me. Most of all, inside of me."

"And I!" cried another guard.

"Peace!" cried one of the prisoners. And "Peace!" cried a hundred, five hundred, until all the air was sibilant and aflame with the word.

"I want peace!" a prisoner called hungrily. Another took up the cry, "I too want peace!" And a thousand echoed. "And I! And I!"

"Tell us, old men, how can we find peace?"

"Peace," said old Melchior softly, "is where the Child is, and where the Child is not, there is no peace."

"Where the Child is," murmured Balthasar, "there is peace."

"Where the Child is not," whispered the little fat man as though from far away, "there is no peace."

"Who is the Child?" asked the guard with gray lips and feverish eyes.

The big man sat staring into the darkness. "The Child," he said softly, "is the straight look in the eyes of men, the straight words on their lips, the straight thoughts in their hearts."

"The Child," murmured Balthasar the lean, "is the love each

has for another and for all others, love that is patience and forbearance, and sternness, too; love that is fellowship, which makes dead stones bear fruit and makes three men a host."

"The Child," said the little man, with his pale little eyes burning, "is the hunger for life that creates life. The Child is itself that life, and men die to achieve it, throwing away a lifetime for it in one glowing moment, or laying aside, one after another, through slow years, the shells of life that are not life, in order to find that which forever makes, forever builds, forever grows into new and higher forms."

The dark room was no longer dark, the dead faces were no longer dead, as the three old men chanted:

"The Child is power, transforming weakness into strength, defeat into victory, death into resurrection."

"The Child is law—the sower reaps, the killer kills himself, the golden calf shrivels and is dust in the nostrils; he who subdues the wolf in the heart inherits the earth."

"The Child in the end, as in the beginning, is love—love that is free and gives freedom, freedom to crawl or to soar, to build or to destroy, to live or to die, but, above all, freedom to choose between darkness and light, and, choosing, to grow."

Guards and prisoners were one now, a single mass of white-faced men with eyes that glowed and hands that reached out darkly for hands to clasp.

The guard with the whip threw it from him as though it turned. "How shall I find Him?"

"How shall we find Him?" echoed a thousand voices.

"Come with us," said big Melchior. "Perhaps there will be a star again."

"There is always a star," Balthasar declared, "if you really want it."

"And there is always the manger," murmured the little fat man.

"A star, a manger, a Child."

Somebody laughed, and suddenly everybody was laughing, not in derision now but in exultation, relaxing after unbearable tension, laughing the free laughter of the morning wind in the apple trees and the evening wind on the quiet sea, and the laughter of boys and girls tumbling in the hay, the laughter of lovers, discovering new beauties each in the other.

"Come, children," said the big old man, "let us set forth. It is the hour of stars."

TO COME UNTO ME

ROBERT NATHAN

THAT YEAR there were very few houses for rent anywhere; and people lived wherever they could. Only the rich were able to buy an entire house, with wood and plaster walls, a rose garden and a bathroom. Nevertheless on Christmas Eve both rich and poor enjoyed the spirit of the season; for the rich gave each other gifts and the poor were delighted with the sight of the Christmas trees which, painted white, blue, and even green, and decorated with colored lights, twinkled everywhere along the public highways.

At the house of a very famous man a party was in progress. Since this man was the president of a motion-picture studio, his guests were for the most part motion-picture actors and actresses, which is to say that they were the most beautiful and famous people in the world. This did not make them as happy as might have been expected; and they joined in the singing of Christmas carols with hearts no less lonely and empty than those of poor people who also wished to be loved.

Among these famous and beautiful people were two children, named Henry and Lettice. Everybody in the world knew what they looked like, what they talked like, what their favorite games were, what they wore and what they liked to eat. But what no one knew was what was in their hearts, because their hearts were the hearts of children.

And so, while the fiddles scraped, while the great singers sang, and while the footmen passed about among the guests with glasses of champagne and punch, and little sandwiches in the shape of snowflakes and crescent moons, and gingersnaps for the children, Lettice went tiptoeing to Henry in one corner of the great room and asked him, "What are you doing?"

To which Henry replied, "Nothing."

However, nothing to a child is so crowded with dreams as *nothing*. And so, when Lettice said, "I know a wonderful secret," Henry followed her out of the room and down the long hall and out into the garden, prepared for all the beautiful things without a name which he had been dreaming about.

But all he saw at the end of the garden was a kind of stable, with a little light over the door.

"I don't think that's so wonderful," said Henry.

"That's because you don't know," said Lettice.

"Don't know what?" asked Henry.

In answer, Lettice opened the door of the stable. And there, lying in a crib made of an old manger, was a baby.

"Now what do you think?" said Lettice triumphantly.

"I don't think it's wonderful at all," said Henry.

"Do you think maybe it's Baby Jesus?" asked Lettice.

"I don't know," said Henry. "I never saw it before."

"I wish it was Baby Jesus," said Lettice, "because then we could pray."

"You can pray if you want to," said Henry, "on account of you wouldn't know who it was till afterward anyhow."

"I can say now 'Now I lay me' and the Lord's Prayer," said Lettice.

"All right," said Henry. "I don't mind."

So the two children knelt on the floor of the tool shed, in front of the baby, whose father and mother, having no other place to live at the moment, were helping the cook at the big house wash dishes in return for a roof over their heads.

"Our Father which art in Heaven," said Lettice. "Hallowed be Thy name...."

And all around them as they knelt, the invisible air was peopled with the unseen faces of the past, with saints and captains, beggars

324]

and kings, with the smiling children, the dreaming children into whose hands, year after year, God had delivered His world, into whose hearts, endlessly renewed, He had put His love, into whose keeping He had given His Son.

For it is in the hands of the children that all things are placed, both good and evil, the poem and the sword, the knowledge of distant worlds, the hope of peace and the fruitfulness of earth.

"I pray the Lord," said Henry, "my soul to keep."

In the big house they sang "O Little Star of Bethlehem" and Lettice's mother and Henry's father wondered where they were. And in the kitchen the two new helpers smiled at each other across the soapy water. They did not expect very much for their child. Perhaps he might grow up to be a good carpenter.

EPILOGUE

THE LIGHT THAT NO DARKNESS
CAN PUT OUT

HARRY EMERSON FOSDICK

WHEN the early stories about Jesus' birth took form in the early church they emphasized the fact that it was night when he was born. The shepherds were keeping watch over their flocks by night; the Wise Men were following the star through the night; in Herod's gloomy midnight councils all the little children of Bethlehem were to be slain, and every way it was against encompassing darkness that Christ's coming shone out.

When people now say that these are dour times in which to keep Christmas, they forget this basic fact about the Christmas stories. This is indeed a dark time, but if what those first narratives say in symbol and what Phillips Brooks long afterwards sang of Bethlehem is true,

> "Yet in they dark streets shineth
> the everlasting Light,"

then all the more this is a grand era in which to understand what Christmas really means. In easier times we left the night out of the picture and made of the Christmas season a light-hearted holiday of festival and merriment, but now we are back where Christmas started—with its deep, black background behind the Savior's coming, like midnight behind the star.

Nearly a hundred years after Bethlehem the writer of the Fourth Gospel was still thinking of Christ's advent in terms of light shining in darkness. John, too, lived in a dour world, in Ephesus, where the goddess Diana was worshipped under the image of a meteorite stone, and in an age shadowed by paganism and violence. Yet something had happened to him that, as Clement of Alexandria later put it, had "changed sunset into sunrise." Christ had come, and all through his Gospel, John speaks of him in terms of light. "In him," John writes in his first chapter, "was life; and the life was the light of men . . . the light shineth in the darkness; and the darkness apprehended it not." That last phrase is a mistranslation; scholars would now substantially agree, I think, with Dr. Goodspeed's better rendering: "The light is still shining in the darkness, for the darkness has never put it out." That fact John proclaims with amazement and gratitude—the night so black, the radiance of Christ at first so limited, he stands in awe before the fact that after nearly a century the light is still shining.

Surely, that is a Christmas text for us now. Not after one century, but after nearly twenty, we still can say at least this much about the radiance Christ kindled in the world: The darkness has not put it out.

Note at once the contrast between John and us with regard to the place where the emphasis is put. We are tempted to be obsessed by the darkness. This is a gloomy time, we say. John, upon the contrary, takes the darkness for granted. Of course, darkness! What kind of a world do you think this is, he could say to us; stop fooling yourselves with sentimental optimism; the sin of the world is beastly; the plight of the world desperate; man's moral depravity and incompetence profound—of course, darkness! So John took the world's black night for granted, and with amazement and gratitude emphasized the light. *There* to him was the astonishing fact, that against the night a guiding star had shined, that into the gloom a flaming hope had come, and that all the hosts of evil had been unable to quench it.

As we translate this way of looking at Christ's coming into the terms of our experience now, consider first that it presents us with a great heritage—the continuing influence of Christ—to which we ought to give our personal faith and allegiance. There can be no wiser counsel in a dark time than to get our eyes on whatever light there is in our heritage, believe in that and follow it. A friend of mine was once lost in the woods in the Adirondacks, and as night came on, completely bewildered, he climbed a tree, and there, far off and dim, he saw a single light. It was not much, but it was something to center his faith on, and guide his steps by, in the night. Well, in our heritage there is a great light that the darkness has never been able to put out.

This is true in our national life. When I for one think of these years ahead, when the use we make of America's predominant power will have such fateful consequences for the world's future, I am more anxious about this nation than ever before in my life. So Lord Milner said once, "The last thing which the thought of the [British] Empire inspires in me is a desire to boast—to wave a flag, or to shout 'Rule Britannia.' When I think of it, I am much more inclined to go into a corner by myself and pray." So we had better pray for America now, that the best in our national heritage—the light there—may be seen and followed. For with all our materialism, our greed, our selfish nationalism and isolationism, there is, in our American tradition at its best, a light—men and women to whom America's power has been a sacred trust to be used in the sight of God for the good of all mankind. Remember John Adams, a founding father, saying, "I always consider the settlement of America with reverence and wonder, as the opening of a grand scene and design in Providence for the illumination of the ignorant, and the emancipation of the slavish part of mankind all over the earth." God grant now that we may believe in that best of our tradition! As for Christians, what a heritage we have! Illumination did come to the world in Christ, and amid the blackness of our Western history his radiance has spread, in every generation some men and women rediscovering him and his way of life and so producing the noblest character that shines amid history's cruelty and gloom; and the most amazing fact about it is that all the hosts of darkness have never been able to put it out.

They have tried hard enough. From Herod's bloody plot to slay Bethlehem's children, to Caiaphas and Pilate, the Gospels portray the mad endeavors of dark powers to put out that flame of life and hope. In *Othello* you recall the fateful hour when the jealous Moor comes into Desdemona's room to slay her, and, extinguishing the candle, says, "Put out the light, and then put out the light." So, more than once in the Gospels and in subsequent history, one stands, as it were, with bated breath as the powers of evil seem about to quench the flame that was kindled at Bethlehem.

About thirty-five years after Calvary the Roman historian Tacitus wrote in astonishment and indignation because the Christian movement had gone on so long unstopped: This "pestilent superstition," Tacitus wrote, "though checked for the time being, broke out afresh, not only in Judea, where the mischief started, but also at Rome, where all manner of horrible and loathsome things pour in and become fashionable." So, from the first, to a scholar like Tacitus it seemed incredible that the flame Christ kindled should go on burning. Here is the marvel of history, not that the world is dark —it always has been—but that we have a radiant spiritual heritage, coming down to us across the centuries, that all the hosts of evil have not been able to quench.

In this congregation this Christmas Sunday I want some personal decisions made, some serious self-committals here. In our world now antichrist does loom, dark and terrifying. Take a good look at him—antichrist incarnate and black as midnight! Some things are being done on earth this Christmastime so hideous that the mind recoils, seared and blistered with shame, and turbulent with indignation. All the more shall we not say, Still in the darkness the light shineth—in *that* I will believe. Christ never seemed to me so important as now when antichrist is so black. A friend once asked William Howard Taft what he thought about the League of Nations, and he answered, "Well, the best things of life get crucified and put in a tomb. But they always have their third day." That is a creed for Christians now. To be sure, darkness! To be sure, crucifixion and the tomb! But still the light that the darkness never can put out—in that I believe.

Consider again that not only does this truth present to our faith a great heritage of spiritual illumination, but it presents a supreme personality in whom the victory of light over darkness was actually consummated. The New Testament keeps coming back to that. It was dreadfully difficult then to believe that Christ's way of life could rise triumphant over the world's evil, but still, in one place that actually had happened. Christ himself presented an achieved victory—not simply an ideal, not merely an argument, but a fact, a resplendent, undeniable triumph of sunrise over night. So John pictures Jesus himself saying, "In the world ye have tribulation: but be of good cheer; I have overcome the world."

As Gladstone said, "One example is worth a thousand arguments." In every realm the final proof is commonly reached not by debate but by achievement. It cannot be done, men say of things seemingly incredible, as only forty years ago they were saying about aviation; and they keep on saying it, theoretically arguing with persuasive plausibility that it cannot be done. And then it is done. That is the answer. How many arguments in human history have been suddenly stopped not by opposing arguments but by a shining fact: it has been done.

So this light we are talking of at Christmastime is a fact, personally consummated in a life. On a priori grounds a life like Christ's, the Sermon on the Mount incarnate in a man who was crucified and yet who has gone on and on, the most potent spiritual influence that ever came to earth, is utterly incredible. No argument could ever have made it plausible. To tell the tale in advance of its happening, a man born in a manger, dying on a cross, distinguished only by love and humility, who shakes the world to its foundations and two thousand years afterward is the criterion by whom millions test the characters of men and the policies of nations—that is the wildest impossibility that could be presented to the minds of men. But the argument against that has long since been stopped. That has been done.

How realistically true in many realms this fact is of which we now are speaking! You cannot educate the masses, men once argued; only the privileged classes produce minds that are worth educating; the masses of the world must be left as they are—illiterate hewers of wood and drawers of water. So they argued, and they were never fully answered by opposing arguments. How could they be? They were answered by lives, like Faraday, underprivileged, coming up out of unpromising circumstances, and yet becoming one of the most creative scientists of his time. So, our modern democracies have opened wide the doors of education to everybody, persuaded not by debate but by example that we can never tell where the great minds are coming from.

Here lies the ultimate solution of the Negro problem. The Negro is essentially an inferior race, men have argued; racial equality is absurd; Negroes have no place except in menial tasks, and can never rise to take their place beside the white man. So the argument has run, and no opposing argument can ever answer it. But then Marion Anderson sings, George Washington Carver becomes one of our greatest American scientists, a Negro girl at Yale wins first prize in the annual competition of young American poets, a New York Negro tops the list of citations for meritorious police duty, a new Liberty ship named the *Booker T. Washington,* christened by a Negro woman, sails the seas with a crew of white and black commanded by a Negro captain. That is the answer. Always the arguments of sceptics run on and on until they fade out in the light of fact.

All such illustrations are small and partial examples of something everlastingly true that makes Christmas forever worth celebrating. This is a dark world, men think. I should say it is! But something else is really here—a new kind of life that did come into the world in Christ, and that, as John said, is the "light of men." No longer a matter of theoretical argument, that is an achieved victory, an accomplished fact. If anyone says now that light cannot conquer darkness, the answer is, it has been done. To which, then, are we giving our faith and allegiance—to the night or to the sunrise? ...

To be sure, there is a stern aspect to light. It is not simply beautiful; it shows things up. Sometimes when light shines it is terrific. This boy, with soiled face and hands, who does not wish to cleanse himself, would be glad to have his mother look at him in the dark—he can get by there—but in the light she will see the truth about him. Light is not simply lovely; it is a judge, falling in silent condemnation on the things that it shows up. So John puts it, "This is the judgment, that the light is come into the world, and men loved the darkness rather than the light, for their works were evil."

Stern though this truth is, however, our hope is there. We would never know that anything is crooked if we had never seen anything straight. We would never know that anything is evil if we had never seen anything good. We would never even know that it is dark if light had not come. Take a lovely home this Christmastime, radiant with the fairest meanings that family life can know, and put it beside an embittered home, harsh with discord and distrust, and it is the lovely home that shows the bad home up. We would never know how bad a bad home is if we had never seen how beautiful a good home can be. In every realm this is the judgment, that light has come into the world.

Granted, the stern aspects of this truth, yet it is our hope, for when lovely homes have once appeared there is something in mankind that cannot escape taking them as standard. They become the criteria by whose arbitrament we judge all other homes, and we are unhappily dissatisfied when we fail that test. When Christlike character has once appeared, creatively beautiful with humility, humaneness, and goodwill, despite ourselves and all our evil that kind of character moves up into the central place and becomes the judgment seat where other character is tried. Yes, when once the world catches a glimpse of itself organized for peace instead of war, something happens that all the forces of darkness cannot prevent: that vision becomes the standard of our judgment, the criterion of our endeavor, and short of it mankind will never be content. So John was not dreaming. He was dealing with everlasting fact. When light comes it stays; it shows up evil; it becomes the test and criterion of hope and of endeavor; and not all the darkness

[335

in the world can put out the light of a single candle when once it has been lighted.

This has been the faith of those strong souls whose wisdom and sacrifice have won for us whatever good we have achieved on earth. Lord Shaftesbury is typical, writing in his diary after a hard fight in Parliament for a bill to improve the condition of the poor: "I was defeated last night—cast down but not destroyed. The stillest, darkest hour is just before the dawn. Righteousness will prevail." So may we keep Christmas in our hearts this year! The light is still shining in the darkness, and the darkness can never put it out.